BEYOND
RECALL

Also by Gerald Seymour

Harry's Game
The Glory Boys
Kingfisher
Red Fox
The Contract
Archangel
In Honour Bound
Field of Blood
A Song in the Morning
At Close Quarters
Home Run
Condition Black
The Journeyman Tailor
The Fighting Man
The Heart of Danger
Killing Ground
The Waiting Time
A Line in the Sand

Holding the Zero
The Untouchable
Traitor's Kiss
The Unknown Soldier
Rat Run
The Walking Dead
Timebomb
The Collaborator
The Dealer and the Dead
A Deniable Death
The Outsiders
The Corporal's Wife
Vagabond
No Mortal Thing
Jericho's War
A Damned Serious Business
Battle Sight Zero

BEYOND RECALL

Gerald Seymour

HODDER &
STOUGHTON

First published in Great Britain in 2020 by Hodder & Stoughton
An Hachette UK company

1

Copyright © Gerald Seymour 2020

A CIP catalogue record for this title is available from the British Library

Hardback ISBN 9781529385977
Trade Paperback ISBN 9781529385984
eBook ISBN 9781529385991

Typeset in Plantin Light by Hewer Text UK Ltd, Edinburgh
Printed and bound in Great Britain by Clays Ltd, Elcograf S.p.A.

Hodder & Stoughton policy is to use papers that are natural, renewable
and recyclable products and made from wood grown in sustainable forests.
The logging and manufacturing processes are expected to conform
to the environmental regulations of the country of origin.

Hodder & Stoughton Ltd
Carmelite House
50 Victoria Embankment
London EC4Y 0DZ

www.hodder.co.uk

For Harriet and Georgia and Alfie

PROLOGUE

Location: Delta Alpha Sierra, June 2017

He thought he might have to kill her.

She came up the gradual slope of grit and scree. Because there were thorn bushes and tufts of yellowed grass, her livestock went ahead of her, shepherded by two dogs that alternately walked close to her heel and charged to head off attempts by the more independent goats to break from the group. The thought of taking her down distressed him.

He would have been described, he reckoned, as a kindly boy: twenty-six years and four months old, with no history of vindictiveness, cruelty, or violence that could be called gratuitous, that had found its way on to his personnel file. Enjoyed his work and considered good at it by his superiors. He was used to making fast judgements on what confronted him. He lay cramped in the hide that he had fashioned in the night's darkness, a few stars to give him enough light to burrow under the lip of earth and stones. He had used the excavated earth to build a shallow parapet and was protected by camouflaged scrim netting that would – hopefully – prevent light reflecting off the lenses of the optics he had brought with him. The problem that faced him was that the goats and the dogs seemed intent on moving in a straight line that ended at his hide. If they kept going, the four dozen goats and the two dogs and the one girl would meander or stamp right over him. The goats would scatter, the dogs would set up a chorus of hysterical barking, she would scream, and the cavalry – hers, not his – would come.

He had been trained to kill, and had both the kit and the expertise.

His decision. Not one that could be shared, kicked around the briefing room. The guys in the unit, and the girls, liked to think of themselves as an élite collection of individuals without the constraints of laid-down procedures. They were supposed to think, weigh up consequences, then act. Instructors had drilled into him the techniques of punching, eye gouging, heel-of-hand chopping, bollocks kicking, everything that would incapacitate an enemy, and he had fired thousands of rounds on ranges from his assault weapon, and had been in the buildings where they did short-range pistol shooting. He carried pepper sprays and grenades that did smoke or flash-and-bang. There seemed to him an inevitability about her progress up the hill towards him; she might reach him in five minutes, or in ten if the goats found forage.

A mobile phone was in a pouch sewn into the upper arm of his tunic. A short wave radio was at the top of the rucksack he had carried into the hide. He could have sent a message telling Control that he was about to be compromised, might have to bug out and fast. The sun was behind him and threw shadows, but the ground above and below the lip that he had chosen was well lit. With his gear there was no chance of him slipping away unobserved. They were Shami goats. He knew enough of the Syrian culture, had been lectured on it, to recognise that these were prized beasts. They were tall, had fine coats, red and black and brown, and had distinctive drooping ears, mostly white. They were top quality and valuable, treasured for the quality of the cheese and yoghurt made from the milk taken from their ample udders. These goats would not have been left in the charge of an imbecile kid, nor one who would plant themselves on a stone and drift off into a fantasy world of boys or girls, of peace or war, of . . . She would be bright, and looked bright, and there were moments when the sunlight caught her face. She drifted after the herd and sometimes bent to stroke her dogs' heads and seemed alert, and he saw worship in the dogs' eyes as they looked up at her.

Why might he have to kill her?

Because this was Syria and the village she had come from was at the bottom of the slope, adjacent to a main highway, and was half an hour from a front line that had not been stabilised. The road had, Control had briefed the night before, a 'specific strategic importance'. Away from the road, out of sight and dumped there as a sort of after-thought, was a village: probably home for centuries to a community of people existing from hand-to-mouth agriculture. Now, at the arse end of the war, it was a cluster of untidy single-storey concrete blocks built without a planner's pattern, with water from a well and intermittent electricity that probably came from a dangerous tap into a main cable running north to south on the road's verge. It would have been visible, of course, to helicopters or drones, but it seemed to have missed out on the agonies of the fighting that had rolled backwards and forwards across this God-forsaken landscape. She had been early from her hut and had gone with the dogs to the barricaded pen where the animals were kept during darkness, and had started out in search of food for them. The rest of the village was now awake and on the move. Control had said that it was necessary to learn about the village, who visited, where its allegiance lay: there should be eyes on the ground because satellites and drones did an imperfect job. Human Intelligence ruled, and it was the trade. Where did its loyalties lie? He was supposed to find out. There were alternatives to killing her.

He could bug out now and emerge from his hole like a startled rabbit and load up his rucksack and rifle, his binoculars around his neck, and get to the top of the slope and forget about her and the dogs and the goats and ignore all hell breaking behind him and start to tramp across featureless ground, without cover or hiding place and no chance of a rescue Chinook, British or American, getting to him within a fifteen-minute window. An alternative was an immediate response demand for the Hereford gang to belt out of their discreet lie-up bivouac, leave dust trails as they came to lift him out . . . and the whole business aborted. Which did not take into account what would have happened when the dogs barked, and she screamed and the boys down in the village – some of them already wandering and stretching and spitting and pissing over by the goalposts of their stone-littered football pitch – heard them, heard her. Most had assault rifles hanging off their shoulders. Trail bikes were outside some of the houses, and Toyota and Nissan pick-ups haphazardly parked. Women were appearing, carrying bundles of clothing towards the river that skirted the far end of the village, near to the football area, and one spotted the girl and shouted to her, and she answered in a sweet singsong voice, and there was cackling laughter and waving. When the dogs were frenzied, and when she screamed, then the hordes of Hades would come in pursuit. Within two, three, minutes, before the Chinook was even airborne and before the Hereford boys had clanked up their engines, he would have been hunted down.

Not simple, the matter of killing and silencing her and not bringing all hell down on his head. He would have shown out. For his unit, the big disaster was to compromise a mission by being discovered . . . and an even bigger disaster was to be captured or killed. Better, marginally, to be killed, even though his gear would be worth a fortune to a village community such as this. What would they do? What chance of them making him a cup of tea, giving him a bacon sarnie, and driving him fifty miles across the desert to the Forward Operating Base where he worked? What chance of them rating him as an item of value, establishing him as a British soldier and trussing him up like a Christmas turkey, taking him down the main highway, south, to where the Iran boys were thought to be establishing a garrison camp. Better to be killed, he estimated, than handed over to them . . . might live to tell the tale, might not. And the Resistance to Interrogation courses they'd sat through promised only a taste of an end-game for a prisoner.

And the other boys, Arnie and Sam, would they give him fire support if he killed her and needed close-quarters backup? An unlikely scenario was that the two men he had tabbed with from the Chinook drop-off would go on the regimental roll of honour for an heroic rescue. Arnie was likely to be half a mile to the west and with a view, just about, of the football pitch, and Sam was at the far side of the road junction, and neither had an eyeline on him. He was not good with words, had not had a testing education

– not necessary for his trade. He knew of no word that summed up the degree of catastrophe that he faced as she came up the hill ... She stopped. The lead goats were within a short stone's throw of him, and she was a long stone's throw farther back. She bent, then knelt, started to pick at a smattering of wild flowers that, somehow, grew among the stones and the gravel, and he thought there was serenity on her face. She stood, and delicately held the flowers, gold and violet, then pushed on because the goats were outstripping her as they climbed. Through the screen of scrim netting he had a fine sight of her. A tall girl with a ramrod back, ebony hair showing underneath a claret-coloured scarf. Dark eyebrows, dark eyes and a strong nose, and a mouth that seemed to move, as if a song was being mimed or a story recited. She wore a jacket of heavy red material and a dress that was brighter than her jacket, and he had a peek of flesh below the hem and saw her sandals. In one hand she grasped a light stick, in the other she held her flowers.

It was his duty to prevent himself being captured; to preserve his freedom he would shoot – or kill. He could have screwed a silencer on to the barrel of his rifle or his service pistol, but the goats would have run and the dogs would have surged at him and the boys below would have heard the dulled reports, and the women who had gone towards the river would have sensed chaos. He supposed he could strangle her.

She might have been nineteen years old, or twenty. She would have spent her life out in the open air with the goats and the dogs. She would be strong, would fight like a cornered she-cat, and his chance of strangling her, pressure on the windpipe until her resistance froze, was poor. He was getting round to telling himself that he had very few options. He used his mobile phone to send a text. Banal, short, he was possibly compromised. He might have to shoot his way out, not good and not definite. She had a sweet voice and he imagined the feel of her skin under pressure, then the convulsion of her fighting him off, and he was uncertain whether he could reach his pistol from the holster, club her insensible. The flowers were bright between her fingers and her lips still moved

... He was supposedly a high-flier in the world of covert reconnaissance, one of the best on the team, and he was trusted to succeed. He had no idea what he should do. His rifle was loaded but the safety was on. He probed one of the outside pouches of the rucksack, searching for a pepper spray and a smoke grenade.

If he did not kill her, if she raised an alarm and brought the boys sprinting up the slope or chasing on their bikes and in the pickups, and if he were captured, then his name would be reviled in the unit. Few would speak well of him if he were killed and his gear lost ... He tried to control his breathing, a thumb resting against the safety lever on his rifle, his body coiled, ready to propel himself from where he was hidden, gather up his kit and start to run. He could smell the goats. He lost sight of her because their noses and mouths filled the arc of his vision and one goat had taken hold of the netting and was trying to chew it, and he was clinging to it. He heard the soft growl of one of the dogs. The noise it made was like faraway thunder and he thought the hackles would be erect on the back of its neck, and next was the smell of its breath but it was pushed aside as more goats came to feed off his scrim net. He clung to it.

She was above him and used the lip of his hide as a seat. She seemed to flick her stick at those goats that had been at his netting; they moved away but he still heard the dog's wary growl. He hardly dared breathe. Her ankles were in front of him. He saw the scarred skin and the bulges of her bones and the dried lesions where her sandals would have rubbed when it rained. Her ankles were tough and strong, and he doubted, for all his fitness training, that he would have been certain of outrunning her. Inside his boots, he moved his toes to ward off cramp, but a tickling in his nose had started and he gulped and tried to hold down the need to sneeze. He wondered if it was dust at the back of his throat or whether an insect had crawled into one of his nostrils. One hand held the rifle and had the thumb against the safety, the other had come off the butt of his pistol and he eased it with painful slowness to cover his mouth and his nose and wondered, if he had to, whether he could suppress the sneeze into some sort of grunt.

Might be the same noise as a goat made, might be similar to the rumble from a dog's throat. His body had stiffened and his breath was held and he needed to swallow, and had only her ankles to look at. A hand came down and scratched her foot. She sang softly to herself, not a song of joy but a lament. A small clear voice.

He had planned to kill her, but had not known how to, or when. The moment came without warning. He was mocked.

She sneezed. And again. What he had tried to avoid, she did. She lowered her head. He saw her scarf and the hair under it fall free to rest on the dirt in front of his hide. He saw her mouth and her eyes and they seemed to linger at a point where the scrim net had the greatest rip from where the goats had chewed it, and he heard her chuckle. A little trill of laughter replaced her song. It was as if she was teasing. He would have sworn that she knew he was there, knew he represented only the slightest danger, knew she would not betray him. Light bounced in her eyes, and her lips were curled wide. She whistled, then pushed herself up. She called to the dogs, and resumed her song. He sensed the sadness of it. She made occasional clucking noises that brought the goats back to her and she whacked a few of them with gusto. She moved on. When she was out of sight she could have gestured to the boys below, those with the wheels and the assault rifles, or she could have signalled to the women at the river's shallow pools, pointed to where he hid. . . . Down the road, towards the Iranians, he heard the sound of artillery firing, and he thought there were also the sounds of larger explosions which would be the Russians' strike jets. In these parts, the war was seldom far away, and he reflected that the village was fortunate to have stayed clear of it, so far. Her dogs were at her heels and she walked well, loping to keep contact with her goats. Probably premature, but he texted again. Reported that a possible danger situation had receded, no exfiltration procedure was warranted. She had gone to the left of his hiding point and was tracking along the rim of the slope and sometimes he heard snatches of her song. She didn't look back.

The sun climbed and the day wore on and he had hours to kill before dusk, when he would go to the right of the village, towards the road junction, and search out a place where a camera could be sited. He would take samples from the soil and the dust from the concrete blocks so that the surround for the lens would be of the same texture when the technicians built the device. Then, under cover of night, he would set out for the rendezvous point where either the Hereford guys would be waiting for Arnie and Sam and him or the Chinook would come in. Several times he saw her but she never looked back to the place where mischief had played at her mouth, where her eyes had been bright with the fun of playing with him.

Would he have killed her for the sake of the mission? Taken her life if it had helped him to go free? Might have, might not have, felt lucky the decision had been spared him.

I

For Gaz, the island was his new home. He worked on the garden with a bitter and frantic intensity. To a stranger, anyone ignorant of where he had been and why he had been there and what he had experienced, it was the sort of exaggerated effort of an incomer to ease himself towards acceptance. A man arrived and set up home and offered himself for casual labour, and undercut existing rates charged for maintenance work, attempted to be a friend of everybody and offered a familiarity that was almost heathen to the remote community of Westray. If Gaz had been one of them, prodding to be welcomed into the inner tribal heart of the island – and there were enough – he would barely have lasted the first winter. Those were the men and women, who came on a boat in the spring and thought it would be fulfilling, a tapestry of dreams, and talked of a former life until they were shunned. They barely survived the first of the autumn storms that gathered strength out in the Atlantic before breaking on the archipelago of Orkney, howling and endlessly beating on buildings. The first storms brought a level of rainfall unknown to the new settlers. In place of the dull and dreary summer drizzle came the ripping power of near horizontal rain, torrential and frightening. Work would dry up, but a post van still struggled along sodden roads and delivered utility bills, and food was expensive, and . . . they were usually gone by Christmas. Very few saw out their first winter, returning to the mainland on a tossing ferry, having survived the Pentland Firth's fierce currents, would land at Scrabster and would say 'Thank God to be out of there. Pretty enough when the sun's shining. Miserable people, all wrapped up in themselves and not reaching out with help and a welcome. And the weather, it's something else; bloody awful wind, and rain. Older and wiser and glad to be out.' Gaz had been on Westray, a thin and twisted finger of land jutting into the sea and boasting eighteen square miles of gale-scraped land, with idyllic beaches and sheer granite stone cliffs, for two clear winters and he valued each day he survived there, and the place had a particular and especial importance to him.

Gaz was working in the garden of a holiday cottage halfway between the island's most notable ruin, Noltland Castle, and the sole hotel at Pierowall. The cottage had a decent enough view of the bay and anchorage on the north-facing side. A combination of a mild winter, a strong Gulf Stream, and fair sunshine along with rain-saturated ground, meant that he had a day's mowing of a rough lawn, hedges to be trimmed and beds to be weeded. The owners, a Glasgow family, would be up in a week and would stay a fortnight, expecting the garden to be manicured. Some occasional residents allowed their grass to be cropped by grazing sheep, others objected to the excreta deposited and demanded that the place be mowed, and were prepared to pay for the privilege. Gaz would mow all morning. His shadow was thrown behind him as he made neat lines on the grass, and he wasted no time because the forecast, as always, was variable and warned of coming squalls, with more expected in the coming days. He was a practical man, good with his hands and willing, happy, to work on his own because that was the style of his old life ... It was old, that life, and he hoped it well behind him, but sometimes it seemed to nip at his heels – and lurk in his mind. The island was his refuge. It was a convalescence. He took one day at a time and had done since he'd arrived, a foot passenger on the ferry from the mainland to Stromness, then buses and ferries, and then a jolting journey by air: it had not bothered him because back in his life there had been many turbulent flights.

He had enough gardening contracts to see him through the short summer months, and when the autumn came and the winds gained strength he could move inside; he was a careful decorator, steady and painstaking. Those who owned second homes on the island and visited rarely, seemed to enjoy the smell of fresh paint when they deigned to come. He could also do basic electrics, rewiring and rudimentary plumbing. Gaz had learned to be alone and to solve problems by fast analysis and decision taking. He did not need to pass difficulties up a chain of command, but he could repair a fusing power supply, fix leaking taps and cisterns, and could strip and service a mower. These skills did not mark him out on the island. They were part of the way of life there. To him, the mower was no easier, no harder, to strip and reassemble than any general purpose machine-gun, and the isolation he lived with alone in his rented cottage was no different than that he had experienced in covert observation posts. That was the world he had put behind him, but their demons were in pursuit.

No cruise boat was due that day. There was a murmur of the tide pushing the stones back beyond the island's cemetery, and oystercatchers came and went and screamed at some imagined danger, and cattle grazed, and seals slept on the rocks and in the seaweed. He was alert to danger, had lived with it pretty much all his adult life. But, in former times, he had been amongst men and women who had shared the risks and could talk about them with gallows humour. That was the world he had fled when he travelled north, carrying his rucksack on to the ferry and never looking back at the diminishing mainland shoreline. Leaving it lost in mist and hoping that memories would become as vague, ultimately be forgotten.

He realised, and it would bring a sardonic smile to his face, that he had been from the start a mystery figure in the Westray community. As intended. In the shop, to his neighbours on the nearest farm, and the more distant ones, and on the rare occasions he went to the hotel bar, and to his customers, he volunteered nothing about his background. His reticence permitted rumour to go free range. Some sidled questions to him, others were more direct and sought information: he was not rude, never offhand or dismissive, but always deflected the enquiry. He was good at it; his previous life had taught him the discipline of secrecy. In the first winter there had been a persistent beat up the path from his iron gate with invitations to join any one of the myriad of clubs that succoured the island people through the darkness of the long winter. The second year few, other than the most insistent, had come to his door. Now, he was left to himself, tolerated, accepted and greeted with a certain warmth and an understanding that he must be a man 'with a past', who had perhaps escaped from an old episode in his life. He was talked about, he was quizzed, and he smiled and changed the subject, and worked hard which was a requisite talent for being accepted on Westray, population a few shy of 600. The postman, of course, knew a little more than most. Brown envelopes still pursued him, and on them was his name: Gary Baldwin.

No one on the island called him 'Gary', nor was he, in this society, 'Mr Baldwin'. He introduced himself as Gaz, which was what he had been called from far back. He was not paid by card or by cheque but asked for cash, using it for buying food and small items of equipment for his work. He was of average height, and had average features and his hair was of average colour, and his eyes seemed unremarkable and there were no features on his appearance which stood out. Not being noticed had been a hall-mark of his craft. He spoke with a quiet voice and in two long winters and one full summer none on the island had heard his voice raised either in laughter or anger: there was a Birmingham accent, supposedly the West Midlands whine, but not pronounced. He'd had, as a child in an anonymous tower block in the Aston district, no knowledge of his father, and not much more of an idea of who his mother was. There had been a succession of 'uncles' who visited or took up temporary residence, and a legion of social workers who called by. He had been five years old when his life had altered . . . an 'aunt' had come, a relation of his mother. His few possessions had been packed in a small case of imitation leather. A spattered Land Rover had parked at the entrance to the block. An overweight couple, cords and tweeds, had panted their way to the door. They were friends of the aunt, he was told, and he left with them and his mother had shrugged and looked away. He remembered everything of the two-bed flat, but a keen memory for detail was a skill that he was to practise in his work . . . what he did before the experience, the illness, then the flight to find a refuge.

The wind buffeted him as he steered the mower, and the storm edged closer. Too many memories and each time he was less able to run from them.

"Morning, Knacker."

"And morning to you too, Boot. Keeping well?"

"Not too bad, thank you."

"Glad to hear it."

Knacker gave his coat to the long-retired company sergeant major of the Coldstreams who did duty at the door of this upper-floor dining-room where intelligence officers, past and present, gathered to swap tales. He handed over his phone and accepted the receipt for it, and registered the respect in which the NCO held him, and then had turned to face old Boot, a long-time colleague and now said to be in poor health. He gazed inside the room, started to nod greetings and let go of Boot's limp hand. Gerard Coe – rather good in the Gulf, once – was at the bar and had lost too much weight and too quickly – and saw others that he'd want to talk to. Just in time, not late because that would have been an act of disrespect, and he was rewarded with eye contact from Arthur Jennings, low down and bowed in his wheelchair but who maintained an unimpaired mind. It was the first Tuesday of the month, a locked-down date, when the Round Table met.

Knacker eased away from Boot but gave him a soft smile as a parting gift. He thought, Boot was on borrowed time and might not be long with them, but his reputation was well burnished, as bright as Coe's, as were the credentials of all of them, veterans of espionage, who came – by invitation only and access jealously guarded – to the upstairs room in the Victorian building on the Kennington Road. They were part of the Secret Intelligence Service, with good links but still regarded with well-founded suspicion, kept at arm's length, funded by proxy, rarely seen in the building at the top of the road and overlooking the Thames. He

reached Arthur Jennings whose parchment-textured skin seemed
to crack in pleasure, his eyes rheumy in delight. Knacker crouched
beside the wheelchair and allowed the talons of Jennings' hand to
grip his shoulder.

They were there, at least a dozen of them that day, because of
Jennings. He was their founding father: had made his name (to the
select few who knew anything of him) while working out of Beirut.
He had become a legend of manipulation and success and extraordinary bravado melded with a ruthlessness that would have
seemed brutal to anyone of a squeamish nature – and was a deity
in the life of Knacker. There would have been no Round Table but
for an evening of binge drinking led by Jennings – an endless
supply of brandy sours. The refrain was that their Service had lost
its edge, was no longer a risk taker, had ditched the role of playing
the desperado. The Service, they said, was 'withering on the vine',
and something must be done to rectify the weakness. An association of like-minded men, and a few women, was built around an
image of a table, round, and on that table – sketched by an old
China hand – was a 'bloody great sword, sharp blade, unsheathed'.
Arthur Jennings, in good voice in those days and with no audible
alcohol impediment, had quoted from Alfred, Lord Tennyson. *For
many a petty king ere Arthur came Ruled in this aisle, and ever waging
war Each upon other, wasted all the land: And still from time to time
the heathen host Swarmed overseas, and harried what was left.*

The upstairs room with its nicotine-stained prints and panel-
ling, and tackily painted woodwork at the windows was not
Camelot, but did the job for them and would have been well swept
for recording devices by the Coldstreamer and his people. At face,
their coming together was of little more significance than a Rotary
or Probus group in a small market town, but such a view would
have sold short the expertise of those who would take their place
at the table where the sword – bought on the cheap from a theatrical costumier in Greek Street – dominated the centre. They
believed in the Service's 'loss of clout', believed that the fresh-
faced graduates now dominating the headquarters building were
unwilling to travel the 'extra mile', were wedded to the strictures

of analysis. 'The slide has to be halted in its tracks,' Arthur Jennings had said. Tennyson had written *And so there grew great tracts of wilderness, Wherein the beast was ever more and more, But man was less and less, till Arthur came.* Arthur Jennings – now frail but not feeble – had summoned an image of a glorious and triumphant new world of espionage, compromise, deceit, and above all of success. They cost little, they were discreet, useful. They worked, as Arthur Jennings had said, 'ahead of the sharp end' – some of the claims were at the edge of justification but much was truthful. All of their membership, with their cover names of Tennyson's knights, would have seemed to an outsider to behave like school-boys, but a point would have been missed. Or several points.

And were deniable. They brought in defectors from across cultural and military frontiers. Agents were run on tight leashes, were seldom allowed to walk away from treachery. A glass was raised to his memory when an asset was captured, tortured, eventually executed or died under the rigours of interrogation, and when the glass was emptied the file was forgotten and the casualty became a fast-fading memory. It was as it had been before.

Over a buffet lunch, Knacker would hear the gossip of colleagues – not indiscreet, but valuable, and nuggets of recently learned tradecraft would be exchanged, and enemies' weaknesses and strengths evaluated. In the centre of their round table was a narrow slot and when they were called upon to eat, the theatrical sword would be lowered into it. Grace would be said – not of a religious nature, but an Orwell quote: *People sleep peacefully in their beds at night only because rough men stand ready to visit violence on those that would harm us.* It was the anthem of the group along with the historic poetry, and seemed to provide ample justification for the bending, fracturing, of official Rules of Engagement. Then, Arthur Jennings would be helped to lean across the table, and he'd puff and pant, and draw the sword clear of the slot – an Excalibur re-enactment, and then the business would begin and the swapping of confidences.

Arthur Jennings, mouth close to Knacker's ear, voice a guttering growl, asked, "Busy? What do you have? Up to speed?"

"Not as of this moment, Arthur. Sort of parked up in a lay-by."

"It'll come . . ."

"What I always say, Arthur . . . Get up in the morning and don't know what a new day will bring – out of a clear blue sky, that sort of stuff."

"Good boy."

They were called to order by Hilary, decent-looking woman whose last agent had been a Chinese air force pilot in an interceptor wing, dead now but valuable while he had lasted. Would have been roughed around before his trial, then taken out into a gaol yard, kicked into a kneeling position and then shot in the back of the head with a .38 calibre. He had done a good job for her, and earned her plaudits. Clapping broke out in the room and Knacker stood and carefully removed Arthur Jennings' hand from his shoulder . . . It was the way things happened, least expected and out of that 'clear blue sky', and then a dawdle would become a sprint.

Knacker's special talent was to squeeze the usefulness of an asset till the poor bugger was dried out, finished and condemned, and done without clemency.

In a first-floor office in the Lubyanka, Lavrenti was briefed on his new job. He was wearing the fatigue uniform, combat medal ribbons on his chest, and had flown down from the north the previous day.

To his mother, Lavrenti was a hero and she would hiss with sympathy each time he raised his hand to the grooved line in his cheek which he had told her was the result of crawling under fire through barbed-wire entanglements. Now a major, he was to his immediate superiors a coming figure to be humoured and treated with respect. He was regarded by his peers in those sections of FSB where he was known, as an officer of influence and prospect, not one to be crossed, and no offence should be given him. To his father, nominally retired and with the rank of brigadier general, he was the meal ticket to a dynasty of financial advantage and an opportunity to advance good links with the present apex of the regime.

Lavrenti was thirty-two years old. His father had been thirty-eight when he was born, far away in the death throes of the failed Afghan campaign, and his mother was thirty-six. His had been a difficult birth and the experience was not repeated. An only son, an only child, alone on the fast track, all their efforts deployed to propel him through èlite schools and an élite college.

He had served two years in the north, far beyond the Arctic Circle, because his father had demanded the opportunity for him. It was a hideous place, awful people, and almost as grim as the sand and the shit and the company of his previous posting . . . The future looked better.

He would return to Moscow. Would head up a new section, reporting directly to the senior officer of a directorate who had once served as his father's chief of staff. Would have good 'opportunities'. He understood that there would be considerable financial benefit in this new work: monitoring private enterprise in the capital. With power, as he was well aware, came the ability to create fear. He would see that truth every day and witnessed it now as he sat in a barely furnished room, a colonel fawning over him.

He was tall, blond, carrying no surplus weight, working out in the gym had become the necessary therapy of those two years in the north. Pale blue eyes, usually hidden by lowered lids, a square and strong jaw, a facial tan flawed by the fucking scar on his cheek. Had a past that very few knew of, had a hidden shadow that burdened him . . . They talked of how it would be and he sensed the friendship he was offered.

He did not easily accept friendship. Lavrenti was curt, to the point, businesslike. His work was praised, what he had achieved in the north and – of course – his record in a combat zone. His previous work on the staff members of foreign embassies in Moscow and their locally employed personnel was lauded, also his 'investigations' of foreign journalists who went home with the precursors of breakdowns speeding them to Sheremetyevo and the flight out. He accepted coffee and water. No alcohol, no cigarettes. There would have been a packet in a drawer of the colonel's desk, and a bottle and glasses. He would accept no favours from this man, wanted not the slightest baggage. Matters were concluded; he would return north, pack up, then transfer south. Would he, please, pass on to his father – Brigadier General Volkov (the name meant 'wolf' and was appropriate) – good wishes and best regards?

Lavrenti would not commit himself, shrugged, a finger worrying at his scar, stood and walked out.

Her name, Faizah, meant she was 'victorious', a winner. The customer jabbed a finger at the 'special of the kitchen' on the lunch menu she had offered him. Little in her life that day, or any day in the previous two years, told Faizah that she was not anchored at the bottom end of existence, was a scarred failure. Hers was a familiar name in the distant central deserts of what little remained of Syria, her former homeland, after the devastation of war.

The four men at the table had come to the bar for three consecutive days and each time she had served them drinks, then food. They must have liked her, had tipped her well. They were Norwegian, in Hamburg to see a demonstration of an engine suitable for powering a twenty-metre fishing trawler, were going home that evening, had come for their final lunch. Not that they needed to see the menu because they always chose the same – *schnitzel*, with Flensburger beer. They were looking at an iPad open on the table. There was a chorus for more beer to be brought . . . Perhaps they liked her out of sympathy. She was a migrant far from home and – obvious to them – damaged.

She scribbled their order on her pad but suddenly her expression froze, as her eyes locked on their iPad. It showed a photograph of two men in uniform. Behind them was a rotund figure, a smile on his face and wearing a military beret. It was the nearest figure that riveted her. He wore officer's insignia on his shoulder, a camouflage tunic, open at the throat. His hair was hidden under a high cap, gold braid and a badge on a blue background and a top of deep grass-green. He stared at the lens, at her, and his eyes gouged into her mind. There was no smile at the mouth and the lips were dried out and his expression held contempt, perhaps arrogance, and there was a narrow line where the knitting of the flesh had been clumsy, running from near to the lobe of his left ear and down his left cheek, disappearing into the folds of his tunic collar . . .

Blood draining from her face, a hand catching at her mouth and a chill on her neck, and feeling that place on her chin where the wound had been opened and the dirt and dust had been absorbed before it had been treated. The Norwegians had sympathy for her, acknowledged that she would never be classified as 'pretty', carried a wound on the chin that would go with her to her grave . . . as the scar on the officer's face, in the photograph, would last for the remainder of his life.

"You all right, kid?"

"You seen a ghost? What is it?"

"Heh, what is the problem?"

She collected herself, a migrant waitress in a bar on a side street off the main drag to the *Hauptbahnhof*, managed a brittle smile. She asked them in her halting German where the picture was taken. She tried to sound offhand, but failed, tears distorting the image on the iPad. They all peered at it, bemused by her reaction. What was the website? She was told. What was the picture? Told that also. Who was the man nearest the camera? Given his rank, but not a name . . . And then, politely, one of them gestured towards the glasses on the table and tapped his watch to indicate that time was limited if they were to eat and drink before catching a flight that would lift them, via Copenhagen, beyond the Arctic Circle and home.

She handed in their order: four plates of *schnitzel* and four more glasses of Flensburger. She told the manager that she needed to get out of the bar. She worked hard, she slept in a garret of the building. She did long hours that she knew to be in contravention of European legislation. She was paid below the minimum rate. A fuss was made but then her employer noted a steeliness in her eyes and gave his permission – but not for long, to be back by late afternoon. Another girl carried the beers to the table and the Norwegians broke off from conversation and stared as she walked out of the bar and into the rain, no coat, no umbrella, but a mission . . . the wound on her chin would never be forgotten, nor the line on the military man's left cheek.

She walked briskly, the pavement puddles splashing under her feet, drenching her ankles. She knew where she would go, and what she would say, would be ashamed of herself if she did not take the chance.

Delta Alpha Sierra, May 2019, the first hour

First light was a dirty opaque wash. A storm blew. The sound of explosions was distant.

Rain would come later, not the sort that fell at home, pattering down from dull cloud, but torrential, slashing through clothing and kit, and running into his hide. Gaz, with a corporal's rank in an obscure and understated unit, had been, with two others, dropped off in the small hours by helicopter – and had walked the last four miles.

Ahead of him and hard to follow were the outlines of the few buildings that comprised the village. Because its name, Deir al-Siyarqi, was usually written only in what the military categorised as 'worm scribble', it was listed in the letters of the NATO alphabet. Where he was, a call sign. If threatened, Gaz, or any of the others, could press the panic tit and broadcast an emergency call from Delta Alpha Sierra and know that a big bird would be tasked for immediate response and would likely come with a pair of Apache flying close fire support. He felt a wariness, the caution that went with the loneliness of deployment as a recce guy. Should have been a piece of cake, they had said at the briefing at the Forward Operating Base.

Gaz lived with jargon, the script of the Special Reconnaissance Regiment unit which he served with, and was regarded – he acknowledged it, but humbly – as one of the best at Close Target Reconnaissance. It was about a camera battery. Too much of his work was determined by the miniaturisation of batteries, how long they would last, and how often the bloody things needed replacing. To get good quality pictures beamed back to the FOB required a battery capacity that could not be sustained if the camera and its lens were housed in minimum space: this one was in a hollowed-out breeze-block. Not ideal, the best was not often the easiest. He rated the combat as seven, perhaps eight, miles down the road, and thought there might be mortars in use or small calibre artillery, but vicious in intensity, was unsettled by it.

He had walked in through darkness, the wind stinging dirt against his body. The others would by now have been on the far side of the village, south of it and to the west. The camera was built into a low wall, once the base of a superstructure beside the main highway where someone had probably tried to set up a soft drinks stop. Perhaps they had also sold fruit or vegetables or bottled water, or fags; the war would have killed off the chance of a budding entrepreneur making it rich. The road bypassed two indistinct front lines – a combat no-man's land. Seemed months since he had been here to extract a single breeze-block and return it to the Base, since the technicians had worked on the colour and the texture of the concrete dust, since the camera had been mounted to keep watch on the road. They – staff and intelligence back at the Base – wanted warning of any probing advance by the Iranians up the road because this was their sector. Gaz came every two or three weeks. He had modified and deepened his hide and made it, admitted with a suspicion of pride, a work of art: his art was that of the Special Reconnaissance Regiment. Sometimes the hit men, the Hereford gun club, drove them in but more usually the helicopters did the lift and left them to walk the final leg. Always in darkness and weather not negotiable. He would arrive during the night, lie up for the day, then go forward when the sun had sunk beyond the village, do the work and then get the hell out, taking everything that had been in the hide; including his waste and his food wrapping. Four pick-ups, lights off, swept off the main highway and careered down the sloping track towards the village. The dogs barked and charged at the wheels.

The mission to the village, the change of batteries and the collection of the camera images, had become almost routine . . .

Also routine would be the presence of the girl, and her goats and her dogs. Not that they spoke, or touched, and barely made eye contact. Everything he knew about the girl was listed in the debrief sessions back at the FOB. Twice he had moved the hide but she had come looking for him and the goats had always gathered close and grunted and he had caught the merriment in her grin. It had seemed easier to move back to his first hide, the best, and allow the goats to forage near him, and hear her plaintive songs and know that the dogs would guard her with their lives. At that distance, less than a quarter of a mile and with the spreading light helping him, he saw the village youths as they cut the pickups' engines, jump out and scurry into doorways. Easy enough for Gaz to believe that they'd been down the road to the Iranian camp and had shot it up and had a fun deal out of the experience, then had made it back, and the follow-up firing that came after them would have been random and not aimed and frustrated. It was bad news, like tugging at an elderly lion's tail and believing the beast too moth-eaten and toothless to respond. Bad news and likely to be a bad mistake. The gunfire was closer, he was sure of it. He had the new and fully charged battery in his Bergen bag and enough water and dried food to see him through the day, and had the panic tit . . . But the dogs had gone quiet and the firing of the mortars and artillery still seemed far back. It was unusual for Gaz to feel apprehension and he hoped to shrug out of it. The wind steadily rose and blew eddies of sand and grit.

It was because of the storm. It was better for Gaz since he had come to the island than it had been before. The place he had fled to was a refuge, almost.

The force of the changed weather would not reach Westray for three or four days but the advance warnings were already over the bared hillsides, where sheep and cattle fed, and the long stone walls that would have broken the backs of the builders more than a century before. Where washing was hung out, shirts and underclothes, sheets and towels, flying horizontally, and the singing had started in the overhead cables.

A psychiatrist, hired for him by the unit, had said that the black dog days were pretty much inevitable. Powerful medication might block their access to his mind, but would send him to a state of vegetative collapse. Did he want that? Or would he prefer to live with the demons? He'd refused the medication and the next best thing that the psychiatrist had offered was long-distance flight; to head away to a place that was remote, where his history was not known, somewhere he could bury the hours of the day in agricultural and handyman work. He had hit a girl. The girl, Debbie, had thought they were an item, a relationship developing faster in her mind while he was on deployment than he had reckoned for. A nice enough girl and thinking him a catch; pressure building on him but unable to talk about the 'what' and the 'where' of his work, and memories spiking in his mind, and her not understanding. Had hit her in the face, sobbing as he did so, and it was a piece of luck that he had not broken the bridge of her nose and left her disfigured: if he had, it would likely have been a prison sentence . . . would have been shoved into a closed van, put in the wire cage and off through the gates and behind the high wall, and would have joined the scores of former servicemen for whom black dog days were classified as post-traumatic stress disorder. The unit, his former home and his only surviving family, had pushed for a psychiatrist to speak for him, an attractive woman with a winning smile and skilled at shifting the magistrate's prejudices. He should go away. He should grab the chance. He should find a place where stress did not eat at him day and night. On her advice he had made a quite sincere apology to the girl from the dock, and had travelled to the far north and had immersed himself in gardening work and minor property repairs and dog walking . . . but it came on bad when the storm winds blew.

He was slumped on his spade, vulnerable and weak, a shadow of what he had been. The storm made chimes of memory ring in his head, hard enough to split his skull apart. Stress was to be avoided, the psychiatrist had said and smacked a fist into the palm of her other hand, avoided like the plague. He should run from stress, she'd said, not permit it to confront him. If he were free of it for a long time, years not months, then there was a chance he could put the experience behind him, just a chance.

In her cell block, she was ticking off the days. Natacha had only those left to serve that could be counted on the fingers of one hand. She wore a soiled tunic, and a drab prison skirt. She was filthy from dirt and sweat and she kept her hair hidden in a light wool cap.

She had been given a four-month sentence, all of it to be served in the bleak red brick prison in old Murmansk. Probably one of the first buildings put up in the city on the inlet to the west of the Kola peninsula, the extreme north-west of the Russian land mass. The cell stank of the urine and faeces and period blood of the five women she shared it with. There was a murderess and a brothel owner who had refused to pay a cop-bribe, a seller of heroin powder, and a thief who had burgled her way into foreigners' Radisson hotel rooms in the centre of the city, and there was a girl similar in appearance to herself who had painted slogans denouncing the President as a thief. Natacha had been told often in the last week that she would be missed . . . She was slight, bony, with a flat chest and a flat stomach, and she might have a dose of HIV or might not but had not bothered to be checked. She would be missed because she possessed a smile that few models on the cover pages of fashion magazines could match, and with the smile she made them laugh. She had a mimic's eye for detail and screeches of laughter came from their cell when she did her imper-sonation of key members of the prison staff, and she was, in a quiet way, anarchic in her sense of defiance: not political but merely to point up the pompous stupidity of the rule book.

She had been caught selling 'phets and weed down by the Murmansk railway station. Her boy had been with her but had run faster and there was snow on the ground and the trooper had slipped, then regained his feet and she had tripped him, and her guy had legged it away. She had not named Timofey. Not a love-match, but a relationship of convenience and comfort, and they would have had to beat her one step short of unconscious for her to give his name. The days were ticked, and now Natacha talked about the dilemma of her hair, and they laughed fit to burst. Should her hair, a scrubber's blonde, go purple or larch-green at the end of the week when she went free. It would be a big decision, green or purple – but might depend only on which was easier to lift off the shelf in the Magnets store on Poliarnye Zori, and Timofey would be waiting outside and they would be gone – and she would not be back, not to the gaol. They challenged her. She was adamant, would colour her hair and would sell wraps and skunk and smack, and might hitch up her skirt in a police car for cash, but nothing serious.

"Better believe it. . . . You don't see me again, none of you, not ever. Nothing serious, nothing that rocks them, so I do not come back." She flashed her smile. "Counting the hours till I am free and able to enjoy again the wonder and beauty of the streets of Murmansk."

Murmansk's winter has six weeks of no sun, just a mix of total darkness and charcoal-grey gloom. Murmansk's summer has six weeks when the sun never sets and the city is bathed in perpetual light. Far to the north of the Arctic Circle, Murmansk can also experience rain in January and snow in July: a contrary city.

Murmansk has a population, sinking, of almost 300,000, and is big on sexually transmitted disease, ferocious seasonal mosquitoes, drug abuse, and the architecture of Stalin, Kruschev and Brezhnev. The Putin legacy is a couple of modern hotels, low rates of occupancy and high rates.

Murmansk, one day but not tomorrow, could have a glittering financial future as the hub of oil and gas exploration, except that the Fatherland, as represented by the ruling class in Moscow's Kremlin, cannot filch the necessary infrastructure technology – even with its army of expert hackers – from the West's engineers. Not for want of trying. While that is on hold, the purpose of the city is to be home to the navy's Northern Fleet.

Murmansk was founded as a naval base in 1916, in the final throes of the Czar's rule, because the deep inlet on which the city was built never froze, even in the depths of winter. Government resources are rich when it comes to the fleets of hunter-killer and long-range missile-firing submarines. In strategic terms, Murmansk is a big player in international military games, and nuclear missiles are stacked in bunkers dug out of the perma-frost ground. When the Soviet Union seemed destined for defeat in World War II, and the German war machine pressed closer to the valued nickel and iron ore mines of the region, British, American and Canadian convoys fought their way through bomb and torpedo attacks to bring military supplies to Murmansk and to stabilise a front line to the south during the 900-day siege of Leningrad. The life and atmosphere of the city is supposedly dominated by the experience, and on a bluff above the drab living blocks the Alyosha monument was built in memory of those killed in defence of the port and its resources.

Murmansk's main street of Lenin Prospekt, designed on the grand scale of public buildings when Josef Stalin ruled, is where the new palace of the FSB is located with 15,000 square metres of offices and holding cells built over eight floors. The vast size of the building is justified, the FSB spokesman has said, because of security dangers in the region. A reported toxic dump for nuclear waste and bristling with modern warfare, it is natural that the security police would send their best and their brightest to Murmansk.

"Murmansk?" Knacker murmured into the phone.

In a building halfway between the pub where he had attended that day's Round Table lunch and the headquarters of SIS, a member of his staff had taken a call from the British Consulate in Hamburg, the northern port city of Germany. It would have been filtered fast through several of the agency's arms: the triggers would have been the war in Syria; the village of Deir al-Siyarqi, with its call sign of Delta Alpha Sierra; the massacre; the date; the accusation; the photograph from a Norwegian-based amateur commentary in both Russian and English, sent from a harbour town near the border shared with Russia – a photograph, and a denunciation. Knacker had been in deep and fruitful conversation at lunch with the man who had run a penetration into the political élite of DPRK and with a woman who had compromised a senior official on the treasury side of the Islamic Revolutionary Guard Corps, the Quds crowd, and basked in justifiable pride at the achievement. Both assets faced, in Knacker's opinion, an 'uncertain future' and both should be kept in their place. The Coldstreamer had discreetly summoned him from the table. A phone had rung with a sharp request to extract him. Knacker had taken the call, had slipped the phone into secure mode, and was relayed the guts of what a Syrian-born waitress had come to the consulate and said. He remembered her, would have been hard not to.

"She is definite in the identification?"

He was told that the girl was adamant.

"Forget the photograph of this Russian officer. Have we been sent an image of her?"

They had. The photo of the girl, as supplied by the consular officer, was on the screen in front of Alice, and Fee had good sight of it.

"Does she carry a scar on her chin? Size of a fifty pence piece?"

She had. It had healed but not well.

Knacker slipped back inside. He whispered apologies to Arthur Jennings and was gently quizzed. Something of interest? He said that it might be. Was it those bastards, the usual ones, he was asked. It was, always them, always the same bastards, always the Lubyanka boys. Arthur Jennings was holding a cheese knife and stabbed it into the table, tearing the plastic covering, watched it quiver.

He was gone and left a slack grin at the mouth of the Round Table's founder ... He was Knacker because of his reputation to recruit damaged personnel, get one last mission from the wretch. Like a man who went round farms or gypsy camps and took away lame horses and would get them one last time between the shafts of a carriage, tighten the harness, crack the whip. Cat food if it failed, or, if it went well perhaps another season grazing in a paddock. And who would his new bedfellows be? The usual point of concern when a mission was at the embryonic stage: who would help it along and who would stand in its way, who was an ally and who was the enemy? Strangers would lurch out of any imagined mist. Might help, might hinder. Always the way with his work. He turned the word over in his mind as he stamped off down the pavement: Murmansk. He had just the man for it.

He held the phone. What he had looked forward to, like a talisman, through the despair of the late afternoon and early evening as the storm curdled over the horizon to the west, was the arrival the next morning of Aggie. She would have come on the plane from the small sister island of Papa Westray, or hitched a ride on an open boat, both rough and turbulent but both usually running whatever the weather.

"Sorry and all that, Gaz, but you know how it is . . . Just a foul summer dose of 'flu. Best to see it out and get it behind me. Give it a few days, and I'll have shaken clear of it. Look after yourself, my big boy. Bye-bye."

The phone purred in his ear. She did not say, not ever, that she loved him. Did not say that it hurt her to cry off from travelling to see him . . . She made pottery for sale in the hotel on Gaz's island, and was a dab hand at simple watercolour paintings and designed her own cards with illustrations of her island views. She would have been four or five years older than Gaz and he had met her when a gale had damaged her roof and it had needed a partial rebuild, and the weather had been foul and it had needed strength, ingenuity and luck to keep the tarpaulin in place while he had done the work, and she had paid him in cash and he had been captivated. She had been on her island three years longer than he had been on Westray so was a veteran and took the bad times with the good; unflappable, unfazed whatever the elements chucked at her, and seemed not to share any of the black dog days he entertained. It had been weeks before they had kissed and months before they had gone to his bed – probably too much drink taken that evening in the Pierowall hotel bar, but not regretted. Most weeks she came on the twenty-five minute ferry link or the two-minute fixed-wing flight, and greeted him as he met her as if it were the one thing – a kiss and a hug – that she had most missed since last seeing him, but she would call and stand him down and sound relaxed about it, no huge deal. Gaz had told her that she was the most important woman he had known in his adult life, had tried to tell her about previous relationships – all in the disaster folder – and been shushed. She knew he had been a serving soldier, not what he had done and not where he had been, and she did not know any of the detail of the psychiatrist's assessment . . . and of her he knew next to nothing. Easier. What he did know was a verdict on him that she had given a friend in the bar who had told him on one of the rare times he was there by himself, and this woman had passed on Aggie's description of him. 'Nice enough, and bloody useful round the place, but I don't really know him because he wouldn't let that happen. A guy you hardly remember, see him and think he's all right but the memory is sort of vague. Something happened but I don't know what, and he'll not tell me, and I don't ask.' What he had learned about black dog days from the few therapy sessions he had gone to before the uprooting and the journey north, was that no one outside the experience gave a toss what he and other sufferers went through and in military terms it was still 'Get a grip', and the days of a diagnosis of 'lack of moral fibre' still lurked. He needed her, and with a storm coming he had counted on her presence to help him through. Sometimes, when the weather was bad and his bungalow seemed to shake with the wind's buffeting he would sit on the floor in the hall and let the draughts whistle round him and put a blanket over his head and just shake and tremble. Sometimes – if the tremors were slaughtering him and his legs were weakened and his head in torment, he would go out – likely having the back door open – and trudge up the hill and past the Noltland ruin and maybe start to run, pounding ahead in the darkness as they had done in the fitness sessions before being accepted into the unit, and he would run until the lighthouse beam caught him and then keep going until he was at the edge of Noup Head. He would hear the waves crashing on the rocks some 400 feet below and sway on his heels and let the wind shake his balance. When the lighthouse beam came round again it would fasten momentarily on the narrow ledges to the left of where he stood and show him the white bodies of the gannets. They were never blown off their roosting points and it might be the only place where he could fight his way through the black dog sessions. With the gannets, up on Noup Head, were guillemots and kittiwakes and fulmars, and farther to the right where the ground dropped towards a bay there were old rabbit holes refurbished as homes for puffins. Once – only once – he had seemed to stumble and a gust of wind might have come at him at a different angle, and he had lurched towards the edge and had regained his balance. Had Gaz saved himself by regaining his foothold? Had the wind shifted and veered off him? Had he struggled to prevent himself being pitched over the cliff? Was he resigned to ending the agonies? Not sure . . . And it had passed and he had turned and gone back towards the ruined castle with the wind hammering at his back. It was about controlling levels of stress and minimising them. Hard to do, but it was why he had fled to the island.

He sat in his chair with the lights off and the bungalow creaking and it would have been good if he had a dog, by his feet or on his lap, and he hoped to sleep – not dream and not remember.

2

Four days of hell, and then a minute in which it seemed to Gaz that a cloud had lifted.

She was coming first thing the next morning, had a ride on a boat that needed a minor repair done in the Pierowall harbour, and she was bringing stock for the hotel's gift shop. In the kitchen he shrugged into full waterproofs, nearly dry from the day before. It was lunatic to be out on such a day but he was a man persecuted by the weight of obligation and must get up the hill and beyond the castle and repair a paddock fence that had come down because of rotten posts. He would do it because he had promised it would be done, and the weight of the wind would make his efforts ludicrous but he was driven, could not escape a sense of duty.

In Gaz's life Aggie shared twin roles. She was both lover and carer, companion and therapist. She would have acknowledged the first, was ignorant of the second. Fetching the tools from the shed, which shook in spite of the steel-woven cables anchoring it, he was belted by the wind and rain splattered on him. No man and no beast would have volunteered to be out that day. Gaz thought that love came to Aggie on a 'take it or leave it' ticket, but to him it was precious and his life had had little of it.

The friends of his 'aunt' were Betty and Bobby Riley, childless, with a 200-acre farm east of Stoke on Trent and off the A50. A new life. Nothing had prepared him, aged five, for rural life. He had gone to the village school, arriving first because he was taken directly after milking was finished and last to be collected, after the second milking in the afternoon. Different to other kids and never belonging; every mother within miles would have masked her mouth and gossiped about the child now living at the Riley farm . . . he knew some said he was bought for cash. A rough and ready life, without frills or luxuries, and a gruff fondness shown him but not open love. Treated, in fact, like one of the dogs, cursed at, head ruffled and given a decent place by the fire in winter – love of a sort. He had understood it best when one of the older dogs, bad hips and sagging on its haunches, had been taken outside by Bobby Riley who had carried a shotgun and had cartridges in his pocket and put a spade by the kitchen door. Just one shot in the early morning fog, and he'd returned for his break-fast, nothing said, but dirt on his boots and the smell of the discharge on his hands, and his eyes swollen. That sort of love was shown him. Nor was his mother ever spoken of, and he had never returned to the tower block. At first he had been driven to school and back, then had walked both ways, at least an hour, then had bicycled. Then there had been a comprehensive in Stoke and a school bus . . . there were girls there, and he was ridiculed for his shyness. What love he did know as a teenager was for the isolation and the quiet of the farm, and most of his spare time was spent out in the woodland beyond the fifteen-Acre. He knew the haunts and habits of badgers and foxes and occasional deer, and the rabbits: killed none of them, never used a snare or a trap or a net.

He worked hard at the fallen fence. There would have been time on the Orkney islands when all the barriers that marked a division of property or ensured livestock kept to their own patch were dry stone walls. Stone, there to last, was a currency. The cemetery close to the hotel was filled with headstones, functional and dignified and scoured clean by wind and rain. Many of the men buried within sound of the sea and close to the calling gulls would have shortened their lives by building stone walls, back-breaking work. What had he, Gaz, to complain of as he hammered three new posts into sodden ground, then tapped home the staples? The men and women who had been where he had – the Province, Afghan's Helmand, and in Syria – did not complain, thought it diminished them . . . but that was before and this was now.

He worked steadily. He did not hurry. When he had finished he would tidy away his tool bucket in the back of the pick-up, and go home. He had a radio that he rarely listened to and a TV that was seldom watched, and he would get the place as presentable as was necessary, not that Aggie would have noticed.

One day, not soon, he might try to share with her what had happened in a storm in a place far away . . . but might not. It would open the can, let the worms wriggle free. 'Be careful what you wish for', what a teacher or a sergeant, or the psychiatrist assigned to him, could have said. He might one day, but not soon.

Time to be killed before he went home, before she came, and the gale to be endured and the rain to be sheltered from. He drove to the castle. He had no reason to be there. He would go inside, often did, through its low entrance and duck through arches, and would hunker down in what would have been a great hall where a man of authority would have held court. Where such a man would have believed himself in a safe haven, even if his future was death on a scaffold . . . He would sit there, contemplate, and be the better for it because Aggie was coming, a dose of the therapy he needed. Had found, inside those strengthened fifteenth-century walls, what he looked for, reckoned himself secure from the reach of his history.

Faizah was busy in the bar with customers. Early lunches for office workers and the visitors who flocked to Hamburg. A popular haunt, and the artefacts of the harbour and the traditional trades of the city were prominent, gave atmosphere. Impatient customers flicked fingers for her attention, and a shadow came across the door.

The door was held wide as if a potential customer needed more light to see better inside, and a gust of wind – carrying diesel and petrol fumes and the scent of the street – riffled her hair and lay on the bare skin of her neck, and tickled her scar. There were many times when the bar door opened, heavy and antique, and men and women hesitated there, but she sensed the difference. Had been waiting for someone to come, four days and four nights. She looked up, stared at the door, and a customer was snapping at her: how much longer before she took his order? At first she could not see the face because the light was behind it. The bar was kept low lit because the owner thought that enhanced its atmosphere and its replicas of ships' figureheads and coiled ropes and imitation firearms. She knew it was what she had waited for.

It had not been easy for her at the consulate on Hohe Bleichen.

"I don't know why you have come here. We're only a consulate."

Where else to go?

"The sort of people you are asking for, we don't have them here."

A message should be passed, responsible people should be contacted.

"And we're about to close. We're not open all day."

She said why she needed to speak urgently to people who would understand.

"I don't really know what I should do, and anyway I'm due to collect my daughter from nursery, and I only do part-time."

She had exploded. A gabble of names and a village that was Deir al-Siyarqi, her finger pressing at the scar on her chin, and no tears, just a hard-fought calm, and the controlled anger of Faizah must have struck at a place of pain. A telephone was lifted. First call was to a woman, demanding that she cut short her art class and get to the kindergarten to pick up a child. A second call to Berlin, and delays and impatience, and obvious transfers, and finally . . .

". . . I don't know who I am speaking to but don't dare to put the phone down on me, just don't. There is a young lady here with a story that would freeze blood, and I believe each word she has said to me. And you will listen to her, hear me, listen, and you will do what is needed. So, here she is."

Nothing prepared. Did not know where to start and a woman's voice on the phone that was accompanied by a metallic humming and she assumed her words were being recorded. She was rarely prompted, not interrupted, and she told it – most of it. She spoke of the boy, the British soldier, and spoke of a man whom she had seen that day when she had been a witness to an atrocity, and now she had seen his photograph, on a Norwegian site and in military uniform. She told it as she remembered it from two years before and did not doubt her recall of each hour that it had lasted, all as sharp in her mind as a knife's blade. Her name was taken, the address on Rostocker Strasse. It would be passed on, but no promises given for the attention her story might receive. The wait had started. She had thanked the consul who had shrugged, held her hand longer than necessary as if to signal that all that was possible had been done and something might happen – or not. Faizah had gone back to work and for four days and four nights had noted each time that the old wooden door of the bar was pushed open.

Her waiting was done. Not a tall man. Looked like a bureaucrat and she had experience of them in Hamburg as she had endured the hoops and jumps she'd passed through and scaled to achieve refugee status in Germany. A senior bureaucrat and with a good suit on him, a laundered shirt with a sober tie, and polished shoes. She saw his face, his little moustache, lightweight steel-framed spectacles, recognised him. A smile slipped to his mouth. She remembered him from a Portakabin, Gaz taken away by medics, and her fingers holding her wound because the makeshift work he had done to cover it was loosening. Then he had had a sympathetic smile, and she might have believed it had she not seen his eyes, cold as when the winter settled on the Norder-elbe channel: they had raked over her. He passed her, went to the bar, would have asked for the owner, who gestured towards her, would have said something but not entered into a debate or negotiated for her time. Had gone to a table where a single customer lingered over his coffee, and was invited to vacate the place, and must have looked for a moment into the intruder's eyes. He pointed to the seat opposite.

She left her order pad on the counter, wiped her hands on her apron, and joined him. He took her hand. Said what his name was, that he had come from London, that her story had taken time to find the right pigeon-hole, and apologised for the delay.

"If you need a name to call me by then it's Knacker, don't ask its origin. What I want to say is very simple . . . We don't forget. Days, months, years go by and events seem clouded in a haze of time, except that we have not forgotten. We have a message for such criminals: *Never underestimate the long reach of our arm.* Tell me."

She pointed across the bar, showed him where they had been sitting and talked of the Norwegian customers and their iPad and what she had seen, and described a photograph.

Lavrenti, the major, walked through the empty rooms of the apartment. At his side was his mother. It was well placed in the Arbat district, where prices were steep even by Moscow's current standards. Irrelevant to him. Bought outright and valued at $8000 a square metre it had a wide living area with room for dining, a kitchen, two bathrooms, two bedrooms, and a small balcony which would be good in summer and not collect too much of the winter snow. It would be taken by his mother; she would order the curtains and rugs, would furnish the apartment down to the cutlery, the crockery, the bed linen and towels: most likely she would choose the shower heads and instruct on degree of hot water.

In the Lefortovo interview rooms, he could call in a man or woman who needed reminding of their status in the new society. He could sit at his desk after the individual had been kept waiting for a half-hour or more in the entrance hall, after he had been marched along corridors with no decoration, no markers as to where he was in the building, after he was brought to the room and was seated on a hard, straight-backed chair and ignored. No acknowledgement, no courtesy. Could keep a person fidgeting, uncertain and with morale slackening, and would have a closed file in front of him and seemed to busy himself at a computer screen which was, of course, out of the subject's eyeline. Then, eventually would start with a cold, monosyllabic voice and would play the bored official and deal with questions of identity, addresses of domestic and work life. Any interview carried out in the recesses

of the old Lefortovo gaol added to the sense of intimidation, inse-
curity: as intended. The building was part of the legend of the
state's control over Muscovites ... there he was free from any
oversight. A suspect might denounce him, with threats of legal
action in the courts, and the complaints would be dismissed. His
job was to protect the regime from foreign espionage, to keep the
regime safe from dissidents, scum, internal agitation, to continue
the supremacy of the high-fliers of the ruling group, and to work
on a career path that would take him, Lavrenti Volkov, into their
ranks. Very simple. In the interview rooms of Lefortovo gaol he
worked assiduously towards those aims. He had been to the shit
heap of Syria and commendations said he had displayed courage,
leadership and ingenuity. He had been to the city of Murmansk
and his record there showed diligence, single-minded devotion to
the aims of FSB ... There was a threat, there must be a threat, it
was essential that the threat existed, was alive, and was massed
across the frontiers of the state: across the Norwegian border, up
the E105 highway. If there was no threat then the work of FSB,
Federal'nya sluzhba bezopasnosti, was unnecessary. The organisation could be wound up and its high-ranking officers sent to work
in industry, or drive taxis, and anarchy again could rule as it had
in the days before the rise of the President. It would not happen
on the watch of Lavrenti Volkov, and in the meantime he worked
with assiduous devotion, and his career prospered – as had the
career of his father, the brigadier general.

His mother chattered about orders for Scandinavian furniture,
not much of it because the new cult was for minimalism, and the
imported TV, and the German kitchen units, and. ... He never
criticised his mother, could still recall the scent she had worn,
from Paris, the day he had returned from Latakia, the Syrian port
city now taken over by the Russian air force, and she had hugged
him as if he were a precious toy, and the perfume had stuck in his
nostrils, but he had not choked on it, had told her how wonderful
it was to be home after a half-year of duty. Nor did he ever contra-
dict his father, high ranking, the best of connections, but who had
fought in the failed Afghan intervention. His father had guided his

path of advancement: to whom he should duck his head in respect, who was a drunk and a fool and to be ignored, who was a drunk and an idiot but should be listened to, and who was a coming man and who was vulnerable and slipping back. And he never complained about the close attention of his two minders, Boris and Mikki, sergeants in a unit once commanded by his father and now middle-aged and clinging to the last scaffolding of impor- tance, drivers and fixers and the street rubbish that he would soon seek to discard. His father had organised their recall to uniform for his duty in Syria and they were supposed to have 'watched his back' and made sure he came home in an aircraft seat and not in a bag; never complained about them because they harboured the secret of a long day in a faraway village, were witnesses. No complaints were made of their work, slovenly, untidy, the least that was acceptable.

His mother said that the apartment was a fitting home for an FSB officer with the best prospects of promotion, a future . . . He would be monitoring foreign diplomats, those from the west European nations who were most hostile, and would be directing the programmes designed to make them uncertain, paranoid: threats to family pets, burglary of homes and the parasite fear that came from burglary, and the opening of windows in the depths of winter and changing alarms and inserting porn clips on a family's desktop, and the harassment of locally employed workers. He told his mother that he was grateful for her attention to his new home.

Outside, Mikki was slouched at the wheel of the Mercedes saloon, and Boris ducked his head when he opened its door for Lavrenti's mother but not for him, respect denied him. They had been there, were witnesses. They went to lunch, a new Italian restaurant.

He should have felt strong, in control of his destiny, but did not.

A printer spewed out the picture.

Leaning forward, peering at the uniformed shoulders and the broad cap and its FSB insignia, Fee said, "Cheerful looking cove, I'd say."

Alice pointed. "And that's the line on his face, what we're told to look for, but you could miss it if you weren't close up."

"Have to know him, have absorbed the sight of him."

"Not just a glimpse. Would need a decent eyeball on him."

Going south on Kennington Lane, away from the monster building of mud-yellow and lawn-green that was forever Ceauscescu Towers and home of the Service, was the office known to those who needed such information as Knacker's Yard, or more simply as the Yard. Its door was sandwiched between the entrances to a taxi company and a fish bar and was opposite a tailor specialising in serious alterations. Varied punters seemed to come and go and it would have been difficult to single out that particular door, no number and no name-plate, but a bell and a spyhole, as in any way out of the ordinary. It was. Inside, with a television monitor to aid him and a lens trained on the street, was the same Coldstreamer who fronted up security at Round Table meetings. If he had a firearm it was not admitted to, but certainly he possessed within easy reach cans of gas and pepper spray and flash-and-bang grenades. On the first floor was the Yard and the windows had blinds permanently down but behind them and out of sight were steel plates. One open-plan area and a plain desk that was Knacker's, and two work surfaces that were the territory of his only aides – Fee and Alice. Other Round Table specialists had a room farther back on that floor and two more had the upper storeys where sleeping quarters were available. Knacker used to say that contamination from the employees in the main building was better avoided if these 'knights in armour' (or hooligans) were separated from the herd.

"It's not just the girl – where Knacker is."

"Too right, there was the recce boy."

"What are we looking for from him? What can he do for us?" Alice asked, rolling her eyes. Knew the answer but would be amused to hear it spoken out loud.

And was answered. "I seem to remember this morning that Knacker called it 'strategic policy advantage', what we'd be after. Doing harm to this fellow, this Major Lavrenti Volkov, nailing him down, and banking a dividend from it. Why we need this Orkney recluse . . . I mean, we'll not get any moralistic crap out of Knacker. It's for advantage, beginning and end – and what else?"

"Our guy did a runner, 'getting away from it all', that stuff. A sick man . . ."

Fee shrugged. They had done well, located a website far to the north and close to a sensitive Russian border and had queried a hack, and been economical with who needed to know and why. A picture had been sent, and a name and a rank and a location where this officer currently served. A file was up on Fee's screen. Where the two women were, so far, the business seemed just the area of trade that Knacker was known for, and relished.

"Yes, I heard he was sick, our guy. He has to do the ID, get the eyeball, but we'd not trust him to do the heavy lifting, kill the bastard. Likely would funk it . . . and there are attractions in using Syrian cowboys. What a strike for them, right into Kremlin land. Imagine word of it sneaking into all those sullen refugee skulls in the camps for dispossessed: be a time for trumpet and tympany. What an encouragement for all those poor beggars who reckon they are losers . . . and could be, the ultimate aim, the start of the quagmire involvement of the Russians just when they are getting packed up and ready – mission accomplished – to go home. It is attractive and can be done, but right at the start the lad has to do the identification. In and out."

"Makes sense." Alice grinned.

He stayed motionless. Gaz had his knees up and his arms hooked around them and struggled to keep his breathing steady. Had no need of a forecast, had sufficient experience of the storms to know that it would rise to a crescendo that evening, then break and be gone. During the night it would hammer in. And the black dog would come snorting at his ankles. He stayed in the tomb-like hall of the castle and little light penetrated the small sockets where the wind funnelled and the rain spat. The islands were about history.

If he had not accepted that events long gone dominated the islands then he could not have settled on Westray. History, to Gaz, was relevant because it gave him insights into the pecking order of importance, where his own life stood – and where he had been and what he had done, had witnessed – and not done, while clinging to his loaded rifle. Had not done anything that marked him out and was no longer a player in the shaping of events. Might one day say something along that tack to Aggie. Might try to breathe into her ear a little of a philosophy he hoped would protect him from the dog.

History was the lifeblood of the Orkney islands. Men and women had lived their lives, brought up children, buried their parents, on the wind-scraped land since the peeling back of the Ice Age. Skara Brae, a settlement of 5000 years before, had been exposed when waves had hit the shore and washed away the sand that had hidden a civilisation. The Ring of Brodger and the Ness of Brodger were rated unique in Europe, and walls there had been built forty-five centuries before to a thickness of fifteen feet. Christians had come 1400 years before Gaz's arrival, and the sites of a long-gone and disciplined people had been reactivated by Vikings who had scratched the name of a woman on a wall in a burial chamber, dubbing her 'most beautiful', and a saint had been murdered by axe blows on the orders of Earl Hakon 900 years ago, and his name "Magnus" given to the cathedral in Kirkwall. Mediaeval disasters had come and gone, and in more modern times naval catastrophes had wounded the prestige of the Royal Navy and the supposed safe anchorage of Scapa Flow . . . the sinking of the *Royal Oak* from a German submarine's torpedoes eight decades before, and 1200 men on board and two in three drowned . . . Gaz knew the marker buoy and knew the location of the grave of the saint, and the last resting place of so many whose lives had barely scratched on history but who still had outstripped him, Corporal Gary Baldwin, Special Reconnaissance Regiment, (Discharged Medically Unfit for Duty). Behind him was an arch and scratched in the stone was the message from many hundreds of years before: *When I see the blood I will pass over you in the night.* The history of the islands swamped him, but Aggie cared not a damn for it. Nor did the religion's carved words impress her, and she'd have rejected that promise of protection, and a message on a haven.

She would be with him early in the morning and then the storm would move on and he would be saved from the demons. He sucked deep breaths and sought to stifle the tremors . . . She had no respect for the history. Not the first time or the second, in his bed in the bungalow, but the third time they had been together. Her initiative and him wet with hesitancy, and nervous because stripping there was beyond the rules of his life, and her discarding and chucking fragments of clothing towards the cattle who came to watch the antics. Sex at the Knap of Howar, and her on top and him underneath and his body afterwards alive with the welts of nettle stings, and below them were the clean stone walls, sunken, of the homes built some 5,500 years before. Those who had lived there would not have exercised inhibition and Aggie had aped them, and brought him along with her, had taught and freed him, and he had imagined the smells of the fire and the scents of sweat and dirt, the tastes of their cooking, and the sea had burst on rocks below them. She had laughed and eased off him and taken the rubber, folded it, put it neatly in her bag for disposal and then had gone in search of her clothing and had dressed herself . . . There had been no other real love in his life. He'd thought their loving beside the settlement's walls and doorways and stores was to test him, see whether she thought him worth pursuing, and had never told him how she rated him . . . He could picture each stone in the wall closest to him, could hear the cries of fulmars and terns, and could feel the shame of that long-ago day which bred despair. He had done nothing, in his hide above the village, had been a watcher.

It was a horrid storm that came to Westray off the Atlantic, and near as awful as the one that would have gathered strength over the uplands of the Jabal al-Ruwaq and above the headwaters of the Euphrates, but he believed himself safe and Aggie would soon be with him, and the pull of brutal history, recent and long gone but not lost, would be a little more behind him.

Delta Alpha Sierra, the second hour

The wind and the rain came towards Gaz.

It was just past dawn and he was dry, comfortable and fed, and ready to receive his usual visitor. Then he would sleep, then doze, then spend the last afternoon hours getting ready for dusk and the move forward in darkness to the wall where the camera was and would settle down to the intricate work of prising open the breeze-blocks and extracting the battery, replacing it . . . just about routine and he could have done it with his eyes closed and his mind dead. Except that he would not be sleeping, nor dozing and he had the feeling, strong, that a bad day beckoned.

He lay in his dug-out cavity and was sheltered behind a scrim net in which he had woven lengths of desiccated thorn. No sun had risen behind him but there was always a possibility that light might reflect off his binocular lenses. Gaz was careful, took precautions. Did not hurry when it was not required and followed all the basic laws for the preservation of his safety. He reckoned the detonations of ordnance were creeping closer, mortars and artillery, and sometimes he saw the vivid flashes of the explosions. He blamed the Special Forces people.

Because of the location of the village, Deir al-Siyarqi, the Hereford mobile teams had spent time here. The village was sited in naturally dead ground, hard for strangers to know of its existence. It ran alongside, but was out of sight of, a main highway. The village and its people offered a chance of quiet but comprehensive surveillance of the road. Not everything was done by electronics and satellite photography. The need still existed for a man to be down on his haunches, chewing grass and seemingly half asleep, counting armour moving along the road: see whether it was Russian armour or Iranian armour or Hezbollah armour or Syrian armour, and identify troops on the move. A man chewing on grass, or a camera built into a wall, did a fair job. The village had survived previous campaigns when ISIS had pushed back government troops and was best when it stayed anonymous and barely figuring on a military map. The Hereford heroes had brought some old weaponry and done some training with the kids, bored, then flattered and then pumped up with silly courage. They would – the village teenagers – have thought themselves invulnerable, had been taught tactics by one of the world's talented units, would have thought themselves beyond and upward of the standard of bee's bollocks . . . They would have gone down the road that night, Gaz's bloody luck, and shot up the tent camp of the Iranians. The equivalent of taking a broom handle, finding a hedge with a hornet nest in it, and giving it a serious whack. Gaz had watched the manoeuvres of Russian troops and those from the Iranian units and the militia from Lebanon and the regular units of the Syrian government. His skill was to be motionless on a hillside, unseen, monitoring and recording and reporting: it was the work of the Special Reconnaissance Regiment. He had a combat rifle and a cluster of grenades but did not expect to use them. He was there to replace a camera battery, supposed to arrive unseen, carry out his task, slip away.

He saw the girl. She had the dogs with her. The older village women were already heading for the river, carried buckets. Some boys were on the move and were loading into pick-ups and might be going farther up the road, perhaps had work to get to. Her dogs were always at her heel. He had known this girl for months, had seen from the cheekiness of her smile, the mischief in her eyes, that the secret of his hiding place was known to her. Although she often sat within a couple of feet of his netting, close enough to reach out and touch him, near enough to whisper a confidence, they had never spoken, her to him, him to her – and it made for a sort of comfort. Gaz was certain that she went back to the village and never blathered that he had been there, was still there, never boasted of her skill at finding him. He would have known . . . The boys from the village would have come out and stared up the hillside and then edged closer, overwhelmed by curiosity . . . a village elder would have come with fruit and a soft drink . . . and the Hereford boys would have been told. It would have been fed into the debriefs that he was compromised and should not go back. She had kept her secret, had walked near to him and shown him the cheekiness, and had kept it close – and he did not know why.

With the dogs, she had gone to the pen of old thorn and had swung back the builder's pallet that doubled as a gate and the goats were gambolling, crazy and excited. He wondered if she had already eaten, what breakfast she took . . . Occasionally she would bring some grapes for him, and from a fold of her skirt would put them down beside his head, and then move on with the goats. Music played, then was cut off by a belated call to prayer. She ignored it, and let the goats and the dogs lead her . . . Then she heard the explosions, and he saw more detonation flashes. Villagers, some half-dressed, were spilling from the doorways and cocked their heads and listened. Every action had consequences, what Gaz had been taught, and he watched and felt that the day would go bad and could see the dull shapes of the personnel carriers coming up the road in convoy.

Perhaps he could have moved then . . . packed his Bergen, stowed his kit, tidied his hide. Crawled out and up on to the plateau where the ground was flat grit and there was no cover, no trees, bushes or rocks. She ignored the rain and had a heavy scarf across her hair and shoulders, and carried a light stick, and bulging at her waist was a plastic bag of food and water. He thought she would have heard sufficient shell and mortar fire to accept a fatalism: would get on with her day and hope that a storm from rain or wind or ordnance would pass her by. He saw the convoy coming on at speed up the road but still short of the track running down to the village, easy to miss, and Gaz reckoned one of the jeeps – in the faint light and with rain and dirt in the wind – carried a Russian flag tacked to a radio aerial.

Once a soldier in the Soviet army, now a veteran, Jasha had turned his military skills to those of a hunter. Decades before, he had lost most of the flesh, part of the muscle and some of the bone in his left leg from one of those shit little mines that the Afghans had scattered close to the Soviet base at Kunduz. He could walk, in a fashion, but not fast.

The bear, too, was a veteran and wounded.

They watched each other. About forty paces between them,

and the bear would have known who he was. He called it Zhukov: a good name for a bear. He would have stood some two and a half metres high and might have weighed almost half a ton. Its coat was a rich mahogany brown, its eyes seemed black and had a lifeless coldness, and Jasha thought that the beast would have torn a man to pieces with the long bent claws of its right front paw. Any man would have had to shoot Zhukov between the eyes, and drop him as dead weight if he were that close . . . any man but not Jasha. He was in his middle sixties, had been a sniper in a regiment of mechanised infantry, had been invalided out and had come to Murmansk in search of some form of hunting therapy while his wound seemed to heal, then went gangrenous, seemed to improve then deteriorate. And Zhukov, his supposed friend – only friend – was in no better health. Both damaged, both suspicious and introverted, and both with the easy habit of killing.

The bear might have wished to end the hunter's life because it was in perpetual pain and savage tempered, could have done it without difficulty. Jasha might have wanted to kill Zhukov out of pity, out of boredom and the need for splurged excitement, and had a rifle in his hands, cocked, the safety on and a bullet in place.

But both, in their differing ways, held the other in respect. He accepted the bear wandering close to his cabin, and the bear tolerated the old man intruding on its space in the tundra wilderness of the Kola peninsula. For a full half-hour, under light rain, they had eyed each other. Jasha was usually the first to break off and to go home, and he assumed that Zhukov would feel an honour satisfied and would resume the search for berries, the staple of its diet. A year before, Jasha had gone into Murmansk and had taken himself to a veterinary surgeon and had slapped down a wad of notes and had asked for a tranquilliser dose. For how big a creature? Big. Big enough for a cow? Big enough for a moose. To pacify it or to knock it out? To shut it down, at least a fifteen-minute dose. Money talked and a dart came with the dose and was loaded into the Dragunov marksman's rifle. He had shot it, the same range as he was now, a good hit in the left shoulder, and the animal had reeled around, had staggered and snarled, had shown teeth and one claw set, but only one. The other front leg, just above the pads, was coiled in a tight knot of barbed wire that had pushed aside the fur and punctured the skin, and had made a wound that was infected and coated in rust. He could have shot it with the wire still attached, could have ended its misery, instead had gone to Murmansk and flashed the money at the veterinary surgeon and had told him the requirement was to sedate a full-grown male moose. He had approached the prone creature with apprehension and had noted the malevolence in the eyes and sensed it wrestled with the power of the drug coursing through it. He had taken a deep breath and had knelt on the ground and used pliers to pull away the wire and blood had flowed. He was not a sentimental man and was familiar with pain, and they were the same pliers with which he had taken out one of his own back teeth, but tears had flowed while he had performed this crude surgery. Five loops of wire had come free and the wound was open and the summer flies swarmed and he had seen then that the bear had already chewed away half of its paw and half of its claws, chewed and worried at them. He had laced it in disinfectant and had realised that the bear's breathing quickened and had seen the first twitch of a back leg and the first movement of the tongue across massive yellowed teeth. He had given the animal the name of the most distinguished of Stalin's generals, a man of iron will . . . Zhukov. He had gone back to his cabin, his refuge, that he had found as a wreck, had insulated and made dry, and had barricaded the door and the windows. The bear had come the next day, and the evening of the following day, had sat on its haunches outside the door and Jasha had peeped through a spyhole and realised that the rest of its foot was now eaten off. A stump had been left at the height of the wire wound. His intervention might have achieved nothing. But the flesh seemed clean and the bear snorted regularly with a hiss of breath to drive away the congregation of flies, and it had watched Jasha's home, then had seemed satisfied that it had located a benefactor, and it had gone. He had seen the bear many time since, had noted the limping gait and the curve of the wounded leg as it put less weight on the ground, and

the way it sucked and spat to remove dirt: the pink flesh had disappeared, replaced by a coarse leathery cover. The hunter was
familiar with the single paw print with the pads and the claws, and
in front of them the smooth mark of the self-inflicted stump. It
was a fine animal . . . It might stalk him, it might be his friend. But
he would kill it if that was the requirement, if the pain ever became
unbearable. The wire would have come from the work of the
border troops. The border troops had brought up wire when they
had reinforced the fence that separated the Murmansk district on
the Kola peninsula from Norwegian territory. They'd have
dumped it. He hated them.

The hunter, Jasha, had no woman in the city down the E105
highway. Nor did he have a drinking friend there. His business
contact was an agent who sold the pelts that he brought in from
the wild animals inhabiting the tundra of wild grasses and dwarf
birch and cloudberry. He killed his animals for the trophy heads
that could be mounted on walls in lodges and hotels and which
were popular in St Petersburg and Moscow. He lived amongst the
shy, cautious lynx and Arctic foxes and the elusive wolverine, and
there were moose and reindeer and the one bear, Zhukov, that
fascinated him.

The bear never acknowledged him. Often, when out with his
rifle and going in silence and using dead ground, he sensed he was
being followed. He thought the beast dominated him and often, in
his refuge home, he would talk softly to it, call it by the name he
had awarded it, have a conversation, and be convinced of his own
insanity. It had watched, it had shuffled round, shown him its
back, and turned away to feed off a branch of berries and he was
losing sight of it.

"Heh, Zhukov, heh. Friend, I will see you. I hope to. I have no
other friend. Stay close and stay safe."

Down at the main rail station, near to the harbour and the docks
– with the rain heavier – Timofey had come to trade.

The arrival of a train from the south always lifted his spirits and
was as good a place for him to make money as any in Murmansk.

Twenty-four hours from St Petersburg to the Murmansk station, and thirty-six if the train had come from Moscow. Best was when young naval recruits were on their way to Severomorsk up the coast. They would buy. Timofey wore a thin windcheater that barely kept out the fine rain, faded jeans, and trainers that were scuffed and stained. His hair was fair and cut haphazardly and followed no style, but he had a strong face and high cheek-bones and a jaw that jutted and his eyes had that detached look as if his attention was far away as he hustled to get among the mass of the young military guys who stretched and coughed and smoked and would be allowed a few minutes to go and relieve themselves before the final part of their journey, to their ships and their barracks. In better times he would have had Natacha beside him, using her smile to attract the guys in uniform who yearned for the comfort of a wrap or a pill. He worked among them, dealt only in cash, had no time for change, and stuffed the money into his hip pocket; in his jacket's right-side pocket were the pills and in the left-side pocket were the scraps of paper with the twisted ends. It was not easy for him because not only did he have to do business, but he had to avoid arguments with the smart-arse kids who wanted to bargain, and had also to be aware that the military police would be looking for him, or others like him, and would come piling in with their batons and their handcuffs if he were too prominent.

His phone rang. He let it ring at first. Too busy trading. He let it ring as long as he dared because if it went off for too long then he'd attract attention. He pocketed cash, handed out pills, and that day they went better than the wraps. He moved fast and could hear the NCOs bawling at the kids to get on the buses. A queue had formed near him and he was circled by purchasers. He sold well, but Natacha would have done better. She would have been in there with her smile and the float of her eyebrows, the pout of her lips, and every kid would mentally have stripped her and would be groping for money and she would have given a tiny wiggle of her hips. They would all be submarine boys if they were in transit for Severomorsk where the hunter-killers were docked . . . and she talked heavy on submarines and had cause . . . and his phone kept ringing deep in a pocket and he had no time to answer, and a few of the NCOs were pushing in among the kids and heaving them towards the buses and the rain slopped off his hair. He had sold all of his pills, and only a palm full of wraps was left. A petty officer was in front of him. Eye contact made. The man thought Timofey was scum. His eyes and his sneer seemed to pose a question and he fingered the top of a truncheon fastened to his belt. Which would he prefer? Would he prefer a crack of the truncheon on his shoulder-bone and then his shin-bone, or would he prefer to back a discreetly palmed percentage of his takings? Timofey despised the sort of man who wore a uniform, held power because of the baubles on his chest. He was a free spirit: he slipped away, and the phone still trilled in a pocket.

Timofey's car was parked in a side street. He drove an under-powered Fiat 500, long past the date when it had any value other than for scrap. The car was good for Timofey and Natacha, painted a dull grey, hardly noticed, and would take him now to the gates of the gaol because this was the day she would be freed. He had not been to the trial and had not visited her in gaol. Would have been too easy for the bastards if he had done, would have identified himself. She would not have expected him to come, and he would be round a corner and beyond the cameras and she would exit though a small door in a big gate and would walk away and might just spit in the gutter and would go round that corner and the engine would be running, the passenger door open. She would slide in, would lift his hand and lay it between her legs, and he'd rev the engine and they'd be gone. He had missed her, had missed her bad.

He answered the phone, and heard heavy, gasped breathing. Timofey's father was a drunk, a certified alcoholic. Most of his cronies in the block were drunk most days from cheap vodka. It sounded like his father was having a panic attack or was afraid or merely drunk.

"Yes . . .?"

A silence broken only by incoherent grunting.

"What is it? Are you too pissed to say? Why did you ring?"

He was answered. One word. Foreign, awkward on his father's slurred tongue, and the obvious fear made its sound more indistinct. "*Matchless.*"

"Say that again."

"*Matchless.*"

In Timofey's language, honed in a tower block close to the church of the Saviour on Waters, that word was a clusterfuck moment.

It was the first time that Knacker had done it, woken a sleeper.

It had taken a committee meeting in emergency session. He had spoken to them with his mobile on 'secure', and Alice had given a presentation, and Fee had contributed with sharply constructed personality pictures of those involved. The matter had been tossed briefly in the air . . . the date and circumstances of the recruitment of a family in the then Soviet military port of Murmansk: their lack of use in half a century; the cost of maintaining their payment structure; and the risk that what had once been a sound signing might now be long past its date, the equivalent of a kettle made useless by aging limescale . . . The committee's vote had been four to two in favour of Knacker's request. The family in Murmansk were, in present-day terms, a 'waste of space', contributed nothing, and should receive a sharp tap on the ankle, that would jolt them from slumber. One member of the committee had said, 'Wake a sleeper, and he belches, goes for a shit, looks in the mirror, and either runs a mile or is the individual you always wanted on board. One of the two, but you have to wake him to find out.' They would need to send an agent to administer the kick. Alice had said that such an individual had been identified to do the donkey leg, and Fee had said that Knacker was on his case, should have it wrapped in the morning. They were working hard on the logistics, travel schedules, and pulling in increments. A parting shot: "This is all worthwhile, the effort of it and the sleeper woken?"

From Fee, who had worked a dozen years for Knacker: "If it works then we will pocket a grateful ally, small scale but well positioned, and because those people have long memories, the friendship and gratitude would linger over generations. In a heartland of Syria we would have assets and we would have a take on the movement of Assad forces and Russians and Iranians and Hezbollah ... If it does not work out, then we will have lost next to nothing, might just have burned the sleepers. We should go with it."

From Alice, who had been in the Yard with Knacker for fifteen years: "We send a man, known to us, and he links with the sleeper and is ferried round and gets a decent eyeball on the target. Then all he has to do is clarify the identification and give his location, and we get him clear. We have a good candidate for the role. A follow-up team moves in, does the necessary. Not connected to us. Decently removed. Early days, but looking good. Better, looking very good."

All passed to Knacker, all predictable. His girls, Fee and Alice, could have extracted teeth from the committee without anaesthetic and were persuasive, and it was the sort of operation, small mission, that Round Table people were ideally suited for. Knacker supposed there was a file tucked away in the archives that carried the details of scores of sleepers tucked in their beds, snoring softly. Some would have been signed up for money, and God alone knew that Knacker was hardly generous with government funds. Some would have hated whatever regime of the far left or far right they confronted. Some would have been compromised, barbed hooks gone into their flesh, and he had dealt with that level of recruitment in Ireland and men had wept to be free of him and had not had their eyes dried or a sympathetic smile, and most were now dead. And some were afflicted with ego and the thrill of living the lie and cheating on friends and neighbours and employers and family, and had their vanities expertly massaged by Knacker. The girls had done well to dig out the sleeper, identify him, and start the process rolling. The codeword for shifting the wretch in Murmansk from his pit was *Matchless*.

He took a taxi. The girl, sweet soul, had said she would go back to her waitressing. He asked for the airport, the private side out amongst the warehouses.

A storm was coming up off the North Sea and must be channelling down the Elbe estuary. He was dropped off at the warehouses. Stood and peered about him and wanted to be greeted. A flashlight was shone at him.

"Are you the one they call Knacker . . . the name I was given."

"It's what I answer to."

Knacker assumed the pilot to be former military. No laundered white shirt, no gold bars on epaulettes, no clip-on black tie. He wore one-piece overalls in a dull olive and had no rank badge and no ribbon strip and displayed no name tag, but had dark glasses half-buried in his hair. They walked together and turned a corner and in the lee of a hangar was a two-engine Cessna. To Knacker it looked pitifully small and he saw the wings flip a little in the wind.

"Your girl told me where we are going."

"Good."

"I have to say, it's where the weather is tonight."

"That so?"

"Myself, I wouldn't put my cat out in it. We might bump a bit."

"Will we get in?"

"Can but try. Not exactly bulging with alternative strips. But yes, probably."

The winds lashed the island with the force of a scouring brush. The rain flushed the land clean and would have been running in rivers down lanes and creating waterfalls off the hills. The rain was a drumbeat and the wind made songs in the overhead wires.

On the floor, beside his bed, Gaz lay in the foetal position.

Those who were not among the island's incomers were familiar with the ferocity of the storms that battered Westray and all the other Orkney islands. The few trawlers and crab boats would have been anchored close to shore in the bay in front of the hotel and the cemetery. The farmers would have been careful to ensure their livestock could weather the blow. The island was battened down and the school would be closed the next morning . . . and work for a handyman was suspended. A rug was rucked up by his body and he lay on his side on the hard smooth surface of the vinyl covering the floorboards. No one on the island knew that Gaz had been a soldier, had served in the desperate combat areas of Syria, of Afghanistan, or of Northern Ireland. He never talked of it, changed the subject if asked about his past, nor spoke of illness or the help of the psychiatrist, had told nobody of a girl getting punched and a policewoman slapping on handcuffs and time in the cells and in the dock. Had never spoken of the day that a storm – the same winds and the same rains – had come to a valley and a village close to a main highway that was believed to be of intelligence-gathering value. He did not know how Aggie would get across in the morning and expected the mobile to trill in his ear and to hear her voice telling him, *Sorry and all that, Gaz, just can't make it. Won't last for ever. See you soon* . . . She had not rung and his phone was beside him. Nor had he eaten that evening nor drunk anything, and was a grown man and a wreck.

It came as a low rumble at first, a thunderstorm far away and the clatter distorted in the wind. He strained to hear better. Fixed-wing and likely circling to locate the strip on Westray island. Coughing and louder, an engine straining at the limits of its power. The wind-sock would be horizontal and the wind coming across the runway. Gaz evaluated . . . He would have said that he knew by face each and every islander, some better than others, but knew each well enough to nod and wave, including the kids and the old people who hardly left their homes . . . and had known by sight every villager, resident that day in Delta Alpha Sierra, knew their trades and their habits and the routines of their days, and had watched them and stayed hidden from them – and realised a simple truth. An aircraft coming to Westray on such a night, in pitch-dark blackness, with a minimum of navigation lights and with wipers on the cockpit windscreen barely able to clear the rain and give the pilot what visibility he needed, meant a matter of life and of death. He straightened his body and then edged across the floor, did a leopard crawl that he had perfected in a former life, unforgotten, and reached the window and dragged aside the curtain. He wondered for whom the aircraft came. An emergency: a man or woman or child would be in that half-world that was divided by the two extremes, by life and by death. Who had fallen, who had suffered a coronary, who was a stroke victim, who was in such danger that a doctor and nurse had been despatched from Kirkwall on the mainland and sent north to Westray, risking their own survival? He saw the lights. They were low and seemed to waver, to dip and toss and swing to the side then jump, then fall. He wondered which of the islanders had suffered the calamity requiring a flight on that bad a night. Or who was about to be born?

A matter of life and a matter of death for one of their number. The aircraft lights seemed to drop, fall away and the engine roared in the night.

3

A car braked. He heard a door opening, splashed puddles, a door slamming shut. The car pulled away. His gate, for want of oil, groaned as the wind buffeted it, and slammed it shut. Footsteps on the gravel.

There was an old knocker on the door, rarely used but serviceable. Two loud raps. Gaz knew what defined a stranger: was a front door locked in the night hours? Islanders, those with pedigree stock who might have a grandfather buried in the cemetery down on the shore, who knew the land and its people and the history, would not have bothered to fasten a door, turn a key, push a bolt. That night, Gaz locked the door, a defence against the demons who hunted him. He had been in the darkness when the car had approached, come warily up the track. He did not have anything in the bungalow that was worth stealing and seldom had more cash than what his wallet held. He might as well have left the door unlocked, but had not, and he had believed himself more secure behind the newly fitted mortise . . . He realised a truth. He had thought the aircraft landing in the night, in the teeth of the storm, was a matter of life and a matter of death. But the rap was on his door. Gaz's life and Gaz's death. His vehicle was parked at the bungalow's side. If it had been the islander who managed several jobs, among them the Westray taxi service, then a clear question would have been met with a certain answer. Was this resident at home? Was definitely at home. Gaz was on the hall floor. The door handle was not tried but he heard impatience expressed through a hacking cough and a spit, then a curse, then stamped feet. Another rap, and another, and a shifting of squelching shoes. A voice from far back, then it had been sparse with words, just enough to nudge along his story as told in the Portakabin where the debrief had taken place. Not a shout but a voice competing with the wind's howl and the downpour of rainwater from the overload in the gutters.

"Come on, Gaz, open the bloody door. Raining out here if you didn't know. I'm Knacker, met you that night at the FOB, heard your story, the eyewitness account. Flown in through a bit of a squall, and come to see you. A little proposition . . . Like I say, it's raining. I'm already half drowned. Gaz, get a move on."

He reached towards the key in the lock, groped and felt the jamb until the chain was in his fingers. The door was locked but not chained. Had been chained for the first months he had been on Westray, but six month ago he had abandoned that level of security. He fastened the chain. Then, only then, did he turn the key and ease the door back as far as the chain permitted. A man stood on the step. The security light at the end of the front wall of the bungalow lit a shoulder of a sodden raincoat, but most of the face was in shadow from the brim of a trilby hat, and rain ran off it in rivers.

"We're not going to mess about are we, Gaz? Tell me that we aren't. Famous for hospitality aren't you, up here? Getting out of this shit would be a small mercy."

Of course, Gaz remembered him, remembered his face and the sound of his voice that was so bloody calm, and the eyes doing a stiletto job on him, and remembered also two women who had hovered in the background, one behind Knacker and one behind Gaz: a pretty woman and a butch woman, neither in uniform, both with leather shoulder-holsters and handguns draped on their chests. A tape had turned and he had told his story, the story that had near destroyed him, and he had hidden from it.

"I cannot see what business I have with you."

"Easier if I'm inside, hopefully with a fire lit."

"The past is done, I don't live there."

"Just a little matter, something simple and quick. Better if it were explained."

"You should go away." A quaver shook Gaz's voice. "Should leave."

"A bit of business to run by you, Gaz. Something that's worthwhile. Did I tell you it's raining out here, or did I forget to tell you, and blowing a bit."

"I have moved on. I have a new life."

"Better if I tell you, face to face, what we're looking at. Wouldn't want you to think, Gaz, I haven't more in my life than pitching up in the night, in a serious storm to look up old chums, or reminisce old wars. Never was good at nostalgia. Am I going to charge the door, break it down? No ... but would enjoy helping you with your road back."

"Would you go away? Please go away."

"Read your notes, Gaz, and the diagnosis. I could do you more good than you sitting on your backside in the dark, frightened of your own shadow. I reckon I could put some purpose your way, better – short-term, long-term – than a bottle of pills and hiding."

"I want nothing from you."

"I saw that girl today. Pleasant kid. Attractive if it weren't for the scar. Brave as a lioness, of course. Not hunkered down and self-pitying. Do I need to remind you of what she did? What do you think, Gaz? Memory drooping, is it?"

"Just go. Go back where you came from."

"Forget it ever happened? Be nice. Forget that place? Forget what was done? Forget the perpetrators? Keep on mowing grass and mending leaky roofs, and doing some bog standard plumbing, or electrics? An option, Gaz, turning your back on it. Or, should I tell you what I want of you?"

"Nothing for you to say to me."

"Certainly comes down here, the rain ... The girl, Faizah, has helped us discover the Russian who was liaison, and we've done the checks. Got a name and a work location, and that's where we need you on board, Gaz. Need you doing what you do well."

"I'm not listening. I'm hearing nothing."

"I'm cold, Gaz, and wet, but this is too important for me to be worrying about myself. He's in Murmansk, the Russian with a shed load of guilt ... All we want from you is that you pop in there, use a few of the skills you're noted for. Have a look at him, identify him for certain, copper-bottom stuff. Come on out after marking him. He's a major in FSB and thinks he's clear, why wouldn't he? But he'd be wrong, and that's not your problem, that's mine. It's not a big ask, Gaz, and you'd be well rewarded: not cash, wouldn't insult you, but pride and respect and the knowledge that you didn't walk away when the chance was offered. Get that chain off the door, be a good fellow."

"Go back where you came from."

"I'm doing you a favour. Mean it. Can't spend the rest of your life cowered in a corner. Chance to get your esteem back. Think on it. Come and get me when you've had the think ... into Murmansk, yes? Sort of job we do well. Out of Murmansk? We're putting it all together. Just think on it."

"Go away." A choke in Gaz's throat.

"A cup of coffee would be welcome, while you think."

The man sat down. Put a hand out to steady himself, his fingers going beneath the puddle, lowered himself, and sat. The rain doused him and he reached up to steady his hat so the wind would not take it.

"You've had my answer. Go."

Gaz closed the door. He left the chain on, but turned the key in the lock. The weather was as bad this night as it had been that day in the village. Would he weaken in his resolve? In a few minutes, the man would be gone, would be bashing at the door of the Pierowall hotel, demanding a room and warmth, and then he would not have weakened, but he remembered the girl, and how it had been.

Knacker sat on the path.

Gravel gouged his flesh. The rainwater lapped round him and his shoes were filled and his trousers and jacket clung close to his body and his raincoat no longer gave him protection and he kept his trilby hat low over his eyes. He was confident.

There were times when James Lionel Wickes, Knacker to all who were important to him excepting Maude, would have broken down the door and grabbed by the throat a man who prevaricated, and squeezed to inflict pain, and times when he would have pushed his fingers into his hip pocket and extracted a wad of notes and paid them without equivocation, whatever was required. He was familiar with winning, was rarely disappointed. He had no doubt that his target would weaken, that drama was avoidable and a bucket of rainwater on his skin and wind on his face would hurry the process along ... Always won and a slow smile at his mouth, disturbing the dripping water, as he reminded himself of the shock, the horror, the squeals of other parents when he had tripped his closest rival in the school Under 10 sack race, flattened him, and crossed the tape first. His own parents had run a market garden in the West Midlands, fancy flowers and cacti, now managed by Knacker's younger brother. Last time he had been there was for his mother's funeral seven years back ... Had joined the army at eighteen and transferred to Intelligence after basic training ... with a slight detour. Had enrolled at Sussex University, had done a solitary week in International Relations and seen his fellow students legless and pissed, and had heard out a lecturer talking of the aims and benefits of the course. Had packed his bag at the student hostel, taken a bus into town, past the Dome and right into Queen's Road and then pushed at the door of the Recruiting Office and signed the form ... expected and demanded that others match his commitment ... A reputation was quickly forged. A few labelled him 'eccentric', most rated him 'difficult', all agreed that he 'delivered', and the name of Knacker came fast, from the early days in the fag-end of violence in the Province.

He talked to the girls, to Alice and Fee. Almost dozed, could have slept anywhere. Heard what was achieved, nailed down and in place – did not query them or second-guess.

"And you, Knacker, how's your evening going?"

Told Fee he might later have a cold, and that it rained where he was and a wind blew.

"You're not going to get your death? Christ's sake, can't you find some shelter? And the boy? Eating out of your hand?"

He was just gathering up a few loose ends, which would satisfy her. He was known for his annoyance if ends were not tied.

"Just checking, Knacker, he's not messing you, is he?You're not doing this with kid gloves? Doesn't he remember what happened there?" That was Alice, a dear girl with an accent from a stone-wrapped village near Bath, petite and looking like a chocolate box cover portrait, and ferocious if challenged.

Told her he was fine. Told them both that all was well. Told Alice where he would be in the morning. Told Fee where she should be.

He sat and could not quite control the shivering as the wind bucked him and each time he moved the security light was triggered and he had not heard Gaz padding inside the bungalow nor the flush of a toilet and imagined him still crouched in the hall and tortured. He knew of the man's illness, its symptoms and had with his legendary discretion briefed a magistrate who would hear the assault case. It was a foul malady and had brought down many outstanding soldiers, as Knacker knew. He sympathised with sincerity. But he sat on the flooded path and waited and thought he turned a screw remorselessly ... he was confident of the outcome. Wondered how the target was, the man the girl had described, considered how his evening was going while in the comfort of ignorance of what would await him.

His father was out for the evening, his mother entertained friends.

Lavrenti had stayed in his room, risked annoying her. He watched TV. A ridiculous game show but in the isolation of Syria he had seen canned episodes and in Murmansk had become almost addicted. He was not out, dining and dancing or in the new cocktail bars, because he had no friend to be with. At least in Murmansk, as in Syria, he would have the sidling company of Boris and Mikki, a few paces behind but close enough to mind him. Not that either would drink if he did, would not match glass for glass, but would be there to heave him up and lug him back to the car, and might take off his shoes or boots in the apartment room north of the Arctic Circle or in the prefabricated cabin where he lived on base, alongside the Iranians. They listened to his monologues, grunted, laughed when required. Company of a sort.

The ripple of voices was easy to hear, even above the game show track. Four of his mother's friends had come for the evening, and two had brought daughters. No other men of his age regarded Lavrenti as a friend. He had thought that the kids in the teenage ice hockey team were buddies and they had played well in a league, and he had even believed that his future might be in the professional game, had dreamed of it. He had been dumped. No ceremony, no bullshit, just told that he was inadequate to progress to the neces- sary levels of fitness, skill and motivation. His mother had wept, his father had growled a refusal to intervene. Had no friends in the college for FSB graduates because there the brigadier general had clout and he was marked down for fast advancement, and others oiled to him but would never be friends . . . and no girls.

His mother called him from the salon. He ignored her. He detested her scheming for his advancement. He had no friends because he lived outside any loop where he might have found them. Often he had wondered whether his posting to the liaison role with the Iranian troops of the Quds unit was an attempt by superior FSB and army officers to keep him beyond sight, and whether the posting to Murmansk was dictated by a worthwhile job or 'Send the little shit somewhere, anywhere, where we don't have to see, hear him'. His mother called again and he recognised the higher pitch in her voice, annoyance. He had changed out of his uniform and wore jeans and a T-shirt and his hair was a mess, uncombed, and his feet were bare. If his father had called him he would have run to be beside him, would not have dared to act otherwise. He was the son of his father, always had been, still was, would be as long as his father's name was known in FSB circles.

She called again, louder. The four friends, would have been honoured to receive such an invitation. Not talked about, but slyly hinted at by his mother, was the relationship between the briga- dier general and the President, a personal friendship . . . and proof was always in the pudding. A barbecue a few years back, six or seven, and his father heating up the charcoal, and Mikki ordered to the kitchen to help his mother make sandwiches and nibbles, and Boris sent to the hypermarket for more beers and soft drinks.

The *dacha* his father had acquired was on a turning off the Uspenskoye Highway, the fast route to Moscow, and half a dozen kilometres away and off the same road was the Novo Ogaryovo, the rural home of the President. No caterers that night, and no fuss and no entertainment except for a string trio out of Crimea, and *he* had come. Without a great cavalcade, only a knot of noisy motorcycles and *he* had been wearing leathers and a helmet with a tinted visor as had his escort who would have been from the Presidential guard. His father had been hugged and his mother's hand shaken. Lavrenti had been in the background, told where to be, and for a moment his father had pointed to him and *he* had looked that way and identified him, and Lavrenti had blushed and ducked his head in respect: it was the closest he had been. *He* had stayed a couple of hours and eaten well and then the leathers had been zipped tight and the helmets were on and the visors dropped and the air had filled with the noise and the fumes and they were gone, and *he* was merely an anonymous figure in the midst of the bikes, and Lavrenti's father had never referred to the occasion again, nor had Lavrenti's mother. He had understood the message . . . his parents existed within an inner circle, were 'untouchables', were to be deferred to, and their status would last as long as the regime of the President survived . . .

A clutch of great leaders had been abruptly removed from supreme office – Gaddafi of Libya, Mubarak of Egypt, and a leader in South Korea and another in Brazil and another in Malaysia, Zuma in South Africa and Mugabe in Zimbabwe, and the president of Ukraine had suffered the rank indignity of fleeing his palace and having to be lifted to safety by Russian helicopters as the mob closed in on him, and Saddam had swung on the end of a rope. And Assad of Syria would have done if Russia had not preserved his rule. A simple lesson to be learned: the regime should be protected if influence and privilege were to be preserved, and there were many lampposts outside the Kremlin walls and in the Arbat district with ornate frames from which ropes could be slung, and many trees with decent branches off the Uspenskoye Highway . . . His mother was at the door.

"You should come, please. It is rude if you do not."

She tutted at him for his appearance and his no-show, but would not criticise him to his face. He pushed up from his chair, and doused the TV sound and followed her into a corridor, and along it, then seemed to remember his position and status and walked tall. He would be charming and would be cold. Would be polite and would give nothing. Lavrenti, at thirty-two, had no regular girlfriend nor an identified mistress, nor did he give any sign of latent homosexuality. He followed his mother into the salon. He was introduced to the four ladies, his mother's guests. He knew them, of course. He knew all of his mother's friends. They were the wives of the men who had clung to a vestige of influence during the anarchy of the years before the current presidency, then had nailed support to the new man, and were rewarded. He shook hands and his smiles were sparing, and then he was introduced to the two daughters. Easy for Lavrenti to appreciate this was a throw by his mother that had been difficult while he had served in Murmansk, in the far north. One was tall and blonde and the other was short and blonde, and both wore clothes and cosmetics to impress. His mother had had no wedding to organise and no grandchild to swaddle, and his father no chance to see if *he* would come out from his home on the Uspenskoye Highway and grace a reception with his presence if only for half an hour. Both the girls were pretty, both stared at him and the taller seemed indifferent and the shorter made little pretence of disguising disappointment, and both were at least twelve years younger than he was. He had not spent a night with a woman since he had flown to Syria, had never slept with a woman with mutual affection, not without paying. The girls, would have understood that he had no interest in them and only met them in deference to his mother; perhaps he seemed old beyond his years, perhaps weighed down by some burden; neither competed for his attention. So, both started on a mutual conversation about music, then films, then shopping, then food, and saw him off. He read them. When they went for whores in Murmansk, Mikki drove and Boris selected who he would go with, and paid: never the same one twice.

He was polite. He pleaded workload to his mother's friends and slipped away. Back in his room, Lavrenti returned to his game show. He took his bag from under his bed, and began to pack the few clothes he would need for his short return to the north. Not the next day but the day after, but he packed anyway. How would any of these women, old and fat, young and skinny, understand if they hadn't been there, no chance of obliterating the memory . . .

Love on a wet evening. Timofey panting, and Natacha squealing and pleading for more effort and short of it for months, and the noise from both of them would have barely been obstructed by the thin walls of an apartment, the only one in Murmansk city that understood the significance of *Matchless*.

Timofey lived with his father in a building that had been put up in the Kruschev era, five storeys high and with brick outer walls, better insulation than the concrete-framed ones of later Soviet days. He knew his father sat outside the door and waited for him to finish, for her to be as satisfied as she ever was. Clothes were scattered and the light burned above them and no curtains were drawn and if neighbours in other blocks feasted on the sight of them then they'd be lucky, what she said. He wore heavy rubber as protection; she might be infected and might not, and neither knew. A final grunt and a last squeal and both sagged.

Matchless was a bell pealing inside the recent history of the family. It was the code word given to his grandfather and to his father and passed down to him, Timofey, with due and secret ceremony inside that same apartment, accompanied by the killing of a full-strength vodka bottle, on his sixteenth birthday. *Matchless* had stuck with the family. Natacha knew of it because his trust in her was total, and he had no secret from her . . . and she knew of the bank account and the monies that stacked up there and were added to each quarter. Nothing had been asked of the family since the day the deal was done.

They did not do, never had done, what the books called

'foreplay', and did not cuddle and kiss afterwards. She rolled off him, he reached for his cigarettes and for a Zippo lighter, and he lit for both of them, and they would have heard the bell ring at the front door, and then the shuffle of his father's feet.

The start? The British destroyer, *HMS Matchless* – crew of around 190 – had sailed as convoy escort to Murmansk. It was 1942, deep midwinter ferocious weather, continuous air and submarine attacks to be fought off, but the cargo of ordnance and equipment had reached the Soviet port and the young sailors were allowed a quick sneak ashore. They had some wounded merchant seamen onboard, plucked from the sea, and local nurses had turned out on the quayside to treat them. An Oerlikon anti-aircraft gunner from *Matchless* had been told in a mess-room by a chief petty officer that these Russian girls went like 'fucking rabbits': aged eighteen, he had been tested in battle and not found wanting and had met one of the girls huddled in the cold, smoking behind a crane stanchion and the price of it had been a bar of soap. Done standing up, and quick because of driving sleet, and done with the minimum of exposed flesh, and he'd thought her a great girl, and she had been his first. She had told him her name, forgotten by the time he struggled back up the well-iced gangway with his trouser buttons still unfastened, and he had egged the description to his mates, and it had seemed unimportant that he had told her his name, Percy Wilkins. A year and a bit later, and while the lad was in the Mediterranean, on resupplies to Malta, a chum had put into Murmansk on a minesweeper. A young woman was on the quay, holding a baby in her arms and asking in fractured English if Percy Wilkins of *Matchless* was on board. Months later the chum met the Oerlikon gunner and told him of the encounter and they had a good laugh, and the chum had said 'the little sprog's as ugly as you, mate, which is saying something', and it was just a story, good for fifteen minutes of fame. Timofey had heard it all from his grandfather and his father, and they'd have heard from the contact point – vodka swigged – half a century before. The matter moved on to the world of sleepers and clandestine banks – and this, too, the grandfather and father had been told – when the middle-aged one-time gunner, now a factory welder, had boasted of his fast and fumbled shag to a chuckling audience of veterans in a British Legion. Now it was the height of the Cold War, of an arms race, of rabid suspicion, of fertile intelligence gathering and, up a circuitous trail, word of the exploit had reached a Whitehall office, and a bright spark had sensed a possible opportunity for insertion when precious few existed . . . It had taken some effort to track down the former nurse and her bastard child in the city of Murmansk but a Swedish crane engineer had proved a dogged investigator, and a Finnish naval architect who designed deep-sea trawlers had met Timofey's grandfather, a dock stevedore and now in his late twenties, had bought him with promises. Had told him the damned obvious: a spy in Soviet Russia would be inter-rogated, tried in secret, shot or beaten to death. Had shown him a copy of a bank statement from an address on an island in the British Channel, Guernsey, that listed an account and his name, and the first dollop of bribe cash. What did the grandfather of Timofey, the son of Percy Wilkins, have to do? Nothing. Sit tight. As age advanced and already limited faculties failed, the account passed to Timofey's father. What did he have to do? Nothing, wait. One day – perhaps – the code word would be used, *Matchless*, then payback time would commence. Timofey's grandfather had been dead for seven years; his father soon would be as alcohol ravaged him. Every year, a stranger would meet the nominated member of the family and would show a single sheet of paper with a printout of the accrued sum, allow it to be seen, digested, and then a cigarette lighter would be produced and the corner licked by flames and the charred remains dumped.

Voices beyond his door.

He removed the protection, pulled on his trousers and a shirt and a sweater, and stubbed out his cigarette. He did not kiss Natacha, nor compliment her on her loving, tousled his hair. She would follow him.

No names given. Their visitor could have been Italian. Timofey dealt to foreigners in the summer months if they came to the Kola peninsula for hunting, fishing, hiking; many required smack or

skunk or phets as distraction from the mosquitoes and Murmansk's
lousy standards of cuisine. His father was drunk, barely understood. Natacha stood behind him, wearing her trousers but not
much else, and the Italian did not blink or gape, or fluff his words,
only smiled and continued to say what would be required, and
when . . . and finished with a few words that left a sour taste, and
Timofey understood their warning.

"Please believe me. The people who make requirements of you
are not a charitable organisation. You might consider going to
FSB and confessing the involvement of your family in criminal
espionage and hope to win clemency from your courts. You would
not get it. The length of your family's conspiracy would come into
the possession of FSB and the monies you have already been paid
that lie in a foreign bank. If you survived the beatings you would
go to a harsh regime camp for twenty years, twenty-five years, and
there would be no move to bargain for your freedom and swap
you."

A figure was written on a notepad sheet and shown to Timofey.

"That is how much is currently held in the account. A good
sum. Unwise to jeopardise your ownership of it."

Timofey said, "What you ask, it is for very soon?"

"Very soon."

Natacha said, "But fun, exciting. An entertainment."

"Be careful, I urge you."

The Italian messenger slipped away, a door closing on the
landing and the slight sound of feet on a long staircase. Natacha
did a little dance and he stood for a moment, sombre, then joined
her and together they danced and Timofey might have said that
the adrenaline running in him gave him a greater sensation than
what he'd done with her, and the dance became faster, wilder, and
his father lay on the sofa moaning for drink.

Timofey cried out, "It's like we slept, year after year, and they
came and kicked our arses and woke us, and we don't know what
will happen."

Natacha shouted in his ear, "What I said, fun and exciting, and
dangerous."

They danced till they dropped and sprawled on the floor, and his father snored . . .

The hunter stood statue-still and listened.

He seemed to hear the wind in the trees and its flight across the scrub and over the rock, and the patter of rain falling. Jasha was a man who had been in military combat and whose ears had withstood the blasting of artillery and mortars, and the echoing explosion close-up of the RPG–7, but his hearing had survived intact. He had come out to shoot an Arctic fox. The pelt would pay well, and if the head were detached then it could be mounted for display in a trophy room of a multi-millionaire, for dollars, not the valueless rouble. He had put down a duck's carcass in the hope of luring one into the arc of his rifle's aim. He would have made more money if he had trapped it, then drowned it in a rain butt, then skinned and cleaned the undamaged fur, but trapping seemed to him to break the concord he had with the beasts living around him. He would get less money but regarded an accurate single shot as more honourable . . . he did not know another hunter who bandied such a word. He thought he heard a hiss of breath. It could have been the wind blowing or the rainwater tipping off the scrub's leaves. Or it could have been the bear. He would not smell it. He would hardly see it in the shadows that on such a night played deceitful tricks, and the low bushes were constantly moving. But he might hear it. He did not like to believe that the bear stalked him.

The success of the original Zhukov and his ruthless views on the necessity of taking casualties, his belief in ultimate victory, had made him too valuable to be purged, as was the fate of most ranking officers. So, Zhukov was unique, a winner whatever the setbacks. Losing a front paw and the claws in the pads and having a stump had not deterred the bear. But it was an animal. The purchase of the incapacitating drug, its use as a sedative, and the risk to Jasha's life, and the work he had done on the wound and the extraction of the barbed wire, and the dosage of steriliser – all he had given was low down in the beast's psyche of gratitude. Jasha thought it followed him that evening.

The Arctic fox had not come. The duck lay fifty paces from him, untouched. Perhaps the Arctic fox knew what Jasha did not. He might be the last to know that the bear trailed him.

Was the bear short of company? Was it tagging along with him? Did it resent his intrusion into its territory? Would it come after him and use its full techniques of innate fieldcraft, then – at the right moment – charge him? Accepting the old wound, Jasha was a fair mover over broken ground, had a sniper's mentality, was lightly built for his height, and Zhukov would weigh a little below 400 kilos and could move on three pad sets with the quiet of that same Arctic fox that had avoided both bait and bullet. He did not think the bear would register an act of kindness; more likely to resent him, an intruder. Yet, was still, in a fashion, Jasha's friend.

Jasha, turned, slowly and carefully, and listened and took a step forward, and another, and broke a twig which was a rare mistake for him, and then hurried, expecting all the time that a huge dark shadow would come behind him. One blow of the stump would fell him, one slash from the claws of the surviving pad would lacerate him. He returned to his hut, fed his old dog, lit a lamp and put a post against the door, and thought he had made himself a prisoner in his own home deep in the wilderness between the frontier fence and the distant winding road to Murmansk: was alone, did not know whether he was followed or was stalked. Bad times. What he had known as a soldier soared in his mind. Always for a sniper, without comrades close and with enemies near to him, there were bad times and none of them forgettable.

Delta Alpha Sierra, the third hour

Gaz had a grandstand view as the cordon closed round the village. Could see the homes and the alleyways linking them, and the small enclosures of dried thorn where the animals were husbanded at night. Looked on to the football pitch and the one pool in the river that was deep enough for the women to wash clothes and bedding. All were surrounded. He watched with big binoculars.

Possible to have a moment of doubt as the convoy had

approached the track; there had been hesitation and a late swing of the wheels. But the village was in trouble when the vehicles swept down towards it. He could see and he could hear. All done with the precision of a planned military operation, and Gaz assumed that a detailed briefing had been given. He estimated a minimum of 100 men were deployed. Iranians, and not the ragtag stuff that he had watched from his covert points earlier in the year. Disciplined and organised, in uniform and carrying cleaned weapons, and on two of their trucks were heavy machine-guns. A little cluster took his eye. Customers – military intelligence and the Sixers – always wanted to know most about Russians. The Iranian commander walked with them. An officer strutted, and Gaz recognised the rank insignia of captain sewn on the arms of his camouflage tunic, and thought his cap, drooping in the rain and ruffled by the wind, had the badge of the FSB. Blond hair peeping from below the cap and an assured, tanned face and a pistol slapping against his thigh. A pair of men slouched behind him, carrying assault rifles, and the power of his binoculars showed Gaz that neither was where he wanted to be. The weather blistered on to them.

His training had taken over. He had observed the military stuff, and at a slight cost . . . The girl had been on her way up the hill, following the charging goats, spooked by the arrival of the vehicles. She came up the slope's loose stone and weed and mud with a sure step and the dogs kept close to her. She turned often enough and looked back down at the village, a few houses with smoke coming from chimneys made from cooking oil tins. He sensed her indecision: where should she go, what should she do? Her family would now be trapped inside the cordon.

Some boys had run, before the route out of the village was sealed. A few carried rifles, but most were unarmed and half-dressed, some still in their nightclothes and barefoot. Other boys stood, irresolute, did not know what would happen; mothers were hissing for their kids to come to them, small children clinging to their long skirts. A dog sprang forward near to the commanding officer. Gaz had identified him from his markings as a major and reckoned he was from the Quds section, the best they had in the ranks of the Guard Corps. How would a dog, big enough to take down a wolf, with yellowed teeth and a screaming bark, know that a Quds officer was an exception to the cohorts of incompetents Iran put in the field. The dog paused in front of the Major, and the rain had flattened its fur and it might have been preparing to leap at the officer's throat. A single bullet was fired, but it did not kill the dog. It whimpered, Gaz heard it, and it dragged itself away, its back legs paralysed. A local man, dignified, came forward to speak to the Russian officer. Might have been a part-time *imam*, might have been a teacher, might just have been the man with the biggest number of goats. . . . He expected to be treated as an equal, delicately shuffling past the crippled animal, but was barged aside, stumbled and almost fell and clutched for support and found the arm of one of the minders following the Russian captain, and was shaken off as if he were a fly or a mosquito.

The girl was close to Gaz. It was a familiar place for the goats. For them it was of no matter whether it rained, or whether the wind blew hard or wafted over them. It was where they were used to congregating, close to the entrance to his hide. They would mill about her, and the dogs would be close against her ankles. Anywhere else would have been better. He could not protect her. As an individual, Gaz was well armed, but not against 100 men and vehicles with heavy machine-guns, and without the help of Arnie and Sam who were away on the far side of the cordon and could not help him. He thought she came to him for safety. A mistake. How to undo a mistake? Did not take him long to ponder it. Must suck it and hope . . . Not an option to curse her from his hiding place and threaten her, or cajole her in whatever language they could muster between the two of them. Tell her words to the effect of 'Get the fuck out'. They had never spoken, had played a children's game, had made an art form of it. Could do nothing. He texted the Operations Officer at the FOB. Weather was foul, cloud ceiling was bouncing off the ground, wind was heavy and in gusts, and visibility was pitiful. If he bugged out then he would have to lug his gear over open ground and he'd be spotted and it would be like one of those smart Boxing Day Cotswold hunts, but a fox would stand a better chance than him. Would not have been so much of a problem if the girl had not been close with her goats and her dogs. They'd be talking at the Forward Operating Base about REDCON, Readiness Condition, and whether they'd risk a Chinook to get near to him, or send in the Hereford gang on wheels. Difficult . . . He sensed her fear as she stared down at her village, her family home.

As the rain bucketed and wind chopped at them, the Iranians divided the villagers into a group of women and children, a second group of older men, and a third group of the kids – the cocky little guys who had been out in the night to get themselves some fun and now were facing a reckoning. The Russian watched and sometimes called and sometimes gesticulated, seemed to have an opinion on how things should play out.

Beginning to feel the cold, and yearning for a hot drink and warm food, Knacker sat on Gaz's gravel path, would not weaken.

The rain had not lifted and the wind had not lessened and the first smears of dawn light appeared on the horizon ahead of him, above the white caps of the sea. No one who knew Knacker would have believed he would jack in a gesture for the sake of personal comfort. He did not call out, never tried to draw his target back into conversation. He would let Gaz, first-class boy, and admired and pitied, twist and toss in the pain, self-inflicted. Tough old world, always had been and always would be . . .

His name had been made in Northern Ireland and he had caught the late days of the 'armed struggle'. Was a sergeant in the Intelligence Corps. Had run a man in Lurgan and another in Londonderry and each had reached beyond the limit of safety and their 'legends' were becoming frayed. Should have been pulled out and left to enjoy the small sums of cash paid them. Neither had been permitted to break the link and his heavy pressure had ensured they stayed in place, continued to report. Had gone a yard too far with them, a month too long, and each had been pathetic and terror-ridden by the time they were picked up by the opposition's security apparatus, which was a one-way trip to a ditch and then a tout's grave. On the bright side, and what marked out this young sergeant, were the rewards: a 1000lb bomb of chemical fertiliser mixture intercepted on its way to the new shopping centre in Londonderry, and in Lurgan a safe house identified where a 'big boy' shagged his slag and was lifted off the bed and sent down for a twenty-five-year stretch . . . a local policeman had done the honours with the name. 'His talent is to pick up an old horse, one that should have been put out to grass, and work it till it drops, then drag it off to the knacker's yard, and with that talent there is no room for charity – but he gets things feckin' done. He's never far from that Yard, is a proper knacker.' The name had stuck, and the reputation with it . . . All a long time ago and the young man had been noticed, demobbed, and poached.

The first cars of the day went along the road below the track to the bungalow, and he expected the rain to ease soon, and the storm to have blown itself out by midday. He sat bolt upright with his legs folded and resisted the chance to stretch. If he were watched he would show nothing of discomfort, but he shook his head and water cascaded from the rim of his hat, and he allowed a finger to pass over his small brush moustache and squeeze it. Nothing, of course, with Knacker, was as it seemed. The island hotel was down the road and the car that had picked him up at the airfield – not an approach and landing he would want to repeat quickly – had taken him there. A room had been booked and he had dumped his bag. The room had been available to him all through the night, all through the hours that he had sat on the path, inflicted remorse on the young man, but the point would not have been made with emphasis, such clarity. *Am doing you a favour . . . a chance to get your esteem back . . . he's in Murmansk, the Russian with a shed load of guilt . . . pop in there, identify him for certain.* He could see over the roof of one of those small chapels that they seemed fond of and past a pier and on to the surge of the waves that menaced the shore, and had a view of a small boat pluckily making progress and throwing up spray and coming on a course from another island, an outline in the mist.

He was confident of the outcome of his visit, that his journey to this remote corner was not wasted, that a man could be prised out of his refuge, and it was a mark of his style that he could do a piece of theatre. Sitting on his backside through the night hours of the storm, taking a soaking, was just footlights and greasepaint. Gulls screamed and rose and fell along with the motion of the boat, and he saw the post van and heard cattle away to his right, bellowing for attention. To some, a God-awful hour of the morning, but that time of day when Knacker liked to be alert, a good time for getting business done.

A pick-up came to the gate. Gaz watched from a window.

She'd have come on one of the crabbers that worked between Westray and the Papa Westray islands. It would have been a wretched crossing, but she never showed fear of the sea, was careful of it but did not cringe. She was good with the men who had lived their lives out here, and always had something to say to them, and her place amongst them was respected. Aggie fitted . . . slotted in better than Gaz did. At the gate she looked for him and saw him as he lurked at the window and she waved cheerfully. She wore bright orange heavy-duty outer clothing, and her hair tailed out behind her. He was blessed, knew it. Gaz could not have said why that woman had crossed a turbulent sea channel and come to see him . . . and she tripped on the man. The light was poor and his coat was grey on the grey gravel and against the grey rendered wall, and with grey skies over a grey roof. The man's arm came up and took her hand, steadied her. And she was apologising, fussing, and helping him to his feet.

She was startled, seemed to stammer a charge of questions: who was he, why was he there, what was his business, when had he come, why was he sitting in the rain? She was given an explanation, clear above the wind, and he believed he was supposed to hear it.

"I came to see Gaz – he's really Gary Baldwin, but from way back and to us, his friends, he's Gaz. It's about where he was before and what he did. We've done our work, my dear. Know you as Aggie, know enough to trust you . . ."

He still held her hand. Gaz recognised it as a master-class. Words spoken calmly, as if nothing was extraordinary and where they met was commonplace, and sodden clothing only a minor inconvenience.

"He's a very brave man, one I am proud to know. That bravery, Aggie – I hope I may call you that – was demonstrated where he served, what he witnessed. It's not a conversation piece and he may have withheld that part of his life history from you. He witnessed an atrocity, saw it stage by stage and could not inter-vene to prevent its outcome. He was deeply damaged by the experience. I am showing my trust and would be seriously embar-rassed, Aggie, if that trust were rubbished . . ."

The worst of the storm was moving away but blustery winds left rain water running off his coat and from the brim of his hat, and Aggie's clothing dripped. Knacker's eyes were on hers, holding them as a stoat would have locked on a rabbit's, and still with her hand in his. Gaz remembered him . . . unemotional, brisk, and to the point, directing him along and not permitting him to slide away into graphic detail but seeming more interested in rank badges and unit insignia, and disappointed at the absence of photographs, and all done fast: not forgotten and a part of the nightmare of the black dog days.

"There was a particular officer present through that day and Gaz watched as he carried out acts of violence that can only be described as evil. We have a partial identification of the offender, Russian military, but we would require – before we can take more appropriate action – a specific identification. We want to put Gaz into the city of Murmansk – quite close to a friendly frontier – have him take a good sighting of our suspect and then slip away . . . We'll have a face and a name, and then we'll do the necessary. That's later and does not involve him. Getting him in and getting him out, we do covertly, and I would want to assure you, Aggie, that we have a reputation for competence in such areas, not easily gained but deserved. That's what we're talking about and Gaz is quite naturally wary of an old world he hoped was behind him . . . If there was another way then I would not have come banging on the door, but there is not. I want to see a brutal and sadistic rough-neck face the consequences of his actions, and I need Gaz's help. He'd be away only a week . . . My own opinion is that carrying out this task would be a help to the convalescence he needs. Not walking away but going forward when he has to. A girl witnessed what he saw. She's stepped up to the plate, and Gaz wouldn't want to turn his back on her. Not often a man has a chance to 'make a difference', strong ambition but rarely an opportunity. This is it, an opportunity . . . To tell you the truth, I'd be more than grateful for a cup of tea."

They turned together, in unison, and came towards the door.

He unfastened the chain, opened the door. Knacker stood back. Gave them space and Gaz hated him for it because that was acceptance of victory. Aggie took him in her arms and hugged him, squirming close. She had come through a storm to be with him and not many from Westray or the adjacent island would have hitched a lift in that pitching swell, had done it to be with him. The loneliness clawed at him. She broke away, went to the kitchen and he heard her begin to rifle in his cupboards for mugs and milk and tea bags.

Beside him, Knacker had started to strip. Water lapped on the linoleum. Raincoat dropped and shoes shed, and suit trousers and suit jacket and shirt and socks and tie, and a vest and underpants that seemed to Gaz to be from a different age, heavier than anything other than what Betty bought for Bobby Riley . . .

A week after Gaz had done his school-leaving exams, Bobby had slipped in cattle shit in the yard and had fractured his pelvis. A month later, while Gaz and Betty managed the milking, the hobbling Bobby had entertained men in suits who came to consider buying the farm. Gaz had shown one of them around the acreage and talked of the wildlife and pointed to a den and a sett. He was an army officer, on leave and doing the driving for his brother, the moneybags. A decent guy, and interested in the terrain and giving Gaz time to explain. The sale went through fast, and Bobby and Betty had gone to a bungalow in Criccieth on the Lleyn peninsula and the parting shot had been that "You'll be all

right, lad, never in doubt you'll be fine, and us – never want to see
a field or a cow's arse again as long as we both draw breath." Now,
more than ten years later Gaz didn't know whether they were alive
or dead, didn't know that old-style underpants like Bobby's were
still worn. The Stoke-on-Trent recruiters had put him into the
Logistics Corps and told him to be 'patient'.

Aggie had scooped up all Knacker's discarded clothes and put
them into the drier, and gave him Gaz's dressing-gown, and
passed him a mug of tea. Neither of them had flinched, looked
away, registered a reaction while Knacker had been naked: Gaz
had noticed. He was good at noticing, always had been.

She said, "You'll do that – you will, won't you?"

Gaz nodded.

Aggie kissed him and he saw the fleeting, half-hearted smile of
Knacker, like taking kids' sweets was nothing to be proud of, and
was kissed again. He went into the bedroom to fill a grip, and the
drier churned in the kitchen, and he heard his Aggie and his
tormentor talking history: she was on Orkney's old monuments
and he was gently explaining his love of the Roman artefacts that
the archaeologists dug up near Hadrian's Wall. He could not have
refused, wouldn't have known how, and remembered the officer
– what the officer had done.

Doubt from her, fleeting, "You'll be all right, won't you? Just 'in
and out'. Yes?"

And remembered how it had been and how the illness had
scourged him and felt Debbie's chin against his fist, and the pain
of the handcuffs on his wrists, and the shaking and shame of
standing in the dock of a magistrate's court, and coming to the
island and the hope that the past was buried deep and could not
resurface.

"I expect so . . ."

4

Gaz walked down the path to the gate, over the gravel where Knacker had sat through the night, and Aggie trailed after him. The island's taxi waited for them and Knacker was by the open rear door, and his clothes – after a fashion – had dried in the machine and were almost wearable.

The wind had dropped and the rain was now far out to sea, and the sun glinted between powder-puff clouds. Gaz thought the weather had been a theatrical effect and exploited by Knacker, as if the limit to his resources was not easily measured. He had been told to leave the bag he had packed but had been advised what to wear. *Just bring some rough ground walking boots, what you're comfortable in.* No clothing. *All will be given you.* Passport, papers and credit cards? *Not necessary, we handle all that, and a float for cash. We've had a passport put together.* Which meant that his acceptance of the job had been taken for granted and that no one had ever seriously considered that he would stand up at his full height and say, 'Sorry and all that, but I don't care a flying fuck for what happened at that village all that time ago, and have no interest – none whatsoever – in seeing a young Russian officer, FSB you tell me, face any form of justice, of the legal kind or extra-judicial. So, please, get off my property and travel back to where you came from because I have important work to be getting on with, decorating and home repairs and mowing. Goodbye . . .'

What to say to Aggie? Usually, when uncertain, he said little, less if possible. He thought that Knacker had played her consummately. There were anglers who came to the Orkneys for wild brown trout, and none could have coaxed a beast on to a barbed hook with such skill. She had floundered and had spoken the spiel,

and he had not been able to fight her. Her use was over. She stood
by the taxi, her head drooping, and had learned much of him that
he had wanted concealed, and had blurted out that he should go
as asked. Maybe she appreciated that what was done and what
was said could not be revoked.

Knacker said to her, "Thank you Aggie, and I'm obliged to you
for making my clothes presentable. We'll take good care of him.
Have a nice day."

She caught Gaz's hand, squeezed it. A kiss and a cuddle beside
the taxi with old Lachlan eying them? Did not seem appropriate.
Gaz nodded to her. He felt haunted, and betrayed, and isolated.

They drove away and Knacker said that he'd a bag to collect at
the hotel. Gaz knew Lachlan because he did pickups for the
holiday owners that Gaz worked for, and some crab fishing, was
useful at plumbing and helped kids with football, so the news of
Gaz going away would be round the island, and round again,
within the hour. Saw Murdo out with his sheep but close to the
road and he'd have seen Gaz, and saw Lisa who cleaned many of
the houses where Gaz worked. The whole island would have
known that an aircraft had made a sharp descent at the core of the
storm overnight, and known that if it had come for Gaz then there
was much he had hidden from them. At the hotel, he sat in the
back of the taxi while Knacker went for his bag and to pay his bill
and Lachlan waited for him to speak, but he didn't oblige.

He thought of a great man who used to slip away from the
islands 1000 years before, so Aggie had told him. The times of
Sweyn Asleifsson, cunning and clever, and living as a pirate off
deceit and subterfuge, using an island as a safe haven; a predator
and a plunderer, and taking Ingirid as his wife after slaughtering
her lawful husband, and unable to settle and restless and chasing
excitement and the whiff of risk, probably chained to his past and
unable to put down roots, and talked of but rarely seen ... Gaz
doubted he would last long enough as an Orcadian to feature in its
past, be subject to a saga.

Knacker came out, carrying a grip, had changed from his suit
into casual dress, an olive-green wax coat and rough corduroys

and heavy brogue shoes, a tattersall shirt and a flat cap and might have been going to a gymkhana. They were driven to the airstrip, out on the northern shore, and the wind-sock hung limp. Knacker seemed to add an extra bank note to the sum required for payment to Lachlan and murmured something about meeting Gaz when he came back, made it sound as if he were off for a visit to a mainland dentist. He carried Knacker's bag, because he was a subordinate, no longer a civilian handyman and running from the past. Back in uniform and subject to those disciplines and Lachlan's eyes seemed to beseech an answer. Gaz asked his own question.

"There was a hard man here, centuries ago, Sweyn Asleifsson. What happened to him – I never read that, his end."

"You'd not want to know his end. Safe journey."

"What was his end? In his bed?"

"And with his woman warm beside him? Want to believe it . . . He went away, didn't have to. Should have stayed for a harvest. Went over the sea and seemed to win a battle but not a war, died fighting. The last man to fall. It's in the saga . . . No good came of him."

On the island, as Gaz had learned, they told stories as if the events had happened yesterday, and they had read them in a newspaper or seen them on a TV news bulletin . . . had a different sense of the past. A young pilot greeted them and seemed to carry Gaz farther back in his life and he climbed up into the Cessna as if he were scrambling on to a Chinook ramp or into a Puma hatch. They took off. No bullshit from the pilot and no nostalgic looping circle of the coast line so he might spot his bungalow or find Aggie making her way to the hotel where she'd offload her pottery, no chance to spot the various properties he looked after and the lawns he was supposed to cut. He wondered if he would ever come back, ever want to, and left behind in his temporary home was little that was precious to him, nothing that was permanent. Knacker was on a call, less than a minute, and his hand shielded his words, and all that Gaz heard of it was ". . . good luck then, Arthur, and give it them hard . . ."

He was on his way and Knacker said nothing to him but sat beside the pilot, ignored him . . . He could remember the officer, the Russian, would never forget him.

The girl who worked for Knacker handled the wheelchair as if it were a shopping trolley. Fee brought Arthur Jennings to Ceausescu Towers. Arthur had been in many corners of the world that he'd have laconically described as 'tricky', but being pushed across half a dozen traffic lanes from the railway station to the main gates was an awesome experience, except that he felt safe in her big, muscled hands. Known to all who worked closely with her as Fee, but born Tracey Dawkins, she glowered at motorists and some yelled obscenities that she seemed to relish . . . Arthur knew she lived in a housing authority flat in Peckham, and her mother was across the landing – how had that been fixed? Arthur always chuckled at the details of Knacker's legendary ability to circumvent bureaucracy. She had been a persistent school truant, a serial shoplifter, and a magistrate had sent her towards the army rather than a custodial sentence. Had gone into the famed and secretive 14th Det as a clerk, and not looked back. Knacker was a renowned talent-spotter. It was said she had chased after him for a position: 'even wash your scrubby smalls, Mr Knacker', and all the usual civil service employment boards had been ignored. They made it across the road and she laughed out loud and Arthur grimaced. At the gates it was not necessary to identify themselves. They were well known to the pair festooned with kit, weapons, and body armour.

"Good to see you, Mr Jennings. Not keeping too bad, I hope."

"Hanging on, thank you. Managing, thank you."

"You're looking well, Miss Dawkins. That was an expert display in pedestrian protocols. One of the best."

"Fuck them. You boys been eating too many sandwiches?"

Both were laughing as she scribbled names on the sheet, and winked, and a side gate was opened for her to manoeuvre the wheelchair through, and she'd have put money on it that one of the armed guards would have said to the other. 'Means something's happening if old Jennings is in to see God Almighty. Something tasty.' Usually the first to know. She'd hand him over to one of the Director-General's personal staff, who'd take Arthur Jennings up to the fifth. The D-G would want to run a rule over a mission that had the potential of a damn great blow-back in their faces if it exploded – as most of the worthwhile ones did.

"You talk rubbish. You talk vodka shit."

But Timofey's father persisted. "Not too pissed to realise this is danger. Too great a danger. I say ignore it."

And Natacha laughed and pirouetted. "It would be fun and entertainment, and if it hurt them then it would be pleasure."

His father could barely stand and would have known that if he slumped back on to the couch he would lose the argument. "You know nothing. What is asked of you, you don't know. You get involved and where does it end? You would be fools, and it involves me."

From Timofey: "And we get paid. We get money, more money than we have, and with money we can be somebody."

From Natacha: "Hurt them, damage them, make them squeal. Those weeks in the cell, with those women, all we talk about is hurting them, but don't know how . . . This is how."

Like kids around a clown they circled him and confused him and he found it difficult to follow what they said and his eyes had glazed, and the effort to be coherent was supreme. "It would be treason. You know that word, *treason*. Know what they do to a traitor? They beat, they torture, they make a man scream to die, and keep him alive, and beat him some more, and if he lives he goes to the camps. How long survive there? My age, what of me? In a camp, a labour camp, a strict regime camp, every day worse, then praying to die. For what?"

"For what? To have money. Money is a reason. It is not political, it is for money."

"Maybe go stand in Lenin Prospekt after it is finished and watch big men, fat cats, come in their chauffeur cars, see others chucked away and disgraced. Maybe watch it."

His father cried, tears running on his cheeks, and he was turning and reaching out for something to grip, "You should not do it, must refuse and . . ."

He fell, or might have been pushed. His feet tangled. He was spread-eagled on the couch. Timofey and Natacha ignored him and the argument was over. His father whimpered, and might have wet himself, but neither his son nor his son's girl noticed him anymore, did not even seem to smell him . . . They left him on the couch. The apartment was in his name. He was the rightful tenant, but he was expelled from the bedroom which they now used. He had to sleep in the living area and they might be watching TV or might be cooking and drinking and might be playing music loud, and he was no longer allowed access to his own room. The father of Timofey had only the bottle for solace and had only the money that they gave him after they had been out to sell weed or 'phets. If the FSB investigators came for him and locked him away then he would not even have the bottle. They were back in the bedroom.

He cried out, "It would be a conspiracy that betrays the state. You would be idiots . . ."

Beyond the door, still ajar, he was answered only by the grinding of the bed springs.

"So, Arthur, where are the miscreants of the Table taking us?"

Arthur Jennings answered the questions posed by Richard Carter, Director-General, God Almighty. "It's about a village in central Syria, Dickie. Has a strategic position, excellent for monitoring traffic down a main highway. Can get better results with ground-based cameras, local input or covert use of recce troops than from drones and satellite facilities. When the war was still being fought there we identified its importance. Took action – you'll know what I mean if I say Knacker was involved."

A dry smile, equivalent of a Martini barely stirred. "I would."

"Special Forces called regularly there, we had the villagers on board and . . ."

Gaz watched her walk towards the building. He had been kicking his heel at Kirkwall, principal town and principal airport of the

Orkneys, for near to two hours. Knacker was long gone in the Cessna – and he'd seen it take off and head south towards mainland Scotland. Would he see Knacker again during the mission?

"Of course, but when we're farther down the road, I'll see you then – just have, for now, a few loose ends to tie up. It'll be good, plain sailing, and you'll be well looked after by the lady. She's Fee, that's what she answers to. My name for her, and with a slight adaptation of the old rhyme: *Fee, fie, foe, fum, I smell the blood of a British man,/ Be he alive or be he dead,/ I'll grind his bones to make my bread.* Probably substitute *Russian* for British and you'll get the drift. Quite passionate and very focused, and I rate her. She was a clerk at Ballykinlar in the Province and years after I'd transferred to the Service in London, and she lapped up all those silly stories about me, decided she wanted to join me. Took leave, this is fifteen years ago, followed me out of the Vauxhall building, accosted me in the street. What do I do? Well, for a start I gave her a photo of a section head and asked her to find me his address. Two mornings later I am crossing the road from the station and she's close to running me down on a bicycle and she palms me Danny Williams' home address in Wimbledon, SW19. Not bad, and I took her on, and fought through the appointment boards. Couldn't be better . . . Not everyone's cup of tea, but mine. My workload goes well with her, and she was at the FOB with me in that unpleasant bit of Syria, knows her Russians and their security apparatus and their strong points, and their weaknesses. Don't worry, Gaz, she'll look after you. See you when I see you."

She came around a corner and had a guardsman's stride and her skirt was rucked up above her knees to accommodate it. Cropped hair and no make-up. She opened the door, came in thrust out an arm.

"I'm Fee, and you're Gaz. Good man, glad you're on board."

She shook his hand, a bone crusher.

He said, "I did not know what other options were around."

"None – except that you could have stayed curled up in a corner, no hope and no chance and no future, and not wanted. Hardly an option. At least, now, you're wanted."

She lit a cigarette. Puffed, exhaled and the cloud near oblite-
rated the No Smoking order on the wall. She took a laptop from
her shoulder-bag. No jewellery but a tattoo high on her left arm,
almost at the shoulder and it showed a small heart, size of a fifty-
pence piece, an arrow stabbing through it. She hardly seemed of
romantic inclination, and he wondered what was the shape, size,
species, of her lover. She had the laptop powered and flicked keys
and he recognised the attachment providing the necessary security, and plugged in a cable with an earphone link and handed the
earphones to Gaz. He watched the screen: saw a harbour filled
with yachts, and launches roped to marina piers, and a narrow set
of steps leading up from the sea; then a cobbled street and cheerful
window-boxes of flowers lightened the screen, and a building that
had been recently pointed between traditional stonework; and saw
the name of the bank, and a commentary gave its Channel Islands
location, and its name, and a printout was displayed and a deposit
had been paid into an account for Gary Baldwin, aged 29, d.o.b.
1991, and a passport number, and also displayed was his signature. He was credited with £10,000. The account number filled
the screen for five seconds then disappeared but he had memorised it, and she switched off the laptop, and took out her
earphones.

"Don't get on a high horse. It is not disrespectful, nor does it tie
you in. It's a simple contract and you do a job and are rewarded
for it. Not an insult and we are not concerned with maudlin patri-
otism, but of gaining strategic advantage. And if it doesn't work
out there's enough to pay for a quite respectable funeral."

And she smiled grimly, and he laughed, and could not remember
when last he had, laughed as he had on that morning before he,
and Arnie and Sam, had taken the lift into the storm and towards
the village . . . But he reckoned she rarely joked, might have meant
it.

"More coffee, Arthur?"

"Thank you, no."

"Press on then."

"Managed to get a bit out of hand at a time when we were changing the batteries for a covert camera, and the local boys had over-judged the support we were prepared to offer, and went and shot up an Iranian compound down the road, which led to consequences, dire ones. The battery charger was in a hide when the al-Quds boys came calling, was a witness . . . Sadly the experience left our boy rather scarred, and . . ."

Delta Alpha Sierra, the fourth hour

The girl was in front of him and the goats milled around her, and her dogs snarled, showed their teeth if any of the beasts seemed about to break away to find better grazing. He could not tell her to shift, could not break their mutual silence, so he huddled in his hide and used the binoculars. He had tucked all of his gear into his Bergen, and the waste and the urine in the bottle, and all the food packaging. The cordon line, down the slope in front of him, was 100 yards away and the centre of the village was 200 yards from him, and the football pitch half as far again. He was stuck fast, and realised it. Not that there was, yet, much for him to see, and anyway the weather misted the view and the squalls of wind raised clouds of dirt and the rain was constant. The texts came in: always calm, and designed to reassure, and that was part of the discipline of the controller back at the Forward Operating Base. They were good, tried hard not to foment panic.

But stark messages reached Gaz. He was told that the Chinook on stand-by was grounded by weather: he doubted if the cockpit crew and the gunners would stay down if his life, and those of Arnie and Sam, were directly threatened, but that's what he was told. The Chinook was a noisy old beggar at best, and he'd have to be well clear of his present position or fifty IRGC would be looking to blast it as it came in. Told that for the Chinook to move would require an escort of fast fixed-wing and, or, Apache gunships, and they'd need visibility for close support – which did not exist. Two sets of wheels from the gun club were on their way but navigation would be shit, and the fast route was over open terrain and not metalled roads . . . and if the fixed-wing aircraft were to drop ordnance around him, create a little sanitised zone and take down half a company of al-Quds 'martyrs' then it would need ministerial permission . . . so, his situation was under review. The girl, looking down, had a better view than he did. But he saw enough, didn't like what he saw.

The Russian officer had pulled up a khaki scarf from his throat and wore it across his mouth and nose, and had the peak of his forage cap low on his forehead, and idled and seemed surplus. The two other Russians, Caucasians, stayed close to him. There had been some tugging matches between the Iranians and the village women. Same reason and same result and a mix of force and verbal violence was used. Teenage boys had been secreted behind older women's skirts. Not the older kids, the ones who had been down the road in the pick-ups during the night, with AKs, and had a bit of *craic* and now looked full face at the consequences: some of them had legged it out and some were sitting in the dirt and had their hands behind their necks and were kicked or hit with rifle butts if they shifted. The boys taken from the women were twelve or thirteen years old. They were pulled clear, and once a rifle was aimed at a woman but then her arms were clubbed and she loosened her grip and howled at the wind.

The girl, in front of him had started to shiver and her shoulders convulsed and every now and then she started keening then would suppress it, then succumb again. He wondered if there was a particular woman that she watched, or a boy, or an older man. If she screamed, if she rose to her feet and her goats scattered and her dogs barked and if she started down the hill, then she would achieve little more than draw attention to the ridge and the lip above his hide. Gaz thought she had not yet been seen and that the men who had made the cordon and those inside it had more on their minds. He was cold and rain drove over her and her animals and spattered through the scrim net and on to him, and he felt trapped and was irresolute . . . It was his training to think on his feet, to be responsible for himself, not to follow the normal army strictures of 'wait out' until told what to do. He did not know what was best for him, the prime chance of ensuring his safety. His breathing came harder.

A man was helped down from the back of a lorry. He wore faded jeans and a military tunic too big for him, and needed support because his head was covered by a sack with small eye slits. Two of the Iranian troops steadied him when his feet were on the dirt, then led him forward to where their commander waited. The Russian officer edged closer to the commander. Gaz realised this was the start of what the Sixer at the FOB would have called the 'business part of the day'. In his youth on Bobby and Betty Riley's farm, in late spring when the crows had fledglings, a hungry buzzard would fly close to the nests, and all hell would be raised as the crows went airborne to fight off the hawk and the cacophony was desperate . . . this was the same. At the sight of an informer, coerced or a volunteer, the women started to yell abuse at him, and punched with their fists and chucked insults, some of which Gaz understood but most of them were beyond the range of the local tongue taught to the recce boys. The man seemed to cringe and the escort held him upright and he was lectured by the commander and then dragged towards the corralled group of young men. A woman crouched briefly and threw a stone towards the informer; it missed, but the reaction was swift. A rifle cocked and a single shot fired in the air, high above the women: more sign of 'business'.

An informer was detested and an informer was feared. Gaz, in Northern Ireland, had monitored the Republicans still keeping the embers of the Troubles alive, and he had served two tours in Afghanistan and had been camouflaged in ditches and on the fringe of maize crops and had watched compounds. There because the naked eye saw more than a drone or a satellite lens, there because of the word slipped to his bosses, or the intelligence people, by informers. Informers gave access where not even Special Reconnaissance Regiment eyes could go, and the fate of such a man or woman was non-negotiable. Likely to be pain first, but gratuitous and inflicted long after contacts and codes had been extracted along with fingernails and toenails, and cigarette burns, and then they would be killed for maximum humiliation. In front of Gaz, the girl had started to shiver and he heard little gasps of breath from her and the dogs at her ankles took her cue and growled low and the goats were restless and Gaz had a tight hold of his weapon . . . Knew he could not outrun a horde of men if they came chasing for him; he did not have an arrival schedule for the gun club on wheels; and the weather would still prevent close fire support from the air . . . Bad times, and worsening.

The first of the boys was singled out. He was pulled clear of the group sitting in the driving rain while the wind buffeted their hair and tugged their clothing, and a red mark was painted on the boy's forehead. He was dragged nearer to the football pitch and stood there with a guard. Not alone for long as the informer moved towards another who wore only boxer shorts and would have come late from his bed.

It had an inevitability and the girl stayed close to him beyond the scrim netting, and suffered.

Arthur Jennings said, "The village was razed, you might consider it a 'war crime', Dickie. But people, in my opinion, are amazingly resilient, rather like the weeds in the cracks in my front path, they come back, those that are left. The village will one day be re-populated and life of a sort will resume. And, as we well know, war gutters out – not that we have much to be proud of in that area – and the Russians are still there, and the Iranians, and the Hezbollah still strut in that territory, and the Assad regime is unchallenged, Moscow's marionette . . . We know all that. What remains, is the value in strategic terms of that community alongside the highway. What is available from there is raw and uncontaminated intelligence: who uses that road, how often, for what purpose? A north-south link and we should have access to what the road traffic can tell us. Am I talking about putting a team of recce boys on the ground as a long-running commitment? I am not. But we need to insert a team and give the locals the equipment we would want utilised. Dickie, you and I are of the generation that recognises the importance of Human Intelligence. We have a rare chance to acquire some very fair results because of the Russian who was prominent on that day. He became a focus of hatred for the survivors. He is an FSB officer, a gilded youth. Lavrenti Volkov. His father was a brigadier general in KGB, then figured in the early days of FSB before nominal retirement and is on the periphery of a group close to the President. He is currently a major and has a future as part of a dynasty of influence, control. We aim to take him down, I correct myself, have him taken down, but first we put a man close enough to our target to make a positive identification."

Lavrenti bridled, "I don't have time."

"Then you make time, find time."

He faced his father, was a little taller than the older man. "A Jew, a little businessman, a nobody. Why should I meet him?"

"Because of what he has."

"Maybe, maybe when I have finished in Murmansk."

He saw colour spread in his father's cheeks and realised that a rising temper was only narrowly controlled, but he did not back off, and the veins protruded on his father's forehead. They had a scant relationship, he had never been hugged and held by his father, seldom been congratulated for any academic effort at school, and his ambitions in hockey had been ridiculed, and he had known that his entry to the élite training college for FSB fast-track recruits had been smoothed. His father's voice rose.

"Not 'maybe', not later. Tomorrow before you go back north."

"There is not time."

"You see him if it means you shit, shower, dress before dawn." A gnarled finger, scarred and narrow to the shape of the bone from grenade shrapnel, poked persistently at Lavrenti's chest. His wife would have told him that he had stayed in his room, when her friends brought their daughters to the apartment.

"And why? Why is it necessary for me to chase after this Jew? Why?"

"I did not think you so fucking stupid. He has holdings north of the Arctic Circle. You know what is there? Are you too much of an idiot to know? There are minerals waiting and begging to be dug from the ground – copper, coal, gold, uranium, tungsten, diamonds. His holding is around an area of the Yenisei River. He is a small man and he bought well. What does he want now?" Spittle spluttered from his father's mouth, some finding a place on Lavrenti's cheeks and nose.

"You know, you tell me." Facetious, sarcastic, almost as if he dared his father to hit him. Never had. Had mostly ignored him. He thought his father would have known about him from quizzing the two minders, Boris and Mikki . . . and once he had finished in Murmansk he would shed them.

"Protection. Wants a roof. Wants people close to him who will watch his back, have influence, keep away the jackals and wolves. Needs a roof under which he can sit. Clear? You give him a roof."

"What is it to me?"

"Fucking idiot . . . What age am I? Past seventy. I wheeze, hack and cough, can no longer run. Death beckons. Dead, I cannot offer the roof. You can. You are the coming man because of my efforts, and fuck-all thanks – and your mother who still has to wipe your arse and also fuck-all thanks. Your future rests with people who make money and who come looking for men prepared to offer a roof. You . . . I tell you . . ."

He thought his father indestructible. Could not imagine life without him. His father made a 'victim' of Lavrenti, and the old intelligence officer was a man happy only in the company of cronies. Over drinks, they would have discussed the bad times in the Afghan war, and the awful times of the Yeltsin presidency, and now talked of financial opportunities and pledged loyalty to the regime that supplied them. Would not have known how to make conversation with his son.

"As you always do."

"First I tell you this . . . you changed, you came back from Syria and were a different boy. We came back from Afghanistan, and had lost, and were the same men but harder, stronger. You are just cold. One day, if you have time, remind me to ask you why you changed. We fought a skilled enemy, you fought peasants . . . What

I tell you, it does not last for ever. The regime will not. When it collapses, and it will be fast because of no prepared and acceptable succession, but a vulture feast on the corpse, the clever man will have his money well secreted outside Russia. Outside, or lose everything. Make what you can while the opportunity is there, get it to London, be ready. Do you hear me?"

Never spoken of before. Brusque exchanges when he returned on the big transporter from the Latakia base, and a grudging acknowledgement of the award of a gallantry medal, along with promotion, but never a table covered with bottles and a detailed critique of how the war in Syria progressed . . . nor ever a mention of a future beyond the life expectancy of the President, almost as if treason were being discussed. As if a cold breeze fluttered on the hairs at the back of his neck, like the past came and charged at him. He submitted.

"I hear you. What is the Jew's name, what is his number? . . . I will call him, I will meet the Jew."

His father, the brigadier general, clenched his fist, clubbed Lavrenti on the shoulder, which was as far as his affection reached.

Arthur Jennings pursued his goal, quietly, held the attention of the man he briefed, and who might – just might – pull the rug from the enterprise.

"We put a man in there who watched Lavrenti Volkov through a bestial and long day. He makes the positive identification and that is all we want of him. Stands across a street in Murmansk and is brought there by a sleeper that we have woken. He's useless but the family are on the books and have been bleeding our resources for five decades, unable to get us decent military stuff from the dockyards, but he can chauffeur our man. What do we get, Dickie, that is attractive? Try this: the friendship of the community when it starts a life again in that place, and perhaps more than friendship – could be devotion, gratitude. Which leads to a small and unremarkable oasis of support for our aims, a warehouse of intelligence on that road, in that area, eyes and ears for the foreseeable future. It's long-term and will pay dividends, cheap at the price and so much more useful than an 'eye in the sky' or some turned clerk in their internal ministry. Above that, we gain a useful location into which to insert special forces or returning regime defectors in the future. A short-term bed-and-breakfast. It's very worthwhile, Dickie, and we'll get our man in just as soon as the planning gets done. He's a good fellow, was with Special Reconnaissance Regiment when he was the witness through a long day. Then invalided out, then identified with that wretched PTSD thing, but we're satisfied he can manage what's asked of him. Knacker told him that we'd be doing him a favour, giving him back self-esteem, but then Knacker always had a way with words. Get him in and get him out, and . . ."

"Sorry, Arthur, but isn't Murmansk quite an unfriendly place, stiff with security and suspicion? And won't this Lavrenti whatever have a concept of personal protection? Arthur, is it not dangerous?"

"Probably you don't want to know more than the bones of the business . . . Except that it's a big prize, and Knacker's confident – as always."

Sitting on a stone and swatting away the horseflies that hovered close, ready to snap at him, Knacker looked out towards the north.

He was alone, not a problem for him. He often felt his own company was preferred to anyone else's, with the exception sometimes of his wife, Maude. No hurry, and the evening light was good and the view stretched far into the distance. Maude was an amateur archaeologist and currently scraped and scratched at mud and clay and stones at a site down the road towards Hexham, and was not yet ready for his appearance and would eke out a few more hours of work, and not take interruption kindly.

Before sitting, close to cattle who watched him as they lay chewing on the grass, he had walked down a slope and reached the temple to Mithras, first dedicated to that all-powerful Roman empire god in the third century. Quite a senior officer had done the honours, the commander of the First Cohort of Batavians, and those troops had looked for divine help when faced with a resourceful, dangerous – and ruthless – enemy. He supposed that it was reasonable for him to assume that such a man who honoured the Charioteer of the Sun would have had a rank and status similar to Knacker's own. He had spent quarter of an hour there and had squatted on the stone parapets of the building, until he had seen a hiking party approaching which had seemed the correct time to begin a more important vigil, the one that cleansed his mind. This was a place he came to each time that Maude was active with her excavation team and when he had worries clogging his clear thinking. He had climbed the slope, left the clean scoured walls of the temple behind him, and had taken a viewpoint where a ridge facilitated a grand expanse of open countryside, and the low light enhanced the distance as far as he could see.

The seat of his trousers would be damp, and the flies would become steadily more aggressive, but this place – between Turret 33b and Turret 29a – along the Wall built with the driving will and perseverance of the Emperor Hadrian, gave Knacker a sense of perspective for his efforts that day, and yesterday and tomorrow. He was above the outer limit of the fort, Brocolitia, where the grasslands still covered the ruins of a great civilisation. The Wall itself, ten feet high and with turrets set along its entire length and with forts built to house garrisons of legionaries and auxiliaries, was a few feet in front of him. The cattle eyed him, would have been cautious of him had he come closer. In front were layers of differing colours and then a growing mist and then a deepening shadow, then a narrowing stretch where the ground merged with the sky and he could see no farther . . . which would have been the problem faced each day, every day, each week and every week, by the officer leading that cohort of Batavian troops. He had a frontier to defend. Facing him, somewhere in dead ground, beyond hills and beyond sight, was his enemy, and Knacker sympathised.

Since he had left the 'bandit country' of the Province, Knacker's existence had seemed to have him peering over the border fences of his opponent – Russia, always, Russia, fucking Russia always – and never knowing what was beyond his knowledge. It would have been the ongoing worry of the commander of a cohort of regular troops recruited from an area of what was today northern Germany and running into the Netherlands. The troops would have been trained, to the highest standards of fitness, and motivated to fight ... but, what if familiarity with the guard duties had sapped their alertness, and what if the best men were drawn away from this part of the Wall and sent farther west where more trouble lurked, and what if the auxiliaries given him as replacements were less efficient? He assumed such concerns nagged in the mind of an FSB commander controlling border troops with a headquarters unit in Murmansk and a line of guard posts and roadblocks watching over a closed frontier zone. How good was the commander of the cohort, and how good at his job was the FSB senior officer in Murmansk? The two men would have a single matter in common and would not have doubted its truth. Both would have understood the *threat*. Always a commander's fear: the threat becoming reality on his watch.

The flies were bothering. The cattle were quiet. A hen harrier was working the ground in the middle distance. A fine looking creature, a predator, and it flew low. Had it been spooked and flown off shrieking, then it would have meant that an intruder, crawling on his belly, was approaching. Would have been a fox in the time the cohort watched this sector, and might in today's territory have been Gaz who had the reputation in his field that many envied. His wife, Maude, might have looked up from the rim of the pit she was working in and might have clucked cheerfully at the sight of it, and pointed it out to her neighbour and they'd have enjoyed the spectacle of it. He supposed himself to be the archetypal intelligence officer, and the cohort's commander would have had one, and it was necessary for him to attune his mind to the business in hand ... getting a man in and getting him out. There was no safety in walls or fences or deep man-made ditches. Knacker could barely imagine the degree of effort, and the cost, of producing this Wall running from the west coast of England to the east, and could hardly have conceived the outlay of the little east German statelet that had tried to build a barrier preventing escape from its sad, malnourished country.

Healthy reflections, Knacker thought. He comforted himself. However great the wall, fence or ditch, it was only as strong as its weakest link. A useful cliché in Knacker's trade. The guard who was reeking with a summer cold or convulsed in winter flu, or dreaming of his centurion's daughter, any of them could be on guard duty in a turret and not see the threat materialising from the gloom, his mind far away before a knife crossed his throat.

He seemed to have spent a majority of his adult life facing the barriers set up by the Russian state. The Service at Ceausescu Towers was obsessed with Russia, the machinations of the Kremlin, its enmity and cunning, its mischief and deceit. Nothing to be proud of but it was the life he led. Farther along the Wall that early evening was his wife. Maude, as she cleaned mud and dirt off scraps of material or pottery shards or found a coin that had fallen from a purse eighteen centuries before, refused to humour him with support for the overwhelming attention given to Moscow matters. She would not permit it as a third person, a decent sized elephant, in her bedroom, her kitchen, her lounge. Had been that way since the first day of their married lives: she on a dig at Herculaneum and him wandering around the drugs fortress of the Scampia development and testing his skills and his nerves, then meeting for dinner, late, in their Naples hotel – and it had rained every day for the week. Back home, she had her own friends on her own terms. Yes, two boys born to them, and for the births of both he had been away, and a conversation – repeated to Knacker – was "Don't know how you put up with him, Maude, I wouldn't – ever considered divorcing him?". She had answered, a reliable source repeated, "Considered divorce? No, never. Murder? Yes, often." But those in the road in the south London suburb of New Malden who had no idea that he was anything other than a common-or-garden civil servant, Pensions or Agriculture and Food, would have made erroneous judgements, not recognising the hidden sinews of the marriage, that had lasted – so far – twenty-eight years.

His work was not talked of, by him, by her, by their sons, now both of student age. She came here, to the ruined wall, as often as she was able, and he would call by when he could hitch a lift or find an opportunity. The pilot had made a deviation, dropped down at Newcastle, and a taxi had taken him close to the Mithras temple. It was a good place for clear thinking.

The tails of the cattle flicked in irritation and Knacker reckoned the flies were increasingly active. Maude would come for him when her digging day was over, not a moment before, and till then he must share the burden of the insects with the herd. He imagined the anxieties of the commander of the cohort based here, with responsibility for this segment of the empire's defences. Imagined his arrogance, and his trappings of power, and the disciplined stamp of the troops on the parade ground, and imagined also the private moments of anxiety. Knacker wore a leather bag across his shoulder, contents delivered by courier to the police office at Newcastle's airport, and in it were aerial pictures and ground-level images of the fence and the cameras and the ploughed strip on the border that now concerned him. There would be a commander there, back from the frontier, and unaware of a looming threat . . . He, Knacker, was not that man, did not have a cohort to lead, did not sit behind defences, did not rely on an untested link.

His eyes were on the far distance, an area shielded in the darkness of the spreading evening. There, hidden from sight but clear in his mind, was the man who Knacker wished most to identify with – perhaps dressed in skins, perhaps naked except for a colouring of blue woad paint, perhaps gaunt and hairy, perhaps as anonymous 1800 years before as a contemporary intelligence officer who sat and chewed his thoughts among the cows. Of course, there would have been, out there among the Caledonian and Brigantes tribes, an intelligence officer of proven worth, or what was the Wall for? Maybe the same damned flies had come for this man as now circled Knacker. He thought of this man, watching for weakness, as his friend, and . . . A horn blasted behind him. Some of the cattle stood and peered towards the road. Knacker pushed himself upright, would not want to keep her waiting. He walked across the field but thought more of his 'friend' than his wife, and the car door was opened for him.

"Hi, how you doing? We've had a great day, good finds . . . And you, your day?"

"Just an average one, not a special one."

And Alice by now would have touched down on an airstrip in Jordan, and Fee would be escorting their volunteered man on the next stage of a treadmill journey, and much was in place and much needed to be done. He kissed his wife's cheek and she drove him away; the painted man would have to wait for further consideration. A decent kiss and cheerful, mirroring how he felt as the mission gathered pace. Would soon be past the point of turning back: always a good moment.

At the gate and after a wave to the guards, and a wink and a nod in return, Arthur Jennings, in his wheelchair, was helped into a taxi by a member of the D-G's staff. He thought it had been a satisfactory meeting, longer than he'd expected and with a sandwich break. Away in the traffic and crossing the bridge, he phoned his protégé.

"Went well, Knacker, in fact I would call it quite satisfactory. I appreciate you are already on course, but the bonus is that you are now sanctioned. Years have not dimmed or withered his dislike of the Kremlin crowd, his contempt for them and their coterie of poisoners. I have to emphasise that he was anxious for the health and the safety of our man, and queried our assessment of risk. I said those were matters taken very seriously. May I rot in hell, but I skated over that, as if going in and out of that place was on a par with taking a train to and from Bognor for the day . . . Of course, goes without saying, he'll be beyond reach and should he miss the schedules then he must rely on his own wits if he's to make it out. His nerve has to hold. But, needs must, he's the only card we have to bring to the table. You'll have evaluated that."

And he rang off. He pocketed his phone and felt alone, rather cold, knew he was prominent in the conspiracy involving the man they'd be using. Had seen a photograph of him. A decent sort of face, which wouldn't help him where he was heading.

She shot better than Gaz did.

No rifles or pistols on his island that he knew of. Gaz was rusty and this was a Walther PPK, a close-quarters handgun, too light-weight for the military.

Heavily built for a woman of her agility, Fee dominated with her presence on the floodlit range. They had given a ride on the Cessna to air force people, technicians muttering electronics and frequencies and degrees of gibberish that were a foreign language to Gaz. Had over flown the Orkneys, and might have gone over his home but he had not looked out, nor looked over the smaller island of Papa Westray for her place, nor for the ancient settlement site where she had loved him and which had been a bagful of treasured moments. Then out over the sea again until the Shetlands were reached. Gone across the infrastructure of the wilting oil industry and surplus rigs in postcard-beautiful bays. A loop across the isolated light on Muckle Flugga and land on his right and the ocean going away to a far horizon on his left, and passed the big golf ball radar domes perched on a summit, then a turn and a fast descent, and another bay that faced out to the North Sea and a single scarlet-painted trawler tied up at a pier. They had landed as the afternoon gave space to evening. It was not his way to query what happened, and she had slept on the flight, and there was nothing that he needed to know that was worth waking her for.

The shooting was at twenty-five paces, not stationary targets, but silhouette figures coming from right to left and vice versa, and it was aimed shooting or fast response and suppressive, and through a whole magazine.

At the airfield, they were met by a military Land Rover. Now he was given information, of no interest to him. They were on Unst, they had been over the sophisticated early warning system of RAF Saxa Vord. In their wisdom, confident in the ending of the Cold War, Whitehall warriors had shut the place down and flogged off the RAF's personnel accommodation. The officers' mess was now a bunk-house. At considerable cost, the base had been dragged back on line. There was an old range, and an instructor had issued weapons to them both.

She had a greater number of central hits than he had. He thought he had enough holes in the cardboard targets to drop a man, close down the threat. He had been a good marksman in Syria, but other skills were higher on the list, and self-taught ... He had gone into the Logistics Corps and was neither popular nor disliked, hardly noticed and could drive a three-ton truck adequately, and they'd had an exercise on the Brecons where there was sparse cover. A sector was marked off and the instructors played the game and went and had a fag and a brew, and a whistle was blown and the veterans went out to find them. Thirty had started and twenty-nine were found. In growing frustration the search for the last one had gone on for another hour, and a whistle had been blown and the transports' engines had been cranked up, and he'd stood up and brushed old heather and dead bracken off his body and they'd have damn near gone over him a half dozen times. His skills were under-stood and he was transferred to Stirling Lines at Credenhill in Herefordshire, and put into the training wing of the Special Reconnaissance Regiment, alongside the Special Forces of the gun club, but shooting was not the priority. Concealment ruled. They finished. The weapons were cleaned, then handed back to an armourer. He turned away. A trudge back to the Land Rover. How did he feel?

"All right, thank you."

What sort of weapon did he want to take?

"No sort of weapon. Nice of you to ask. No sort."

It was considered necessary, Knacker's opinion and hers, for him to have a means of self-defence, a back-stop option.

"I'd rather not, so let's move on."

She bit on her lip. He thought she'd do that rarely. Said nothing and did not argue. His defence was concealment, an ability not to be noticed, and he relied on such talents, and standing up in

downtown Murmansk with a peashooter handgun and a magazine of nine rounds was ludicrous. He took a last look at Muckle
Flugga, isolated and on a crag and jutting up beyond the last cliff
face on the west of the island, and saw gannets circling, and Gaz
would have bet money – all of that £10,000 – that had he been
there, hidden and covert, Knacker would have found him. They
were driven across Unst, came to a quayside, walked together
towards a trawler bathed in bright lights.

Two men were on the quay and two more worked at the main
mast where a new sail was being hoisted, and farther down on the
quay were the ragged remnants of an older sail, a pretty scarlet but
with slashed rents. He assumed they had come in that morning
and had been at sea in the storm and must have had a pocket
handkerchief of sail hoisted and assumed they'd pitched through
the swell and the white caps to meet a timetable set for them. Work
stopped. He was watched closely. He thought they evaluated him
She spoke first to them. "Hi, boys, sorry and all that if you had a
bastard of a night but appreciate that you put in the effort. This is
your passenger . . . treat him carefully as there's nothing in his
history about riding a million dollar yacht. See you on the other
side, boys."

With the ripped sail were also tangled ropes and broken wicker
crab pots. Their faces were drawn with sleeplessness, all unshaved,
and they wore damp clothing, and all smoked and all held coffee
beakers. There was a small Norwegian pennant attached at the
back end of the trawler.

She said to Gaz, matter of fact, like nothing was that important
a deal. "They're going to ferry you to Norway. Why? Good question but a good reason . . . You go in one way but we don't reverse
it. They're going to lift you out from Murmansk. They need to
have a look at you because they take a hell of a chance getting
involved with you. The FSB who look after all forms of border
control in Murmansk, land and sea, would take a bad view of their
facilitating the escape of a high-profile fugitive. They'll decide if
you're worth the risk to them. Have fun, Gaz."

She walked briskly away, and a hand was given him. He stepped down off the quay and on to the decking, which was where it all began, he supposed, the real stuff. It would have been reassuring to have had a Walther PPK in his belt and against his hip, but he had declined the offer, and ropes were loosed from the quay and an engine throbbed beneath him.

5

"We'll see you, man."

"That'll be good, and I'll see you guys – I hope."

He hitched his bag on his shoulder and walked away from the fishing boat and down the quayside. He saw Fee ahead of him and she scratched behind her ear and then kicked at a pebble, and was gazing at the skyline, and showed little interest . . . Might have convinced a rookie that she cared nothing about whether he was on time, or late, or whether he was washed out with sea sickness and about to jack it in, chuck the mission over the side of the quay where the weed floated. She'd care . . . Gaz supposed there should have been a customs officer or an immigration functionary standing with her and waiting to check his documentation. There was not, nor any sign of one hurrying to intercept him: that would have been her responsibility. Would not have lasted half an hour on Knacker's payroll if she could not deflect such interest. She greeted him.

"A decent ride?"

"Decent enough."

"Anything left in your guts?"

"Guts are fine."

"Rather you . . ."

This was Kirkenes. The guys had told him it was a fishing port, with a booming marine repair yard, and a small dry-dock. The guys had also said that the town was dull, like 'one horse and one street', and had been rebuilt after the war, had been flattened by Russian aircraft during the German occupation, then the Germans had been pushed out and they'd bombed the place even flatter to make it uncomfortable for the Russian invaders. He had been told this in low, considered voices as they had swung into the fiord leading to the town and its harbour. They had been dour men at the start all weighing and judging him. Was he worth the effort? Worth the risk of going to a penal colony for twenty years? Did he have that sort of value? It was a grey, oppressive morning, the sort of day that indicated summer had given Kirkenes a miss . . . The guys must have been happy to have him as a passenger, and with a return booking because that was what had been called out to him as he had walked towards Fee. Good guys, using basic transport. Little luxury in the common sleeping area below deck. They'd seen him off with a noncommittal slap on the shoulders and a brief hug before he'd climbed up a couple of steps and then stretched out for the quayside. But they expected to see him, which gave comfort – and a back-stop was agreed.

He walked beside Fee, matched her long stride. If he'd have allowed it, she would have carried his bag.

It had been explained to Gaz: why four Norwegian fishermen would hazard their freedom, involve themselves in UK black operations. It had been explained as the trawler had ploughed on in what they called a 'moderate swell'. One of the younger guys had done it as if nothing he said was remarkable. "About the second world war. Everything is the second world war. Finished seventy-five years ago but nothing is changed and the allegiances still rule. Old loyalties and old loves, and old gratitudes count now as they did then. The time of our grandfathers. Everywhere you go in your life today you can look over your shoulder and see the results of that conflict. There was the Shetland Bus. You would not know of it. Small trawlers sailed to and from Norway and berthed in the Shetland Isles and they brought back from German occupation the refugees and the agents who were considered important to the resistance, and returned there in desperate winter seas, with the same agents, this time with weapons and explosives. Only went in winter because of the darkness and when the seas were worst and when the Germans could not fly and did not have patrol craft out . . . All of us had grandfathers who sailed on the Bus route. The message came and of course we would answer. Can you understand that? Now, you as an island people are in decline. We have an abundance of oil and gas and can build a superior infrastructure and have as generous a welfare programme as there is in the whole of Europe. But neither situation allows us to ignore a call for help. It is unwritten, forged in iron, and still lives. But we look at you, assess you, because it is a big thing that is asked of us. At the end we will tell you whether the old friendship has a greater pull on our loyalties than common sense . . . What is asked of us is not easy and the penalties for failure are big. You know that, of course you do. The same as for you."

One speech and no theatrical gestures of friendship, and no emotion shown, and Gaz had believed each word he was told and had imagined small boats, inshore trawlers, buffeted by winds and tumbling through the white caps, and had felt stronger, a little.

He had realised he was being examined all the time he was on board and supposed he had passed some test – as he had done nine years before when he had pitched up at Stirling Lines, home of the cream of the Special Forces, and had been thrown into the rigours of training required by the instructors of the Special Reconnaissance Regiment. Had been told the majority of the intake would fail, and might have been the youngest to reach those heights in the selection process. There had been a girl there. A sergeant's daughter. Good enough looking, seeing him as a catch, but no special commitment returned by him. More important was the passing of the brutal tests inflicted on them. Each week seeing more of them carrying a bag to the minibus and taken to Hereford rail station, returned to unit, failed. Not Gaz . . . Did well enough in Close Quarters Battle Training and high marks in Close Target Reconnaissance and better than useful in Unarmed Combat Skills, and passing out. Off to Londonderry for the first operational posting and familiarising himself with working the housing estates where hatred for military was ingrained. Where, if trapped, he might shoot his way out and might not, in which case he would end up a bloodied corpse. Had rather enjoyed it, had handled the pressure and had been praised in the laconic shorthand the unit used. Had done time in the Province, had gone back to the camp in the west of England, close to the Welsh border, to find the sergeant had moved on but his daughter had stayed, seemed to expect him to move in with her. She was Debbie. Had done it, moved to her one-bed place. Shouldn't have, but had ... all the boys shagged available girls. Part of the way they all lived. Nice girl ... and what had happened was not her fault, was his. He had gone to Syria. Not like the Creggan and the Bogside in Londonderry, but big boys' games.

The boat crew had made the one speech, none of it repeated, and mostly he had huddled below deck and tossed with the bunk's motion and only been out on deck at dusk going into evening and had seen one whale and two pods of dolphins and once they had been buzzed by an eagle that had come low over them, hoping for fish carcases to be thrown its way. What irked him most was that bits of the plan they were putting in place had already been decided before they had his arm-twisted agreement to be a part of it. Could he have refused? Not worth even scratching it over in his mind.

She led him to a car, where a driver waited for them. She opened the back door for Gaz. The driver didn't speak. Gaz thought he was treated like he had the plague, was dangerous to know. The light rain had flecked his hair and dampened his anorak. He slung his bag ahead of him and climbed in. He reckoned he was being given all the attention due a 'fatted calf', pampered, cosseted and good for a week-long feast. Would he be remembered the day after the table had been cleared and the guests had burped and farted and staggered off home? Not likely to be. They drove away from the quay and towards a sprawl of buildings. Saw his target and the wire-fine line on his face that had seeped blood, could see him clearly.

The Jew stood. The meeting was concluded.

The Jew had been 'invited' to Lefortovo because the gaol and its section of interrogation rooms was the place where Lavrenti was most comfortable when in the capital and needed to meet strangers. He very seldom entertained in the bistros of the Arbat district, or in the dining-room of a larger hotel. To have control and to feel the exercise of authority, he chose one of the small, soundproofed rooms inside the gaol. Here, he could be confident that any individual he met would be unnerved, anxious, and there-fore likely to put themselves in Lavrenti's debt . . . Not this man.

The Jew had explained his position in the fields of Arctic mineral extraction, had outlined his proposed understanding, and now expected the major to 'piss or get off the pot'. Implicit in what Lavrenti was offered was the Jew's confidence that it was 'take it or leave it' and that there would be a queue of other men inside the Shield of the State, the *Federal'nya sluzhba bezopasnosti*, who he could turn to if this agreement were not accepted. The man wanted a roof; word would have passed to him that a rising star in the firma-ment could provide the necessary guarantees, a solid and progressive roof, a *krysha*. Also implied was the unstated and unarguable fact that the Jew took a chance with this young man and banked on his reputation to survive and to prosper. It was a long-term arrange-ment that the Jew looked for, and one of mutual benefit.

It was the usual tactic of Lavrenti, when a man was in front of him, across a bare desk, that he said little, aimed to increase the discomfort of his visitor . . . not so that morning. The Jew had his cigarette packet on the table, along with a chunky Marlboro lighter, and would soon – likely – ignore the No Smoking sign and light up, which would activate the alarms. The Jew seemed to feel he had given enough of his time, looked for confirmation and was ready to leave. The deal was for ten per cent, rising to fifteen per cent of anticipated profits.

The take-out was small initially, but the major was not yet in the giddy circles of those adjacent to the seat of power, the court of the Czar, but would soon be if he worked and exercised influence. The offer meant he was, as yet, taken on trust.

The Jew did not have any small talk and seemed puzzled that more questions had not been asked, but the detail was run through and Lavrenti stared down at the table. No paper record and no bugged recording of this conversation would exist. He had exer-cised his power many times in small rooms such as this one before going to Syria, and they would again be his fiefdom when he returned from the short visit to Murmansk. Now he was alone, faced a significant step into unknown territory, would no longer be the protégé of his father and feed from the old man's hand . . . It had been another bad night.

It was hot that day in the small interrogation areas of the Lefortovo, the air-conditioning was off and the windows were sealed, and sweat beaded on the back of his neck and threatened to break loose on his forehead. In the night, fleetingly, he had felt the cold on his body when the wind had driven the rain against his camouflage gear and the wet had penetrated and the chill had gripped. He remembered each hour, each minute, at the village, and what had happened and what he had done.

This was the future . . . a deal to provide a roof and protection to a little Jew who would trick and bribe and evade responsibility for revenue payment and he would assure the success of the programme, and would live well off it – as his father had done with other cash cows. Now the Jew stared at him, looked hard into his eyes, showed little respect.

"Are you all right, Major?"

He said he was well, and yet could not meet the penetrating gaze of the Jew.

"You were far away; were you listening to me?"

He had listened.

"You are, Major, as I am told it, a decorated and experienced officer. Served in Syria, a fine record there. Perhaps finance and mineral extraction are alien to you – perhaps."

He could deny that. He needed to show himself to be well on the ladder and advancing towards the highest rungs. He knew the question that would follow and never answered it whether it came from a stranger, the Jew, or from his family, even his father, the former brigadier general.

"How was it there? As bad as we assume, or worse?"

He said, seemingly offhand and bland, that it was a necessary act of policy and the commitment had suited the state at that time, that it was finished and not to be pecked over.

"I hope it was for some purpose . . . You found it hard, saw bad things? Was your role dangerous, did . . .?"

Lavrenti slammed his fist on the table. "I don't fucking talk about it. Don't."

And he stood, and faced the Jew. The man showed no astonishment at the sudden, unprompted explosion. If he then had doubts as to the wisdom of putting his protection in this officer's hands, relying on protection under this officer's roof, he made no sign of it . . . What was not said was sufficient to deflate Lavrenti.

"Well, Major, you have much to think of, and no doubt would be pleased to have time to consider a response. What a privilege to have met you. No hurry, nothing immediate is required, maybe in a few months . . ."

The cigarettes were pocketed and the Marlboro lighter. It was as if the Jew had come to a car showroom and had browsed and looked at brochures, then decided that he did not like what he saw, would go elsewhere, but without wishing to cause offence. Lavrenti pushed a button on the leg of the table, at knee height. An escort would come and lead the Jew out of Lefortovo. He had never before reacted in such a way to mention of his war service in Syria, had not acknowledged the stress caused by what he had seen on one day, and what he had done on that same day. Within an hour his father would have been told and within an hour and five minutes the brigadier general, retired, would be on the phone, blaring questions and criticism at him, and he would deflect. Nothing of that day had left him, and more often his nights were spent tossing and sleepless. He went out into the corridor, locking the door behind him. He walked briskly. Uniformed men in the corridors stopped, stood sharply at attention, saluted him, and from behind open doors officers saw who passed them and called out greetings as if he were the man everybody wished to count as a friend because he owned a future. A guard at the main gate offered good wishes and asked when he would be back, but he did not answer.

In a restricted parking area, a privileged space, the car's engine was idling, Mikki at the wheel and Boris standing by an opened rear door. They talked and laughed, and saw him. It would be a fast drive to the military airport, then all three would be on a flight, duration 150 minutes, going north to Murmansk.

He had not lost his temper in that way before, had not shown such weakness . . . The images clung at his throat.

They went at speed and a cloud of dust billowed behind them. Alice, petite and pretty and with her hair trailing under the rim of a combat helmet, half of her face covered against the dust and sand by a khaki scarf, and the skin below her throat masked with the shape of an armour-plated jerkin, and with trousers in olive green flapping on her legs, was with the Special Forces. She was taken into Syria, across a border marked only by a single strand of barbed wire, now long buried in dirt and sand. A few such routes, listed only on the covert maps. existed for mutual convenience.

She was driven – three vehicles and one passenger, her, with machine-guns festooned on them all – towards a sanitised but unwelcoming refugee camp where they would collect a guide for further incursion. The escort had given her headphones and a face microphone so she could communicate, but remarks were kept to a minimum because her business was not for sharing, and procedures in this hostile environment were best kept private. It was 'wild west country' and the warlords of Syrian militia and the Americans and the Russians ruled the ground along with the Hereford people. There had been times when the British would have met up with Russians from their Spetsnaz teams, cans of strong beer broken open, and fags exchanged, but relations now were guarded, though the understanding of free passage along selected routes still held.

Only Knacker would have granted such opportunities to a low-ranking official. Alice spoke well, had a decent accent and a reasonable Oxford degree in Modern History, but working to Knacker and answerable only to him, she was entrusted with work far beyond her pay grade. Her family had wealth, a certain influence, a home on the hills above the Regency city of Bath . . . and her lover, sometimes passionate, sometimes noisy and sometimes raising eyebrows, was the formidable Fee. They were a solid item. Four months after teaming up domestically and living in Fee's housing association apartment in south-east London, Alice had been driven by Fee to the west country. She had been dropped down the street and out of view of her parents' home – and Fee would have gone to the shops – and she had walked the last 200 yards, and had believed that her mother and her father were too hidebound in their attitudes to accept the relationship, bless it. It had been a hideous wet day, biblical torrents rushing down the street, and Fee had driven to the house, and had been waved in along with their daughter. A few frosty minutes and news of a problem with an electric kettle had surfaced. Fee, huge and muscular and with a gap between her teeth and cropped hair and a bulging backside, had produced a screwdriver, had re-wired the kettle, had programmed their televisions, had fixed Alice's mother's mobile phone. Since then, Fee had been up on the roof to check for loose lead, had cleaned out gutters, had re-plumbed a shower unit. She was now adored and was greeted on each visit with a fresh work list. . . .

They had clearance of a sort, but had been fashionably economical with detail, to drive away from the camp and into the harsh hinterland of the country where grief and brutality and mourning and cruelty were the popular pastimes. Had she used a firearm? Once or twice, a laconic answer. She had an assault rifle across her lap loaded with twin magazines, and a leather pouch filled with grenades, and a medical pack strapped to her hip.

The camp was beyond a hillside, a collection of tented streets, and hanging above it was a pall of smoke from small cooking stoves. A Red Cross flag hung limp by the gate. The Amman based station that looked after Jordan had done the leg work. The guy in front of her, normally crouched behind his weapon and scanning every summit, every ridge and every bend in the track, gestured to her. A lone man sat beside the track, 100 yards from the camp entrance, his head down so that his features could not be recognised, and would have heard their engines rumbling along the track. The man pushed himself up and came loping towards them.

He was watched by the guns, fingers on triggers and weapons cocked. It was bad country and only a fool would not have been suspicious of a supposed contact, his motives and loyalties. He was frisked, searched roughly – would be their guide.

Alice shook his hand firmly. The man pointed away to the east and the wheels spun and they headed out across open country . . . Sort of everyday work, Alice was giggling to herself, to go off-road and fetch herself three killers, not squeamish men, from a village. Down to her to select them. Not work for a recce man with demons in his head who might falter when a trigger needed pulling, but for guys in whom a desire for revenge burned brightly – a mark of the responsibility that Knacker dumped in her sweet little lap where the automatic rifle lay.

Delta Alpha Sierra, the fifth hour

Gaz watched, could not take his eyes from the scene.

He watched, had readied himself, was coiled as a crushed spring. He could have burst from his hiding point, shouldered the Bergen, then run into the rain and the wind that streamed over the flat ground above the rim of the slope, and he would have to have gone fast because there was no cover. He prepared to break out and quit because he was uncertain how much longer the girl could endure what she saw. If the moment came when she could not absorb more of it, and screamed or shrieked or yelled, then he would have to take the gamble, and run. More likely scramble, hunched low and have the rifle ready if it were necessary to give suppression fire. It was a bad option, but all options were poor.

He could have reached under the net and touched her hip, could have felt the sodden material of her jacket, and the dogs hard against her would have snarled and showed their teeth, and might have savaged him. He did not know, God's truth, whether he should reach out, envelop her and bury her face against his shoulder and twist her so that she saw nothing . . . Not out of sympathy but because of the risk that she might yell defiance or abuse or agony at them. The goats, sweet and gentle, took their mood from her and stamped close against her, ignoring the dogs. She would have been justified in standing, howling, losing control. Not easy for Gaz, and he was trained and she was not. Hard for her. He thought that if he had gripped her shoulders and pulled her down towards him she would have fought him off. Reckoned he would have failed and he was on his side and had no room to manoeuvre. If her discipline cracked then they would come for her, for him . . . The Special Forces vehicles were reported to be on their way and they'd be heading into bucketing rain, scouring winds.

The hooded man, the informer, had already separated the young men of the village who had been too slow to evade the closing cordon. Those he had identified squatted in a small circle, their heads bowed under their bound hands and blindfolded with strips of their clothing that had been ripped to make a length of cloth sufficient to go round their skulls. Now the turncoat, what Gaz would have known as a 'tout' during his time in the Province, loitered by the circle – might be glorying in the power given him, might be as trapped himself as any man who betrayed family, friends, comrades in arms – and then pointed, condemned the first.

A rope was thrown up and looped over the crossbar of the nearest goal on the football area. Two of the Iranians caught it and started to loop the noose, and another had brought a wooden chair from a house.

And women in their group and hemmed in by rifles, loaded and aimed, had started to moan, a premature keening wail for the dead. Gaz gazed down at the Russian. Would have been an intelligence officer, and most likely from the FSB ranks because they were used in most of the close liaison jobs. Iranians would operate under the supervision of a Russian, he would have his own bodyguard team with him to keep his arse clean and safe, and if push came to shove then the assumed wisdom of the men and women who tasked Gaz was that the Iranians would be 'good kids', do as they were told. The Russians had the big artillery, the fast jets that could plaster down ordnance and gas, and the helicopters. They ruled if an officer decided to chuck in his weight. Would he now intervene or would he accept that all was ordained? And what would the girl do if they went ahead, stood the boy on a chair under the crossbar? He had a tight hold on his rifle and a strap of the Bergen was over one shoulder, and there was a pistol in a holster on his hip, and smoke and flash-and-bang were hooked on the front of his camouflage tunic. It was impossible for Gaz to see the face of the boy under the blindfold, and the rain peppered him and the pennants on the aerials of the Iranian personnel carriers were rigid.

The Russian officer stood with arms folded. His legs were a little apart and he might have rocked on the balls of his feet, and the wind rapped him and rain streamed on his face but he made no movement. He neither wiped the rainwater from his face, nor tugged his headgear lower, nor did he intervene. The Iranian commander was close to him and seemed not to need to give orders, as if decisions of protocol and procedure were long taken . . . The girl in front of him shook and little spurts of breath dribbled at her mouth, and Gaz thought this was the beginning, the beginning of the beginning. The boy would not have realised what was intended for him until two fists, one on each side of him, grabbed his arms and lifted him up and started to march him away from the group – from the other kids who had loaded into pick-ups and driven down the road looking for fun, like it was a night out in Stoke-on-Trent but better because they had firepower and a base to shoot up. Consequences far to the back of their minds.

Gaz watched. The girl watched. Neither of them shielded their eyes, did not look away as if that might be – God alone knew how – disrespectful to the kid. The Russian did not move and the two men behind him were expressionless, as if this was a part of a day's work, might have been right.

The kid was lifted up on the chair, and might now have realised what came next for him. Would have known for certain when the noose made a necklace over his head and under his chin and the knot was tightened. An NCO was in charge of it. The kid was supported and the far end of the rope was knotted at the top, by the crossbar's angle with the upright post. Gaz saw the NCO look to his commander and received nothing that told him anything of 'enough is enough'. Might have looked for confirmation at the Russian, and might not. The NCO had his hand on the chair's back and ducked his head, the signal, and the steadying hands freed the kid's trousers and the chair was pulled from under him. The boy kicked a long time, his body dancing and spinning, but found nothing that was a haven for his weight, and was suspended and was strangled. The Russian officer now looked away but his minders did not. Gaz had seen sniper kills, and had seen advancing *mujahidin* cut down by machine-gun fire in a maize field, and had seen others caught on an open hillside by mortar fire as bombs rained down . . . had not seen anything as played out as the death of the kid from the rope on the goalpost crossbar.

It could have been her brother or her cousin, or could have been the boy she hoped one day might be her husband, but she did not cry out. It was a start and would be worse, and Gaz was its witness.

"When will Knacker be here?"

A reasonable question, a blunt answer.

Fee said, "He'll be here when he's ready to be here."

They had come along the coast, had passed ship building units and tanks for bunkering and a mountain of crab pots and their orange marker buoys, and one hotel, and then the driver had taken a sharp right and had gone up a narrow street of bungalows. Their destination was the one that did not have kids' bicycles and skate-boards outside, was also the one with a pocket handkerchief of uncut grass. He had followed her inside, had dumped his bag in the back room offered to him, had seen there was another bedroom in which her clothing was spread messily. He had showered, shaved, put on clean jeans and a shirt from his bag. In a dining area at the back, blinds down and the lights on, there was a screen and a projector. He had expected that Knacker would do the briefing. She did it well enough. He did not complain, nor did he take notes, but he absorbed. Maps on the screen, from her phone. They showed the border, the territory beyond the closed area, and a single highway leading across tundra to Murmansk.

Next, the maps showed the position of a roadblock far north on the highway, but back from the frontier, another at Titovka, and the barracks and headquarters of the 200th Independent Motorised Rifle Brigade. Then, photographs of the fence flashed up, concrete posts and stock-proof wire mesh capped with razor wire: sections with cameras were marked and those with tumble wires, and the ploughed strip behind, and the depth of the closed area. The picture taken from a blog and showing a hatchet-faced officer. Gaz betrayed himself, a sucked intake of breath, and he could see the line of the scar. Another picture, from stock files, of the new FSB building on Lenin Prospekt in Murmansk. An image of a man, probably middle forties, a cigarette drooping from his mouth. And a young man . . . fair hair, his attention seemed far away, but piercing eyes and a determined glance . . . Gaz always looked first at the eyes. He assumed them to be the sleepers, now woken.

"What do we have on the older one, what name, what reliability?"

Fee said, "It would have been his grandfather who was first recruited, then tucked up in bed, allowed to sleep. Handed down the contact to his son. We have no reason to imagine him to be other than reliable, solid and probably looking forward to some distant day when he can get on an Aeroflot going anywhere in the west, and then hightail into Guernsey and draw out his loot. Goes without saying that we are co-signatories and have to sanction any withdrawal. The young one is the grandson of the original asset. We assume him to be hard-working, a graduate, anxious to prosper his career. From what we know of them, they're a typical Murmansk working-class family, except that grandfather's own dad was an anti-aircraft gunner on a destroyer putting in to Murmansk during the Arctic convoy days, taking advantage of local generosity. The communications we have had from our courier have been necessarily bare, but nothing that indicates alarms. They have been told what is expected of them – where, when, they meet you. Where I come from, Gaz, south London, we've a sense of when it's going down the pan. Seems good, right now, from what we know."

"No disrespect to you, but when do I see Knacker?"

"Busy man, has a plateful."

"Doubt he has matters to concern him that are more important than putting a man across the Russian frontier to spotlight a target."

"You will see him before you go."

"And the aim of recognising the target?"

"Running before walking is seldom the best way to progress, Gaz."

In Syria, at the Forward Operating Base they worked from, the briefings were of extraordinary detail with sand models of locations and ample aerial photographs. Timings were down to minutes and behind every operation was a backup force of the Hereford people and their rough terrain vehicles and the Chinook crews who would go through hellish levels of weather to get to them. He had never felt alone there until the day he was marooned on the hill above the village. He would be alone here.

She said, "Don't go all fragile on me, Gaz, just don't. You go in and you do your recognition and you bug out when you have an idea of locations and of his work schedules, and we have the people to do what else is required. I advise, now, a bit of sleep if you can . . . What else have I to say?"

Gaz did his rueful look. "Something about not getting caught, something about consequences . . . and something about making a difference."

"I won't, but Knacker will, when he gets here."

The coin was small and a dull colour, once clean silver, but now ingrained with centuries of mud, a *denarius*, minted six years before Hadrian's death: it rattled feebly in Knacker's trouser pocket when his fingers played with his loose change. He carried £4 and 98p, and this one coin was – Maude had told him – worth

£60 in a reputable auction room, but she had nicked it. A present for him. Not many said that romance intruded deep into the lives of Knacker and his wife. A pizza eaten on a bench in the gardens beside the abbey in Hexham, and then bed in the guest house and her 'tired', and him glad of no interruption to his thoughts on the mission ahead . . . She had woken at two in the morning, had used a sharp elbow to rouse him, had grinned, had left the bed and rooted in her jeans and had produced what had seemed a scrap of dried dirt, had told him its history, and that it was an unforgive-able felony not to declare a find. Had turned off the light, had gone back to sleep. In the morning she had scrubbed it with his toothbrush, let him scrutinise the face of the Emperor, and the goddess, Pietas, making a sacrifice on the reverse side . . . A hurried breakfast, and she had dropped him off and gone back to her dig. He let his fingertips caress the surfaces of the coin. He had told her only that he would be away a few days, that it was an insertion initially – not where, not when, not why.

He was back on the Wall. Close to Mile Castle 35, sitting on the old stones that the 6th legion's stonemasons would have shaped when the foundations were laid, and ahead of him was flattish moorland and cropped grazing and one isolated farmstead. They did sheep here, not cattle, and none was close to him. No flies to irritate or disturb his concentration . . . Out there by the horizon and beyond it would have been an intelligence officer who probed with his intellect this section of fortification and had a life's inten-tion to find the point of weakness. Knacker identified with him. Did not know if the man had had a name, only that Mile Castle 35 would have figured in this man's analysis: dressed in cured skins in winter when snow and frost were on the ground, and near naked in summer with woad paint for decoration. Unshaven, tresses of hair in a tangled mess, and clever, capable of deceit, and painstaking, all of which Knacker reckoned he possessed in plenty. Nothing greatly had changed over the many centuries.

Today, on the fence to the north-west of Murmansk there would be a static line of border guards, and a closed strip with entry forbidden behind it, and military patrols, and also a small army of agents and assets, not easily identified, who watched and reported. The Romans, to counter the threat of infiltration or attack, used the *exploratores* who roamed on horseback, heavily armed, over the Wall and beyond the horizon. Had also the *speculators* who did the covert stuff and might pose as deserters, refugees, merchants . . . and would face a bad death if identified. Merchants were the best in Knacker's opinion for that work. Brought grain, fetched precious cloth for the wives of the barbarians' top men. It interested Knacker that from time far back men had practised those same arts of warfare, had realised their value, had wanted to put a man beyond reach of help. That day, and preparing to be launched, he had Gaz to play the part of one of the men that his predecessor, out beyond the mist and the vague edge where cloud and ground met, would have waved off.

Had that man, nineteen centuries before, set off with a light heart and a smile and a cheerful step? Unlikely. More likely barely coherent, his gut twisted in fear, his bowels loose, and death might be by beheading and it might be by the form of crucifixion popular at the time for setting an example. He turned the coin in his pocket. Then, and now, men could be bought and relied upon for the heavy lifting, and the one pushed off and sent towards the Wall would have been given, or promised, a tiny purse of these coins, the one that was in his trouser pocket. In this age Gaz was shown a link with a Guernsey bank set among narrow cobbled streets and with hanging baskets of petunias, and a man giving the spiel who seemed as trustworthy as any country church deacon. Money had bought them in the Province and Knacker could have listed the others from new Russia who had taken his shilling, his coinage. He had no duty of care. None of them at the Round Table believed in that baggage.

He sat on the stone and stared, and waited. There would be a blast on a horn and the sound would be carried to him on the light wind, and no rain was forecast for that day, and brightness was expected. Maude would be able to dig and scratch in peace. The driver from a Hexham taxi service would take him to the airport and the pilot would ferry him to the front line. He thought himself refreshed, at peace, and a few sheep stampeded away from him as he stood, stretched, coughed. It was not right that men such as himself, from the Round Table, should be burdened with matters of conscience; they should be allowed to get on with their work. He'd give their man a little encouragement talk, always thought it went down well . . . Always the Russians in Knacker's life. Their borders and their defences and their *exploratores* and their *speculatores*, and, in comparison with their resources, he was just an innocent abroad, a painted man. He did not know whether they knew of him, had a file for him.

He gazed out a last time, then glanced at his watch and reckoned the taxi was either there or near, and slowly trudged away from the wall and the ruin of Mile Castle 35. It would be good to be up to speed, running, starting out on the mission – not, of course that Knacker would be setting foot into barbarian territory.

The kids did business.

Natacha accosted. Timofey carried the stock in a shoulder-bag and took the money. Both reckoned themselves good at personal security, and both would have said they had learned lessons from the last time, when she was caught and he'd legged it into the pitch darkness. There was supposed to be, this time, a fast bug-out route to take them away from the selling pitch and up a steep slope, through a jungle of bushes and small trees, across a road and then into the warren of lanes inside the housing complex. This was not where they had been busted, at the railway station, and where the buses and coaches parked.

Each of them had a good view of the steps leading to the monument. The walkway was wide and open and it would have been hard for the police to approach them unseen, difficult even for the FSB people who sometimes took over from the police. It had been the FSB who had arrested Natacha: he had evaded them and she was close to it but had slipped and gone over on an ankle and that had given the bastards the chance to dive on her.

At the edge of a wide space of concrete, backing on to the

undergrowth and the high apartments, was a peculiar black shape, curved in a half-circle, five or six metres high and seeming to have small covered windows that were similar to those in a pilot's cockpit. On the front of it was a gold-coloured eagle mounted on a pristine scarlet base. The monument was important to Natacha because of the plaque set into brickwork at the back which carried the names of more than 100 men lost in a submarine disaster. Natacha's father's name should have been there but was not . . . should have been, because of the loss of that vessel, the monstrous *Kursk* – sunk with no survivors in August 2000 out in the icy Barents Sea. Her father's name was not there, should have been, and he was as dead as any of the men, who had sailed in her. Natacha liked to work close to the conning tower of the submarine, recovered from the bottom of the Barents, along with the bodies, and the rust scraped off it, and new paint applied, and a permanent memorial to those sailors of the Northern Fleet, as her father had been.

It was bold of them to trade in daytime, but it was a part of Murmansk – poor housing, poor pay for those in work, poor expectations – where money could be taken. Customers did not expect to hang around. Service on the nail was wanted. They had their regulars, men and women and boys and girls. In fine rain, buyers shuffled close to them. The city had a name for hard drugs, and Murmansk had as high a number of HIV addicts as any town in the Russian Federation. A new customer sidled close. The Italian.

"I have a flight in an hour."

"We will get our money? The extra money they will pay us?"

Timofey reckoned the Italian despised him. Had no reason to believe this, but he seemed to look across the open concrete and towards the section of the conning tower and to linger on Natacha's legs. He gazed at the Italian. Was told with a disinterested shrug that 'money' was the affair of others but he assumed obligations and promises would be kept. A slip of paper was passed to him, pocketed.

The Italian said, "Where you have to be, and at what time. You meet this man and you do what is asked, and you will find his employers grateful. I came here after visiting your father. Your father was drunk. Your father told me you would be here ... I would like to warn, dear friend, that these people for whom you work, who have woken you, are most trustworthy. Rewards for completing the task they give you. Quite unpleasant vengeance if they are betrayed. Easy to understand. Be there, do as you are asked."

He was gone. Striding quickly, and he would have had to work hard to have thrown off the inevitable tail that local FSB would have placed on a known diplomat travelling to Murmansk from the capital, and slipping away from whatever legitimate business had brought him so far north. They went on selling and the rain had come on heavier and the mist settled low above the apartments and customers came and went and the slip of paper was crumpled in Timofey's pocket ... He would do what was asked of him but only for the promised money.

He could not see Zhukov but knew he was close. He could not hear Zhukov but believed he was watched.

He was at the back of his cabin where he had dug and hoed the scant soil to plant summer vegetables. He had potatoes and carrots and cabbages growing. Near the cabin were dense dwarf birches and he should have been able to see a creature as large as the bear. And there were sufficient fallen twigs and dried leaves to mark where it moved.

Jasha was not a man easily unnerved.

He was military by training. He was now in his middle sixties, and a wound received in Kandahar, southern Afghanistan, had halted his ability to run. He had learned to swing his hips and bend his back and scurry at speed. Ugly but effective, and what mattered to him was nothing to do with a parade ground and everything to do with a degree of agility. His leg hurt him but he accepted the levels of pain and was thankful his own fragmented muscle caused him less agony than the wire would have done that had dug deep in Zhukov's leg. He could accept pain. In midwinter, a tooth had broken and the pain had run in rivers and it was when the track was blocked by snow so he had removed the tooth stump and its root with a pair of old pliers, and had survived. Pain he understood and reckoned to cope with, but he was uneasy about the hidden presence of the bear. Jasha had never established, enough to take a liberty with it, whether the creature regarded him as a benefactor or an enemy. He abandoned his vegetable patch.

He stood by the door of his cabin, strained his eyes, his ears. The old dog lay on its bed of hessian sacks . . . He had seen the sacks outside a store in Murmansk, piled in a basket, and had thought they might have a use, had picked out a couple and thrown them in his pick-up and driven off; had felt remorse, had paid for them on his next visit to the city. Jasha was a confused man, and sometimes he chuckled at the thought of it – not that day. The dog was too old to accompany him when he hunted for a full day, went after the Arctic fox or the lynx, but it guarded his cabin. The dog growled. Not loud, but soft, like a light flashed to show an alarm. An intruder was close. He was unnerved. Jasha had faced ferocious tribesmen in combat, but always they would show themselves as they edged closer, looked for a killing shot or, better for them, the opportunity to take a prisoner. The dog showed its teeth and sunk low on its sack bed.

He would have liked to talk with the bear, with Zhukov . . . What he knew of combat was that a tracker followed an enemy and waited for a sign of weakness. He had his rifle with him: had taken, in the last several days, to having the weapon with him when he went to dig in his garden or to clear back dwarf birch saplings, or to empty the bucket that he used inside the cabin. He went inside. In two days' time he had an appointment in the city for the sale of pelts, now well dried, and for the heads of two foxes which would fetch a good price, and he would have to leave the dog to fend for itself for a few hours.

Jasha closed and barricaded the cabin door behind him, using the table and the chair. Rain dripped rhythmically from the roof and misted the window panes. He sat in his chair and faced the door, his rifle on his lap. The dog, an old and treasured friend, came off the sacking and sat close to his knee. He heard nothing and saw nothing. His fear seemed to shame him.

She was told to stand on the steps of the hotel. The evening was closing down and the clouds nibbled against the sea horizon behind her, and the wind blew at the soft rain. In spite of it being high summer some of the passing cars used their headlights and the tarmacadam glistened. The man she had met in Hamburg had greeted her at the airport, had told her again that she should call him 'Knacker', had shared a taxi with her, had booked her for a single night into the hotel by the shore and along from the harbour. He stood close to the girl but behind her, would have been in shadow. In the middle of the day the woman from the consulate had come to the bar on Rostocker Strasse, and had paid the owner for her time and had taken her to catch a flight through Copenhagen and on to this edge of the European mainland. She could have refused, had not. He, Knacker, had told her that this journey for which, in a quiet voice, he thanked her, was the last time she would be involved in a matter of retribution . . .

She would never forget. She had heard people discuss death, talk of bereavement, when they were waiting for food or drinks to be brought to them in the bar. Usually, they spoke of 'moving on' and 'putting all that behind us'. They had not been where she had been. To have refused to come would, in Faizah's mind, have been a betrayal of the village she had once been a part of. She saw him. Felt for the first time, the only time, a weakness in her legs and seemed to shiver on a warm evening. He walked well and she thought him a stranger in the place, and he looked once behind him and a woman – stout hips and tight trousers and with a street-light showing up a tattoo on her arm – waved him forward. Seemed as manipulated as she was. Dressed casually, he came forward warily and reached the far side of the street. No traffic to hold him up but he looked both ways as if that were routine, necessary or not, always careful, and crossed – would have been told to, and then looked up and was in front of the steps leading to the hotel's entrance. Recognised her . . . where they had been and what they had shared. Of course he recognised her. He rocked on his feet, hesitated, and climbed the step towards her. She had been told that she would see him and had asked why she was brought the long distance from Hamburg. Knacker had said, "It's to encourage him, my dear, simply that. Encourage him."

To hug her, to kiss her, to shake her hand, to stand awkwardly in front of her. Options that faced Gaz. Remembered how it had been on the last day, all through the hours that he had been with her – and remembered also how it was when he had been in the hide and she had come close with her dogs and her goats, and never a word spoken between them. He had been in the room in the safe house, he had lain on the bed and stared at the ceiling and had not slept and had tried again and again to memorise all he had been shown . . . He had not thought of Aggie. Nor had he thought of the gardens and homes where he was booked for work. Nor had he considered the rumour mill that would have been grinding the length and breadth of Westray, and thought his life there already fractured. The puppeteer was Knacker . . . Gaz saw him standing in the darkness at the side of the hotel entrance and beyond the throw of the interior lights. He saw the scar on her chin, where the skin had folded back, where her finger now went, nervously. He stood in front of her. He thought her aged and her skin had lost most of its lustre and her eyes were dull. He reached out his hand. One finger of his joined with one of hers. Each finger hooked so that they did not drift away.

She said, "You are going to Murmansk, where he is."

"Yes."

"Where the Russian officer is."

"Yes."

"He could have stopped everything."

"Could have, probably . . . chose not to."

"I have been brought here to 'encourage' you."

"It's what they do – they believe if I am encouraged then I will do better."

"What do you do in Murmansk?"

"I am supposed to watch the FSB office in Murmansk. To see him. To follow him. To learn his home and his work schedule. Then I come out."

"Finished? See him, walk close to him? Then, come out?"

"That is what I am told to do."

"You identify him, where he believes he is safe. You can get beside him. You can shoot him, strangle him, stab him, beat with a bar on his skull until it breaks. Not kill him?"

"No."

"You remember it?"

"Yes. Very well. It is not my business to kill."

"You are a soldier . . ."

"Was a soldier. Not now."

"You will *help* to kill?"

"I do not know what is intended. Perhaps others will be used to kill. From my information, perhaps."

"You will not kill him? Only *help* to kill him? Should I go with you? I could kill him. With my hands, with a gun . . . You saw him, saw what he did."

"I just do my job," he said flatly.

"I hope I encourage you to 'do your job'."

She turned away. The colour was back in her face and the light in her eyes, and he thought her glance ravaged him and was intended to. Gaz bit at his lip. She went into the hotel's foyer, and Knacker came from the shadows and gazed impassively at him. He thought his words had been pathetic. The woman, Fee, called from behind him. He went back down the steps and crossed the road and might have been run down because he looked neither way, and a horn blasted him, and she was stern faced and made no comment and they went up the hill together towards the safe house. He supposed he was 'encouraged', and the next day he would go across the border, and remember, all the time, what he had seen that day.

6

They were parked up in a four-wheel drive. Gaz was in the back.

The clothes he wore had been given him that morning. Cross-country gear and his own boots, and breakfast had been cooked by Fee, and a single cup of tea ... He was shown again, on a laptop's screen, the border and its hinterland, taken by a drone camera.

They were deep in a pine forest. A Norwegian was at the wheel and his name wasn't given and Gaz assumed he was from their border control unit, roped in for the ride, and to offer advice. Fee sat beside the driver. Knacker was alongside Gaz. Gaz assumed the girl, Faizah, was now surplus baggage. They'd likely have pushed some bank notes into her purse for a taxi to the airport and she'd have already caught a flight south, then a Hamburg connection. Her job had been to hustle Gaz: she'd done that successfully. He had slept poorly, but could not remember the last time he had slept well – might have been the last night before deploying towards the village, Deir al-Siyarqi, more than two years ago.

Had slept well then, hadn't known what would hit him in the next hours, out of 'the clear blue sky', unexpected and where all the bad times sprang from. Had been looking forward to seeing the girl – no name and no talk and a herd of goats and two dogs – and her playing the silent game with the raised eyebrow, the sharp light in her eye, and sharing his secret. A different girl on the step of the hotel, brought to Kirkenes with the express task of stiffening him. Army people called it 'moral fibre' – it needed to be strong, dependable, and they'd reckoned she could toughen him. Nothing about him sitting with her and asking how she did, what her life was, would she ever go back? Only her lecturing him on the constraints applying to any trooper, corporal, sergeant or officer in a unit specialising in reconnaissance. Left a bad taste, sour, and should have been better because of where they had been and what they had seen.

The drone, of course, had not crossed the border. He was shown the fence from an elevated angle, could see where pine trees had been cleared and the ploughed strip where footprints would show up, and the track of crushed stone that was another 100 yards back and used by patrol vehicles. The Norwegian said how often they came by, and had unfolded a map which had the camera arcs marked, and he'd pointed to a section where a bend in the fence left dead ground . . . a small length but with tumbler wires. Beside the Norwegian was a clear plastic bag holding strands of animal hair. He spoke quietly, never looking at Gaz, as if the sight of him would contaminate: he would have been just one more of the foot-soldiers that Knacker had rounded up. They were on the northern section of the wire, and it was explained that farther south the frontier was first in the centre of a river, then halfway across a wide lake, as big as an inland sea. Where their interest lay, marked with a streak of red, was outside the eyeline of the nearest watch-towers. Gaz did not query the intelligence the Norwegian brought: how recently had the length of wire been surveyed, how long since the patrol patterns had been logged, had this location been used before? Had to take it on trust.

He was asked if he wanted to stretch his legs. Knacker assumed he did, had already opened the vehicle door.

Something that Gaz loathed: the final talk before a mission, when a spook would tell them all how important it was, what a difference it would make. He stood on the edge of the clearing and they would have been 100 yards back from the frontier fence that was shielded by the pine forest where no birds sang.

Knacker came close. "I saw you wince. Don't worry, you'll not get a portrait of our monarch or the Union flag, and how we're all reliant on you. Take it as read. What matters are my assurances. We don't send you out bare-arsed. We've done our best, which is a good best, to ensure you have the planning and backup you deserve. Why you? You are the only one we have, as an asset, with the knowledge and the qualities to do what is asked. Interrupt me any moment you want to . . ."

Gaz asked nothing, busied his mind memorising what he was told. He shook his head. The rain was lifting, the clouds breaking and the wind dropping. Flies were gathering.

". . . We had this sleeper family in Murmansk. Been there for ever. Codeword *Matchless*, and that was the name of a Royal Navy warship doing Arctic convoys, and a seaman came into the port, sneaked ashore during a blackout, had his leg over. He never went back but word reached his mates on another convoy that 'herself' had been down on the dockside with a little bundle all wrapped up and needing a dad to be shown off to . . . Bit of a yarn but twenty years later the intelligence people had a whiff of the story and some digging was done, clever stuff, and the girl was identified, and her little bastard, and they were signed up. Good people and brave, because they faced a miserable death if they were caught after taking our shilling. Yes, we paid them. Money into the account each quarter, and it vegetates in the Channel Islands, and they sleep, sleep well and are not disturbed. Moved through the generations and contact with them is through the Italian embassy in Moscow, and a SISMI officer. We have no reason to believe that the family are not receptive to being woken. We see them as reliable, hard-working, fond of this bank account where their wealth accrues, though not yet touched. The contact has assured them that a substantial bonus applies to this work. They meet you at the rendezvous point they have been given. You will have trekked to get there but you have all the necessary skills to achieve that. They take you into Murmansk. You will be placed in the vicinity of the FSB building on Lenin Prospekt. Play it how you wish to play it, Gaz . . . Identify him, tail him, the major, establish his place of residence, and that is pretty much it. You leave the rest to us. Get this down your throat, Gaz – and I am not merely urging you to go the extra mile, get this . . ."

Nothing to say, he listened.

"It was a war crime. It was a job for the International Court of justice. It was the marker laid down by a civilised world that such behaviour was unacceptable. War crimes are only applicable to the team that loses. They didn't lose, they won. They flattened the country and slaughtered the opposition and gassed them, and clapped their hands and cheered for Victory Syria Day and not a prosecutor in sight. They won. Except that *we*, non-combatants, do not see it quite in that light and have our own end-game which will bring gratification to the few who survived. That brave and rather attractive girl is one who, I hope, will feel a tad of satisfaction, and the others who survived. Do we do this, Gaz, because we like to donate comfort and love to victims with a munificence based on vengeance? Not really. It's about gaining friends and allies and putting them in debt to us, and that way we thrive. As I said, you leave the rest to us, and don't worry your pretty head about what the rest entails. Mark him for us, Gaz, as you used to mark for the snipers, or for the drone strikes. Give us the opportunity to finish it, Gaz. I think Fee brought a thermos of coffee, and probably some biscuits."

Knacker stood back. Not a man who regularly congratulated himself. He had been listened to, had been heard. It was his familiar speech on the eve of a mission, the last hours before a man was put in harm's way. Minor variations, but done many times. Earlier in his life he had stayed close to the border and had watched his agent go over or under or through a fence. Or had seen him into the departure hall at an airport. Or had been on a platform when a night train pulled away, his man settling into a seat and ticking fast in his mind the details of the legend, a lifestyle story, he'd been provided with. There had been a few men, and one woman, who had believed they possessed the strength of will to change their minds late in the day, to step back, and say to his face they were no longer prepared to go, wanted out. None had succeeded. He had ridiculed them, had praised them to the hilt, used the poetry of inspiration, had threatened . . . Quite a considerable armoury of tax investigation, job loss, consequences that were brutal and which he would not flinch from employing. They'd all gone . . . a few had even come back.

He seldom lingered in the past, just a fast kaleidoscope of faces that seemed to blur the image of Gaz in front of him. There were enough of them who had gone boldly forward with his soft-spoken encouragement trilling in their heads. Some had died beyond the reach of help after experiencing the violence of interrogation cells, and some had gone to the penal colonies, and some would emerge as broken individuals, but Knacker could comfort himself that, the end had always justified the means. A couple lost in Iran and three in the Damascus hell-holes, but the outstanding majority had gone into the territory of the Russian Federation. In his experience, the men he sent put on a show of confidence. There were those who were traitors to their own regime, who loathed it, or were keen to accept Knacker's money, intelligence officers or scientists, one from the military general staff. And some who worked in telephone exchanges or in central banking. Some would earnestly say to him, 'I think I've done enough . . .' He'd respond, total sincerity, that their safety was his paramount concern and '. . . just one more time, friend, just once more, then we'll call it a day . . .' They all did, and there was always a moment of reflection at the Round Table, when a new casualty was spoken of, a pause in laughter and gossip and a raised glass. And life moved on. His hand was in his pocket and his fingers played with the coins – sterling and euros and Norwegian kroner – and they rested on the one that Maude had stolen at the Wall. He liked that thought, being a Pict or a Cantabrian painted with woad, not wearing a suit and a waterproof against a change in the weather and pushing men forward towards that great Wall, or a simple fence, all in the interests of the greater good.

"Little bit more time to kill, and I'm relying on Fee having that flask, and those biscuits . . . then I'll leave you with her and our good and competent local colleague. Just have to get back to town, tie up a few loose ends . . . See you when you come back out . . . First, a splash of coffee."

He always tied loose ends, left everything tidy; Knacker believed in the value of tidiness. The coin was between his fingers and that evening he might get one of the girls to clean it.

"We'll miss you, Major, miss you greatly."

Many had echoed that, all lying bastards: he knew most would be anxious to see him gone. He represented power and influence beyond a level they could attain or dream of.

"Congratulations on your new appointment, Major, we have been fortunate to have you here."

Murmansk had a fine new headquarters building, but it was a backwater and those who wished to earn promotion would want to be out of the place fast. Only an imbecile would want to be here in this city where for six weeks in summer there was no darkness, and for six weeks in winter there was no sunrise. His mother had travelled north for two visits in the twenty-three months he had been stationed there and he had seen the lustre leave her face and she had seemed to shrivel in the wind. On each occasion rain had fallen steadily. There was nothing to show her and she had remarked, when standing at the foot of the Alyosha monument, that she would have preferred a postcard of it to seeing it for herself.

"We hope you will have pleasant memories of the city, of us, Major, and remember us favourably, and we hope you will speak well of us and our work in Moscow."

In the capital there were fine shopping opportunities, and worthwhile work and a chance to bead his gaze on the faces of the fidgeting men over whom he exercised control. And status. And the regular chance to manufacture an excuse to take a free flight down to Sochi where there was always a vacant villa or an apartment belonging to a friend of his father. The brigadier general had never come to see him. His father distrusted the navy, was an army man, had no interest in the affairs of the Northern Fleet. And work involving drugs dependency in the city would hardly have held his father's attention, nor anything connected with the so called 'green lobby' that complained endlessly about the alleged dumping of nuclear waste from decommissioned submarines. He hoped he would never again have to deal with security problems involving the frontier, or monitoring foreign diplomats and occasional tourists, or the difficult relations with the naval security people, an arrogant crowd. His father had sent the two minders who lived in a neighbouring block and drove him around and mounted a loose guard over him.

"A privilege to work with you, Major, and our thanks for your insights."

He would go out of the door and his desk would be cleared and the hard drive on his computer cleansed of his own work and a new man would soon have his feet under the table.

"Your replacement, Major, was here the day before yesterday. Seemed efficient and interested in his work. A wife and two children, and looking forward to our winter sports."

No backward glance from him when Mikki and Boris travelled with him to the airport, and his few personal possessions would have been crated and would go south on the train. There had been no gathering of colleagues at the main entrance to see him off. Most of those serving in Murmansk looked for a lifetime of sinecure and making enough money to buy an apartment without a mortgage between the railway station and the Prospekt. Would be excited to handle a case history of the eco-people who tried to bring law suits against the government and needed warning off. He could have had the boys park his official transport at the back of the building where the cell block was located and where the closed yard and high gates prevented scrutiny. Lavrenti preferred to use the front entrance, the limited spaces for senior officers, to make a statement of his importance.

He sat alone in his room. The matronly woman who typed for him was in an outer office, the door between them closed. When he had first come to Murmansk, the same woman had managed to beard him in the staff canteen; sitting with her had been a girl in her early twenties, his assistant's niece, and the introduction was blatant. He had, scarcely polite, turned it down. Had flushed red, had indicated that there was a significant 'other' in Moscow. It had been a poor lie . . . His phone did not ring, emails were no longer copied to him, and the room was bare of anything personal except for the last item in the room that he would take away with him. A monochrome photograph, enlarged and framed with an aged gold leaf effect which had been hard to achieve in Murmansk, showed his father beside the barbecue, the President, smiling in front of him. Lavrenti never referred to the occasion and was not in the picture, but everyone in the building on Prospekt would have known of the picture and his assistant would have spread word of it. He would take the picture down the next day and it would go in the cases to be sent south . . .

His father had phoned him. Not a happy call. Cold, clipped, demanding an explanation why a roof had not been supplied to a coming man who had the opportunity to exploit mineral and oil deposits. He had blustered, his father had been incisive in his criticism. The situation with the Jew was to be rectified as soon as he returned to Moscow – not a matter of debate. He would sleep badly again that night. His assistant had prepared digests of ongoing cases, investigations that he had worked on, and the following day he would meet his successor and be shot of his responsibilities.

He stared at the desk, then at the empty screen, then at the closed door – and could not forget what he had seen, what he had done. No one in the headquarters building would miss him when he was gone, and the loneliness crushed him.

He had sagged off the sofa bed, and dropped down on to the rug beside it, and his elbow hit a bottle and toppled it . . . another day had started in the life of the woken sleeper.

The apartment was quiet. Next door, through a thin wall, music played, but the kids had gone for the day and had switched off the radios and the TV, and he had not heard them when they had come out of the one bedroom, his bedroom, and taken any food that was in the old refrigerator. They had enough money, because one was a thief and the other was a whore and both were criminals, but they had not bought a new or even a reconditioned refrigerator. He lived from the scraps they gave him, and most of his money went on cheap booze. He was thin and gaunt, and had dreamed of being even thinner and even more drawn in the face and with his skin hanging off his bones. In his dream, he was shuffling in a line of other *zeks*, wearing the prisoners' flimsy uniform, near starved, and coughing half his guts up and labelled as a man who had betrayed his country.

He cared little for his son and cared less for his son's girl. His wife was long gone, had given birth to the one child – named Timofey which meant 'Honouring a God' – and had left him to bring up the brat. And his sisters had gone. Anyone with a brain left Murmansk. He remained, and a few of his drinking partners; he loved them but had never told them, never spoken of a bank account abroad or of a codeword, *Matchless*. He feared that he might reveal his secret when drunk, pissing against a wall beside them . . . He would go to a prison camp for the rest of his days if he were caught as an enemy of the state, would rot there, and die there. He loathed his son, but could not drink without the money his son gave him. Loathed the girl who some days would come out of the bedroom – naked – and parade in front of him as he lay on the sofa bed, flaunting her tits and her arse, hated her. He did not wash. Did not eat, and had tipped over the bottle and its contents had slopped on the rug.

On television they showed films of FSB men and women when they charged out from the shadows and surprised traitors, handcuffed them and bundled them into vehicles. The television showed films of traitors in the courts, in a cage and facing justice. The films made it clear that the FSB always caught the spies, the traitors. It was on the television.

He would report the treachery. He would save himself. He would go into town, to the Prospekt, would find an officer, would tell him of the Italian's visit, would stress his own loyalty – would not go to a penal colony up in the tundra, and would be rewarded, and would have drink – and would get back his own bed. He dressed in what he had worn most of the week and drained what was left in his overturned bottle. He would save himself.

★   ★   ★

Down by the Stroitel stadium, where they played ice hockey, junior league matches, the kids waited.

In Timofey's life and in Natacha's, going down to the stadium and waiting there was as dangerous a time as any. Freedom on a knife-edge because it was the one occasion when they were not in charge; they were there because they were told to be. The stadium, for a reason that neither could explain, was the location chosen by the Chechen boys from St Petersburg who drove up to Murmansk with fresh supplies: they had the best product. They were reliable, their prices were consistent, they were careful with their security. Wild and small and swarthy and from the Caucusus, their cruelty and brutality were unmatched. It was said that even the gangs in St Petersburg and Moscow were nervous of the Chechens. They waited.

Time drifted. The product that the Chechens brought to Murmansk was the best on the market. Timofey and Natacha had their regular customers. Never a complaint about the quality of the cut, never an accusation that the weed was augmented with fine sawdust, domestic flour or dried grass cuttings. If the Chechens in their large black van with privacy windows were late then the kids did not complain. To insult the travelling suppliers, or to antagonise them, would lead to bad consequences. Only a lunatic would trifle with the Chechens. It was the world in which they lived, but in the slow build-up to sex the night before, while the old idiot grunted and heaved and cursed in the living-room and failed to sleep, they had murmured what they would do with the money lodged in the foreign bank account, and that would be increased as a reward for the services they would provide as 'sleepers'. They considered Red Sea resorts, the Italian coast or the Costas. Timofey carried a thick wad of notes in his hip pocket, she had more in her shoulder-bag. This was more important than where they had pledged to be later in the day; they were in place and with the money, looking out for the arrival of the Chechens, and also for the police.

They sat in the Fiat 500 – and smoked and talked and she nuzzled his neck and his hand lay on her thigh, and they kept a look on the mirror and the road behind the parking area. Maybe, Natacha whispered, there would be an opportunity, later, to get new wheels, something bigger and more comfortable than the Fiat. They had only each other, no one else cared a pinch for them. His father was a drunk and ... her father was dead and in a shameful suicide's grave.

She seldom told the story of how the death of the *Kursk* had killed her own father, safe on dry land when the explosion had ripped the submarine apart. He had been in the arms of his girl and had not set an alarm, had been in the warmth of a bed when the crew had stumbled from the apartments in the closed naval town of Vidyaevo on an August morning and gone to the buses that would take them to the quay where the submarine was moored. Some vessel. The height of the fourth storey of the building in which she now lived with Timofey, and as long as two football pitches, and they had sailed early with their Shipwreck and Starfish and Stallion missiles to exercise out in the Barents as if the enemy – NATO forces – were targets. First they would make an attack using a torpedo that weighed five tonnes and which was powered by hydrogen peroxide H2 02 propellant ... She knew every detail of what had happened. At the moment her father had been stretching, yawning, considering the brilliance of the fuck he had enjoyed, that torpedo had exploded. The *Kursk* had gone down, its hull broken open. Her father, and his girl – who would be Natacha's mother – did not learn of the *Kursk*'s loss for several hours. He would have pleaded influenza, and there were no telephones for the use of junior crew so he could not call in sick. Her father, after the persistence of the rumours sweeping the garrison town, had realised all his friends, colleagues, the boys with whom he laughed, joked, drank, were dead. He lived because he screwed this girl. He had taken a length of rope and had gone to the edge of the perimeter and had hanged himself. Natacha was a survivor of a sort, and managed, because of Timofey, to stay strong. And, that morning, if they were impatient, if they bugged out because the contact was late, then they would never again have the chance to trade with the Chechens, and might pay a high price for their disrespect – so they waited.

Gaz had sat in the vehicle, eyes closed and body still, and used known techniques for relaxation. There was a tap on his arm. The Norwegian to see him on his way. Gaz had no complaint that he had not seen Knacker, nor that Fee stood back and was half masked by the trees and did not speak and did not wave. No one in the regiment, about to climb up the ramp of a Chinook or scramble into a Special Forces vehicle and head off towards the sharp bit, wanted chaff talk that fogged concentration. He hooked the small rucksack over his shoulder. A change of clothes was in his bag but he was now in combat and camouflage gear and his only weapons were a flash-and-bang, and a pepper spray and a single smoke grenade. His clothing was sanitised, all labels removed and – if caught – he was expected to keep his mouth shut for thirty-six hours which would give time for what he knew to be buried, disguised. It was said within thirty-six hours, if you blundered into a patrol anywhere, here or Syria or the Province, the captors would realise the significance of who they had. After thirty-six . . . not worth thinking about, and the stuff he carried was for escape, creating diversion and chaos and having the bottle to break and run. But that, too, was chaff.

The Norwegian was older than Gaz – grizzled beard, cropped hair, slim and tall and fit. He led the way, carrying the small plastic bag that contained the animal hair. Gaz did not turn to see if Knacker and Fee watched him go. When they had worked out from the Forward Operating Base in Syria, and the same in Afghanistan, the Sixers always stayed back and the contacts were brought to them in a secure place. He assumed that Knacker was, in their books, a proven Russia expert, but would have bet that he had never been there. Might have looked out across country and at watch-towers, might have peered through high-powered lenses at an expanse of treetops, might have watched distant cars on the move . . . the Sixers were supposed to stay safe.

In a low voice, barely more than the sound of the wind in the leaves and on the fronds of the pines, the Norwegian explained why he carried the animal hair, and why he had with him a square metre of heavy leather. Made sense to Gaz. They were at the edge of the tree line. The fence was thirty yards of open ground in front of him. The Norwegian held his arm as if he did not want him to charge, not until he was pushed forward. From under his coat he produced two metal discs, each the size of a large Frisbee.

"I won't see you again, friend, but I wish you well. It is right that you come out another way because this is a valuable place and should not be abused. You are like a bear. A bear does not recognise a political barrier. Goes to it, assesses, crosses it and has a coat that is strong, and protects it. We believe we know the patrol pattern and that this is a good time. You cross. You run after returning to me what is mine, and you do not stop. You go across the patrol track, then right and you will see a tree, quite tall, killed by a lightning strike. Beyond it, on lower ground, is a small lake. You take the left side of it and will see an animal track that veers to the right and you follow it, and you come to the road. That is the main highway from Kirkenes to Murmansk. On the far side, going down a little hill, is a picnic site, a pull-in behind the trees. There used to be benches there when the idea was to develop cross-border relations and have a friendly place for Russians and Norwegians to stop, take a pee, eat, then drive on. It is not used now because relationships have changed, changed considerably. You do not expect charity there, friend, but it is where you will meet your people. I wish you well. You are ready?"

"Ready."

The Norwegian glanced at his watch, stood erect, listened. Gaz heard only the light patter of rain and the wind blowing in tree-tops, was passed the sheet of hard leather, and breathed hard, and considered. Then, with no ceremony, he was pushed in the shoulder and went forward, stumbled, regained his balance ... and realised he was at war, a lowly and deniable trooper, lurching towards a frontier barrier. A few strides and the fence was in front of him. The ethos of his former unit was to merge and blend, to observe and note, to slip away and report. What action was taken was not his responsibility. Did as he was told, obeyed orders and it was for others to decide what use was made of the information he provided. He did not pilot a drone strike and did not nestle a sniper's rifle against his shoulder. He did not have to look into the faces of the relatives or the comrades-in-arms of those whose lives were snatched because of the reconnaissance he was expert at. Comforting? Sometimes ... What he had often hidden behind was the screen of professionalism. Like now. Like getting across open grass, thick and tufted, and seeing the fence looming high over him and razor wire strands up to his waist, and among them tumbler alarm wires, then four more stands, then short crossbars on each post and attached to them was more wire that projected a foot on each side. The concrete posts holding the barrier were solid and newly made. Saw that, and saw the ploughed strip beyond the fence where footprints would show, and he'd not have the time to smooth the dirt and lose the shape of his boots in the ground. Then a vehicle track, and patrols would be alerted by the tumbler wires, then the sanctuary of the tree line ... No time to consider the finer points of ethics ... A last thought and not of Aggie, not of Aggie taking a picnic with him on the cliff edge, but of the girl, and her scarred face, who had come to encourage him and the contempt in her voice when he'd explained his role, what he did and what he did not do. He heaved the sheet of hard leather over the wires' cutting edges at the top of the fence, and jumped. The fence rocked, and he swung his legs.

A hissing voice, urgent, behind him. "Go. Keep going."

They were thrown from behind him. Done expertly, landing not by chance but from a practised drill. Two metal pieces, the size of dinner plates, lay on the undisturbed ploughed strip.

He landed. The fence was violated, the wire loosened and sagged. Professionalism kicked in, like he had not been away two years, sitting in the shadows, agonising over his past. By now the alarms would be chorusing and lights flashing. He stretched forward with his right leg and put his boot on to the nearer metal plate and felt it sink, and stepped on to the second, and balanced and rocked and crouched and reached to pick up the first and threw it, and saw it fly well above the drooping fence. The Norwegian was on the far side of the wire, freeing the leather, and starting to scatter the hairs from his plastic bag, long and coarse. Gaz did the last stride and was beyond the ploughed strip and turned and groped for the second plate, and could see that the imprint it left was that of a huge beast with claw indents that went down a quarter of an inch. Clever and simple, and good enough for a cursory check. He threw the second plate over the fence and the Norwegian scurried to pick it up, and was gone. Left behind was the buckled fence, the traces of brown bear hairs impaled on the barbs and also the creature's prints.

Gaz ran. Went fast for the tree line. Head down, searching for stones on which to land, and rock where he would not leave a trail. Kept running, and veered to the right as he had been told. Saw the tree. Dark, bare, dead, it seemed scorched as if the lightning had burned all sap and life from it. He headed for it . . . tried to gain strength to fight the fear that welled. Had dismissed the girl with her goats, and Aggie who was bent on rescuing him, and even Debbie who was a good kid and sorely tried and whom he had hit. He thought of the target, the officer who had come to the village.

Delta Alpha Sierra, the sixth hour

The body on the crossbar no longer kicked, or twitched, just spiralled.

Gaz was trained to observe, accepted that life was gone. He watched the troops who were not part of the cordon, those who had fanned out and were starting to search the buildings. It might have been that either the commander or his Russian captain were behind schedule, that time had slipped, and the example to be made was not yet nailed down. Troops approached the group of kids, who sat, hunched, round shoulders, blindfolded heads, hands tied at their backs. Until the Iranians reached for them they would not have known if they were to be taken. The one with a football shirt was lifted up and held. Gaz had the glasses on him and recognised the badge on his shirt was that of Bayern Munich; the shirt would have been a top possession, and would have come into Syria with aid parcels from Germany: not sending their own sons to fight in a messy mid-east war, but happy to send a football shirt over. The kids did not know, but Gaz did, where they were going to be taken. He knew ... and the girl probably knew, and Gaz reached forward and stretched his arm far enough to hold her wrist, and held it tight.

He said nothing, nor did she.

What they had seen was that there were now four ropes looped over the crossbar of the goalpost. A man from the Islamic Revolutionary Guard Corps carried a sledgehammer and tent pegs. The ropes had a noose at the short end; after being slung over the crossbar, the other end was fastened to a peg which was then hammered into the soil. More chairs had been brought out into the rain and the wind. The corralled women, with the small children, were not blindfolded and they might have been intimidated by the aimed rifles during the first killing, but no longer. They had begun to whistle and shriek and the sounds of their voices filled the valley.

The one who wore the Bayern Munich shirt kicked out as he was carried. Gaz assumed that his blindfold had slipped. The kid would have seen the goal where he'd believed himself the Lewandowski of the village. Seen the ropes and the chairs, seen the body suspended, feet making slow circles and reversing, and would have seen the hooded man who stood near to the commander. Gaz could not have said what was best. Best to get it over with, take the inevitable, hope it would be quick. Or best to fight, howl and lash out, try to break free only to be clubbed and taken to the football goal and heaved up on to a chair? Gaz had no opinion, hated what he saw but could not look away, and held the girl's wrist. Had he been able to, Gaz would have smothered her, lain on top of her and twisted her head so that she saw nothing, and covered her ears so that she heard nothing. The cordon of militia guys was perhaps a 100 metres from him and seemed uninterested in a group of goats, would not have seen her, nor her dogs. If she yelled at them or stood and screamed curses then they would come, fanned out and scrambling at speed, and he would have no possibility of breaking out, and she would be shot down. For him it would be worse; to be captured was the foulest nightmare of Special Forces troops. If she did sacrifice her cover and scream abuse she would achieve nothing. He held her.

The kid with the football shirt, Lewandowski's name and number – nine – faded on the back, was hauled past the commander. His arms were bound and he was held by two men who dragged him towards the football pitch, his legs seeming to stagger and slip below him. It might have been an act and might have been an accident. The kid had control of his legs and could pivot on one and lash out with the other. He had good purchase . . . Go quickly, or go with a fight? Gaz did not know. In Londonderry once, up in the Creggan estate and in the roof of a derelict house, he had seen a child, brought by his mother to waste ground for a kneecap punishment – would have been labelled as anti-social which might have meant vandalism, or might have meant he'd called a local strongman 'a feckin arsehole', or might have meant stealing. Little more than a kid and going to be shot in the kneecaps, from the back, and hadn't fought, had just lain there and waited, like he was drugged. He would never run again. The Bayern kid's trainer caught the Iranian officer on the side of the cheek, and the kick had enough power to twist the man's neck and topple him so that he staggered and might have gone down had the Russian not grabbed him, held him upright. Gaz thought it a powerful enough kick to have loosened teeth, might even have damaged the ligaments holding the jaw. He was held but they had no grip on his legs and he managed one last kick and caught the officer's groin. The officer jackknifed, and the pain would have been severe. Clever? Maybe . . . Worth doing? Perhaps. The commander squirmed: nobody laughed, not like they would have done on an English cricket pitch. Maybe the kid had not thought it through, maybe he hadn't reckoned on consequences, just launched fury as a response . . . the consequence might have been coming anyway and all he'd done was hasten it.

They were all on the chairs under the crossbar, and all quickly had the nooses slung around their necks. The women and the children had troops close against them, chest to chest, and were spitting and were being whacked with rifle butts, and the noise was of pandemonium. Gaz held her wrist so tightly that he might have snapped the bone, and she whimpered and so did the dogs, quietly but in distress.

There was a crack. A crack like a rifle-shot.

A crack that was carried on the sharp wind to Gaz, and he squinted to see what had made the sound and saw the chaos and then the scrum of movement between the goalposts. Four boys had been hoisted on the crossbar. Too much weight. Chairs dragged clear, the crossbar snapping. The roped kids falling and militia around them and the commander back on his feet, hobbling and gesticulating. They used bayonets on the bound kids on the ground, using the blades as if they were clearing rough ground.

Gaz thought there was more to come, that the killing had only started, and he could not look away. By text he was told to hold his ground . . . he was a witness and therefore valuable. Not intended that a Special Forces team having carved a path through the depth of the storm should then get stuck in a fire-fight against an al-Quds unit. He held her wrist and she did not fight him, and he thought his strength leached.

Had Alice been on the phone, when the three were brought in front of her, to her lover, confidante and fellow journeygirl for Knacker, she would have said, 'No lie, Fee, but they look proper evil bastards.' Hereford boys escorted them into the tent, were wary of them, with good reason.

And Fee might have answered her: 'Evil is good, rack it up, and a little cunning to garnish it – where they're going.'

The contact they had collected on the way to this shanty town of hovels for displaced persons quizzed each of the men in turn. Their recent histories were laid out. Common for the trio was an ability to focus on the flight from the village of Deir al-Siyarqi during the critical minutes before the cordon around the village closed. All those who had escaped from their homes and had run, half-dressed and fresh from sleep, across the football pitch and up the dried river-bed, had been pursued only a few hundred yards before the IRGC people had given up and had loosed wasted shots after them. They had gathered in the far distance, had hidden and had watched until dusk. None of the three had returned to the village that night, and in the morning they had watched as the birds circled in the air and the pall of smoke was not yet dispersed. One had lost his parents, one had lost his parents and two brothers, one had lost his wife. The camp where their credentials were examined by Alice for suitability was eight miles from the village that had been their home. The flotsam of the war in that sector were kept there, supplied with minimum nourishment and basic shelter. Alice had been driven there fast, the vehicle kicking up dirt from the open ground, to the rim of a plateau. The regiment guys had been reluctant to stop there more than half a minute. Time enough for her to soak up an atmosphere, and flick images of what she saw on to her phone. There had been drone pictures for her to sift through but nothing as cold and comprehensive as seeing it with her own eyes: all the roofs blown off or sagging, all the walls blackened from fire damage. The mound of the mass grave was still prominent, and she had stood for a few seconds where she imagined Gaz had been hidden, and from which he had seen the day play out . . . They had then driven to the shanty town where the detritus of the seven-year war were living out their lives. Quite moving, actually, not that sweet Alice with her face of extreme innocence and a scattering of freckles, gave time to senti-mentality. She thought the men fitted Knacker's requirements.

She would have said, had she been on the phone to Fee, 'I think they'll manage a good job, and go through shades of shit to get there to do it. Will be a painful job on him when they know where to go.'

Fee would have replied, 'Painful and slow and him wishing he'd not been born. Well done, girl.'

And that was Alice's business completed, and she could get back on the road with her escort, and the three chosen men would be moved by the man who had brought them to this sprawl of shelters, and they'd call him FoxTrot which was F for 'Facilitator'. FoxTrot would shift them in a camper wagon across country, through back roads and tracks to the Lebanese border, bring them to Beirut where 'sympathetic local assets' would provide cash and travel documentation in the names of three citizens from Beirut, and they would fly north. The beauty of it was that they had seen Alice but did not know her name and she had spoken to them in Arabic, and could have been German or Dutch or Swedish, and the regiment boys were in *mufti* and did not have to speak and were masked. Fee was right to praise her; it had gone well. They left in a dirt cloud, and she'd be back in the Yard in the morning. It had gone well at her end, but that was the easier one, by a country mile.

She texted Knacker, spare with detail. *Three on the move.* Told him all he'd need to know. Alice reckoned him a good guy, the only man she'd follow into hell.

Knacker and Fee sipped apple juice. He rarely drank alcohol and she could do without. Some teams were used to being pissed up when an agent was launched, but he thought that irrelevant and juvenile and had trained his girls to follow the stricture.

They talked the price of king crabs. The red king crab, with a body size up to eight inches across, three pairs of legs and one pair of claws – currently marketing at $26 a kilo – was classified as an invasive species and one which brought big profits. Fee had done the homework, had brought the Norwegian fishing boat scuttling across the North Sea to Unst in Shetland. The creature, ugly as sin and a delicacy, was in big demand in St Petersburg and Moscow: wanted in all the pricier restaurants in which the new rich flaunted their wealth. The usual top fishing ground was the Kola fiord leading down to Murmansk. Except that this was not a natural species for those waters and pollution was thought to have ravaged stocks this summer season. A plane from the south flew in to Murmansk most days to collect the wriggling brutes in their last throes of life, and went home empty. A hole in the market led to opportunistic advancement. Norwegian waters did not have a fleet of dirty naval carcases leaking oil, chemicals, even radiation poison. It had worked well and a hole was filled. Knacker and Fee sipped their juice. It was the sort of wheeze that Knacker liked . . . up their noses, pinching their bollocks. Doing them damage and them not aware of it. Knacker had seen his people off across some miserable border, and some came back and some did not, but the usual result was a paper of some significance going on to the desks of 'customers' in the selected Ministry offices north of the Thames, or across the Atlantic. The purchase of red king crabs in Kirkenes harbour had made a dent in the cash float that Fee had brought, and he would sign it off. Cheap at the price. He did not laugh out loud because this was only the beginning, most certainly not the end of the beginning, not while his boy – a reluctant hero – was on the move and heading for a rendezvous.

"Would you like to eat one of the bloody things tonight, Knacker?"

"Wouldn't mind that. But spare me having to watch you pop it into boiling water while alive."

Gaz paused by the tree. Used its dead trunk to shield him, the basics in avoiding 'silhouette', and listened. He heard the rain dripping off the leaves and branches of birches and pines, and heard the ripple of the wind above him, and the shrill call of small birds – and did not hear the cacophony of barking dogs, nor sirens, but might have heard the distant throb of a vehicle engine.

Almost laughable . . . Gary Baldwin, Gaz, a guy invalided out of the Special Reconnaissance Regiment, certified as a sufferer from post traumatic stress disorder, an island recluse who scratched a living from handyman jobs, was the invader – a solitary one-man-band invader – of the country with the largest land mass of territory on the planet. He thought his incursion was so far unnoticed, but doubted that the quiet and serenity around him would last. He pressed on.

Old skills were resurrected. He moved at a loping pace and hugged cover and clung to the edges of the tree line and did not use the open spaces of heather and low scrub where he might have gone faster but would have left a more marked trail. He had never worked in similar terrain. The ground was either rock-hard with a flimsy layer of peat compost sitting on top of granite formations, or it was a bog and his boots went into liquid black mud, and the trees were dwarf height and dense where they had taken root.

He thought they had been at the border later than intended, and tried to make up time. He concentrated on each step in front of him. Where to let his weight land, how to lift a boot from the bog and not leave it sucked under, avoiding brittle branches . . . There might have been the sound of a jeep's engine, but he would not have sworn it. He considered how he would be met, how greeted, how they would be. Responsibility for the pick-up, he assumed, would have been delivered into the hands of the original recruit's grandson. Gaz knew little of Russia, and the sociology of life in the western sectors of the country, but understood there was an undercurrent of resentment from the young against the dictatorship, what a lecturer had called the culture of kleptocracy, and another guest speaker had described the country as a 'mafia state'. The grandson would be young, idealistic, educated, and would be a free spirit – would think that he was doing something for the future of his family, his friends and his neighbours, for society. He had heard of the Pussy Riot group, and knew protestors were banged up in gaol, that elections were rigged, that dissent was not tolerated . . . Knew there had been no inquiry into the actions of a Russian officer on liaison duty with Iranian militia troops during an atrocity of which he was a witness. So, a kid who was prepared to help the agent of a foreign power was likely to be a boy with high principles, a total contrast to himself. Gaz did not champion human rights, equality issues. He had been working out of the Forward Operating Base in central Syria at the time of the last UK election and it would have been possible to use a postal vote for the constituency of North Herefordshire, where the barracks at Credenhill were sited, but he had not bothered. He expected that the boy sent to meet him would want to quiz him on politics and talk of persecution, and staying outside gaol ... and again he concentrated because the lake was in front of him.

He went around the north side of the water. A fish jumped, broke the surface and clattered back and sent spray flying. The ripples spread wide. He no longer heard what he had thought might be a jeep's engine. And found the animal track.

The Norwegian boys on the fishing boat had given him a crash course on the ground he'd face, and the wildlife. Might be a bear such as the one that might have broken the fence behind him, might be moose or reindeer, might be a small pack of wolves. He took the path. Had walked for an hour, gone more than two miles, and he thought he was late for the pick-up, went as fast as he dared, but trying to avoid leaving a trail of heavy boot prints. Thought he noted a shape far back among the trees in shadow, and turned fast, but registered nothing, and twice more. Was sure that something, or someone, kept pace with him and was on a parallel path, but never heard and never saw ... Now heard a vehicle, a straining lorry engine. He quickened his pace.

It would be good to meet the contact ... In Afghan and Syria they often went with a local man, might be a policeman and might be a collaborator. Was never supposed to be fully trusted, but all the guys and girls went overboard to make the man driving them into a friend. Would try to read him, and see if there was sincerity in his eyes or shiftiness. The driver could nudge the mission towards success, what some in the SRR even regarded as glory. Flip the coin, see its reverse face, and the man might be subject to a raft of pressures in Syria. Could be that his whole posture was counterfeit, or that his family were the bargaining chip and would be wasted without cooperation, could be that the opposition made a better offer. Could be that the driver would arrive at a pre-arranged roadblock, get out of the vehicle and walk over to his father, his cousin, his uncle, his wife's family and deliver Gaz – never did know and always better to get a ride with the Hereford lot or a lift in a Chinook. He was hurrying, was late, reckoned the contact boy was anxious, afraid, and pacing, cursing.

Through the trees, Gaz saw timber lorries on a road and

climbing an incline, then quiet, then came into a sad and disused picnic lay-by. As it had been described. Collapsed timber tables with benches – might have been damaged by the weather and might have been vandalised. A surface of chip stones was carpeted with vigorously growing weed. He crouched down, still inside the cover of the low trees. Saw layers of dumped plastic, bags and wrappers and cartons. Looked for a car, and looked for a boy.

Like a kick in the stomach. Before being pushed out of the regiment, he would have easily settled himself and hidden away, waited for a contact to show. The lay-by was empty and nobody walked in circles, smoking, checking a wrist-watch. Birds sang, and a hawk went over and screamed, and a few cars passed on the road that was mostly hidden. He waited for an engine to slow and then the growl of tyres on gravel at the start of the lay-by, and then the pick-up car to come into view. And waited. And wondered . . . five minutes gone, ten, fifteen . . . and cursed. Confidence fled. A car came into the lay-by. Gaz stood. Dumb of him to have allowed doubt. The engine was switched off, and a man, middle-aged, climbed out, stood with his back to Gaz, fiddled with his flies and peed at the matted grass in front of him, shook himself, wriggled his arse, fastened his trousers and was back in the car and starting the engine. The emptiness and the silence returned. Nothing to do but wait – and hope. Sensible, Gaz reckoned, to go through the back-up plan, but it seemed to him to be shot with holes.

7

'Don't worry, shouldn't fret, something'll show up – always does.'
What Knacker would have said if he could have reached him on a
phone. Gaz had been at the lay-by a couple of minutes short of an
hour. He was still hunched in the undergrowth near to the
collapsed picnic bench.

He heard a car's wheels on the stones behind the trees, where
the slip-road came. He braced himself, ready to drag himself up.
He had decided he would stay in cover until the car was at a halt,
then would slip forward; he expected a window to be wound
down, the codeword given, and he'd be inside a saloon, a fast
handshake and they'd be off, the tyres squealing on the loose
ground, and his heart could stop pounding, and . . . A police car
came into the lay-by. It parked some forty paces from him. Two
uniforms on board.

Knacker would have shrugged. 'You'll reckon a way round it
when the pick-up gets to you. That's who you are, what you do.'

The mosquitoes seemed to search for him. Some had success.
Gaz could not stand up and could not flail and could not sit in a
bush and light up a pipe . . . In his trade they reckoned that cows
were bad because they would gather in a half-moon around a hide
dug into a hedge, and sheep were crazily difficult because they
were liable to stampede, and dogs were always curious. The
policemen opened the door of the vehicle and were unwrapping
sandwiches and unscrewing a flask.

Knacker would have said, 'Think on the bright side – ask them
for a lift into town, if the contact doesn't show.'

The police were well dressed and their vehicle had been
washed. They settled into their meal, then each had a cigarette,

and then poured from the thermos. They might catch half an hour of sleep. One back-up plan seemed to Gaz to be the most realistic: give it an hour, maximum. Give it an hour and then go through the trees again and look for the animal track and follow it as far as the lake, and forget about the sense he had had that he was watched as he moved but had heard nothing. Get back to the lake and trail around the end of it and go by the little beach in front of where the fish had jumped, and look for the dead tree. Get a bearing off it, reach the fence. Don't worry about prints in the ploughed strip or about leaving torn clothing on the wire, just run at it and jump, roll and fall. Walk back into town. Show up at the safe house and be turning over some variation of 'not capable of organising a piss-up in a brewery', and facing the big man.

Knacker would have said, 'Just needed a bit of patience, and it was all going so well. I'd have thought better of you.'

Would go back to the island and drag the mower out of the shed and start catching up on a backlog of cutting grass, and doing the little jobs. Tell Aggie that he had flipped ... would never have another chance of suffocating that black dog, the one that tracked him each dark night. He tried to remember good days ... Not a whole heap of them. Bad for him to reminisce and hard for him to maintain that blood was not on his hands. He pinched himself. Hurt himself by twisting a fold of skin between his fingers as much as the mosquitoes did on the rest of his skin. He sat, and the insects feasted.

The policemen ate their food and crumpled the paper wrapping and chucked it aside. They shared a bar of chocolate and the tinfoil went the way of the sandwich wrapping, and they both swallowed from a plastic bottle of soft drink and dumped it with the rest of their garbage. Then they settled back in their seats, closed the doors and windows, and prepared for sleep. Enough to make a man cry.

Knacker would have said, 'Remember you're the best, Gaz. Not just because you were the witness, but because you are top of the tree. Why we chose you.'

And he stayed put, could not work out an option. Instead, he focused, remembered the target, why he was there providing a meal for mosquitoes, saw the face, needed to cling to it.

Not much to fill the boxes. The music centre and the widescreen TV, then into the kitchen.

Lavrenti could have called Mikki or Boris, told them to get off their arses and come up to the apartment and take over the packing up. Or at least politely request their help. Did neither. The removals company had assumed that he would not himself – Major Lavrenti Volkov – do the work. It had been explained that the company was not responsible for breakages if items were not correctly wrapped . . . He was losing his temper: two plates were cracked and a glass broken. But still he did not call them.

It mattered little how much he damaged. His mother would replace everything when he returned to the capital. Settling him into life in the Arbat quarter of Moscow would be her next project. There, he would be shot of Mikki and Boris, would tell his father that he longer required them. A big step for Lavrenti. A plate slipped from his hand, landed on its edge, and the pieces scattered. He kicked out, lashing then into the wall.

This was a good apartment by Murmansk's standards. The landlord would have hoped for some personal advantage to come his way if the rent was at rock-bottom, and the maintenance charges waived. He was another who would find that patronising an officer of FSB carried a bad kickback. The window had a view of the docks: idle cranes, moored and rusted hulks, a destroyer awaiting cannibalisation. Not a cruise liner in sight although they had been promised, and the wind rippling the oily water. Through the same window, in view if he pressed his nose against the glass, was his official car, black and polished, and leaning against it were his minders.

They would not be worried by Lavrenti. Both were Afghan veterans, devoted to his father. They'd have licked his backside. They'd have been overrun, so the account went, when the local bastards surrounded a patrol that was edging down an incline of loose rock. Twenty men, an under-strength platoon and all of them from the security division. Calm words from his father and a call to get close, to keep up the volume of aimed shots – not enough ammunition to blast away on automatic – stay low among the rocks and believe ... A Soviet flag was tied proudly to a thorn bush. His father had called in an air strike. Had called it in right above them. Who believed in God's hand? None of them, before the jets arrived from the strip at Jalalabad. All of them, when the noise of the explosions died and the smoke cleared and they were free to finish the lives of the wounded *mujahedeen*, most of them had already gone to their God. The Russians were all alive, considered that their officer had saved them. Mikki and Boris were not loyal to Lavrenti but to his father. They lounged beside the big car and smoked and must have reflected that they lived a pretty good and prosperous life.

They had done jobs for his father, and chauffeured his mother, and provided protection during the wild years when the old regime collapsed. His father had done well, and the muscle he had brought to a killing ground had been supplied by Mikki and Boris. It was natural that as his father climbed he would need reliable men to watch his back against revenge and jealousy. The boy going to Syria, and his mother in tears, and his father, gruffly anxious, had sent them to stand alongside his only child to protect him. They had been with him that day, had seen it, watched it, but had not taken part in it ...

He drank with his friends, fortified himself.

Whenever life was so bad that his future seemed eaten up, and he had no booze money, he would lurch up the hill, and know he was free of his son – the rat Timofey – and of his son's girl, the whore. Always there were friends at the Alyosha monument, and always they were generous with what they had. It was a steep climb for him. After their own drink was finished, they would wait till it was quiet and the front plinth of the monument was deserted, and then the youngest and the fittest would dart forward. At the front of the monument, where gaudy wreaths were laid, were usually fresh fruit and newly cooked scones, and bottles of vodka. Those who came to stock up the offerings, in memory of the heroes of the Great Patriotic War who had died in the defence of the city, replenished the vodka bottles. The young drinkers, the fastest on their feet, would ignore the fruit and the scones. A bottle of real stuff, Stolichnaya 100 proof, ABV 50%, would be brought back, replaced by one filled with tap water, and they would drink happily until it was drained.

Today he wanted proper vodka, not the shit they were used to drinking. He needed to fortify himself, not that any of his fellow drinkers, riddled with alcoholism, would have understood his problem. They had been told often enough of the wrongs done him by the vermin who had taken his home, his son and his son's whore, but they would find it hard to comprehend what he intended – when the drink supplied the necessary courage. To stand outside the big building on the Prospekt and tell the first officer he could grab hold of what his son intended. A sleeper, woken, and a foreign power intervening, and espionage. He would tell it because the alternative was a penal colony where there was nothing to drink, and where he would die.

Now he said where he was going, and why. Some shrugged and some looked away, and some thought he was obviously ready for an asylum, and some murmured that it was dangerous to denounce his own son. It would take a quantity of vodka to gain the boldness for that level of betrayal. He would do it. Fuck them all . . . He would.

"It is a secure line at your end?"

"Secure, confirmed."

"Thank you. Good to speak, Paulo. You are going to bring me up to speed?"

"My intention, all you should know. I begin at the start . . . I considered that I had the wrong people and the wrong address, but I knew the name and the address were correct because they had the code. I tell you my friend, Knacker, they were a consider-able surprise to me."

Knacker assumed that Paulo, third-tier Italian diplomat and first-tier UK asset, spoke from the security room in his country's Moscow embassy.

"Please explain."

"Only my opinion but I should not hide it from you. They did not seem to be *suitable*, I think that an appropriate description."

Over the years, Knacker had built himself a network of colleagues. They came from ethnically rich and diverse backgrounds, were cultivated with the care that Maude, when not scratching among ruins, gave to her glasshouse tomatoes. He believed them loyal to him, willing to walk an extra mile or two, and above all they were tasked to tell him the truth. His name was not widely known in the European intelligence community, but those who knew it swore by his effectiveness as a confounder of what was called the 'Russian conspiracy', to dislocate their best endeavours – almost a crusade.

"Tell me."

"I am not a cold water man. I do not pour it with the aim of dampening enthusiasm. The man originally recruited, then let go to his sleep, is long dead. His son – now in his late fifties, early sixties – lives at the address I was given. He is a pitiful alcoholic, barely able to communicate and with severe physical limitations on his mobility. It would be unwise to place any reliability on him. Then there is the grandson . . . he has taken over the family primacy and was the one 'woken'. He is Timofey. Cannot be specific but I am assuming him to be a pusher of narcotics, the cannabis/marijuana field, not the Class A of heroin/cocaine, but perhaps also in amphetamines. He would have no ideological distaste for the regime of authority in Murmansk city except that it is 'authority'. He would be without discipline. Your expression, Knacker, is I believe 'the loose cannon'. With him is a girl. On a table in the apartment, one bedroom and where they live with the father, was a gaol release form. The girl is just back from a detention sentence. I detect she has less self-control than him, more mercurial and harder to predict her actions. They possess a small car – Italian, of course, and therefore utterly reliable in its quality engineering. Knacker, allow me one suppressed smile. They are quite unsuitable for any important work put in their way. You want my conclusion?"

"Why not, Paulo? Are you cancelling Christmas?"

There was no possibility of Knacker misunderstanding the tenor of the Italian's report. He liked the old quip of 'If it were easy, everyone would do it', could hide behind that, but not appropriate to inflict it on his colleague, and knew his honesty.

"It gives me no pleasure . . . it is a difficult town. The FSB there expect the infiltration of hostile agents. They have the Fleet and there are concerns for the security of the naval yards. Also they have the proximity of a NATO border. People live on a diet of suspicion. There is a sizeable apparatus of counter-intelligence. That is the reality."

"The conclusion, Paulo?"

"It is difficult to say to you, Knacker, because I know what is invested."

"Cut to the point, friend."

There was a pause on the line. Expected. Knacker was in the garden of the safe house, and he spoke quietly. Fee watched him from the kitchen, behind the double glazing, and filed her nails. The Norwegian had sent a cryptic text indicating the Russian patrol vehicle had checked out the border fence and had dutifully photographed what appeared to be bear prints on the smoothed ground their side of the wire and had collected the coarse hair deposited on the barbs. From his vantage-point in the bushes he had heard their radio exchanges, and a shout that it was 'another of those fucking bears, big bastard by the print size', and they had set about repairing damage. All satisfactory.

"My conclusion, Knacker, with regret, is that the *Matchless* contact is not supportable. These are not the sort of people who could sustain the necessary actions for a mission of this risk. They should not be used. I urge you most strongly, the advice of a respectful colleague, to terminate the mission. Terminate it. You should bring back your man. That is my conclusion, Knacker. Abort him."

"Thank you, Paulo."

"Please, or it will be tragic, follow my advice."

"Succinctly put. I am grateful – the trouble is that I reckon it too late. From your part of the world, Paulo, 'the Rubicon is crossed'. Appreciate your help. Summary, don't think I can get him back. Have to let matters take their course, and hope. Thanks again."

He smiled to himself, pleased with what had been passed to him. They sounded the sort of people, those kids, that he would have wanted on board. Defiant, outside the tramlines of convention, bloody minded, and above all streetwise – could not have picked better. A rather jaunty step as he went inside.

The police car would have received a call.

A last piss into the undergrowth, a last disposal of rubbish, and the engine starting up. The blue lights came on over the car's roof, and the guys inside had settled in their seats and both doors were slammed. They were off, did a sharp turn and at one point they were within ten yards of where Gaz hid. The car skidded on the stones and made a show of urgency. Gaz watched it go . . . had watched it for little short of an hour. Two lorries had turned in, been there five minutes, then had left. The police car accelerated, disappeared, and he was left with the emptiness that had taken hold of him before it had pitched up, like a mission failed . . .

He caught sight of the girl from the corner of his eye, shifted his gaze to her. She was down the lay-by from him, about fifty paces away. She stood her full height, raised her hand, clenched her fist except for the main finger, held the pose. Perhaps, in the police car, they would have had a glimpse of her in the mirror or perhaps they were already hitting the main road. She lowered her arm and began to brush the dirt and debris from her jeans and her top, and shook her head as if to dislodge any leaves or berries caught in her hair. She looked around, then down at her watch, then mouthed

something which he did not hear. The gesture from the single
finger showed contempt, an obscene insult, and as universal was
Gaz's reading of her lips. Could have been *trakhat' tebya*, could
have been *fuck you*, could have been anything that made her feel-
ings clear for the 'boys in blue'. She tilted her head and stared in
front and behind and seemed for a moment to stamp in frustration. Her jeans were stained in mud below the knees and her
footwear was pathetically unsuitable for traipsing across country.
Her hair was blonde and tangled; she seemed to curse . . . and
then she whistled.

The boy came. Gaz understood. She had come through the
trees to the lay-by but had hidden while the police were there,
had seen them off, had looked around her, had raked the cover
with her eyes, and was annoyed because she had not found what
she searched for, and had whistled to summon the boy. He was
scrawny, pale, muddy, and he had hair cut short. She lectured
him. A wide gesture, waving her arm across the empty expanse
of the lay-by and then her hands slapped her thighs as if to
emphasise her irritation . . . seemed to say this was the place, and
. . . seemed to say that it had failed . . . and started to flounce.
The boy stayed calm. Glanced at his watch, pursed his lips,
would have accepted they had been late, shrugged. Perhaps the
boy reckoned time, early or late, was less relevant than her
response. . . . She stood with her hands on her hips, small and
defiant and angry. He was quieter and calmer, and took a big
breath.

One word, shouted at the emptiness of the lay-by. "*Matchless.*"

Gaz pushed himself up, responded: "*Matchless.*"

Small birds were pecking at the policemen's food wrappers, but
his shout, and Gaz's answer, scattered them and they squawked
and flew. He had not yet shown himself, was still wary. When he
stepped forward that was the ultimate moment of vulnerability, no
going back. And, they could have been turned, and could have
had a better offer, and could have fifty FSB gooks in full combat
gear poised to jump on him . . .

The boy shouted, fair enough English, "If you are here, stranger, and you answer to the word, *Matchless*, then show yourself and we can get the fuck out. We are late. We have hiked ten klicks. There is a block on the road at Titovka. To go beyond Titovka you must have a special permit and your documentation is checked. We left the wheels at Titovka and came through this forest – fucking awful. One last time, are you here, are you not here? We are not staying . . . here or not here?"

Every move he made during his years with the regiment had been planned. Every eventuality was considered. Backup always existed. The whole business was chaos, and he was an idiot for accepting the arm twisting, and . . . He stood up, parting the low fronds and branches of dwarf birch. He stepped forward.

He spoke in English, "I think it is me that you are supposed to meet."

So chaotic that it seemed pitiful to talk in the code of a professional. He walked towards them. A basic law, one that he did not ignore, was to remember that they were not his friends. They were just part of the deal that Knacker had cobbled together. No hugs and no kisses, no small talk. A formal handshake, the girl first and then the boy, and her grip was firmer than the boy's, and they had names. He was Timofey. She was Natacha. Who was he? Good question. He paused, hesitated and wondered how great a confidence he should give them.

Crisp but quiet. "I am Gaz . . . Thank you for coming."

She said, "Nobody thought about the block at Titovka. Titovka is where the army has a garrison. We had to go around the block. We thought of taking a car, hot-wiring it, driving it up here. Would have done but could not see a car to give us that possibility. We go through all shit to get here. It is a closed zone, a security zone. Nobody told us that we had to enter it, we found for ourselves. I ask you, are your people incompetent?"

When he went back, *if* he did, Gaz promised himself that he would repeat the challenge of this girl, Natacha. Would like to see faces tighten, lips compress, all the things that bosses did when criticised, and the biggest insult was an accusation of incompetence.

Gaz said, "Probably, most days, they do their best."

They both laughed in his face. He was asked if he could go through the forest and the bog, where there was no road, whether he would manage rough ground. Poker-faced, he said that he thought he could, would try. The girl led and was light-footed and set a pace. Neither wore the correct clothing or shoes, yet he struggled to keep up with them. Both possessed strength that came from tilting against the state's windmills, the bloody-minded obstinacy required to survive on the basement of society, and the arrogance that came from being unbeaten . . . He knew the young tearaway kids in the Creggan and in the villages up on the hills of east Tyrone, and the ones who would have thought themselves indestructible when they had gone down the road from the village in Syria. It gave Gaz a level of confidence just trying to catch up with the girl and keep the boy from clipping his ankles. He would not be the one who needed to stop and gasp and regain composure, would make sure it was one of them. But he had a question, and it needed answering.

"What's the motive for you in helping me? Because of the old family link, and sleeping but being loyal to an old promise. Is it that?"

The boy answered. "It is the money. Only the money."

The girl chimed in, "What else? If you live here what matters? Only money."

Nothing was as Gaz would have expected it. They went at a pace, skipping and dancing and sliding, slashed by low branches. He thought they were watched, would have sworn to it, but heard nothing and saw nothing and had only his instincts. And, certain of it, he was comfortable with them.

From the boy: "You go after an officer in FSB? What has he done?"

And from the girl: "We hate FSB. Big hate. What has he done?"

"Would take a long time to tell."

Delta Alpha Sierra, the seventh hour

He could not look away. It would have been rank cowardice to close his eyes or bury his head in his hands. Gaz reckoned she no longer had the heart to rise to her feet, have the dogs go with her and stampede the goats down the slope and charge against the cordon line. No point in such an action, except that she would have been shot, would have had the misery ended.

He racked up the number of bad moments with the worst at the top of his list, and the space was crowded. The most recent 'worst' was the death of the handicapped child, probably Down's syndrome. A teenage boy. His mother hanging on to him, holding him tight against her skirt, and other women helping her to control him, but he was strong, fought them, and broke free. Gaz assumed that the girl close to him, surrounded by her goats and dogs, would have known the lad, from the day he was born. This remote village would not have relied on the help of central government in the years before the start of the war. They would have banded together, every woman in the small community helping the mother. The kid ran in slow ungainly steps, his fists clenched. Would have seen what had happened to other boys, not much older than himself, who would have teased and tormented and loved him as part of their community. Now, the boy wanted to hurt the commander and the officer who so obviously had control of the scene and who directed the action. He was shot. A puppy had run with him, had been shot and wounded, squealed, and was shot again. The boy crawled, making an easier target, then howled. Then a rifle, fired on semi-automatic, ended his life.

The killing now became systematic. More of the boys who had crouched with their arms tied and their eyes blindfolded, were heaved up and dragged away past the surviving goal of the football pitch. They were taken beyond the limit of Gaz's arc of vision, but the shots came clearly and were echoed back from the sides of the valley, amplified by the low cloud, and carried by the wind that funnelled through the village. Rain swirled over it. Gaz thought the time for a programme of killing had now started and that vengeance for the overnight attack had given way to clearance. He knew the Russian word for 'provocation' and the phrases for 'unacceptable actions' and 'severe consequences'. He watched the officer and looked for any indication that he had now seen enough, wished to disassociate himself and stand back. What he remembered was the officer's action when the Down's boy had run with closed fists towards him and the commander. The service pistol, inevitably a Makarov, had been as near as made no difference out of the officer's holster at the moment the boy had been dropped, then was aimed when the boy was wounded and before the final round was fired. An academic had come once to Credenhill and lectured them about the emotions roused by combat. Had used the expression 'red mist', had spoken of the threat it gave to police and troops involved in confrontation. He thought the officer was infected with it. Pistol drawn, face flushed, and grenades coming off his webbing, and being primed, and being hurled inside buildings already on fire. Self-control gone. What Gaz also saw was that the two Russian troopers, uniformed and an obvious protection for the officer, had not cocked their weapons; they followed their principal but did not ape him. The academic had spoken of 'attacker advantage' and 'forward panic' as being parts of a crowd reaction. Gaz thought the officer had now lost self-control: he had become an animal in a feeding frenzy, a fox in a chicken coop.

He could not intervene. He texted the FOB what he saw played out in front of him. The cordon stayed in place and all attention was directed inside it. The women were held back at bayonet point, but that would not last, and all of the boys had now been dragged across the football pitch and into the gully at the far end.

The girl was quiet. The animals cowered close to her.

The officer had thrown three grenades into buildings where the interiors were already set alight. From inside came the explosions, then the crack as rifle bullets stored there were detonated. From one, an old man came out on his hands and knees, his clothing alight, and Gaz thought he would have been taken there by his family, hidden in darkness in the hope he would survive. He was kicked, and was punched. The officer lit a cigarette. His minders stayed away from him, like they were not a part of it. Gaz could easily have shot him, but that was not a role that fitted the ethic of his unit. He would have been killed, his gear captured, and the girl would have died. Gaz held the rifle close, would use it as a final act of self-preservation, did not intervene.

It was beyond anything in his experience. He knew it would get worse: the women and the children, and the old men, were still corralled and would not for long be held back by the tips of steel bayonets. The officer used his pistol to shoot into the head of the first hanged boy, already dead, a wasted bullet ... And the wind blew and the rain fell.

Jasha was an intelligent man, had once regarded himself as well read, with brusque opinions, and intolerant of idiots ... but that was before he had become a recluse, a hunter. Now in his isolated world, he was yet another Russian who had been scarred by the awfulness of the Afghan intervention – and had been invalided out. Lost and alone, he had found the cabin and made a new life.

He pushed open the door of his cabin, and was confused. The door had no lock, was secured by bolts on the outside and a bar on the inside. He went in, closed it behind him, and his dog came slowly, stiffly, off its sacking bed, and nuzzled his ankle, and seemed spooked. Not that he was calm himself. He had been out on the tundra, had walked on a stalking trail following the sharp scent left by a dog fox, and at first, had been aware that the bear followed him, that he had Zhukov for company.

He had been a soldier who was always short-tempered when confronting the bullshit of the military machine. The war was so obviously unwinnable; defeat stared into the face of the Soviet Union, his country. While he had the freedom to have himself dropped off by a helicopter and go and find himself a lair to lie up in, and watch a village or a trail used by the enemy, and kill and slip away, live to kill again, he could control his frustration. Until he was wounded, hospitalised ... Trailing after the fox he had been convinced that the bear used a parallel path and he thought several times he had noted a fleeting shadow of the creature, but not heard it, not seen it clearly, not smelled it, just believed with a stubborn certainty that it was there. His army career had ended in a casualty ward. An officer had toured the beds, handed out cigarettes, treated the injured to brief lectures on the justifications for the war – the Soviet intervention in Afghanistan – and how well it went, and how proud was the country, and the Party, of what they had done. Their sacrifice was recognised and . . . Jasha had said to the officer's face that he talked shit, that the war was lost. If he did not believe him, then he should look the length of the ward, and both sides of it and count the number of occupied beds, and note not one was empty. Behind the officer had been a trailing entourage.

He could remember how Zhukov had seemed to wake from the sedation long before the bear had regained partial use of its limbs. A baleful eye, no love, no gratitude, but what he judged to be a degree of magnificent tolerance, and he had thrown the wire, its barbs still holding flesh and fur, high into a tree where it could not again hurt the beast. What did he want from any relationship? A fantasy of mutual respect, a sort of understanding between himself and Zhukov – a dream, but he thought it possible.

The officer leading the entourage was a combat veteran and had bright ribbons on his chest. In tow was a writer from a government propaganda agency, and the *Izvestia* correspondent shipped down from Kabul, and a TV news crew visiting from Leningrad. Jasha, the sniper, was weak, his voice soft, and he would have spoken through sagging breath. He told the microphone and the notebook and the officer's flushing face, that the war was a bloody waste of conscripts' lives, and that the talk of ultimate victory was a combination of imagination and lies. If the wounds on his leg had not been still bloody through the dressings he would have received a stinging slap across his unshaven cheeks. They moved on sharply, scrambling to be clear of his bed.

More confusing to Jasha was his clear view of what he assumed to be three fugitives: a girl who wore light city footwear, and equally light city clothing and who slogged over the uneven ground and tripped on rocks and sunk in the black mud of pools: a boy behind her who cursed and swore when he fell: and between them was a man, a little older with a rucksack on his back, who stepped confidently and wore camouflage. He reckoned he was an intruder, with the kids as his guides, and had scratched for a reason before floating a possible answer. They skirted Titovka where the roadblock was placed. Why would a fit and strong man, obviously a soldier, use that sort of trash for bringing him on to Russian territory? Could not answer the question.

He had been out of the ward within half an hour and had been shut away in a broom cupboard of a room, out of sight of all other casualties, placed where he could not contaminate the faithful ... The officer had been from the political security section, and would have hit him had there not been so many witnesses. The episode accelerated a terminated army career: there were no references for work – he had quit them and all they stood for, had come to Murmansk, and had holed up in the tundra, had regretted nothing. He remembered the officer's face, had not known his name.

He fed his dog. Parboiled meat and rice he had bought in Murmansk when he had met the man who purchased his pelts and trophy heads. Intelligent? He would have shrugged but not disagreed. A sharp mind? He accepted that ... accepted also that the bear, Zhukov, might be admired but not as a friend, and accepted that he had no idea why a man in camouflage was being escorted across this God-deserted territory unless the need was to avoid the Titovka block. More intriguing: who took responsibility for the stranger's journey?

Knacker nurtured the image of the woad-painted intelligence officer who dreamed of incursion and attack, and probed for weakness. Imagined the officer behind the Wall who had the fortifications to back him, and trained troops, and who had to be lucky every time, not just once. Loved the images, and allowed the cavalcade of thoughts to include his wife, Maude, on her knees and elbows and with her rear end stuck up high and scratching and brushing . . . and pocketing a little peck of historic interest – done it for him, in mischief.

How to brighten the coin had seemed a problem beyond Knacker's reach but Fee had showed him the answer on her phone, then had busied herself. A good, wholesome, noisy spit on the *denarius*, then it was wrapped tightly in tinfoil, then put in a Pyrex dish, and steaming water poured across it. Time now for the revelation. She did not ask him about the relevance of the coin, but humoured him, as she usually did. She picked it up from the dish, shook it, unwrapped it, dried it, rubbed it hard, and handed it to him. A little silver coin, with good clear engraving on it.

Knacker chortled in pleasure, took it and pocketed it, said, "Many thanks – always need a talisman when we have a man far from home and going farther."

He sat in the back of the saloon, had a VIP journey to work. Lavrenti had been longer at his apartment than he had expected.

They dropped him at the main entrance on Prospekt. The car would be taken around to the back gates and parked in the yard, but he was free to go in through the grand new doors of the building. The building was huge, dominating Lenin Prospekt: it could be considered a symbol of the state's power, displaying the strength and ability to protect the citizens of Murmansk, or one that was intended to intimidate and to demand discipline. He went inside. Would he miss the life in this Arctic city, and the work it created? He would not. On the second floor, he was met by his replacement who recognised him from a casual meeting in Moscow some months before, and walked with a tall girl, a uniformed captain, a rare female with prospects in FSB. He was close to his old office door and noticed that his name had already been replaced – a fucking insult. But before he was able to snarl a response to what was a serious kicking to his prestige, the captain spoke.

"Ah, Major, you were not able to attend our meeting. We managed without you. You were scheduled to be here."

"What meeting?"

"It is customary, as you well know, Major, for the departing officer to brief his successor on current investigations, where they stand, their considered priority. You were not there . . . I briefed."

"I was packing my apartment. I do not recall any 'current investigations' that were of importance."

She ignored his impertinence. "Hardly fair, Major. Your team have been working hard to ensure progress in several areas of criminality. We regard them as of 'importance'. Is this only a backwater, Major?"

"I was here yesterday."

"The meeting was for today, not yesterday."

He realised he was 'history's man' and noted that the major who would replace him wore no wedding ring, Lavrenti had once received from the captain the certainty of an invitation . . . had claimed that her cooking was good, that she knew a source of fine Georgian wines, had posed an invitation to her studio apartment, and had worn a blouse with a button unfastened. He had brushed her aside. It was common for male and female officers in FSB to pair off, forge relationships. She wore her dark hair short, looked superb in a combat tunic, a webbing belt holding a filled holster at a wasp waist. He had rejected her. Would have gone instead, fast, to a prostitute. The officer beside her seemed to squirm in embarrassment. The captain gazed at him.

"I have briefed, Major, on our work to combat a spike in espionage in Murmansk, and the recent . . ."

"What espionage?"

"An Italian diplomat was in the city two days ago. Is now back in Moscow. Notification was on your desk, not acted on."

"And . . .?"

"The border fence north of the E105 highway was crossed five hours ago. Thought to be a wandering bear that went over, but not thoroughly investigated. You were asked what you wanted as a reaction, but did not answer."

"And – other than a fucking bear and a fucking diplomat – what else?"

"The agitation of a Kirkenes-based eco group. More protests

and because of their report on Kola pollution, nuclear work from the navy, the short-term suspension of the king crab trawler trade. Because of the extent of the damage, a Norwegian boat is due in tomorrow with Norwegian stocks of the creature for restaurants in St Petersburg and Moscow. The group is attracting attention, but you know that. We talked of it."

He felt he could not threaten her, that she would not crumble. Lavrenti said, "I am glad you have plenty to concern you, as I will have in my next appointment. I have expenses to file so need my desk and my computer . . . so kindly find a corner at your work-space, Captain, for my successor, or the canteen."

He waited. They retreated. Were in his office little more than half a minute, and came out with their laptops, and outer clothing, and a coffee flask, and the major carried a photograph of a couple who could have been his parents, but not a wife and children. What he understood of power, Lavrenti reckoned, was that if it were not enforced then it withered, and at pace. He felt vulnerable as he settled in his chair, tapped in, and brought up the record of his expenses. He was both confused and nervous, and did not warm to the list of trivia, what he might have reacted to had he not been distracted – a diplomat, a bear, a gang of eco-warriors and a boat full of wriggling crabs. It was hardly possible for them to have mutual relevance.

No indication that he was regarded as a 'special' man, and deserving additional respect, and leg room. The front seat, passenger side, was held forward by the girl, Natacha, and the invitation was clear. Gaz climbed in, shifted his backside, swiped away the debris of magazines and food wrappers and chocolate tinfoil and pizza packaging. The front seat was dropped back against his knees and she settled in front of him. When the boy, Timofey, switched on the ignition, the motor coughed, spat, then caught. They had been parked in an entry where a track led off the main highway.

He was offered what she called *kosiak*. They were out on the road, and the Fiat shook and rolled and Timofey was getting the maximum from it. Did he want what she called *kosiak*? He thought he should have felt nervous. Rather liked them, and would have been more worried if they were political, ideological refugees from the system of governing their country. There was something brazen about them which he found attractive, and their crossing of the open ground, could have been two hours of it, had impressed him. Done better than he had, and he wore the right gear. Felt confident. The boy drove well and carefully and would not have attracted attention. Did not crowd close to lorries' tail bars or sweep into the centre of the road, engine straining to get past. They were heading for Murmansk and the countryside was the same as that they'd crossed on foot. Dwarf trees, bare rock, boulders carpeted in lichen, and dark lakes. He saw trucks and occasional cars and one convoy of military transport. Timofey laughed, said something to her. Then turned to Gaz and spoke in fractured English:

"In Russian, *kosiak* is a joint, a spliff. I learned that from the tourists I sell to because English is how I communicate when I trade with foreigners. It's what I do, friend, I sell marijuana. I said to Natacha that you were a professional man and that you would not want that smoke – was I right?"

"You were right."

"And you will want to know whether Natacha and I take a joint. No, we do not ... We just sell and trade ... You are in good company, friend."

A hand came back, bony and emaciated, with bitten-down nails, and Gaz gave him his, and the car was driven with one hand on the wheel, and the grip now was iron hard and crushed Gaz's fingers. Then Natacha had swivelled in her seat and a small and delicate hand, like a pianist's, held the two of theirs and kissed them. All three laughed and they careered down a long and winding road.

At last, Gaz saw the silver of the sea ... and he shivered and the cold came close to him. On the floor of a cell he would not be laughing, not holding hands and not taking kisses, not if he were spread-eagled on a pavement, rough hands searching his pockets and fingers going into his orifices and machine pistol barrels gouging the skin on his neck. The shiver had started and he did not know how to stop the chill and the tremor.

She said, "What you have come for? It is important?"

He could have answered that he had come to make the killing of a man easier, make the death simpler, but did not. He gave no answer.

8

The kids had the radio on.

Music that Gaz would not have tolerated in his own car, Russian rock, and booming inside the small Fiat, heavy drumbeats and the thwack of a base guitar. No checking with Gaz as to whether he liked it. He reckoned that the kids, for all the confidence that they displayed, might have been scared half out of their wits, and this was the dose to fire up courage. As Gaz saw it, they were naive, barely more than adolescent, and were way out of their depth.

A light drizzle had started. A sheen was on the pavements and water dribbled round the weeds clogging the gutters. A few pedestrians hurried, shoulders bowed to minimise the rain, clinging to umbrellas because with the rain had come a sharpening of the wind.

They had driven down the fiord and he had looked across and seen an aircraft carrier moored up on the far bank, and cranes, and also a scrapped destroyer and two submarines, one against a pier and another in a floating dry dock. It was natural for Gaz to take in the intelligence sights of the naval port, but he also saw the famed ice-breakers and cargo ships and small tankers, and the water was dark, and the cloud pushing down on it was grey. High above the apartment blocks with their dulled concrete cladding was a giant mountain of a statue that seemed to stretch up from the ground and pierce the clouds. The statue was a monument to war dead, he knew that, had taken that in from the detail given him on the trawler. He saw the fishing port. Lines of rust buckets tied limply together and no movement . . . What did he know of Murmansk? Population 300,000. A community where wages were marked up so people stayed there, prepared to live with six weeks of ever-present day-light in the summer and an alternative of six weeks of darkest night in the winter. No civilian jobs and no private industries, but the state needed workers to keep the place ticking over: naval, security, military, and customs, and all the bureaucracy that went with local government and the power machine far to the south in Moscow. The only homes he saw were squat complexes down on the coast and great shoebox apartment blocks that closed in on each other.

Who was he now? An invalided British serviceman with a PTSD medical history on his computerised records. A Norwegian fisherman, resident in a village up by the North Cape of the European mainland. He had the paperwork to prove it, and an ID card with the boat's name on it, and a twenty-four-hour visa that would expire at noon on the following day. All bullshit because he spoke not a word of Norwegian and would not have survived three minutes of half competent interrogation. But it was thought sufficient to get him through a block in the port area, and into that sector where a trawler, bringing a hold filled with chilled red king crabs, would have tied up. Good enough for a cursory check from any poor bastard huddling at a gate in the rain while mosquitoes tunnelled up his nostrils.

Gaz had not worked a major city before. Had done the countryside of the Province's border lands, and round the farms of eastern Tyrone, and knew the Creggan estate on Londonderry's south side better than anywhere in the world; was at home in the empty wastelands of central Syria, or amongst the maize fields and the poppy plantations of Helmand, but short of knowledge for a dense, closed city.

They passed apartment blocks that had no football spaces, no gardens and no decent walkways, the outer casings of concrete or brick stained dark from air pollution and corrosion. Few shops and with opaque windows anyway, and bus-stops which always interested Gaz, and he could not see any bars – he had started to look for cover opportunities. Realised what NCOs in the unit would have called the 'bleedin' obvious, mate'. He would not be on his own; he would be with them, reliant on their tradecraft, an infant in their hands. They passed a park, its grass overgrown and the bushes ragged, but there were fine ornate buildings with porticos behind a fountain, and a statue of a military man, a cape dangling from his shoulders.

A sneer played on Timofey's mouth as he turned off the road. "That was Kirov, Sergei Kirov. An ally of Stalin, the boss of Leningrad, but in this country, then and today, the top man does not like to see a deputy with ambition. He was assassinated. It is the same in politics as it is in *mafia*. A big man cannot be challenged by a rival, must be destroyed. We survive, Natacha and I, because we have no ambitions. We go our own way, free spirits. If we can sell, can find enough arseholes prepared to buy, make some money, walk away, then we are content. That is why we help you, not because we love you, friend, or believe in your right to bring a war into our country, but because we get money for it. You know what we argue about, Natacha and me? We argue what we shall do with the money. Who knows . . . except in this city there is nothing to spend money on. That man was killed because he climbed too high, was a threat. Who is the man you will kill, friend?"

He evaded. "Not the right time."

"An FSB officer, yes? You will kill an FSB officer?"

"I need to see him, look at him, identify him, follow him home, know where he lives."

"Then you will kill him? Why this officer?"

"At a different time, we talk then."

She said, perky and pleased to interrupt, "I would like to kill an FSB officer – well, kill him a bit and then stamp on his throat, and then hurt him some more, then make him cry that I should finish the work, hurt him that much. I was in the gaol because of FSB . . . maybe you should let me help you."

Gaz deflected, but realised that a gamble of epic proportions had been taken by Knacker Incorporated in packing him off to sea, then into mainland Russia, but he had been only vaguely briefed as to the value of the end product. A big operation and an expensive one, one that oozed risk. He was the mushroom man, kept in the dark and fed on shit. At the finish of the day his role would have been small but pivotal, but Gaz was barely flattered.

She said, "You want to know why my father hanged himself? Why it happened? Why he took a rope to a tree, to end his life?"

"If you want to tell me."

He could have told her that he did not give a damn why her father had killed himself, and did not want to talk, needed to concentrate his thoughts . . . and needed, maybe, to reconcile himself to the fact the plan was rubbish, the method of infiltration poorly prepared, that he was little more than a cloth hung out on the drying frame that spun in his garden at the back of the house on Westray. Too much was asked of him, and he should have refused. He supposed that this evening, or at dawn the following morning, the trawler would tie up in the docks and he would be there and would meet the second man on the crew outside the gate and they would go together back the secure area, and then cast off – would get the hell out, leave this couple alone with their dreams. Could get out then. Would be free, be clear, would have failed.

But he would not: he was trapped, was Knacker's man.

The building blocks were being set, discreetly, in place.

Alice had come to Tromso in northern Norway, and had been lifted from there in a charter, had come down at Kirkenes. Before the plane had lined up to approach the runway, she had been able to see out of the porthole, courtesy of the pilot's manoeuvre, the thick pine forest on the Norwegian side of the frontier, then the scrape in the ground where the trees and foliage had been bulldozed clear – the border zone – and then had been able to look farther inland, out on to the Kola peninsula and had seen more forest. Her view had disintegrated because of low cloud and gentle rain, but she had seen a bleak landscape. She wondered if the tundra wilderness were populated, saw no homes, and no small farms. The only sign of development, other than the border strip, had been the monstrous, nickel smelter with high chimneys spouting fumes, a handful of kilometres into the Russian side. Alice could pick up and discard campaigns, had once been vegan but no longer, had once been a teetotal non-smoker but now did both, had once followed the mantra of abolishing pollution and industrial contamination, and that one had lingered. She thought the smelter a disgrace and its belched smoke a national humiliation for those across the border and the big cats down in Moscow . . . and out there was their boy.

She had no coat, no hat and no umbrella. She walked across the tarmac. Had given the pilot a mischievous 'come on' grin when she'd thanked him for the ride, and he had grinned back. She had chucked off any tiredness from the long flight back from the Middle-East. Fee was waiting for her at the terminal building. From his cockpit, the pilot might have watched her. Not so demure, little Alice, with her freckles and pale face and fair hair tending towards red. They hugged, showing the pain of being apart. They broke and walked towards the transport.

"Get him across? Work well?"

"Yes, he went. Seemed in reasonable spirits."

"Only 'reasonable'?"

"That's good enough. Be more worried if he was dancing a jig. It's a pretty fuck awful place where he's gone. Should be there by now and staking out."

"What's he like?"

"Pretty ordinary. What you'd expect. I mean, he was broken by what happened, what he saw. Wasn't our finest hour, dragging him out of his cave, his refuge, but needs must . . ." She shrugged.

Her own boys, the recruits, and the Facilitator, were due to land in seventy-five minutes. Contact, after a fashion, was broken. She passed no comment on them, was more interested, concerned, about the man that Knacker had brought on board: he'd a skill at that, unrivalled, getting men and women to go farther up the road than was ever warranted by a simple call of duty. Those were the ones Knacker selected, the 'pretty ordinary' ones. Alice did not travel anywhere in the orbit of harm's way on her own, was always accompanied by a close protection team of Royal Military Police or hemmed into the back seat of a vehicle with a gang of sweaty Hereford boys . . . had sometimes wondered how she would be on her own, looking after her own back. Perhaps Fee read her.

"Actually, it's not too bad what's asked of him. The plan holds water."

Drunk, rolling on his feet, clutching at other pedestrians on the crossing the father of Timofey had his eyes fixed on the grand new building on Lenin Prospekt.

Had the traffic been heavy there was every chances he would have been run down. He weaved, lurched, and carried on. He was uncertain of the entrance, where he would find someone to whom he would denounce his son, and the girl who was his son's whore.

It was a heady cocktail that drove him across the wide road. Alcohol, the indignity and shame of the way he was treated in his own home, the insults he faced daily: supreme was the certainty of arrest and imprisonment in a penal colony on a charge of treason, espionage, betrayal of the state. Again and again, he rehearsed, among the vehicles and gripping the arms of fellow pedestrians who tried to shake him off, what he would tell the clerk at the desk, and the gratitude he'd get for his revelation. Better he had never been woken, better he had stayed asleep. He made it across.

His eyes might have deceived him, but he thought three door-ways led into the building. Not four and not two, and he was desperate to piss, but first he had a flight of steps to negotiate. He did not know which door he should attempt to open. He saw a car parked at the side of the steps, two men lounging beside it, smoking. Rough-looking men, but he swerved them, and must have wet himself, and started shouting at them that he had impor-tant information to offer and . . . he was told to 'Go piss yourself somewhere else'. He stumbled and fell and lay on the steps and his hip hurt, and the wet ran down his leg.

He would try again. If he did not try, again and again, then his future was in the penal colony, a certainty leading to his death. Smart shoes came towards him and he clutched at a man's trouser leg but his hand was kicked away; then he grabbed at a woman's ankle and held it for a moment before being stabbed with an umbrella . . . but he had seen which door they had come through. He started to crawl.

★ ★ ★

Knacker looked through a gap in the curtains into the annexe off the lobby, and could see a table and bench beyond the window fronting on to the Kirkenes street.

The one that Alice called the Facilitator was facing him, but unaware of him. Three men were seated at the table, all in profile. All smoked, all drank Pepsi-Cola, wore T-shirts, and frayed jeans and trainers, and the empty tins were stacked in front of them and a tinfoil ashtray overflowed.

After studying them, Knacker remarked to Alice and Fee, "I was at the Round Table the other day. Old Boot was there, not in good shape and not long with us, I fear. I didn't dare engage him in conversation or I would have been deluged with Iron Duke minutiae and Waterloo stuff. Had he been here, looking at those 'hitters', who we intend to let loose beyond that frontier, I fear he would have given us the standard Wellington quote: *I don't know what effect these men will have on the enemy but, by God, they terrify me*. What do they know?"

Alice answered. "They know that they'll be put in the path of the Russian officer who was at the village. They won't see us, and I was not given their names when I chose them. They know they have been chosen because we wanted men who will walk over nails, through fire, for the chance to do the guy some hurt. Frothing at the mouth, I'd say."

Fee said, cheerily, "Remember, Knacker, when we were in Syria, and the gun club boys used to talk about Fire and Forget, the Milan or the Javelin anti-tank missile. Aim it and let it go . . . What we can expect is a right ruckus on the streets of Murmansk."

Alice said, "We'll be long gone, Knacker. Well out of it, and deniable."

Fee said, "But reverberations, Knacker. Heard far and wide."

"My impression of them, Knacker, is that they'll want to get down to a hardware store and get a knife sharpener. Use it to freshen up razor-blades," Alice said.

"I think that's the game we're into, Knacker," Fee said.

He left them. A brisk stride took him out of the town and down to its coast line and there was a fine-looking church there, with a well-tended graveyard and a bench. He sat. He reflected.

Wondered if they knew his identity in the Lubyanka. Wondered if they had heard whispers of a man who was nudging towards elderly and had a silly name. If they had an address in New Malden, and knew of Maude and her hobbies and of his sons. Wondered if they had a file on the Round Table and its ludicrous pantomimes with the sword from the theatrical outfitter, and one on Arthur Jennings, dear man. Wondered if they had a man just like him, and a luncheon club where they performed their own version of pagan rituals. Wondered, most of all, whether they played the sport with any less intensity than he did . . . wondered if they did *not* know of him because he would have been regarded as little more than a nuisance, irritating and easily brushed aside; it would hurt to be so dismissed – and might be justified. He had never received, in all his years in the Service, any form of commendation, never been awarded a medal pinned on him by his sovereign, had never briefed a politician, never even met one for a flaccid handshake. The coins rattled in his trouser pocket, except for the *denarius* cleaned for him by Fee. His fingers rested on it and traced the lines on its face and its reverse and it seemed to show the transitory times of men who sought 'to make a difference'. Some idiot had dropped it in the mud, and such an idiot might have been distracted by anxieties as to whether that woad-painted bastard away in the far distance was confidently plotting incursions.

He spluttered with laughter. It was going to be good: why should it not be?

"I want a bus-stop," Gaz said.

The girl Natacha was deep in to her rant. "You have to listen, because this is why my father hanged himself, died because he could not live while all the men whose friendship he treasured were gone, lost . . . And why I help you. Why? Because it was these people, those in the new FSB palace, in all their palaces, who killed the men who could have been saved on the *Kursk*. Not all of them, but some. They should be alive, some . . . after the explosion and the deaths of ninety-five sailors there were twenty-three who were unharmed and who sheltered on the upper deck of the ninth compartment. They should have been rescued. Who could have saved them? The British could and the Americans could – but it was not acceptable that foreigners save our sailors. You understand why I hate?"

Gaz said, "A bus-stop is always good. No one sits outside if it is raining, but they wait for a bus."

She was passionate, blasting him with her words. "The President was on holiday. In the sun, in the south, resting, still there five days after the disaster: that sort of man, not prepared to interrupt a holiday. And no senior officer dared to ask for help from the NATO navies. Eventually some cracked in their resolve and foreign divers and foreign equipment were asked for but no detail was given of how the escape hatch operated, and the divers were not allowed to fly to Murmansk but had to come many, many miles by sea, with more time lost. It was believed that if one, just one, of our sailors were rescued by a NATO navy then it would be political catastrophe. Such was the language of those who governed us and defended us. A deputy prime minister came to talk with the relatives of the crew at their base. A woman, perhaps already a widow, blistered him with criticism of their lies. Was she heard? She was sedated. A needle was stuck in her leg. The pride of the government was more important than the lives of sailors. It is why we help you – not just for money."

The boy laughed. Gaz thought that Timofey had probably heard the story of the *Kursk*'s loss many times. He needed a bus-stop because there seemed to be no cafés here and no place to wait and watch.

"Eight days after the disaster, the NATO navy opened the hatch on the *Kursk* but all the men who had lived at first were now dead, too late. Three days too late, at least. Killed by carbon monoxide poisoning in pitch darkness and with water all round them and oil in it. A horrible death. Then the President came. He made a big offer to the families: every widow and every mother would get an officer's salary for ten years for her sailor husband or sailor son. How many roubles? The President did not know. He went away. Do you understand?"

It was the way of Gaz's work that there were times when he needed to listen to a tirade or a confession or just gossip in which he had no stake, no interest, but it was necessary to show interest, concern, and not to kill the cooperation of anyone he relied on. The same wherever he had worked. The Fiat was parked. The boy, Timofey, rolled his eyes and had a tired grin. He led them up a side street and out on to the main street, the Prospekt. There were fine public buildings and some flew a flag, limp in the rain without wind to stir it. Timofey led him to a bus-stop and when he looked across the Prospekt he saw the big building which had three prominent towers – at each end and in the centre, and two blocks that were recessed between the towers, and saw a high fence of ironwork and a gate that was guarded. And saw a drunk who was kneeling, arguing with a guard . . . Saw a parked car half on the pavement, two men idling beside it who seemed uninterested in all that passed them by, and the taller one threw down a cigarette butt and the smaller one held a small book of the sort that contained puzzles or word teasers. He rocked. The girl, Natacha, cannoned into him. He looked at the two men by the car, a black BMW 5 series, and the recognition flooded in him. Cold ran on his neck. Gaz knew them. They would not have known him.

He remembered graffiti in a nationalist corner of Londonderry. Daubed after it was public knowledge that Raymond Gilmore, small-time, low-life Provo, had gone supergrass which had meant the lifting of the city's IRA brigade principals. It said *I knew Raymie Gilmore – thank feck he didn't know me.* It had been regarded, by military and bad boys alike, as quality.

He had watched these two on a foul weather day, wind and powerful rain, while an atrocity was played out in front of them. They had seemed detached from the main action and had trailed around the village and across the football pitch and gone down between the buildings, had stayed close to their officer but had neither cautioned nor encouraged him. Gilmore had died a maudlin drunk, his handlers gone . . . The guard on the gate in front of the building's main door was on his radio, complaining – easy enough to read it – about the drunk.

Their presence was the best sign. The bus-stop across the street had a weatherproof roof and sides of reinforced clear plastic. It served several routes ... which was good because that meant it aroused no attention if a bus came and was ignored.

"Friend, you want me to stay?" A whisper in his ear.

It was what he had come for. He was not there to have his hand held, to be dependent on these kids. Before the black dog days he had been able to operate as well in solitary as in company, but before ... "I want you back at the car, able to come quick, just around that corner. Nearer than where you parked, and watching me."

"You take that chance?"

Everything he did was taking a chance. He nodded. He thought the girl did not want to leave him, perhaps feared she'd miss out on the big scene, but Timofey tugged her arm roughly. He was alone ... Women milled around him with shopping bags, and kids who had come from school and larked and swung their satchels, and a druggie who might have been one of Timofey's customers ... He reckoned now that the pair of them, Timofey and Natacha, were better than he'd bargained for and neither would crumple. Hard to credit. He was in Murmansk, a security-dominated city, one where counter-espionage forces were supreme, and he watched the two foot soldiers and waited for their officer.

What to talk about that had not already been exhausted? Not the dour days in Afghanistan, and not the long weeks in Syria. Instead the two minders ignored the drunk who was on the steps and arguing with the guard, belting on about a plot, an infiltration, an espionage event and too pissed to finish a sentence. They talked of their future.

For Mikki and Boris, the truth was that the brigadier general – respected and almost loved – was a different man from the one they had followed through the Afghan intervention. They minded his kid – whom they called the 'little shit' or the 'little bastard' – because the old man asked it of them. The future was soon, pressing. It would be a hotel ... they had enough connections to get the necessary permits and the building resources, and would easily attract a decent 'roof' to shelter under. Where? Boris was from Irkutsk and Mikki had been brought up in the far Far East and Kamchatka. Both had made the decision to quit home, abandon friends and family, and join the military security wing of what was then KGB. Both had been on the personal protection detail of the brigadier general when he was a junior colonel and both owed their lives to the time he had called down the air strike right above where they held out, ammunition stocks near exhausted. Their idea now was to site themselves along the M11 highway, perhaps inside the city limits of Veliky Novgorod, and purchase a property in decline that was close to the Volkhov river and near to the lakes and forests. It would be a good stop-over point in the 800-kilometre drive from the capital to St Petersburg. That it was still a dream and not reality was because of their loyalty for the old man who had taken both of them off the streets when they were raw recruits, had kept them close and privileged. Always they had need of a roof, always they had been protected with one.

They talked quietly. There had been a time in Boris' home city, Irkutsk, when there were gunfights on the streets as *mafia* groups battled for supremacy, and in Mikki's home town there had been numbing unemployment when the regime had collapsed and the factories had locked their gates. They had been fortunate, had been on the winning side when the dust of chaos cleared, would not have been without the shelter given them by their officer . . . Everything they had they owed to the father of the 'little shit', and nothing was owed to the 'little bastard'. They waited for him.

The rain fell. Neither understood why the drunk was still there, had not had his arse kicked. They might have a central building and they might also have chalets amongst trees. It would be a good place, and clean, and used by families. And what pleased them equally was that they would never return to this God-forsaken wreck of a city where it was always day or always night. What helped in the project for the hotel was that each was blessed with a hard-working woman who would turn her back on the city and come with them. Would be better than good and they would be shot of Lavrenti Volkov.

★   ★   ★

At his desk, his door closed, Lavrenti trawled his screen. No matter that the new major and the impertinent captain had had the chance to get to know each other better in the canteen or in a meeting room, or – for all he cared – in a quiet part of the cell block. He would stay in his office, regardless of what name was on the door, until the end of the working day. Phone calls came to him and most involved investigations that he had been a part of, but three were for the new man. His crisp rejoinder was 'Wrong extension, nobody of that name is on this number.'

He found clips of the President speaking in the Kremlin, and more clips of the President at armed forces exercises, and watched him on vacation and fishing or hunting or diving in the Black Sea, bare-chested. He thought the man was his saviour. As long as he lived, and power remained in those hands, small and delicate, Lavrenti was protected. As were many others. Many hundreds of men lived well because the President stayed in rude health. Those who had worked on secret missions abroad, and those who had been in the vanguard on the special units in the Caucasus, and those who administered the regime's justice in the interrogation rooms at Lefortovo, and those who collected the money for providing roofs. It would have been simple to have tapped the keys, to have resurrected the involvement in Syria, plastered the screen with images of Russia's bombs and Russia's armour and Russia's infantry, and with those units of the Islamic Revolutionary Guard Corps of Iran to which Russian officers were assigned as liaison. From the next day, he would be in Moscow, alone, and would offer a curt farewell but no thanks, to the two minders allocated him so many years before because that would denigrate his authority. They knew, they had been there. Had seen it all and had never given a sign. They had been there, a handful of paces behind him, and it ate at him. Voices in the corridor, and hisses of irritation, and they would be waiting for him, would wait until he was ready to leave.

Timofey came to the bus shelter, glanced around it and had blinked, and the cold had touched his neck, and he could not see the man. Had come to look for him, to see if all went well, if anything had happened, how much longer they might wait – and that hour was almost on them when the bureaucrats vacated their premises. Could not see his man, did a raking sweep with his eyes – caught sight of a man in the back of the shelter and realised the skill displayed. How to sit in a bus shelter and have his body at that angle and his head turned away and behind a large woman, and his eyes swept on and relief soared, and admiration and . . . Timofey saw the figure on the step outside the ironwork fence of the headquarters building. He recognised his father.

The guard had called for reinforcements. They were at a door behind the fence, slipping on rubber gloves, were being waved forward. Timofey knew the wide powers and the range of authority enjoyed in the city by FSB. They would not have been awarded such a building otherwise. They dealt with counter-terrorism, and with political dissidents and with supposed corruption in local government, and with drug enforcement . . . everything above issuing the bus timetable for the city. He was rigid, his heart pounded, and he saw his father and the guards who were coming to get him and take him in. It did not take a high school graduate to realise that his father would have gone down to the Prospekt to snitch on his son . . . did not take an intellect to comprehend that his father was going to betray him.

He ran.

Crossed the street, paused in the central reservation and launched again. Cars hooted and bus brakes screamed, and heads turned. Timofey reached his father. The guards, a few paces away, were wary and would have wondered whether the drunk was about to vomit on their uniforms. A pair of men by a black saloon, a BMW, were watching, had found something of interest in a sea of boredom. He bent and his fists gripped the damp coat and he dragged it up, used wiry strength.

"Sorry, my father, a drunk. Apologies to you. Going to get him home. Don't know what shit he was giving you, wasting your valuable time. I look after him. Harmless, a fool. Sorry . . ."

He held his father under his armpits. His father croaked a few guttural words. "An agent was sent. Through the wire . . . A man came . . . It is an attack on FSB . . . Hear me, listen . . . Listen."

Nobody did, and nobody could. Timofey held his father upright and had a hand across his father's mouth.

Timofey said, "Tragic, isn't it? A good man until the fucking booze got him. Sorry."

Did not lard it; apology was already enough out of character in that city. He had a hold on the man and they went out into the traffic and the vehicles weaved round them. Might have, if he had not been watched, dumped his father in the path of any heavy lorry that was going too fast for the brakes to work well on a wet surface. He took him past the bus shelter and tried to see his man. Dragged him back to the side street and the Fiat, opened the door and threw him into the back, and said to Natacha that the 'old bastard' would have betrayed them and was too pissed to make it into FSB and do the snitch. Timofey went back to the street corner where he could see the guard and the waiting car and the two men lounging against it, and had a view of the bus-stop. He checked his watch. It was the time when offices emptied and bars filled, and men came out with the girls they hoped to shag that evening . . . and he only cared for the twin prizes: excitement and money, adrenaline rush and cash. And wondered which officer inside that building was of such importance to the foreigners that they sent a man to find him.

Delta Alpha Sierra, the eighth hour

She didn't cry out loud and that surprised Gaz.

The hours had drifted on and some of the Iranian militia had lit fires to shelter them from the weather and had built little covers to keep the rain off the embers, and they heated food. None for the village women, or the children . . . the men were all gone, had been taken beyond Gaz's vision, and he had heard shots and assumed more executions had taken place . . . from the staccato bursts of firing it had not been a fusillade of weapons on automatic, but aimed.

The goats had moved away from her and seemed to believe it possible to forage but the dogs huddled close. Gaz had released her wrist. He would have liked to have held his rifle in one hand and to have wrapped his other arm round her, give her what little comfort he could. But he did not move and still no words had passed between them and they held this silence. A search party moved in and out of buildings that were not in flames. He saw them, noted them, wondered whether her own home, where the thorn palisade was in which the goats were corralled at night, would be the next to be searched. His legs ached because he could not shift but he had training for it: for her it would have been worse. The text from the FOB told him that a Hereford team was on the way but would lie up until dark. The text also said that the Chinook would fly, regardless of weather, if the vehicles could not get close enough to pull him out, and Arnie and Sam had already moved back and were at the RV point . . . It was just him that was left, and he was the witness.

What happened next . . . important to remember every fucking thing that played out in front of him . . . Rare for Gaz to swear, and it always upset Betty Riley when he did. He had the binoculars on a group of the IRGC as they exited a building and could see that one of them carried – as a trophy – a fag-end. It was a filter-tipped fag-end. The commander was called for, and the Russian officer, and the goons who traipsed after him, sauntered across the dirt. Gaz understood. He didn't smoke but others did. He did not bring cigarettes to the village as a trifling goodwill gesture, but plenty did. Probably would have been when one of the Hereford teams was visiting, doing some weapons training with the kids, lecturing on a few of the combat basics, and they'd leave cigarettes but not be as dumb as to leave a carton or a packet, just a few filter-tipped fags. Would not have been a pack of local Alhamra, red and gold, but more likely Bensons, brought in from Cyprus after a rest & recreation. It was examined. The fag-end was passed from the commander to the Russian officer and he looked closely at it, like he was some goddam detective. Gaz was not sure how a particular woman in the little group that was hemmed in by bayonet points was identified. One moment she was inside the laager the women made, and the next she had been hauled out and was brought to stand in front of the commander and the officer. She was questioned.

The girl in front of Gaz would have known what she said, exact words of the response, a lip reading from the girl would have given each syllable of the answer. Gaz could not hear and did not have the language but the contortion on the woman's face told him enough. She would have been an important figure in the village community and her nightclothes hung sodden on her. The breath came faster from the girl's mouth, hissed through her teeth and lips. The woman's face was inches from the commander's and the officer's. The commander, the senior Iranian, slapped her face, did a double impact job using the outside of his hand for the first stroke and the palm for the second, and the woman shook, steadied, did not fall. There was a moment, huge in the binoculars, when they faced each other and her face was flushed red from the blow. She spat. Twice.

The first was at the commander. A bearded face, half of it hidden by his dark glasses in spite of the low cloud and the rain and the lessening light, but he was fast enough to twist away and the mess went past him. The second spit was at the Russian officer. He had not anticipated it. The spit caught him at the nose and in the eyes, and he reeled back as if punched, and in his anger he seemed to choke for breath.

Gaz heard and saw what followed.

A hand on a holster, the flap already loosed, and a weapon held, barely aimed, pointed in the direction of the woman, of her stomach. No hesitation, and the crash of the shot carried on the wind, and the girl in front of him winced as if she had taken the force of it. The officer had fired at her stomach. The woman rolled, staggered, and then lurched forward, was going down, but her arms stretched forward and the fingers of her right hand caught his cheek, one fingernail sticing down the flesh, through the stubble, and the line was immediate and clean cut. It was big in the binoculars. The officer kicked out at her and caught her shin and she fell to the ground in front of him. As Gaz saw it, the officer lost control. His hand went up and felt his cheek and the blood was already flowing and he looked down and saw it run in the palm of his hand.

He fired again. Kept firing. Fired into the inert body of the woman. No more twitches or spasms, her life was already gone. The officer fired until the magazine in the butt of the Makarov was emptied. Then he kicked her, then, in extreme anger, kicked her again. Gaz thought he might be sick but held it back in his lower throat. The girl stared ahead, never moved, did not even shake, and the dogs were close to her but the goats were roaming, which left her more exposed than when they were thick around her. What struck Gaz was the minders had not moved. Had not taken the empty pistol from the officer, nor had deflected the kicks he aimed at the body, nor had sought to calm him.

And it would be worse, Gaz thought. Dusk was still four hours away and still witnesses lived. He watched the officer and the blood dribbled on his face.

The computer was switched off. Anything private to him was sanitised. Lavrenti rose from his seat and the chair went back hard against the wall and marked the paint: little matter. He hooked the strap of his bag over his shoulder, took his pistol from the desk's top drawer, put it in the bag. A quick look around him and his two-year stint inside the Arctic Circle was nearly done. They were waiting outside, the new major and the captain. He acknowledged them, the briefest and shallowest duck of his head, and neither offered a hand to him as a farewell gesture. Down the corridor. No voices calling out through half-open doors . . . ignored, like he was a triangle of yesterday's pizza. He went down the stairs. Usually he alerted his minders that he was on his way but it had not seemed important, not this time. He had noticed a growing impertinence from them these last days. In the big hallway on the ground floor, a colonel waited to receive a guest. The colonel bossed the headquarters building and the outer doors swung open and Lavrenti noted the arrival of an official from the regional governor's office, and the two men hugged. The colonel would have seen the departing Lavrenti, would have known his tour of duty was completed, but did not acknowledge him. He was about to leave and was fishing the lanyard off his neck that held his local accreditation, and a security man stood and waited for it, and his face was lit in admiration.

"Goodbye, Major, and wishing you well."

Which startled Lavrenti. Something warm and something genuine. He noticed that the security man wore, proudly, a line of medal ribbons. "Thank you, and you."

"Because we need more like you, Major. Combat men. Those who have fought in the name of the Fatherland. Been on active service. Not these desk warriors, fuck them – excuse me, Major – but more who have been at the front line, need them. Done time there."

He was saluted. He went outside, into the drifting spat of the rain. His minders had not seen him. He walked to the gate. The guard there was admitting men and women who were probably in the delegation of the governor's office but had come in different cars. He was delayed but it did not seem important. He paused in his stride and saw, through the bars, that the traffic on the Prospekt was light. He did not look back at the building, had no more time for it, but was unsettled by the greeting as he had given over his lanyard, and the warmth of it. *More like you, Major ... combat men*, and so few knew.

Gaz saw him.

The officer came out, crossed the space in front of the building but could not push past the delegation entering the gate. He paused. Was wearing his cap and his camouflage tunic and had a bag across his shoulder, and his khaki drill trousers were pressed and had a knife-sharp crease, and his shoes were polished. The same glower in the eyes and the line that had been bloodied when Gaz had last seen it and now was faint but visible. Still the goons with the car, as recognisable as the major, had not seen their man. He flicked with his fingers, cracked them, and Gaz watched the response as the goons turned and gazed through the ironwork fence and jettisoned their cigarettes, and . . . Gaz was running.

Out from the bus-stop, along the street and past an apartment block entrance, and to the next corner. Looked for the Fiat, found it . . . a good boy, his Timofey. True to his word. Brought close to the corner, the engine ticking over. The girl was sitting in the back . . . the most chaotic call-up that Gaz had ever done. That it worked was miraculous . . . a delegation had gone through the gate and then into the building via a single door, and the officer had been forced to stand and watch, and his own car had not been ready. He did a sharp, short whistle, and the Fiat was coming fast towards him.

A door opened, foul smell hitting him. A jerk at his arm and he was pitched down into the front passenger seat, cannoned down and was bruised. Had only half closed the door when the boy accelerated away . . . He said it was the black car. They braked hard at the main intersection. The driver scanned. Gaz had seen the officer for a full ten seconds. He had seen the goons, who had once been minders, for an hour, a little more. All put together like a jigsaw. That should have been a moment of rare pleasure for Gaz. Should, mentally, have been thrilled enough to high-five the kids and punch the air.

There had been a four-day stake-out in Helmand, and he had been the lead of a reconnaissance team, had had a full sergeant working to him, and had identified a local hitter, a man with the reputation of having filled coffins to go back to UK for a hearse journey up the High Street in Wootton Bassett: the man was supposed to be an expert in the dark art of building the IEDs that either killed outright or made living a pained misery for survivors. Easiest cliché: *they all look just the same* and might have been true except that Gaz was the one who had detected in previous surveillance stills that the target tied his turban loosely and with a side knot, not a central one, and it had been enough. A man convicted, sentenced, and executed with a Hellfire strike on the compound from a fast jet and all done because the tying of a knot had been picked up by binoculars half a mile away. Knacker and his crowd would not have relied, just, on Faizah's identification, of a Russian officer in a changed location and different uniform. Needed his training, what Gaz brought to the table. Had previous, had form, history ... If Gaz spotted a man, and identified him, working in the sort of theatre that was his playground, then the man was dead. Not, of course, by Gaz's hand, but he had that level of power.

Needed more. Needed a location. Needed a quieter street and a backwater location. Needed a better place for the hitters to get to work. The BMW was starting to move away from the kerb. Timofey had pulled out into the traffic and a car almost hit them, and a collision with a motorcycle was narrowly avoided. Gaz glanced behind him and saw the girl sat on top of a drunk.

Her voice was rich in contempt. "His father. His father went to tell them. His father was too drunk to get a hearing. His father is a traitor to us. This is *his* father. We should put a weight on him and take him to the docks, drop him in the river."

Which he supposed was the way of the jungle they lived in ... an arrogant thought, so he bit at his tongue and said nothing ... just pointed ahead and Timofey had locked on the saloon and followed it easily. It had the speed to surge away from them, but it was that time in the late afternoon when the road filled and the offices slopped out. The shops would soon be shutting, the pavement was crowded. Murmansk was on the march and it suited Gaz well. He had no indication that the saloon's driver used tradecraft, was aware of them, nor did he seem to practise any of the procedures laid down for the evasion of a tail. Their size helped them, a compact little vehicle that could shift between lanes and be hidden by the bulk of buses and lorries. Fact was, it was turning out ordinary and simple. The boy drove well and seemed aware of the risk of showing out, but the drunk's stink from the back was sharp and Gaz was aware of a dilemma: did not know what, in the world from which the drug-dealing kids emerged, would be the fate of a father wanting to tout on his son. Timofey had his eyes on the roof of the saloon and swinging at lights, going right and climbing a steep and narrower road, and going back often enough to his mirror. Asked, "What is it now that you want?"

"I want him to go home. I want to see his home."

"Only that?"

"Yes."

"And he is?"

"He is Major Lavrenti Volkov. He is FSB. Before he worked here he was in Syria. I have to see him, locate him. Because of what happened in Syria."

"What happened?"

"You don't have to know. It is another story."

Timofey persisted. "My father, who did he speak with?"

Gaz said, "He tried to speak with the guard at the gate. He tried also to speak with men who came from the building. Many people came but none wanted to hear what an alcoholic said. Nobody stopped, nobody listened. He had drunk too much, was not heard. If he wanted to betray you, then he failed. That is your problem, and I am not a part of it."

He had said it easily, was practised at shedding responsibility. It was the way of a reconnaissance trooper. He carried no burden of 'consequences', would be far gone from Murmansk when it was decided how to use the information he provided. What happened to the drunk, Timofey's father, was separate from him. By the following day he would be travelling back towards the island of Westray, and hooking up again with a mobile, calling customers, telling them that he would make up the time on their lawn cutting and the repairs he had promised for them, and maybe heading for the hotel and a beer, and might wonder if the mission had cleansed him of the attentions of the black dog days, and would meet again with Aggie . . .

He could see the saloon's roof and remembered everything of the officer: what he had seen at Delta Alpha Sierra and the image of the man this afternoon, smart in his uniform, but wearing the scar of where he had been. Was near to the finish line.

9

Through the traffic, an old, scraped and unremarkable Fiat 500, rust showing at the bottom of the doors, tailed a glossy black BMW 5 series saloon that was the vehicle of a man of substance and his protection went with him. The car climbed, and there was a bend where the road swept to the left. In the back, Gaz imagined the old man had passed out, or worse, or merely slept, but every few minutes there was a muttered curse from the girl who was astride him and Gaz did not doubt her venom, and still the stink ... The road swung, and Timofey followed the bend and the BMW was fifty yards, three vehicles, in front.

Gaz looked down and out across the Murmansk harbour, and saw the hulk of the aircraft carrier that had been mostly towed on its voyage to the Syrian theatre, and mostly towed back and now had cranes alongside, and could see an ice-breaker tied up at a quay, and small trampers, small tankers and beyond them was open water except for one small craft, ploughing through the water. The rain still fell but the wind had dropped and the water surface barely rippled. She threw out a good wake. Amongst the port facilities' decay and the broken ships berthed there, she seemed clean, cared for, like there was a pride about her, and Gaz remembered ... Passing hot cocoa around in the cabin while the trawler shook in the storm, and rolled fearfully, and listening to the boys talking of grandparents in accented English, and realising what their past meant. Hearing stories of men who had battled storms and enemy aircraft, and some were at the bottom of the North Sea. Realising that long-held loyalties still carried weight: only cynics and those who valued their actions that day, not heritage, would have dismissed them. He thought each member of the four-man crew regarded themselves as fortunate to have been lifted from obscurity and asked to carry out a mission where danger was inherent . . . Each of them at some future date might sit on a headland, spray dampening their clothes, wind in their hair, and shout into the skies what they had done that day, that night and that tomorrow. Would believe that the men of the Shetland Bus route would note what they did, would be satisfied. He had liked them, had thought them simple men. And the road straightened; and they climbed some more, and he lost sight of the trawler.

Daft, but he felt emotion. Could no longer see the trawler, and could barely make out the roof of the black saloon. It did not matter whether the plan for the mission was excellent, indifferent or crap poor. What mattered was whether they were *lucky*. Could have had a big team working on it for a month, with a sub-committee overseeing, and a consultancy pulled in for background, and some head-hunting done . . . could have been thrown together on the hoof. If they were to stay *lucky* then they would need to obliterate the chance of a 'mistake'. Everyone agonised about a mistake, and hardest was to recognise it – and the moment it had happened. Gaz dared to think that all of them in the cramped interior of the Fiat were without a mistake, were therefore *lucky*. Had already scratched his head, chipped into his memory, looked for an error but not found it.

The boy drove well. As a career criminal, drug-pusher and with a girlfriend, fresh out of gaol, Timofey was careful not to get too close to the target vehicle. Had once, on the way to the bend where Gaz had seen the fishing boat, seemed to lose the black saloon and another man might have panicked and accelerated too fast or hesitated at the next junction but the boy had stayed calm. Nothing more than a nibble at his lower lip and they had pulled out to pass a slow-moving bus and the BMW was in front of them. He liked men who were cool, calm . . . It was a given for the guys, and the occasional girls, in the unit that histrionics were unacceptable. He'd been dependent on the Hereford teams and the Chinook people when there were engine malfunctions and weather calamities, and nobody made a big deal out of it. The boy checked his mirror often, stayed in touch, was an excellent tail . . . In the scenario used by the instructors teaching vehicle surveillance, there would be two vehicles or three, and linked radio, and a commander sitting on top of the operation and guiding them. If it were pedestrian surveillance then there might be as many as eight of them . . . He had Timofey who sold 'phets and marijuana, and Natacha who sat on an old drunk's torso and might strangle him if he complained, and himself. The fishing boat was in place, and where the BMW stopped to drop off the officer was journey's end for Gaz.

Not for the first time he touched his upper thigh and felt the outline of the doctored papers, and the passport. Reassured. He had memorised where the boat crew would meet him, and they'd stroll together through security, to the quay, board – and sail.

"Do you not talk?"

"Not unless I've something to say."

"Your target, who you go after . . ."

"Not my concern."

"You come here, go after one man – that is an FSB officer. What is FSB? FSB is bastards, big-time bastards. They control this place, take what they want, they are the law and the execution of the law. You go after one man, and he wears a major's uniform but has a German top-range car and a driver, and another. What did he do?"

"Better you do not know."

"But you know what he did, you are needed to identify him. Then others come . . . what do they do?"

"I make the identification, I advise the location, and I leave. Simple."

"And we get paid?"

"Money into your account, generous."

"The people who come, do I help them?"

"I don't know. I know very little. That is the way it is done."

"What did he do?"

"I try not to lie, Timofey. It is good to know little."

Timofey took a hand off the wheel and punched Gaz's arm. Not gentle, not playful. A sharp-edged fist, hard, and Gaz flinched. The road had narrowed and a heavy lorry dragging a trailer was in front of the BMW and slowed it. He felt the motion behind him – the old man had woken, belched, probably wanted to piss, and Gaz wondered what would happen to him – but he did not need to know, did he? And that was his creed and adhered to. He did his own job and went no further.

Approaching the end of the street, Knacker saw the flag, and ducked away.

He faced an ordinary enough office building, a flag-pole angled from the wall above the entrance. The flag had red and blue and white strips, was wrapped around the pole, did not fly with any joy. The Russian flag . . . He had, before setting out on a lone walk, noted on the girls' map that the Russian consulate was at the upper end of a central Kirkenes street. There would be a camera that scanned the street and recorded those approaching the doorway. He thought his face would not have been shown clearly at the distance where he turned on his heel. He had already walked up that street, past the art shop and the stationer's and a couple of fast foods, and he had noted the imitation border markers concreted into the pavement. They were painted in red and green bands, the colours the Russians used on the frontier markers, and were plastered with photographs, in colour, of a benign looking chap who was – had been – prominent in this Norwegian town but had made a visit to Moscow. He was now banged up in a cell block in the Lefortovo: an accusation of espionage, and his home community disbelieving and angry and impotent. Knacker had passed the town's large police building with its intelligence liaison desk, and the big church where parishioners knelt on a Sunday and would have tried to exorcise anxieties about their neighbours, their neighbours' intentions, and would have failed. Knacker left the consulate behind him, always enjoyed a walk, alone, and could reflect. Could think of motivation, why a single enemy consumed his attention. Was parsimonious with that adversary – did not feel the same cold dedication for conflict with Iranians or North Koreans, or the Chinese who were now labelled by the analysts as engendering the greater threat. He confronted Russia, would do so as long as he was employed.

Why? Difficult to answer. Knacker had never been across the borders, by land, by sea, by air, of the old Soviet Union and of the newer Russian Federation. The only citizens that he knew from behind the former or present versions of an Iron Curtain were fugitive dissidents and recruited defectors. The matter of searching for an opposition target was based on the value it carried. Russians were high end. Men talked long into the night of when they had bested that opponent. Legendary tales were embedded into the Service folklore, epic triumphs – and monumental failures. They were the only 'enemy' on the playing field for whom the game's end result mattered . . . with, Knacker's opinion, motivation and going the extra yard. A game with high stakes. They played big, and Knacker had lost men and they had too. He would continue to face collateral as would they . . . but always the notion of victory softened any conscience pang . . . He thought himself a man of decency, would gladly write the chit for a one-off payment for a widow, a grieving mother, a daughter, even a mistress. He thought his opponents arrogant, contemptuous of his efforts and so it was worth administering a sharp kick to these shins. As he walked the wide streets of this frontier community, he could consider that the establishment of a small oasis of loyalty where once had been the village of Deir al-Siyarqi was reward enough for casualties taken.

He was in a fine mood. He kept away from the hotel where the Facilitator and his hoods waited to be called forward. He assumed that Gaz, the reluctant volunteer, was by now on the trail, lead dog in a pack and going hard after a bushy tail, and on board the fishing boat within hours . . . going well.

Not complacent and not chicken counting, but likely soon to be murmured about at a Round Table lunch . . . Going well enough to be shared amongst that élite where the impossible was boasted as normal, why it existed and why Knacker's reputation was rarely bested. Going well and the phone in his pocket would only ring if the business headed for the pan. He was pleased that the Round Table's traditions remained in good hands, was vindicated.

Fingers probed, prodded, used a meld of firmness and gentleness, but went where they were guided and with the required force.

Eyes glanced away from the patient's chest and upper stomach and scanned the X-rayed image that had been taped to the side of a bookcase above a drinks cabinet. Lips pursed and a frown furrowed a forehead. The doctor was astride a stool and his patient – Dickie, Director-General, God Almighty – was propped up by cushions on the chaise longue that had long been a fixture in that office high above the river, looking out on the seat of government on the other side of the Thames. The patient would have assumed himself indestructible but the doctor would have known better.

"All right, give it me."

The doctor did.

"Heavy schedule at the moment. I'll try and fit in the necessary when it's calmer."

The doctor's head shook sharply. 'Immediately' was the response, or 'sooner'.

"Bugger . . . you don't look open to negotiation, Freddie. Can't go this moment, need to put the DD-G in the frame. Allowed that, am I?"

No barter permitted. A few hours, not a full day. If the schedule were abused the chances were high that the destination would be the mortuary, not the clinic. The doctor thought a soothing word might help, 'nothing's for ever, and the DD-G's likely to make a fair fist of things', and the tidbit of the joys of lasting longer, seeing more of the grandchildren.

"Smooth talk . . . Problem is I've put things in place, but they're on a fragile base – one running at the moment. Beyond recall . . . Be here tomorrow, please, and take me in."

The doctor left. The Director-General, an admirer of Knacker, a supporter of all of that ilk, pushed himself uncomfortably off the chaise longue and felt that irritating stab of pain, and rang his PA in the outer office and asked for a meeting with his deputy, early in the morning. Felt angry, then reflected that it was probably never easily accepted that a potentially terminal condition existed deep in the chest.

"Shit, bloody inconvenient. A show running and all out of reach."

He parked the pick-up. It might have been in a restricted area, but the hunter, the recluse from the forest, had no address that would register on a traffic office computer. He went to the hotel and carried a heavy bag. Horns jutted from it, and the hooves of two deer, and the tip of the dark tail of an Arctic fox. Jasha had come to town to do business. There was one hotel in the town that his contact cared to use.

The Azimut had a minimalist coffee lounge and lobby. Jasha came here because it was a hotel that permitted him to bring his old dog. Normally he would have sat with the agent who bought the pelts and trophies, and the dog would have been curled by his feet. He accepted the cash offered . . . not that he needed money. Under his bed in the cabin and screwed down on to the floor's planking was a combination-locked safety deposit box. Each time that he returned from Murmansk it was harder for Jasha to insert the bank notes, denominations of 100 American dollars and 500 Russian rubles with the image of Peter the Great upon them. Jasha could not have said how much he was worth and had never tipped the notes out of their secure box and counted them. His distraction was obvious, and the agent quizzed him.

"Are you unwell, Jasha?"

A shake of the head and an attempt to dismiss such trivia. "No, I am well."

"And soon another winter, and you are not younger, and you live without comfort."

"I am good, and I have pleasant company."

"You have not lured a woman up there, surely not?"

"I have my own company, have my dog, and outside is nature. It is enough."

He assumed the agent thought he lived in circumstances

similar to a serf in the times of Catherine. He was challenged twice more with efforts at conversation, and was vague. They made their farewells. He had the idea that the agent watched him leave and wore that look an old friend reserves for someone not expected to live long. The money was in his hip pocket and he had shouldered the big bag, now empty. He would visit a super-market for essentials, then head back up the road, into the wilderness, to rejoin his own world of the dog, the bear and the creatures he stalked . . . except, the source of his distraction: he had seen the intruders he had noticed earlier on his way to the Azimut hotel.

The old sniper had needed to be certain in his judgements: distance, wind speed, identity of targets – and then act on the evidence displayed. He was not a man of self-doubt. Jasha always used the same route into Murmansk. Climbing the hill before the last drop down to the hotel, he had seen them. A young man with the pallor of a city kid from a tower block, a girl with a stream of blonde hair flying as she skipped over rocks, and a man who Jasha would have said was a soldier. Had seen them among the trees and rocks and heading towards the road below the Titovka roadblock. Had seen them in a small car, a moving wreck, that had struggled up a hill. Had seen the driver clearly, and the 'soldier' had been beside him and the girl had been sprawled in the back. Had recognised them . . . They followed, up to the lights where he was held, a black saloon BMW 5 series, two men in the front in civilian clothes and he thought a uniformed officer in the back, but it had tinted windows. He added together all he'd seen: sufficient to distract him from selling pelts and trophies. He hurried to the supermarket wanted to be home where he had no involvement, was no part of a mystery.

The girl whistled, a sad tune, and Gaz thought her more bored than miserable – and uncomfortable perched on top of the boy's father.

"He makes it difficult for you, yes?"

"He is my father."

"And is a danger to you."

"I don't slit his throat. My father, yes." Timofey jabbed Gaz's rib. "You know about what they call 'sleepers', do you?"

Gaz said, "I know little about anything, best for me."

"You know that a 'sleeper' waits, looks to each stranger who comes close?"

"I would not know, not my business to know."

"Since my grandfather handed to my father, then it was given to me."

"All beyond my reach, not relevant to me."

"Where you come from, in the office there, did many people know of the sleepers, my family. Were we talked of?"

"Outside my orbit – but I doubt it."

"Would people, in that office, have cared about us?"

Gaz weighed him. He was young, had a pretty girl in tow, was a self-employed dealer and probably supplied satisfied customers, and bought wholesale narcotics, and had no politics but dreamed of wealth. Was not stupid, had an obstinacy that came from intelligence ... would believe in the right to be told truths and lies would fall flat.

Gaz said, "It depends what you want to hear."

"What is real. I want to hear that."

"You were not discussed. Do they care? Do they care whether you succeed with what is asked of you? Absolutely, all rooting for you. Do they care what happens to you afterwards, after the mission? Perhaps, if they think you may be useful for another waking in the future: if so, they will hope you go back to sleep and keep out of sight until the next time. Perhaps if they do not imagine that you will be useful in the future, then they will not care, and there will have been steps taken to manufacture a screen of deniability. They are good at using agents with whom they can deny association. It is the trade they are a part of. What I do is not for my monarch, my country: I do my duty as a minor figure. I was a witness. The duty of a witness is to set right a wrong. You understand me?"

"A little, friend, I understand a little of you. Do they care about you?"

He remembered the force of the rain pummelling his bungalow on Westray, and remembered the battering of the wind and the singing in the wires, and remembered the hunched figure on the gravel of his front path. They would have had a file on the levels of his disability, and then they had soft-soaped Aggie: never a chance to refuse.

"I want to believe that they do, but I am secondary to the greater good of the many. Listen, Timofey, we do not turn down what is put before us, we are the willing Joes, we are hooked on the narcotic of it. Why should they care? Bad news? Go and have a coffee in a canteen, then move on. They are good at that, moving on."

"I appreciate the honesty. I enjoy this. To take risk is an addiction, and . . ."

Timofey hit the brake. The little Fiat swerved, skidded, squealed and came to a stop six inches from the vehicle in front, a builder's van with the back door flapping, and one working tail-light. Natacha's whistling died. Two cars in front had also stopped abruptly. Nobody complained. No driver lowered his window and exposed a fist to the rain and gave a finger towards the stationary black saloon. What sort of imbecile shouted obscenities at a car, chauffeur-driven, that carried one of the city's élite? In front of them, traffic rounded the stationary car and gave it a wide berth as a rear passenger door opened. They were in front of a bar, rubbish on the pavement outside its door, weeds growing between the slabs, and graffiti was writ large. Gaz saw the target step out, say something over his shoulder to his goons, then head for the entrance.

A big television screen was showing a football match and in an alcove pop music played off speakers, no one spoke. He'd pushed open the door, paused then heard it clatter shut behind him; the volume from the football was big and the music too loud, and nobody spoke.

He wore uniform. Was *Federal'nya sluzhba bezopasnosti*, had advantages, privileges, authority that no other person in this dreary bar possessed. The men, some standing and some sitting, hung their heads, held silence and did not wish to challenge him with a direct glance. He imagined some had been mid-sentence, and some had been laughing at a joke. Glasses were held tight as though this stranger might snatch them away. His medal ribbons were bright on his uniform. There might have been veterans among the drinkers, and there might even have been fathers of infantry men stationed at Titovka, returned from a town in Syria as he had arrived. No one spoke to him. Fag-ends on the floor were examined in detail, the football was ignored and no feet tapped the heavy-duty vinyl to the beat of the music. A girl was behind the bar, and concentrated on polishing glasses.

He would get no greeting, no momentary friendship here. In Moscow, if he drank, it would be in cocktail bars. In Syria, if he drank, it would be in the sanctity of the officers' mess and surrounded by other FSB personnel. When he was in Murmansk he would drink in restaurants, occasionally, and in hotel bars if he were forced to entertain prominent civilians. He did not know this place nor anything like it.

He looked for company, and would not find it. He carried enough rubles in his wallet to have bought the bar's entire customer base a round of drinks and then keep them in alcohol for the rest of the evening. Behind the bar, above a shelf of bottles containing differing makes of vodka, was a portrait photograph of the President. He, Lavrenti, was a chosen one, and not another man in the confines of the bar could claim that rank. He looked around him. If any had met his glance, had offered him a vestige of a smile, they would have been on his tab and bought a drink. But he had no takers. They would have thought him an enemy . . . He was the son of his father, examined with suspicion. He ordered a drink.

The girl did not hurry but turned slowly, and reached up for a bottle – the Stoli brand – and poured for him. Not a generous measure. He paid, change was put on the counter. He thought he was over-charged.

Neither Mikki nor Boris had followed him in. He would have challenged the girl if either had been close to him. A frisson of fear . . . he drank, slapped down the glass and asked for it to be refilled.

Still no voices around him, only the football commentary and the music at the back of the bar: he saw there, lit, a photograph of the lost *Kursk*, a vase of faded plastic flowers beneath it. He needed to drink – fuck them, fuck them all – and leaned on the bar.

Delta Alpha Sierra, the ninth hour

The texts told Gaz that within two hours the Hereford team would do a two-vehicle pick-up, that it would take a twenty-minute hike across the plain and that Arnie and Sam would be at the same coordinates. Not to leave it until the tight end of the schedule, but to be there with slack . . . Their final message indicated he should leave as soon as there was major distraction down at the village.

But they weren't here, those who tapped out the texts. Back in an Afghan deployment, a guy out alone, on the edge of an irrigation ditch and looking at a path that skirted a ripening maize field. Seeing in his image intensifier night-sight the white shadow of a man advancing on the path towards him, and screwing the silencer attachment to the end of his assault rifle and watching the figure looming closer. The way his position was sited, he would have to exit the ditch, crawl through a thorn barrier and then leg it away, and he'd make a noise like a buffalo on stampede, and then there was another shadow hurrying behind the first. Had to be a *mujahid* patrol checking the edges of the compound perimeter. If the guy did a positive identification then the SAS would go in, or a drone would be fired. The noise of the darkness, insects and frogs and distant dogs, was around him, and the slapping sound of approaching sandals. The front shadow had stopped, then had turned to wave the second figure forward. Had seemed the way that a mission finished and a trip through Wootton Bassett beckoned. They had come on together, the two shadows – and the guy had fired. Two shadows prone on the trail and they would have been five seconds from discovering him. Had got the hell out . . . An inquest had followed. He had killed a teenage girl and a boy who had followed her out of the compound for a kiss and cuddle, and the talk had been of a court martial and a murder trial. Had been a suggestion that a guy in SRR was not above the law, was its servant. The trooper in interrogation had snapped back at his inquisitor. '. . . But you weren't there, weren't there and don't know . . .' The investigation had been stopped.

Gaz was there, and the men and women who sent the text were safe in a Forward Operating Base, behind concrete walls and perimeters of razor wire set with claymore mines. He had just replied that he would 'move when I judge it possible'. Not possible at that moment because when he crawled from his hide the goats would scatter, the dogs would bark, then snarl as they hugged her ankles. He would have said something like, 'Sorry about this, darling – and sorry I don't know your name, but I'm going to run for it and the commotion will probably be fatal for you – and sorry also for what is happening in your village . . .' And had texted that he expected to meet the pick-up point, but a bland answer would have to satisfy them. *Sorry for what is happening in your village* was worse than anything he had seen before. What had happened to the men was now visited on their mothers, wives, sisters, daughters. Women were kept inside a diminishing circle and the tips of the bayonets were pressed against their stomachs. Some were pushed hard enough to draw blood. One at a time they were dragged out of the group. Pulled clear, then led away, had their legs kicked out from under them, then shot while they knelt . . . The village had become an abattoir.

It was the intention, plain to Gaz, that no witnesses should remain alive.

They would have been fighting men, and taken casualties. Had been shot up in the night, would have thought they were deployed against vermin, creatures out of the gutters and the sewers. He watched the Russian officer. The man had a quiff of blond hair and what Gaz could see of his face reflected only the pink hue of sunshine and insufficient protective cream. If a Russian was posted here – so their briefers said – he'd likely have had a decent education. His goons followed him . . . Did he shoot, the Russian? Not always easy for Gaz, because of the strength of the rain and the force of the wind, to follow each detail of the man's hand movements, and sometimes the sound of the gunshots was close to his ears and sometimes distant. He thought the Russian had fired his handgun down into the dirt and it might have been, if he had, to blast the back off a head and kill a woman already wounded. The girl was crying hard now. Not noisily, but shaking, near choking on it. Gaz held her arm. Had no idea of any words, in any language he had, that might have edged towards an appropriate response. Said nothing. Gaz had water with him but did not use it and had not passed its container to her. Two more women shot. His grip was broken, his hand shaken clear. She was pushing herself upright.

He snatched at her. Had a hold of her clothing . . . Could take it no longer, that she would live, perhaps, and others die. She would be the only survivor of the village. The boys who had fled at the start, when the convoy had come, would have looked to save their skins. He thought that the courage she had shown had reached a burn-out point. He clung to her clothing. She wriggled and then lashed out with her foot, kicked behind her.

The force of her heel, held inside a rough strap on her sandals, shook Gaz as it caught him across the nose and lips. His eyes smarted. He clung to her. She kicked again, and then turned to force him. Could not get to his skin and eyes because of the scrim net. What would he have wanted to do? Watch it, or join them? Live or die with them? He would not let her go. If it had not been for the netting she would have had her fingers into his face, and her nails would be in his eyes. She would be free of him and would start to career down the hillside, the dogs running with her. He thought she would be dead in half a minute. He held her and the kicking was more frantic.

Gaz hit her. The sort of smack that might have calmed a child's tantrum. He released his rifle, reached out and used the palm of his hand to smack her face and his other hand held tight to her long sodden skirt . . . it ripped. Gaz saw her bare legs and cursed himself, and the moment passed, and he knew then that – better or worse – he had saved her. He let go of her and she huddled down with her dogs. Gaz knew it was not finished.

The light, miserable all day in that weather, had further deterio-rated. He watched the officer. Would never forget him.

Sure or not sure? Nearly sure or probably sure?

Gaz had had the binoculars on the face of the Russian officer for the greater part of that day. Rain had been carried on the wind through the scrim net covering the hide's entry. At times the lenses had misted, but he had seen the face, stubble covered and showing the dirt stains from the road and then from the grit kicked up by the force of the wind when he walked in the village. He had seen the officer come out of the door of the building on the Prospekt, clean and scrubbed and shaved and wearing a laundered uniform, and had known him best because of his recognition of the two guards who watched him. Was sure. Gaz thought about being on board the trawler, going up the fiord and turning out into the open sea, and the bottle appearing and all of them drinking from its neck, and likely all of them, crew and passenger, legless by the time they tied up at Kirkenes, and him on an afternoon flight out. Might get a light punch from Knacker, might get a bone-crushing hug from the woman called Fee. But had to be *certain*, not *nearly certain*. Did not want to, but had no choice, and told Timofey what he needed.

No argument, and Timofey said that since he would not slit his father's throat, he needed the means to make the old bastard coop-erative, and gave a grim smile.

"You don't talk, you never speak."

"Understood."

"There are enough fools here – behave like one, understand nothing . . . can you do that?"

"Have to look in his face – can do the rest."

The glance over him from Timofey was cursory and there was a dissatisfied hiss between his teeth, but he whipped off his anorak and thrust it at Gaz. He shrugged into it, too small but breaking the khaki and olive colour of his shirt. Natacha started the tuneless whistle, like hope had gone, and Gaz grimaced. Not much else to do . . . except that he had to be *certain* and not *nearly certain*.

They went together. He thought the kid a cocky little beggar. There were enough of them, those kids on the estates he had worked in the Province, the Creggan and the Derrybeg ... kids who could strut because they'd shed fear. The target would be killed, might be done cleanly and might be done messily, but not Gaz's problem because he was only the one who marked the guy – but had to be certain. The rain fell pitilessly on them and they crossed the street and went past the BMW and Gaz didn't turn to look at it, would have seen nothing anyway because of the tinted windows and the fog on the inside from two cigarettes, They walked to the entrance.

"You been here before?" Gaz asked him, sharp.

"No."

"Know the lay-out?"

"No."

"Anyone know you here?"

"Perhaps, perhaps not. Stay close."

Gaz followed him inside. It was like a plague had hit. Almost a full bar at the front and a few scattered in the back area but the only voice was that of the football commentator screaming because there had been a goal, but nobody had seen it. A rock band played over speakers at the back but no one danced. A girl behind the bar eyed them. Gaz would have looked like any gofer who walked beside the boy and stood and waited. Timofey spoke to her, grinned, and might once have traded with her. He was just a step behind the slouched figure in smart uniform, half astride a bar stool with a vodka shot glass in front of him. Across the bar was a heap of change. Timofey ordered. The girl bent low behind the bar and brought up two bottles. Gaz looked at the face, first in profile.

This was not a man who was stared at. To gaze at him was more than impertinence, nearer to an offence. The head swung and looked hard at Gaz who was already turning away. A kaleidoscope of memories charged in his mind. Something about the venom of his look at Gaz, and then a dismissive tilt of the head, and something changed ... The officer was reaching towards his change and pushing notes towards the girl, and pointing at Gaz. In the Pierowall hotel, on Westray, a Friday night, the query would have been: 'What can I get you, chief?' He was certain. He started towards the door, heard Timofey enjoying some banter with the girl before they left together, Timofey passing the bottles to Gaz. They went to the car, stepped into it, and the father was allowed to see what had been purchased and gurgled deep in his throat in response. They drove down the street, past the BMW, and they waited. All that remained for him was to catch up on a location, where the guy slept – where he could be found when the hitters came. Had done well, said so himself, and there was no mistake on his horizon, no chill on his neck.

Mikki and Boris in their car, working their way through a cigarette packet. Mikki had only to make a slight gesture with his finger and Boris would know the significance of what he had seen, what he shared. Not that Mikki had, that early evening, seen the young man, who walked behind the boy, little more than a youth and with the pale skin of everyone from Murmansk. The one carrying the bottles was not noticed, but the boy was. The boy was the cause of Mikki's small movement of the finger, the equivalent of a raised eyebrow: surprise, and something of relevance.

It did not need to be said between the two great cities of their country, that the boy should be of interest to them. They had seen him before. At the gate on Prospekt when they had awaited the officer. An old drunk on the pavement, muttering of a conspiracy. Pissing himself, and a disgrace, and a guard working him over with a toecap. A boy had come to collect him. A polite and well-spoken boy, who apologised, addressing the guard with respect. Here now. A shit bar in a shit quarter of the city, the same boy . . . They did not have to speak. Did not have to say that it was 'peculiar' that the boy had been at the entrance to the headquarters building, now was at this bar where their officer – no fucking idea why – chose to go to drink. Nothing said, but the matter registered – which was enough.

★   ★   ★

Ropes were fastened. The boat massaged the old tyres on the quayside. She had come in with the delicacy of a girl negotiating a rough and muddy path, had weaved between the old cargo vessels and local fishing boats.

Waiting for her were the vans for the wholesale trade of red king crabs. Warm greetings for the crew. This was a place for maritime professionals where respect ruled. The disputes of political leaders, either under the NATO umbrella or facing it, carried no weight. A crane would lift out the boxes of crabs and the ice packed around them would have ensured that they lived, after a fashion, and still had wriggle in their pincers, snap in their claws, and they would make good money. An emergency call had gone to a Norwegian-based boat to supply the crabs because of the efforts of a gang of eco-geeks on the Norwegian side of the frontier, and of allies inside the city of Murmansk. Bluster had proved inadequate and Russian fishing was suspended, curtailed for another week, and then the authorities would claim that clean-up procedures were in place to allay the pollution fears. The dock workers would not have noticed that two of the crew's eyes seemed to rake the high ground short of where the monument stood, and either side of the white walls of a famous church where the road twisted and climbed. Anxious faces, but then remembering where they were, why, and joining the banter of fishermen. All hard men, and brothers of a sort. But a secret divided them.

Out of the bar with not a backward glance.

From the front seat of the Fiat, Gaz had an eyeline on the major. He left the bar and Gaz assumed the talk would have erupted behind him. He knew of such bars in the Province where they could smell out a stranger, would have had Gaz if he had been dumb enough to go in without full back-up alongside him, and no difficulty for the man in this place because he wore uniform. He pondered it . . . thought he recognised some sort of aching and inescapable loneliness, like there was a ball chained to the man's ankle. Knew it himself. The officer had gone into a bar where he would not be welcomed and had killed all the talk, morose or cheerful, had probably swallowed a number of slugs . . . What had been different was the posture of the men waiting for him in the black BMW. At the FSB building they had at least made a play of respecting his seniority and had opened the door for him, but now did not bother to go through the motions of deference. Lavrenti Volkov opened his own door, and closed it himself . . . like a dynasty was finishing. The car pulled away.

A short journey. Might have been little more than three-quarters of a mile. The traffic had thinned. Gaz saw more men in uniform and some walked briskly and some parked their cars, but this was the only BMW with the status of a driver. The block was as ordinary as any around it. He watched. There was one parking bay and two cars were heading for it; the officer's in second place until it accelerated and squeezed ahead. The other driver could have taken a collision, and a scrape, or could accept that he missed out – and did. Gaz absorbed the scene. The girl no longer whistled but the old guy she sat astride had found his voice and gurgled protests. The boy turned sharply, caught at his father's thin hair and jerked his head, was rewarded with a squeal and then quiet. Gaz gestured with his hand, wanted Timofey to stay where he was, slipped out of the Fiat and eased himself towards another bus-stop. They said in his trade that the hardest thing was to do 'absolutely nothing'. To stand on a street corner and have no reason to be there was to invite what they knew as 'third-party notice' when a pedestrian – man or woman, old or young – was suspicious of an outsider on the patch. The bus shelter was good because he could be outside the arc of '10 to 2' vision, was on a periphery . . . 'third party', they were told, accounted for four in five show-outs.

A van arrived. Its bulk swallowed up the space in front of the building's entrance. There was lettering on the side, painted large, but in the Cyrillic that Gaz did not read. The officer had paused at the step in front of the building and would have seen the immediate chaos, and heard the horns going and the shouts of protest of those who could not move their vehicles from their parking places, those who were double parked and needed to shift shopping . . . There was an old mantra: *If you can see the target then the target can see you* but he was well back in the shelter and litter blustered in the wind round his feet. A woman smiled at him and seemed about to start a conversation but he'd looked away, and a toy dog eyed his ankle. The officer greeted the men from the driver's cab, wheeled out instructions, then the officer waved for his goons to come forward, and one of them went inside the building with three people from the lorry. Timofey was beside him.

"You want bad news, friend, or worse than bad news?"

"Tell me."

"It is a removals van. You understand? It is the van that you hire to move your possessions when you are leaving. Is that bad or worse?"

Worse than bad. Gaz stood, watched, and Timofey flaked away from him and he saw him back at the Fiat, bent low and talking urgently to his girl; saw her extricate herself from the back seat, stand and stretch and wipe her clothes. She nodded and straightened and started to walk, passing the bus-stop but not looking at him. Gaz felt a helplessness, like the world had conspired to punch him, count him out.

IO

A dull light burned over the entrance to the apartment block.

The back of the van was open. Two men made a meal of shifting what Gaz reckoned were half-filled cardboard boxes. The goons stood aside and allowed the men to wheeze, move at snail speed from the door to the van, then put down each box, sweat a bit, swear a bit, light a cigarette, chuck it away, then lift the box into the van ... and start again. A woman came out of the door and shrilled a complaint at them but they ignored her. She was elderly, with tinted hair close to her scalp and wearing too much lipstick. She jabbed her finger at the goons having had no satisfaction from the removal men. They spoke to her, and the indication was that it was none of their business. Gaz thought her the sort of old lady who could be a friend. She walked off with an arthritic limp, carrying a plastic shopping bag, hanging loosely off her arm. The woman was as good as ideal for what he needed: there was a drumbeat in his head and anxiety reared. She went past the bus-stop and along the street, avoiding the weeds and cracks in the pavement, was on the opposite side of the road to the Fiat. Gaz eased himself up from his seat in the bus shelter, seemed to look at his watch and despair of the bus he wanted ever arriving, and a couple of other hopeful passengers shrugged with him. He headed for the Fiat.

The window was wound down. He leaned forward and spoke in Timofey's ear.

He gave his command softly. Easy enough ... The woman had left the block with her shopping bag, was probably heading for a near-by store. Had not gone far because walking was clearly painful. Why she was special to Gaz was that she had, barefaced, quizzed the two men who escorted the officer. And seemed satisfied with their answers. Timofey said it would be for Natacha to do it . . . In the back of the Fiat, the old man snored healthily and Natacha had one of the two bottles purchased at the bar unopened at her feet, but she had been generous with the other, a third of which had gone down the father's throat.

He thought the business was slipping. It had seemed almost wrapped and his journey near complete and he had the documentation he would require at the port's security gate, and the trawler would have loaded its tanks and emptied its holds, and they'd have been waiting for him. Would have been as it was in Syria when the guys came back into the Forward Operating Base and did the detailed debrief for the Sixers who were regarded as too precious to step outside the compound and get mud on their shoes. He went back to the bus-stop shelter. It was always good in the debrief when the guys came back and had done well, and there might be high fives and slapped backs. But, other times . . . a surveillance screwed up and a target was lost. There were times when he had not done well, and had not done badly, but the situation hadn't played out as hoped. Nobody to be praised and nobody to be blamed. Crestfallen faces. Saw Alice's and she'd blink and mutter that it was 'no one's fault' and not believe it, and Fee would swear, and Knacker would hear it and walk away. Knacker would leave it for the girls to tidy up. Gaz would go home to the island, and would open up the bungalow and would smell the damp air, notice the grass that had needed cutting before he'd been volunteered, and he'd be back in the dark place where the black dog roamed. He would get confirmation when the elderly woman came back along the pavement, burdened with her shopping bag.

He sat in the shelter and at his feet was the detritus of fast food meals, and a couple of sodden newspapers left in the rain, till the wind had driven them into the shelter.

It was a matter of the time schedules, and what was possible and what was not . . . He would take a sense of the blame if the bad stuff was confirmed, not that it was deserved because Gaz was only the watcher and had done what was asked of him.

The door to his cabin was wide open.

Jasha knew he had both closed and locked it.

He left the headlights of the pick-up on full beam and aimed at the door. The night hours were minimal and the sun would not set but the high trees around his home darkened the clearing except for the cone of brightness from his vehicle. Normally, when he came back from a day in Murmansk, the dog would be barking for him and scratching at the door. He heard nothing but the movement of the wind in the high branches around his cabin He kept a torch in the glove compartment. Used to carry a game rifle in the vehicle for when he came back in the long dusk but had abandoned the habit because the FSB and police units might have found it in a random search and were dishonest bastards, would have demanded payment not to hold him up while the weapon was confiscated and the paperwork checked out ... It was why he detested going into the city, why he preferred to be here, at his cabin, and alone.

Maybe he did not need the torch because sufficient of the head-lights' power went through the open doorway and lit the far wall where his sink was, and the stove that was powered by bottled gas, and something of the chaos inside was visible. His jaw was set and his chin jutted. Jasha was not a man easily beaten when confronted by danger. Could be life-threatening, but would not slap him down if the safety of a friend, anyone who relied on him, was at issue. He took a deep breath, steadied himself. The dog was both a comrade and a friend, and had stayed silent. He reckoned the dog would hear the approach of the vehicle from at least 300 metres and would have worked on the door, heavy scratching. He doubted that the bear, his Zhukov, was still inside the cabin. Imagined it would have forced its way in, used its great strength, its one ferocious set of claws to prise open the door, would have gone inside and the dog would have made a token gesture of resistance and been savaged. He thought that he would find his cupboards emptied and tins holed by claws used as can openers and everything wrecked. He had loved that dog. He had been a puppy, abandoned by the military checkpoint at Titovka and Jasha had rescued it. The dog was his most valued friend, his constant companion. He would bury it that night. When he approached the door, the heavy wood planks hanging crazily, he would pause, hope to God that Zhukov would power past him if still inside. If he were in its path it would kill him . . .

He went through the broken door, entered the cabin. Shone the torch round the walls, and over the floor, across his bed, and . . . The torch beam caught the dog's eyes.

Jasha assessed, his mind a confusion of puzzles. The dog was on its sacking bed and lifted its head, faintly wagged its tail, was palpably traumatised but lived. The table was upturned and his bowl of wild berries and apples was shattered but the fruit remained. The cupboard where Jasha kept tins of food had been dragged open but the contents had not been touched. Every door was opened or broken; he searched but could not see that anything he valued had been taken. It was, Jasha thought, the calling card of a creature that simply wished to know more of him, to learn about him. Jasha understood.

He went outside, switched off the pick-up's engine, killed the headlights and let the quiet and the stillness settle around him. He supposed himself privileged because the bear, Zhukov, tolerated him, and wondered if a madness gripped him, and tears ran fuller, faster . . . And more to confuse him was what he had seen in the city – the small car, three people crammed inside it, the same three who he had seen running across rough ground, subject to military permits of entry and coming from a frontier named as an enemy of his country. Mosquitoes cavorted in his face and he did not know if the bear watched him. It would have destroyed him to give up his home, but it was not asked of him.

He yelled towards the trees and into the rain clouds, "Thank you, friend. Thank you for sparing us."

And he did not know if he was heard, but thought it likely. He nursed his confusions.

★   ★   ★

She was the amoral dealer. The troubled daughter of a man who had strangled himself with a rope. She hated a state that had tossed her into gaol. Natacha, smiling with what a priest would have described as 'an angel's sweetness', intercepted an elderly woman struggling along a pavement, weighed down with her purchases. Done with gentleness, charm and sincerity. They walked together, and she cut her stride to extend the opportunity for conversation and gave no offence, no embarrassment. The woman's answers, faced with rare kindness, flowed.

"Rude and difficult, and never a part of our community."

"Is that so? Not respectful of you?"

"No time of day for me. Military, believes that makes him a czar. No manners."

"And you have worked hard all your life."

"Of course. I was in the office of the Harbour-Master, outside in all weathers, and . . ."

"If he is so grand, so mighty, why is he in that block?"

"I heard it was an administrative error. He fought it, then tired of the complaint."

"And now he is leaving?"

"Yes, on his way. I did not know about the removal team coming, but his men say he will be gone in the morning."

She pouted, played the game well. "You'll miss him? I expect you'll be on the front step with flowers for him, and he'll have chocolates for you."

"Good riddance – not missed by me and not missed by anyone else on our staircase."

"Gone before you have started on your work for the day. I doubt someone like yourself is ever free from work."

"Just bits. Cleaning. Making my pension go further, what with the price increases, you have to work. Not that he would hear me complain. From the bastard Chekist group, a spy in his own country. Complain to him about anything, that he leaves mud on the staircase from his shoes, and he will denounce you. They are the secret police, the new power."

"They are shit. Will he go early?"

"He goes at dawn. First flight of the day. He has two men with him and they take him to the airport. They fly later, and then they are finished with him. They told me."

"Do not love him then?"

"No! They are Chekists, but juniors. They worked for his father and why his father believed he needed protection I do not know. We think that they are responsible for him, are paid even to wipe his arse . . ." She crumpled with laughter. "They carry guns, I have seen them. They despise him. He has no friends, no visitors. People from his work, they do not come. He lives like a hermit. No women come, not even whores. He may be important but he is alone."

"Not moving to a different place in Murmansk?"

"Do you listen to me? I said the first flight in the morning. He goes to Moscow, his men told me. But . . ."

"Yes?"

"Why do you ask? What is your interest?"

"No interest, just conversation."

"Do you look to denounce me? I talk too much? My husband, he said I talk too much. Do you trick me?"

"No, all I do is carry your bag, and help you. If you would rather I did not . . ."

Natacha passed the Fiat but was still short of the bus shelter. Awkwardly, she looked at her watch and her face lit with that surprise always shown when time has flown and suddenly she was late, and she put down the bag. Had done well, carrying it half the distance from the intercept to the apartment entrance, and the van was still in place. She assumed that the men talked with the guards so as to stretch out the job, make sure they had exhausted their evening shift other than the return to their depot. She saw that the elderly woman's face was now wreathed in concern, her eyes flitting nervously.

Natacha turned and walked away. She expected that the old woman was now staring at her back and was fearful, the bravado of her criticism of her neighbour now regretted . . . Too fucking late, sweetheart – and Natacha gambolled back towards the car went to tell what she had learned.

*   *   *

She did it without drama, like it was a conversation and not a description of a crisis. Gaz had come to Natacha. She was by the Fiat and gave her account in a mixture of high school teachers' English and colloquial Russian, which Timofey translated.

Natacha repeated, he assumed, the exact words of the old woman: important that he believed she kept to the script because that way the wriggle room was restricted. Not 'going in the morning' but 'going on the first flight in the morning'. Precious few hours left. Also leaving first thing in the morning would be the trawler. The agreement was that he would not communicate with it by phone, not even in the code they had as basic back-up, because to do so would alert the city authorities. The major's old crowd at FSB, the vast yellow building on Prospekt, would have a forest of aerials and dishes on high ground, there to suck in the scores of electronic messages being sent to and from the city. On the boat he was supposed to sit tight, and come into Kirkenes on the ebbing tide and they would be watching for him, waiting for him. He assumed one of the girls would have a pair of binoculars slung across her chest and when the boat rounded the outer head-land and started the run into the harbour the lenses would be up and focused, and they'd be looking for his face – then his expression – and would read it and would know. He carried a mobile. It had never been used, it held no information other than Knacker's number because he had been told it was only to be used in a matter of life and death. A plane was taking off in a few hours, first of the day, and a target would be on it. Lost. Not that it was Gaz's business to know what was planned in the aftermath of his own mission. He was the man who observed, who reported, who went in fast and came out fast, who did the job and kept it all simple, and then – as the instructor would say, or the unit sergeant – 'got the fuck clear'.

Time to make a call.

Night coming in an Arctic summer, and street lights self-activated and hardly needed, and the words bubbled in his mind. He needed to consider the words, not sound like a panicked kid.

"I need to walk, need to think, and then . . ."

Timofey, now bored, as if the light had been extinguished on the mission, said that Natacha would walk ahead of him, and he should follow her, and speak to no one. He would go back to his apartment and dump his father and get more of the drink down his throat.

Natacha pulled a face, straightened her hair, and started off down the hill. The Fiat accelerated past them. He turned once and saw the two goons by their car and saw an upper window where a ceiling bulb burned. He imagined the target with a camp bed, the echo of bare floors and perhaps a small TV as company for the evening . . . and remembered what he had seen, what was expected of him, what had been done at the village.

Delta Alpha Sierra, the tenth hour

Might not have thought it possible. Might not have reckoned, before the dawn of that day, that it was possible to watch the enactment of an atrocity and have reached a plateau of shocked horror. Not thought it possible that an accumulation of cruelty could become boring. Boring because it was repetitive, had become routine.

He held her, would not let go of her. The rapes had started . . . Some women and some of the older men had been able by weight of numbers to break clear of the corral and they ran or hobbled as fast as elderly legs would take them. . . . Some needed to be distracted from the ritual killings of kneeling men and women and children, and they could take one of the women, sometimes young, very young, and sometimes an ugly toothless old harridan.

Two of the runners Gaz could not scrape from his memory. A woman had broken out, she had long legs and could manage a decent stride within her flowing clothing, and she might have been fun for the soldiers to watch and be allowed to run a few more paces before being dropped, but the first shooter missed with three or four rounds. A militiaman with a telescopic sight on his rifle brought her down and others hurried to finish her with bayonets. He watched, felt it was owed to the woman. Watched also the scurrying movement of an older woman, who could not manage speed but went forward bent low, not running towards the perimeter line of the IRGC men, but making for the football pitch, the broken crossbar. He heard, against the patter of the rain and the bluster of the wind, a chorus of laughter from the militia boys. Gaz understood. She went to where her son was, or could have been her grandson. She found him. Just a flattened heap of clothing, dead and sodden, and she gathered him in her arms. Perhaps a dozen rifles covered her as she struggled to stand upright and still carry the boy. She had found a new strength and staggered towards the commander and the officer. She carried the body to them and Gaz reckoned the officer was starting to slink back and might have been about to manoeuvre himself behind the commander. A small woman, bearing the burden of a bloody corpse, taking it to his murderers, laying it in front of them, by their boots. But, no great gesture, no ultimate act of defiance, she was shot a few paces from the commander, died with the kid in her arms.

These were the highlight moments. Many of the killings were now functionary, and without clemency. Gaz stayed in a scrape in the ground, hidden by the girl, by her dogs, by the goats, and continued to watch.

Held her tight. If she had broken and run, he would have had the Bergen strap on his shoulder and would have set out in as quick and as crabbed a zigzag run as he was capable of. He stayed, clutching his rifle. Three women had been raped. Pinned down, surrounded by standing men, one groping at his belt and pushing others aside and disappearing from Gaz's sight. No screaming. He thought that a woman who fought would not have avoided her fate, and might just have lost some of her dignity – if any remained. Gaz was certain that the officer could have intervened, could have stood his ground and yelled at the commander that the killing should stop.

Had Gaz spoken to her, had she addressed him, had they found a common language of signs and words, had they spoken, then she might have said, 'That was my grandmother who they killed a quarter of an hour ago, and it was my aunt who was shot a half an hour ago. The next one, who they will take out is my mother. See that one on the right of the tall woman, she is our schoolteacher. The father of our imam, he is the old man that the women hold upright because it would be lacking in grace for him to sit in the mud and filth.'

Each time that a rape was finished, there would be a moment when the watchers parted or drifted back and he would see the flash of skin, of upper legs and then would come the single shot ... all done with an inevitability that had led, almost, to the boredom of witnessing a massacre.

He let go of her arm. He cocked the rifle. Left the lever on safety. Took back her arm. Gaz did not know why it was appropriate for him to make it apparent that he was arming the weapon. By now the vehicles of the Hereford mob would be near the rendezvous. They would be travelling slowly across the shifting dirt, but they would be coming. A matter of pride that the Herefords reached the meeting point if the Chinook could not get there, Arnie and Sam waiting, their lights smearing into the mist ... and he had saved her.

The officer walked purposefully around the village, his pistol in his fist, and Gaz saw when a body might have been in death spasms and was rewarded with a final shot between the eyes or into the back of the skull. He could not have given a good answer as to why he had cocked his rifle ... Time slipped and the light had faded, and the officer smoked a cigarette. The commander lit it for him, and the flash of flame brightened on his cheek where the blood was now caked in an erratic line.

The goats had started to bleat, fearful, and the dogs snarled and their teeth were bared. She did not fight him, stayed still, and he did not know what he could do for her other than remain as a witness.

His phone beeped.

Half undressed, Lavrenti checked the text. Did he want food? Was he going out again that evening? Leave for the airport at

06.00, agreed? Might have been Mikki and might have been Boris, both idiots and disrespectful. He wanted nothing, would stay in the emptied apartment, and agreed the departure time.

Another text. His father . . . What time was his flight due to land at Sheremetyevo? If possible he should accompany his father to a lunch at the past senior officers' FSB club. Had he renewed contact with the entrepreneur who needed a roof? Another fight with his father was beyond him, he had not the strength for it. He replied with the time he'd be on the ground and requested a car meet him and take him direct to the venue – and he would, *soonest*, be chasing the Jew for a further meeting.

He closed his eyes. Again the bleep . . . his mother. Two pictures included in her message. She had enjoyed a tea party with a long-standing friend who had moved back to Moscow after her husband's service had concluded in St Petersburg. The pictures were of the friend's daughters – big fucking deal – one was twenty-nine and the other was thirty-two, and both grinned at the camera, and both were on the shelf and anxious to fall off it quick, and their father was still influential in the upper tiers of FSB. He deleted the message. Lavrenti might have reflected that there was a time in his life when the best of times ahead could have been coming home in the early evening to a pretty partner and her kissing his cheek, or mouth, and him offering chocolates or flowers, and some giggling and fingers going towards belts and straps, and elastic stretched, and tongues massaging each other, and then . . . then . . . always *then* . . . and now unattainable. Might have happened before the posting to Syria, before going to the village. Would not happen now.

He flicked the light switch. The half-darkness settled round him. He turned away from the window and faced a bare wall. Against it was his rucksack with his clothes, and at the bottom of it was his service pistol. It was frowned on in FSB to take a weapon home unless the officer had a pressing need for personal protection. He did not have that, only a sense of self-preservation that competed with inescapable guilt.

*   *   *

Knacker said quietly into the phone, "Do it yourself then, my boy, just get on and do it."

The voice came back with a blur of static. "Don't understand what you are saying."

"Words of one syllable. Get it done. Cavalry can't get there, so it has to be you."

"Just not possible."

"Can't see a problem, my boy."

"Not in my field, not my role, not . . ."

"We are not in a fucking trades union, not talking restrictive practices. Needs must . . . Get it over with. I can't hang about, no opportunity for a shop stewards' sub-committee meeting. Flexible rostering, let's call it that."

"Not fair. Was sent to do a job. I've done the job. Sorry if this is not what you wanted to hear."

"You were there, you saw it, and now you're backing off. How many were zapped that day? Want me to tell you? The courage of that girl, her strength. God, I could give her a bloody table knife and she'd get it done, and how. Are you squeamish?"

"I did what I was supposed to do."

"Which was a bare minimum and did not allow for moving goalposts . . . I can't put the people in place that are recruited. Can't be done, not in the schedule. Means, dear boy, that we either have you to do the nasties, or we jack it in."

"It is not my fault – it is not what I do."

"What you do, sorry and all that – as I understand it – is sit on your arse and only get up when someone needs the bloody grass cut, or has to have some new corrugated iron nailed on to a roof. You opted out . . . I pitch up and give you the chance to walk again with some pride, face your demons. I reckoned you had the character not to look away. Gaz, I thought better of you. And that girl, that Faizeh, she'd have thought better of you. All of those poor people who clamour for revenge, call to you from the dark and the cold of a mass grave, aren't they owed something?"

He turned the screw. Not fast, but with increasing pressure, but the call was drifting and should be cut as soon as the message was delivered, rammed down the damn man's throat. A silence greeted him, and a cough, then more silence. He pitched on, charged for the conclusion. Hesitation would have been fatal – a demand for time to chew on the problem, a promise to call back. Not Knacker's way. He knew the answer he would get. A request – take a life – made without hope but from necessity. Turned the screw but . . . for once he anticipated that the famed 'Knacker's magic' was not going to pull a rabbit from this hat.

"Apologies, sir, but I cannot."

"We are rattling round, need to cut to the quick. I suppose you can push off down to the docks and get aboard your transport and sail home, and go back to your refuge, and let's hope the fairies . . . Gaz, I trusted you, and a host of people have that faith in you. Find a way, always a resourceful soldier, weren't you? Do it, take him down."

"I don't have the means, don't have a weapon."

"You were issued with one, a handgun."

"Refused it."

"Am I supposed to credit that?"

"I was offered a handgun and a magazine, and declined to take it."

"Then maybe you'd better find one, a resourceful boy like you." A screw that would barely move through another revolution, and he felt the matter was close to conclusion. The girls were behind him, listening, and knew that the recce trooper was a fish gradually submitting to the strength of the rod and the line.

"The supermarkets, if you didn't know it, are closed at this hour in Murmansk, so I doubt I'll find a handgun among the vegetables or the frozen chips."

"Very witty, Gaz, glad your idea of humour is holding up . . . So, you had better get off down to wherever it is and link up with the transport – and you can tell the guys that it didn't work out, and they can tell you what they risked for old times and old loyalties, and you can wave as you sail away and hope the sleepers have gone back to bed and not been compromised, that their involvement was for fuck-all. Let's look on the bright side: you won't have to face the girl, not confront Faizah and tell her that you couldn't manage it, and I expect she'd be gracious and understanding but she's already on a flight and gone back to where she's attempting to rebuild her life. I'm not sure that I and the team will be here to meet you on the way back, but you'll be fine, you'll find your way home. Good luck."

He cut the call. Knacker raised his eyebrows, as if inviting comment. A meeting would be convened for late the next morning, the Round Table gathering to induct a new member, Camilla Turnberry, tough as an old leather boot it was said, with a deft record in Ukraine. The kettle howled in the kitchen. Sorry not to be there because the gatherings seemed of increasing importance to him, the coming together of the eccentric thinkers. The girls would tell him what they thought over a cup of tea.

He passed the phone to Natacha. He made a gesture with his hands of snapping it in two.

They were on a small platform, overlooking the harbour, grey in the long dusk, and there was a statue near to him of a woman gazing far out towards the Barents Sea – a fisherman's wife, or a sailor's mother. Iron railings around the statue were covered with scores of cheap padlocks and Gaz knew them to be the symbol of lovers, leaving something to be a witness of permanence. He doubted if he knew the meaning of love, maybe never had, and thought that, from what he had said and what he had heard, he would not see Aggie again, tell her anything that mattered . . . thought himself cheapened. What Knacker had said squirmed in his mind. Above them, was a floodlit church: he thought it a place he would need.

She did not break the phone but opened it. She took the card from its innards. Then took her cigarette lighter from her jeans pocket – gave the card back to Gaz and let him hold it between his thumb and forefinger while she flashed the lighter. The flame ate at the card, let off foul fumes, and when it crumbled in his hand and the heat scorched his skin, he dropped it, stamped on it. She went to an overflowing rubbish bin and dipped her hand far down inside and that would be the last resting place, till the bin was cleared, for Knacker's phone. Gaz wondered what a statue counted for, a woman waiting for a man to come back from danger, whether he were included.

He said what he wanted to do, pointed to the church.

"He won't do it, Knacker," Fee said.

"Sorry to be the pooper at the party, Knacker, but I can't see it, not him," Alice said.

"He's not a Hereford boy, doesn't have that ruthless bit."

"Had a pretty high level breakdown, Knacker, went and hid."

Fee poured tea into a mug for Knacker. "Those people, the reconnaissance troops, they lie on their stomachs and watch and report, and they slip away. They're long gone when the serious stuff starts."

Alice added milk. "He'll be on the boat. I guarantee it, nothing on their local news, and him on the boat."

"Just didn't work out."

"Have to get the hitters on to a flight, send them home. God, they'll bloody grumble."

"It was a good idea, Knacker," Fee said. "Just didn't get to take off. He wasn't the man for that job, a bit too ordinary."

He would have disappointed both of them. Did not rise to what they told him, but paced the kitchen of their safe house, and jangled money in his pocket and could feel his coin of 1800 years before, and considered how it would have been for that Roman military intelligence officer who would have had *speculators* out in those empty misted wildernesses. Considered also how it would have been for the woad-painted chap, who he identified with, who would also have had covert agents prowling near the forts on the Wall and maybe farther behind the lines and beyond help. He did not rise, nor did he deny them.

Fee said, "What you always say, Knacker, if it were easy . . ."

Alice said, ". . . then everybody would be doing it. They're not, it's not easy. A fucking nightmare."

He let his fingers linger on the coin's surface. A good legacy for him. Was always tough to do the waiting time.

Gaz sat on the wall beyond the forecourt of the church. The quiet had been around him, broken only by drunks' shouts and occasional tyre screams and a distant siren. Before he had taken a place opposite the front doors of the church he had been able to look down on to the harbour far below. Arc lights lit the bulk of the aircraft carrier and he saw two destroyers of Soviet times now ready for scrap. Saw the tangle of masts and rigging and ropes and nets where the fishing fleet was docked. The boat that had brought him across the North Sea, from Unst in the Shetlands to a landfall on the Norwegian coast, was there, waiting for him.

He wrestled with his dilemma. Betty and Bobby Riley would say, 'If it's right, then you do it, son, and if it's not right, then you don't do it. Don't hold with pragmatics, and no justification in doing something because you've been told to. In your belly you know what is right and what is wrong. Can't escape from the gut feeling.' And a school teacher had said, 'You are your own man, it's not an excuse to say that you were told to do that.' And a chaplain had said, 'At a fork in the road, you make your own map. Go against your better judgements and take the wrong way and you will forever regret it.' And Aggie had said, their fingers entwined and both of them braced against a gale, while they had walked on the cliffs at Noup Head, 'What's done is done, cannot be undone, good saying and true, utterly true . . . you have to live with yourself and your actions. Think how you want to be remembered, and respect yourself.'

The words of Knacker, the man who could manipulate him, purred in his mind. They might, down at the boat, have already eased their legs over the side and on to the quay and begun to amble towards the security check at the gate, and gone outside it and started to linger in the shadows, and they would lurk out of sight except for the glow of their cigarettes and would wait for a taxi to pull up and disgorge him, or a private car to drop him off and then spin fast through a turn and drive away, or they might be waiting for the soft tread of his feet. He'd said, like it was a joke: 'Suppose I get an extra hour in the little whore-house, Murmansk's finest, and miss the sailing time, promise you'll wait for me.' Raucous laughter, from men who harked back to the comradeship of war and a bus route through grim seas, and then solemn faces below the carpets of stubble and weathered skin, and a promise of what they would do. Accepting little was possible if the schedule was not met; one had said they'd not hang about long past sailing time, not invite suspicion, had to be gone, had to . . . He thought of them, and thought of the pilot who had flown him, and the jaunty south London girl who had escorted him, and of the briefer for the fence crossing and the trouble taken there, and of the girl from the village who deserved more than was given her . . . too many to think of. Heard voices and vehicles, and the scrape of a key in the heavy lock of the church door. All wishing him to succeed. Could not tell them, stand there and yell 'It's not my fault. I did what was asked of me. Just bad luck, and I'm not to blame.' Could not shout that, but could not erase what Knacker had said, 'Do it, take him down.'

Natacha came fast towards him. She had left him to his thoughts, had stayed back, now was like a protective terrier and coming close. Her hand went into his arm. The church door was opened wide. A hearse came and bearers lifted out a simple wood coffin. A widow wore black; children stood awkwardly with her, mourners forming her escort. A priest came from inside . . . Gaz assumed that at this hour, on the edge of midnight, the coffin would stay in the church for what remained of the night, that the funeral service would be in the morning but a vigil would start now. He thought this was where he wanted to be. They went inside, Natacha's arm tucked in his. He entered a world of brightness and unreal beauty. The walls were covered in the icon pictures of that version of Faith, Christ images and those of the Virgin, all decorated in the highest quality of colour and gold leaf, and carved dark wood surrounds: a place of majesty, and of calm. The priest engaged him, a look of sympathy and support. Gaz accepted that he had gatecrashed, was a felon in the night to these people, but he used the location, as he had when outside, to assemble his thoughts . . . they were taught in the unit to think on their feet, to back their instincts. His experience, when he had been in hedgerows and ditches and in camouflaged scrapes in the ground, was that a man when isolated must make his own decisions and not bleat for company or help. Listening to the murmur of voices around him, and with Natacha holding his arm, Gaz felt the stress of the day was starting to float away. Knew what he would do, and calmness came; not what was expected of him, but what action he would take.

Gaz eased a path through the mourners, left the family and the coffin behind him. Stole a last glimpse at the magnificence of the icons and went out into the grey gloom of the night; he looked to see if the boat were still visible but could not find it and the mist was thicker and the rain had started again. Only the pallbearers were outside. A clock was striking in the distance, the chimes muffled. Too much time had passed. He turned to her . . . bloody girl thought he was going to smooch her and her face lit up with anticipation, but he put a finger across her lips.

"Something I want you to get me?"

"Get?" Wide-eyed, watching him, like it was a game.

"Get me a gun."

"What do you want? You want a howitzer? A bazooka? Even a tank? Which?"

"Just a handgun, a pistol."

She was laughing, and the pallbearers glared at her, and they'd have heard her inside. She tugged Gaz's hand, and they started to run. Still laughing, chirping, 'Just a handgun, a pistol.'

I I

"The gun, when must you have it?"

She had a good stride and Gaz was stiff in most joints and his muscles ached and his head reeled from tiredness.

"Before dawn." A glance at his watch. "In two hours or three."

"You don't run fast."

"I can run when I have to. Not more than three hours."

"Then you have to run faster."

Her laughter trilled and she quickened the pace. They went up a steep hill, past blocks of uniform apartments where lights burned and TVs shouted. Few cars passed them, fewer pedestrians. She was reaching into the hip pocket of her jeans and dragging out her phone.

"It is not just a joke, you need a gun. Because he is going in the morning and early, you need a gun . . . not to make a joke?"

"No."

"And he is FSB?"

"He is a major with FSB."

"And he is guarded, two men?"

"Yes. It has to be here before he leaves, after that he is beyond reach."

"Not very much time . . ." Again she laughed and the sound was clear, sharp, like the crackling of breaking glass ". . . and only a pistol?"

"You can do that? Find a pistol?"

"Why not? You want me to use it, or Timofey?"

"Not you and not Timofey. I am the dog and it is my fight. What I mean, the job is mine, but I need a pistol."

They had come off the street and were now into a darkened

park area and there were wide, steep steps and he realised they
had done something of a circle because the church was in front of
them . . . They had made a loop and he realised that a foot surveillance team would have been confused, even lost. She had her
phone jammed against her ear, close to her mouth, and she was
giggling as she spoke. Gaz assumed she spoke with Timofey, her
lover and her business partner. One day, if – biggest word that
Gaz knew, *if* – it worked through, *if* he was back on Westray and
then able to make the long journey south and get to Hereford and
take a taxi to the barracks gate, and *if* he were met at the security
check by one of the current instructors, *if* time was found for him,
he would speak about a girl. Tell them about a girl who understood how to use tradecraft to throw off possible foot surveillance
or vehicle surveillance, who had never been on a course, attended
a lecture, or sat an examination, for whom failure carried a penalty
of six months, or a year, in a lock-up. She had inbred suspicion, an
understanding of survival. Would tell the instructor that they
could not have drawn a better stereotype for an SRR trooper than
this girl: jailbait, fun, not complaining, a nightmare for the leader
of a team of watchers. She might have done his job, equalled him
or been better, Gaz reckoned. She clicked off her phone, buried it
back on her hip.

They were close to the severed shape of the submarine's
conning tower. Gaz reckoned she spent time here, thinking about
her father. She would have learned to hate by staring at the tower,
and knowing that authority had condemned those in the crew
who lived through the first explosion. Known the grievances of
the families whose men were abandoned in darkness, breathing
toxic fumes, oily water steadily rising, the cold sapping them, and
abandoned because if foreigners rescued them then national face
was lost. Gaz's resolve hardened.

"Where do we go?"

"We go to our home. Leave you with his father. Timofey and I
go out."

"Go out?"

"We go to get the gun. We do not have a gun ourselves. Only

gangsters have a gun, the Chechens do. Guns cost money in Murmansk. Don't have one, don't buy one, go to find one . . ."

"You can find one?"

"Of course. Come on, you are slow."

They went up a track that climbed above the conning tower and a block loomed above them. The people that Knacker worked for, the 'suits' in the huge building by the Thames – not that Gaz had ever been inside because people at his level in the pecking order did not get invitations – would have to pay big for a gun 'found' at two hours' notice, maximum three. He had stumbled but she had jerked him back to his feet. They came out of the bushes on the hillside and in front of them was a walkway of decayed concrete. Went along it, then into the dimly lit entrance of the block.

"Are you too tired for the stairs?" she mocked, giving his hand a squeeze.

"I am not."

He would have liked to have broken the grip she had on him, but did not think she would allow it. An old man came down the flight of stairs and they almost lurched into him but they avoided the collision; he looked at them and ducked his head away: would have recognised her and thought she brought a client home. Almost what he was, a client. One who would pay well for a quick-delivery firearm. They went up the five flights of stairs and he was reeling when she turned off into a high-ceilinged lobby. He thought she had made him walk up as an entertainment to her. She rapped on a door, used a code drumbeat.

They were let in and the smell hit Gaz. A few words and he was elbowed aside and they were gone, clattering down the stairwell, and her laugh was loud, and he closed the door.

"Just as it would have been," said the engineer to the skipper. "The old men, gone and at rest now, would understand what we face. We look at the clock in the wheelhouse, and the faces of our watches, and the time does not help us. They had the schedule for the Bus back to Shetland, and waiting for a hunted agent to get to the pick-up. Perhaps the snow had closed a road, or he's punctured or there was a roadblock, but he is delayed, and the sailing schedule says the crew cannot wait long for him. A little but not much. Minutes, not hours. Perhaps he comes on foot. I liked him. I am allowed to say that? Probably resourceful, but I thought him also naive, without the killer instinct. A decent man. But … but … I cannot contemplate losing the slot and waiting too long for him. I won't do it. What if we leave without him? I never asked him if he had a secondary plan to get clear, anything else that is possible. I liked him well enough to promise. Will be sorry if we leave without him."

The skipper had no answer, and together they watched the gate and the security hut beside it and the guards under the street light, brilliant and sharp, and the empty road.

He sat at the table in the kitchen of the safe house. No hobbies cluttered Knacker's waking hours, nor was he obstructed by the rigours of crosswords and brain-teasers. Books rarely amused him unless they fortified his prodigious knowledge of the workings and personalities of the Russian Federation.

Usually when he was alone and with quiet around him, except for distant night sounds from the town, and the gentle contented snores from the second bedroom, he relied on summoning up 'problems' to relax him. And relaxed well because 'problems' always came past him. The hitters topped his list. Three who would have gone over the frontier in a week's time and were now, with their facilitator, not required. It would take a charter flight to take them out, and fly them direct to a European hub … Might need deceit to get them on board, dollops of it. Might demand brazen lies because he was told all three were ready to chew carpet tacks for the chance to confront the officer in that atrocity village. Get them on a plane, and somewhere high in the distant void let them discover they were in fact down in Stockholm or Copenhagen, and in time to connect with the Amman leg, or to Beirut, and leave them to rant and shout, and stuff cash into their pockets and … It was a problem but people who mattered would be well clear, and the boy back in his island refuge.

The boy, of course, was also a problem. He did not know the detail of the sailing time for the fishing boat but worked on the principle of 'where there's a *will* there's a *way*'. He assumed the boat would delay its departure for long enough, and the boy would get himself into position, wait for his moment, confront the officer as the man lugged his case out through the front door, line up on him – club him with an angle iron, whatever was available, and leg it, use the sleepers to do the ferrying, and get to the docks and on board, head for the open sea . . . But it all seemed to Knacker that the problem might have 'potential'. *Murphy's Law* was old, tested, never seemed to come up short. It was a perverse rule, and it burdened him too often and the only safeguard that Knacker knew of when confronted with *Murphy* was simplicity. Was it dutifully simple? A man into Murmansk, a sleeper to help him, stand back-stop for him. A change of plan but a military man on the ground and one used to taking decisions for himself. A weapon, club or firearm, whatever . . . To Knacker it could not be simpler.

A simple plan and a simple man to execute it. He disliked complication, and was wary of intellect. Thought the damaged individual he had recruited on that Orkney island was 'simple' to the point of boredom, and yet . . . It was the way with the agents put over frontiers and dumped over borders and wandering, lost souls, in Smolensk or Saratov, in Novgorod or Archangel, in any of those hideous cities into which the oligarchs had not yet invested their loot, that locals would put their necks on the block to help. Useful idiots. His man, Gaz, would now be muddling through alongside the usual misfits and malcontents that seemed always to have a place on the mission expense sheet. But, Knacker was unsettled and a pencil snapped between his fingers. Before his time as a Sixer, before his birth, a politician had been respectfully asked what he feared most in life in government and had replied, 'Events, dear boy, events'. Good enough for Knacker. Could have done with more coffee, for a clearer head – and the snoring was firmer, but regular – and was about to fill the kettle. His personal phone rang softly.

His wife, Maude, from her dig site guest house. Was he all right?

"Fine, thank you."

A pause, and he wondered if a crisis beckoned, or whether she had drunk too much at dinner with her fellow excavators: well, actually something relevant to him, and might have seemed moderately tipsy.

"Very good, what's that?"

He was one of the *frumentarii* and they were originally collectors of the wheat stocks needed to feed the army.

"Yes, Maude. Except that we are not short of wheat where I am. Anything else?"

She continued and, rare for her, there was an edge of mischief in her voice. On the dig that day, the last, they had found part of a gravestone of such a wheat collector, and there had been considerable excitement. The wheat collectors, travelling far and wide, were the most sophisticated of Rome's intelligence gatherers.

"Pleased to hear it. Quite late here. Safe journey tomorrow."

But told there was more. Another group on the dig had found layers of ash, carbonised material, undisturbed for nineteen centuries, and the professor with them had claimed this as proof that the barbarians had broken the wall, had pulverised the defences of a fort, would have swarmed across it, would have slaughtered the legion troopers and their families, and the only survivors would have been taken north, into the dark lands, as slaves. Was that not interesting?

"Tell me, Maude."

She told him. As she explained it, all the might of Rome could be bested when the tribesmen had come, no doubt in secrecy but with detailed planning, had identified a flaw in the Wall, had attacked, had destroyed, had won.

He was cheered. He thought *Murphy's Law* a relegated negative. God, and if he had owned a pot of woad paint he might just have stripped off and daubed himself . . . He imagined the panic and anger that would have spread along the length of the Wall when it was obvious that the savages had come across, done their will, had gone home. She should not have telephoned, that was a rule of their lives, but love and respect existed between them, was not exhausted, and she had cheered him. "Thank you, Maude, grateful."

He turned the lights off, had almost a cheerful step as he went towards the room allocated him, just a single bed. They were in the main bedroom, in the double, undressed and rather sweetly in each other's arms, both snoring. He would have liked to have woken them, Fee and Alice, and told them of the wheat collector, bivouacked on Lenin Prospekt, and of the wily old beggar in his paint and skins, operating from a safe house across the fence, who had just won the day, or the night. He tiptoed past their door.

It was the hallmark of Knacker that he never doubted his instinct, never stopped in mid-stride to tell himself, 'too damned dangerous, too much of a risk, better to back off'. Had not, would not. Had he ever questioned those instincts, subjected them to forensic examination, then the chances were high he would have ended up as a snapped reed. Would sleep well, and on the dressing-table was the silver coin that Fee had cleaned, quite bright and easy to see.

The sofa was free.

Gaz sat on it. He thought the old man, Timofey's father, had rolled off and was now asleep on the floor, half-wrapped in a threadbare blanket. Only one side light was switched on, a bare bulb. It was a dismal room and no effort had been made to smarten or tidy it. It had no mementoes, no little pieces of china or pottery that might have reminded the occupants of 'good times', however far back. The father puffed and gurgled and spittle ringed his mouth. He held an empty bottle by the neck and the second bottle, unopened, stood on a kitchen unit at the far side of the room, opposite the door. He imagined Aggie here ... she would have come in and sworn, then would have looked for a bucket and cloths and any sort of disinfectant, would have rolled up her sleeves and hitched up her skirt, would have started at the sink and the cooker and steadily worked her way through the whole apartment. Then, while it dried she would have carted the furniture – what there was of it – out of the door and on to the landing. Would have tipped it item by item down the flights of stairs, then out into the open, would have piled it high. She would, Gaz knew it, if allowed, have turned his own home into a place for both of them, not just a place to sleep, with clothes heaped on the floor and a sink full of unwashed plates. Aggie had tried to put pride back into his life. She would not have known why, only that he was short of it. The smell around him was of dirt, sweat and staleness, and the place was quiet and the father stayed asleep and the kids had not returned.

Where would they go in Murmansk, in the small hours of the night, to find a pistol? No idea . . . Would not be bought from the deeper underworld because they would have asked him for cash. Exhaustion crawled over him. Needed to eat but would not have dared open the small fridge and look inside . . . Nodded, leaden-eyed, and sank back into the uneven surface of the sofa cushions, and slept. He slept well. Needed to. A creed of the unit was always to grab sleep where it was available.

He felt oddly warm. And drifted . . . and heard feet slithering on the floor, and the bottle toppling, and the crack of a breaking plastic seal, and heard the hiss of the man relieving himself in the sink. Felt a hand on his shoulder and the bottle touch his face, and Gaz thought that it was not his place to fight, to protest. He was the interloper. He slid off the sofa.

His place was taken. The springs of the sofa sang as the man slumped. The bottle might have the top back on or it might not. And the alcohol might have drained into the fabric and padding of the furniture or it might not. Not Gaz's business . . . The man had an account in a Channel Islands bank, one of those discreet buildings back from the esplanade lining the harbour. The account accumulated cash, could have bought a decent flat down near the Prospekt, or a fine cabin across the frontier in Norway. He would never get to draw from it. Best he could hope for was an annual printout that displayed for a half-minute on a mobile phone screen, then vanished. The man had no international passport and his opportunity to get to the Channel Islands was minimal . . . This was the man who had gone to the headquarters building on the Prospekt. To what purpose? To play the tout and the snitch, and to denounce . . . He forgot about sleep.

On the hard floor, Gaz reflected. The man was not his enemy. He had no right to blame him, let alone harm him. A degree of guilt seeped into him. And uncertainties. He could remember so clearly how it had been in the village below him, and he wondered about his duty, how far it should take him . . . Very soon, he expected to see the officer and to have a pistol in his hand, loaded . . .

Delta Alpha Sierra, the eleventh hour

The light always went fast there.

Dusk becoming night, hastened along by the low rain clouds that the wind blustered. The short horizon darkened. In front of Gaz, homes still burned, shadows flickered, but the smoke aggravated what light was left. He knew how it would be . . .

. . . would have sent two vehicles, rough terrain types and armour-plated at the sides, big beasts. A driver and a navigator in the front, though he would have a general purpose machine-gun on a mounting in front of him, and behind them would be the guy with ready access, down by his feet, to an anti-tank missile and the .50 calibre weapon. They would be in darkness and, night-vision goggles to guide them, and would have to reach a set of given coordinates. Would not want to hang around and would not know if they were within seconds of being blasted and an ambush sprung. Would be hoping, fervently and with expletives to amplify it, that the boys would be there, waiting and ready to go. Once they had the boys, they'd burn rubber. The name of the game was *exfiltration*, never straightforward, depending on cool heads, and nerve. Worst was having to hang about because one of the guys was late to the pick-up: when he showed, a late guy would get a bollocking, and singing an aria of excuses didn't gain sympathy. How it would be . . .

. . . Arnie and Sam would emerge from separate scrapes in the ground and hustle forward. No ceremony, nothing said, slinging in the Bergens, grabbing a heave-up. A message goes out over the radio between the two vehicles, pick-up completed. And they know that a force of 100+ IRGC is two miles down the road, and it was what instructors called 'the fog of war'. Another of the instructors' favourites was 'no plan survives contact with the enemy', and this one, Gaz's instincts, would not. No one actually saying that Bravo Charlie vehicle had two on board, not three, and no one drawing attention as the engines revved again that Bravo Foxtrot vehicle had not three, not two, had none on board, and both of them – Bravo Charlie and Bravo Foxtrot wanting to be out of a bad place, and both cutting corners and they'd be gone. Somewhere, across a big void of dirt, they'd likely find a deserted concrete box of a building, and pull up and think of a brew, and find they were one short: 'Where's that arsehole, that Gaz? Where the fuck is he? Thought you had him . . . We thought you did . . . Holy shit.' Thinking about it and attempting to shut out the sights and sounds from down by the village, and seeing the officer striding right, left, any way, a man who has unfinished business to achieve.

He held the girl's arm. The agony for Gaz was that he held her to save her life, and had not factored whether it was a life that wanted saving.

The first time she had spoken. "That is my sister."

Gaz took his hand off the rifle. Her first words.

Said it again, "That is my sister."

The dogs moaned in unison beside her and the goats were close and some of them nuzzled against her head. She spoke as if the outrage and anger had drained from her. He could remember the mischief of the days when she had come close and brought the goats and her dogs, and pretended that she did not know he was there, except for the fun in her eyes. And all that day, all the hours since the convoy had powered up the road, she had maintained the stoic silence: and he had too.

Said it again and without passion. "That is my sister."

What to do, Gaz? Nothing to do. Imagined telling the debriefer at the Forward Operating Base – in the event he made it out – there was a nice girl, quite pretty, who used to come and sit near him, and he knew her goats and dogs. No talk until the village was occupied by a company-sized unit of Islamic Revolutionary Guard Corps militia, and there was a Russian officer there. Tell them that she had finally broken her silence and had said that next in line for martyrdom, after the rape was concluded, would be her sister. First puzzlement, then irritation. 'What the fuck has that to do with you, Gaz?' He clung to her. He was uncertain whether, at any moment, she would bolt. Scream to raise the dead and charge at them.

Felt a weight of shame. Could, or should, have looked away.

But he watched and the stillness of the girl in front of him, not struggling to break his hold, fazed him. Down in the village, a half-clothed girl was dragged by her hair across the football pitch and past the broken crossbar and off towards the gully. She could not have walked tall and proud, but had to scramble, because her hair was held. Three more followed her and before they slipped from view, up the gully and behind the big rocks of the water course, Gaz saw that the officer followed. One of the men trailing the girl had already started unbuckling his belt, and stumbled and tripped and needed to be held up, and there was raucous laughter among his group. The officer walked steadily after them, did not touch his waist, ignored the rain on his shoulders. The goons stayed back, like it was not their business to interfere. The girl did not scream, nor her sister as Gaz held her. He waited. Gaz hoped that the girl could not see beyond the football pitch as the light faded. He had the binoculars, he saw. He thought the goats would soon break because they would have been used to returning to their corral when evening came and the dogs gave them no indication of what they should do. When the goats broke ranks then she would be exposed on the hillside. Nothing he could do. He heard two shots.

She did not have to say, 'That is my sister.'

He tried to sleep, but three more texts arrived.

His mother. Normally, at that hour, she would have been asleep. Had Lavrenti received her text with the photograph of her friend's daughters? He deleted it. Twenty minutes later, the message was repeated – again deleted. And after fifteen minutes, the suggestion that he was out on the town, in Murmansk, with senior officers from the FSB being feted on his last night there, but when he reached his apartment, could he please respond – deleted.

Sleep avoided him, like he had some plague, shunned him. He was no longer restless but lay still and stared at the ceiling, watching a spider progressing across the surface. He wondered where the bastard hid himself away in winter: he had done two in Murmansk, had survived, had worked with a restless energy, had chased environmentalists out of town and then had moved on and been involved in the risks of foreign agents infiltrating the ranks of the Northern Fleet crews and support staff. The reward was that the bastards had created sufficient drama for the fishing fleet to be temporarily confined to harbour while a cosmetic clean-up was done ... Had he been another month in Murmansk the bastard environmental teams would have been in the cells, facing years of detention – no longer his concern. No longer his worry if hostile spies were attracted to the fleet. Also, not his worry, lying on his back on the camp bed, whether his mother entertained a friend who had brought two daughters for inspection. His mother would not have understood. His father might have understood but would not have admitted that such events had ever taken place when he had charge of a unit. No serving officer in FSB, unless they had been posted to Syria, sent to liaise with Iranian savages, would have understood. Not often, now more than six month ago, he had spoken about it to the four walls and the ceiling of his bedroom. Now he hectored the spider.

"If you had not been there you would not know how it was. You had to have been there. The enemy were vermin. As bad as Afghanistan, and the *mujahidin*, or worse. Not just the terrorists, but any people in any village. Not grateful for what we did. Treacherous. Smile at your face, put a knife into your back. What happened that day should have been done months before. Not just there but any village where they hid enemies of our mission. And less trouble came afterwards because the word spread. Other villages refused to harbour terrorists or the hostile elements of the Americans and the British. The whole fucking place, all of that country, should be given up to our missile forces and used as a range. We owe them nothing. We never received thanks. Nothing was done that day for which I have to feel shame. Yes, we inflicted harsh punishment on them, but that village was a nest of snakes. Not just men, young men, the whole population of the village supported those who came and attacked our bivouac camp. They did not come afterwards. We did only what had to be done. I carry no blame."

He said it out loud, and while he had spoken – lying on his back, in the darkness and staring at the ceiling – the spider had moved on and was steadily approaching a crack in the plaster where, perhaps, it had made a home . . . a better fucking home than he, Major Lavrenti Volkov, had. Of course, he carried no blame, need not accept an iota of shame. But he could not sleep.

They were two old military men.

Could once have been in a *Spetsnaz* unit, or in a KGB outfit, or with a paratroops, or just the bloody miserable mechanised infantry. Mikki and Boris did that night what any guys did when the end of a mission was called. Went out to find a bar. Not a smart place, not one with carpets on the floor and padded upholstery: they went to look for a drinking hole where the floor was scraped and stained planks, with crude furniture, and where they were not known. Could do it because their charge – the major – was in his apartment and would be lying on the camp bed, alone, and they had no need to hang around and wait on his whim.

The bar was for veterans. Combat pictures on the walls and a ferocious gang of guys against the bar, and the music was the anthems of marching soldiers, and the place glorified the past. Both men would have cursed that they had only found this glory-pit at the end of the posting to Murmansk: it did beers and spirits and the prices were good and the big guys who served were fast with replacements. They drank well, kept pace with each other and with those around them, and the bar would have been used to welcoming strangers who seemed to fit whatever mould it was that veterans were washed out of. Pasty complexions, little tyres for stomach lines, and an ability to mix, to slot in. A drunk, more taken than they had yet lowered into their throats, quizzed them: what was their business in this crap place?

Easy to answer: on a mission for a senior officer, and Mikki had tapped his nose to indicate confidentiality, and Boris had touched a finger to his lips. Two gestures, enough to satisfy the drunk. And one drink followed another, and bank notes flitted over the counter, and neither had eaten . . . They were not booked on the major's flight but on a later schedule. Their own apartment nearby, one shared bedroom, was already cleared and their own gear all gone on the same van as the officer's. Where to sleep? Who the fuck cared? They were Afghan veterans and here were Syria veterans, and unnecessary to speak of connections to FSB. One of the last coherent statements made by Boris was that, in the hotel they would open off the highway from Moscow to St Petersburg, it would be good to have a themed bar area for armed services memorabilia. . . .

They were free of the shit major from early morning. Good enough reason to celebrate. Would have walked out on him months before – could have been straight after the return of the aircraft ferrying them all back from Latakia a few weeks after the 'incident' at a village close to a highway, and never spoken of. Would have done if their loyalty to his father, to the brigadier general, was not paramount.

It would be far into the small hours, not long before the idiocy of a dawn on a summer morning in Murmansk, that Mikki and Boris staggered out into the fresh air, and a taxi driver fleeced them, and they slept in the BMW. How would they wake to be in time for the shit major's airport run? Well, they would, because they always woke early . . . if they didn't wake then the shit major could rouse them. Not a problem.

★   ★   ★

Timofey said where they should go. Natacha said what she would do. He drove. Up the hill from the Prospekt, on the Sofi Perovskoy, was a narrow cul-de-sac down the street from the Regional Science Library, and at the far end was the best hamburger outlet in all of Murmansk.

All cooked on site, nothing brought in. All done by a heavily built proprieter who did the shift from mid evening into the small hours, and who had gained a reputation for quality. Good meat, the best onion slices and powerful chillis, and sauce if wanted, and at a decent price. The van 'borrowed' power from the local government building. No tax paid, and no civic permission required, because the business was near enough to the police station and close enough to the headquarters of FSB to ensure their patronage. Hardly a night went by, unless there was driving snow at blizzard proportions or the summer's occasional torrential rain, when men and women doing late shifts would not slip away from desks and screens and vacate the custody suites, and turn up at the counter and place an order. The owner, who doubled as chef and wore an outsize white apron, would then cook the order, wrap it, and charge below-list prices for those in uniform or who wore an ID card hanging on a lanyard from their necks. It was a place of confidences between agencies, and of gossip, and a location where deals were done and favours earned. Always there were queues of men and women. The business had its own 'roof' in place, paid the necessary dues and was free of the attention of predator gangs.

Natacha and Timofey had found it and realised that, late into the night and early into the morning, kids gathered here, and were happy to take away a wrap for smoking once they had eaten. They had done good trade. A decent slice of business was available in the shadows beyond the light from the van. Then, change. The new FSB headquarters had been sufficient to drive away the kids. In most weathers, Timofey and Natacha had learned, the FSB people would walk from the back entrance of their building and come with an order: often five portions or even ten, then scurry back. Police used to draw up in their patrol cars at the top of the road and one would go for the order and the other would stay in the car, the radio playing light music, read a magazine or do word puzzles. Other police would come from the central block where they worked. It would be those in the patrol cars that the boy and the girl would target.

"Where will he shoot the officer?" Timofey asked.

"He did not say," Natacha answered.

"If we do this and he shoots and a major in FSB is dead on the pavement and we are linked with the gun, then . . ."

"Then a wall of shit falls on us. I know."

"Did he say they would pay big, extra?"

"Didn't."

"You have been with him – you trust him?"

Natacha's laugh was soft, not a snigger or sneer. "An innocent, troubled. I don't know how he will walk to his target, look into his face. Contact with the eyes, give the target a moment of terror, then shoot. Don't know. But he asked for the gun."

They passed the cul-de-sac and she saw a short queue, and a flash of light as a cigarette was lit.

"It will be good to watch," and the laughter hooted. She had no fear of the involvement and could have talked of the nights in the communal cells, the brutality of the uniforms, and the system . . . Same uniforms, same system, that had left the boys on the submarine to die in darkness, abandoned . . . She lowered the window, spat through it, then flexed her hands, made her fingers supple. Nothing more to be said, and time running. The lights of a patrol car blinded him momentarily, then it parked in the street and the headlights were killed. One cop out and the other staying in, predictable. One cop walking into the cul-de-sac to join the queue and order, and the other content with Elton John.

He edged closer to the mouth of the cul-de-sac, and switched off the lights. He would not smoke in the car and show the glow of a cigarette, and he would duck his head low and keep it in shadow and the street lights were weak. She reached in the back of the Fiat, and pulled a plastic bag from the flap behind her seat, took it on her lap and dragged the tangled mess from it, and swore, and tried to make sense of the wig. Her blonde hair became chestnut and she reached into the shallow glove slot in front of her knees and found the spectacle case. Clear glass, heavy tortoiseshell frames, once used by a theatre group, and thrown out ... She used the forward mirror to check the positioning of the wig, and put on the spectacles and contorted herself so that she could wriggle out of her light poplin coat and reverse it.

She stepped out of the car, and fingered the buttons of her blouse, loosening the top two and pulling the material a little apart, and swung her hips, and did her walk, and went to the patrol car. Behind her, Timofey would wait, his fingers hovering close to the ignition key. He knew what she would do, and neither dissuaded her nor encouraged her: it was their partnership. It would not take long; she might have five minutes or as much as seven or eight. She approached the patrol car, came from behind, and her foot-steps would have been enough to alert the man who would have been soothed by his music, looking forward to his meal, and he would have seen thin legs and a loose top and a flash of skin and the outline of shallow breasts and a cascade of auburn hair, and the distinctive spectacles. She could see the back of his head and the shine of his bald scalp ... It would be done fast, without nego-tiation, no time for him to consider, imagine when his partner would be back from the burger bar and what his wife, likely fat as a barn, would say if she knew. Just a little moment of shock and awe, and wonder. She had not done it before, but had imagined it. Did not seem a problem to her, nor a problem to Timofey who slept with her.

His window was wound down. She reached it, leaned on the frame.

He would have seen her face. No lipstick, no scent, no jewellery; she would have appeared little more than a child, with big academic glasses on her nose. He would have seen the grin, and might have read the offer. She moved fast. Leaning in and showing her cleavage, and the old beggar half jumping from his seat, but restrained by his seat belt. She unfastened it. Natacha reached down, manipulated him. Looked into his face and grinned. He started to pant, might have yelled, might have grappled for his radio microphone and pressed the switch to transmit, might have shouted for his partner, or might simply have thought himself the luckiest bastard in that precinct of Murmansk. All the time keeping her head only a few centimetres from his eyes and his mouth, and only reaching up to remove the spectacles and pocket them, then returning her hand to find the second belt, his own, and feeling him and chuckling. No time to waste.

One hand inside his trousers, and the bastard gasped: would have been her luck if he had seized up, had a coronary. A gasp and a groan, and that was for one hand, and feeling him, and the bastard wriggling and making strange noises like he was fitting. The most important factor in the procedure was that the Murmansk police, who thought themselves the finest in the whole of the Federation's territory, armed their firearms when they left the police stations, went out on patrol. Had a magazine loaded, standard practice. She knew it, and Timofey knew it. She had a hold of the cop and this was the start of the bit, not for long, perhaps two minutes, where her hand should be warm, soft, and caring, and the cop snorted, a bull heading for the abattoir help-less and noisy. He made so much noise that she was fearful of waking half the street. Her eyes never left his. One hand doing the necessary, the other gently moving on him. The 'necessary' was to locate the pistol's handle, and find the clip that held the holster strap in place. He was gone to the world, and Natacha found the pistol.

Her hand closed on it, let the other one squeeze, and slid it past his belly and wormed it down and into her waist, and she thought the bastard was about to spill on her, and used her two hands quickly. She worked the seat belt inside the fastening of his trouser belt, and was satisfied. A little master stroke. Both hands free, a last look into the popping eyes, and she pouted a kiss, was gone.

Natacha was fast, it was only pure shit luck that a cop had caught her the last time. Ran well, 100 metres to cover. Behind her came a belated and furious eruption of anger, like a man woken from a dream into the cool of the night with a mess on his stomach, his flies open and the holster at his belt empty. Bellowed and would have tried to spring up from his seat and fling open the door and chase the bitch, the whore . . . but could not until he had groped in the darkness and undone his trouser belt fast and freed the seat belt.

She was into the car. It pulled away.

Timofey asked, "You good?"

Natacha answered, "Yes, good. It's a Makarov he'll be getting. Yes, I'm fine."

They went away into the night, and fast, and no sirens chased them.

He was woken by the their excited laughter outside the door, trouble getting the key in the lock. And Gaz had that moment when he did not know where he was, and why he was not in a bed. He was sitting upright, and light spilled in from the hall.

He was on the floor. The old man owned the sofa, still snored and wheezed. They came inside and the light was extinguished. He'd had a moment to see the elation on the girl's face, and the look on the boy's that was not triumphant but confident. Timofey had been closing the door when she was reaching into her trouser's waist, and pulled out the pistol and her blouse rode up and must have caught on the foresight. He reached out, an automatic reaction for any military guy, and she passed it to him and her finger was too damned close to the trigger. The boy watched him: he reckoned Natacha looked for plaudits but would not get them, not yet.

Other than on the Unst ranges Gaz had not had a firearm in his hand since the day at the village . . . not when they had shifted him out and 'his feet hadn't touched the ground' which was the hackneyed quote for the speed of their accomplishment. Colleagues, had queued to say what a star was Gaz, how competent and how level-headed. Not had one since he had been shifted on by an obliging magistrate. A few farmers had shotguns on Westray, but he had no need for one and no wish for the contamination of one. It nestled in his hand. Because of where he had been, in Helmand and in that sector of Syria, he knew it as a Makarov PM, an optimistic firing range of fifty-five yards, based on the German Walther PPK – none of which she needed to know – and an eight-round magazine . . . and there was one in place and he made it safe. Detached the magazine, discharged the bullet in the breech, aimed it up at the ceiling and cleared it, was satisfied. The old man behind him had woken, stared at the weapon with saucer eyes, then seemed to crumple as if a nightmare had captured him. Gaz had asked for a weapon, had given a tight timeline, and it had been delivered and the schedule was kept to. They deserved congratulation and he was now ready to give it.

"This is brilliant, really good. It is what I needed and I am grateful."

Instructors at the Hereford place said that a Makarov PM, old as the hills, was as good as anything on the market, another fine design coming off the Izhevsk production line. She pirouetted, he smiled sardonically, as if it were good to be praised but not necessary.

Gaz said, "Not my business and you don't need to answer me: how did you get it?"

She grinned, chuckled. "A cop gave it me."

"What did you have to do to make him so generous?"

Timofey said, "You should not ask, don't need to know . . . You have the gun."

He had started to strip it, used a handkerchief to clean the parts, and then would empty the magazine and reload it, and he reckoned the kids were gold dust, and they'd warrant hefty remuneration, nothing niggardly. Better by far than kids with the passion of ideology . . .

Natacha said, "So, when do we go to kill your officer? I think a quarter of an hour, and then you will be ready, ready to shoot him?"

Gaz did not give her an answer but worked to sanitise the parts, to be certain the weapon would be effective, not jam. It felt good in his hand, and familiar, and there was no backing out.

12

An early morning move out, same as so many in an old life.

Timofey said that what he'd already drunk and the front door locked from the outside would keep his father quiet, collapsed on the sofa. Natacha gazed at Gaz, seemed fascinated by the weapon, had watched without blinking, as he had stripped, cleaned and reassembled the working parts, then emptied the magazine and wiped all the filth and fluff off the bullets' casings. He doubted that he needed to know how a girl with pretty blonde hair and a smile to win hearts, and the culture of the gutter, and with unfastened buttons on her blouse, had lured a cop into handing over his service pistol. Assumed it done with the neatness of a railway station pickpocket, and with fingers on the move. How would the cop report that a bit of a kid – with that smile and the depth of those eyes – had conned, fooled him bad . . . almost felt sorry for him. Past five in the morning. Enough time wasted.

"How close do you have to be? To kill, how near?"

"Not exact, play things by ear. Our expression. Never box yourself into a pre-paid decision. Go with the flow."

As poor an answer as Gaz could have offered, and he short changed her, and knew it, but it would suffice. He asked much of them, and they risked all for him – and for the cash promise – and could go to gaol for most of their natural lives. But they were not his friends, not a part of any unit he had been with. Had he been now in a Forward Operating Base, as dawn came up over the maize and poppy fields, or over the dirt expanses of central Syria, he would have been alongside Arnie and Sam and the others. All good at their jobs, knowing their mission, and each prepared to watch the others' backs. Would have been heading off into the

faintest grey light and trudging to the helicopter pad where the
Chinook's engines were warming. None of that was now in Gaz's
life, just a memory.

They left Timofey's father on the sofa. Gaz was trained to
notice little moments of interaction, was as good at that as scruti-
nising terrain and covert ground. What he saw was the motion of
Timofey's hand across his father's forehead, and the alcohol had
brought a type of peace to the old man's face. Just a touch of the
hand and he remembered a remark about not slitting his father's
throat even though the old guy had been prepared to denounce
their enterprise – and was probably scared half out of his wits, and
with cause. It was a good moment, but not sentimental. Gaz reckoned the kids were as competent as he might have hoped for, or
better. The Makarov was at his waist, and her eyes never left it and
they'd regained their mischief. He did not confide the plan dove-
tailing in his mind because to have done so would encourage
debate, then counter proposals. Kept quiet: Gaz was good at that.

Timofey had a key on a chain to his belt and locked the door
behind them. Gaz had the pistol in his hand. Armed it, checked
the safety, heard the clatter of metal parts scraping together . . .
would like to have fired it first, been somewhere he could gauge
the accuracy of the sights and the strength of the kickback, and
the squeeze required on the trigger.

They went down the stairs. Timofey led and Gaz followed, the
girl staying close as if he was now special, beyond the reaches of
her experience. Little nuggets of information had filtered to him,
and were absorbed. She was joined at the hip to the *Kursk* disaster;
he was the distant product of a sailor's tumble in the stress of
wartime with a local girl, and the boys on the fishing boat were
running down on the time they could linger here. All were bound
by loyalties to men long dead. He supposed that old faiths were
the currency by which Knacker could prosper.

Timofey said he would drive, and Natacha climbed into the
back seat. They would be told when they needed to know. He took
a pair of pizza boxes off the floor in front of the seat allocated him,
and a fag packet and chocolate wrappers and took them to a full

rubbish bin and dumped them. If they had asked him why he did housekeeping for the Fiat, he would not have answered.

Gaz sank down on to the front passenger seat.

He reached across, and took Timofey's hand, and held it tight, then released it. Then turned and took her hand and held it for a short moment. That was his gesture. They were his army, his team, his unit. They were what he had. The engine coughed into life . . . Not for a man of Gaz's rank – corporal and discharged for medical complications – to consider whether the mission stank of old offal, could be justified, would make a difference, was even possible. Most would have said success was unachievable, but they were not the guys who lived in Forward Operating Bases – not the guys who lay on their stomachs with the piss trapped in increasing discomfort in their bladders; not the guys who spent half a day and more watching an atrocity staged in front of them as though they were fortunate to have views from the house's best seats . . . he reckoned himself one of life's small people. They came and fixed things that their 'betters' cared not to spend time on. Small people and the world seemed to need them – as Knacker needed Gaz. Would it make a difference? Decent if it did. Grimaced to himself because the small people were not that smart and not that privileged . . . smart people and privileged people wouldn't lie in a ditch beside a tinfoil package of their own excreta for three days, or more.

As they headed away from their block, he said that he would like a short stop, and for one of them to get him half a dozen plastic shopping bags. Just that, and he wanted them empty.

On the first floor of a public house on a main street on the south side of the Thames, the early team were at work on the room that the Round Table used for their monthly lunches. The management rather enjoyed the secrecy that the 'spooks' visited on them. Word had reached them that today would be a wake replacing the induction of a new member. The deceased was one of the 'old guard', a founder member of the Round Table. Benny Kowalski had had access to the best document forgers in Europe, from Vienna to Helsinki. He had crossed the Iron Curtain, had passed through electronic fences and digitalised airport checks as though they were merely inconveniences. His assets in the east had ranged from army officers, intelligence men of GRU and what had been KGB, and locked in his head, inside an elephantine memory, were archives of names and contact points. At any moment of crisis, it would have been Benny Kowalski who would sidle up to a sub-committee, speak out of the side of his mouth, say if the matter was 'real' or just pretence, speaking fluent English but with a gravelly Polish accent. He had not attended the last several meetings and it was said that cancer had finally caught up with him. There would be much nostalgia at his passing, and Tennyson's verses would be spoken with collegiate fervour. Respect would flow, and a yearning for the 'old days, good old days'. The days before the bloody kids, the analysts, moved in. The supply of alcohol required for such a wake would be a delight to the public house management. Long might they last.

Dawn came, brought a silver shine to the river, and early sunlight slipped into the suite of offices occupied by the Director-General. He'd be gone by midday. His wife had accompanied him in the car that had brought him here. She would wait in an outer office while he dealt with 'essential business', then they would leave together by a back entrance, not making a drama from a crisis . . . She had said, when he had for the third time used the word 'essential' as justification for coming back in that dawn, 'For Christ's sake, you silly old thing, the morning after you're gone the seventy-three bus will still run down the Essex Road, and next month the Test at Lords will still kick off on time. Face facts.'

Miserably, he did.

The Deputy Director-General, in an hour earlier than was his habit, was ushered to the office and they were provided with coffee and a few of the previous day's *croissants* fetched from the canteen below.

"Not sure when I'll be back."

"Not personal, but I'll work on the assumption that you're not, not coming back."

"You'll want briefings. I believe most of your effort is in finance, staff matters, and . . ."

"I'll organise them, thank you. There will be changes. Inevitable."

"Not a case of baby and bathwater. Much of our work here has been exciting, risk-taking, innovative, and effective."

"It has been – much of our work – free of justifiable scrutiny, piratical. Seems to me and others, to have been out of control. There will be changes."

"I hope not to be around to see them."

"First, right at the very top, will be the immediate closing down of the la-la-land world of these Round Table geriatrics. They'll go in the bin, with all their childish rituals. No place for them. Rather nurtured it, haven't you? I trust demolition will be easy."

"Easy to destroy, difficult to build, I used to be told."

"You'll be out of the building when I circulate the instruction. No further resources will be committed to that Round Table. They'll be reined in. If they don't like it then they can go away quietly or noisily and whine or rant, but they are finished. I expect to run a tight ship, one with ethics and accountability. I wish you well. Yes, all of us do, but time for change and the extirpation of self-congratulatory people who are not team players. Good day."

Gone, none of the *croissants* as much as nibbled, and the coffee pot still full. Impossible to have even begun to explain the addictive quality of plans such as those brought to him in the name of Knacker; the risks were intoxicating and the triumphs blessed and the failures heartbreaking . . . All madness, yet he could never refuse Knacker.

The Director-General, still holding that position by a thread, asked his PA to get Arthur Jennings on the phone.

The old woman saw them, or at least recognised the shapes of their heads.

Early on that day of the week she went to the market, always early and always the same day. The black saloon car, German, was parked close to the front entrance of the block: she always recognised a German car and sometimes – making certain she was not seen – spat against a tyre. Her father had been on the forward defence lines of Leningrad during the siege and she had been brought up to loathe all things German . . . But she did not spit that morning because the two minders were in the car.

The windows were misted because there was still a chill in the air. The forecast on the TV was for sunshine in the Arctic area. She did not know why the officer, only a major, had two lackeys who drove him, walked with him, opened doors for him. They slept, lolling against each other. She could hear their snoring.

She had never before seen the two men asleep in the car. And making a noise, she'd have said, that would wake a cadaver in a morgue. Asleep in the car and drunk. She was not a fool: few were in that district of Murmansk, where you needed to be tough and hard and self-sufficient. She remembered the girl . . . remembered her questions. She glanced at her watch, wondered what part she might have played in any event to be staged that morning, shivered, hurried her shuffling step. She had no affection for that officer, could not recall one greeting for her, one moment of consideration, but . . . She went across the dirt path and on to the pavement and crossed the street.

A small car pulled up ahead of her. She recognised the girl . . . looked away, went as fast as old legs would take her.

Delta Alpha Sierra, the twelfth hour

Gaz studied the girl's goats.

Discomfort and hunger had beaten their fear of the noise below in the village. That is where the goats should have been; it was long past the time they were usually milked and they would have been hungry because they had not foraged well.

The girl had not spoken again in her halting English nor in her own Arabic dialect, was still sitting with her knees against her chest and her arms wrapped round them, and the two dogs had now given up on the goat herd and their heads were on her ankles.

The weather was as bad as anything he had known. They had just taken the first big lightning flash. A sheet lit the village and the football pitch where the bodies still lay by the goal, and the gully where women and men and the teenagers had been taken to be killed. Lit it up like it was a technicolour movie frame. Then thunder. Crashes of noise as if artillery were concentrated on the place. The girl did not flinch. The rain came harder, and still one small group of women and children were held inside a wall of bayonet points. There had been rain and wind before, but with the lightning and thunder came torrential rain. Gaz was not supposed to intervene, was supposed to do his reconnaissance work, forge no friendships, have no obligations to those he spied on. He was huddled inside his hiding place and the rain did not reach him. The girl was drenched but seemed no longer to shiver.

He did not need to restrain her. Her dogs kept close to her, their eyes watching hers, and their ears were against their heads as if listening for further disaster. But the goats had started to break away. It started with the kids crying and the older animals no longer nudging them to be quiet, but crying themselves and stamping; the dogs ignored them and cared only to guard the girl.

Gaz watched the Russian officer. To watch him was within his remit. Watching the goats – sweet, gentle, pretty and skittish – was not part of his work, not in the way that the Russian was. The man seemed to have neither plan nor purpose, seemed to have no recognised part to play in the savagery of the day, but yet was willing to join what was being done. He had killed, had shouted instructions, had gone into the gully where the women were taken, and might have fiddled with his belt and his flies as he emerged. The rain had dulled the flames of the burning buildings and the smoke thrown up was thicker. Now the flames guttered and the smoke hung in a pall, too heavy to be sucked away by the wind. At the second or third of the lightning strikes, when the village was illuminated, the officer's face had been turned towards Gaz. As bright as if he stood in clean sunshine, every pore on his face visible, and the stubble and the dried narrow lips, and the cut along the side of his face, washed clean by the rain, only the line remaining. The officer stared around him. The Iranian commander was now busy at interrogation. Huddled drenched wretches, blindfolded, some still in their nightshirts, were dragged before him. The killing lust lingered and the guarded huddle diminished. Resistance had died and no more insults were chucked at the Iranians. Maybe all of them were now resigned to death. Gaz saw nothing in the officer's face to indicate disgust with what was happening around him. The goons followed the officer, matched each step, and held their weapons ready, were as much witnesses as was Gaz.

The intensity of the storm was spooking the goats. Some sounded a trumpet call. Some bleated. Thunder still pealing, and still occasional lightning, and the day at its close was as grey as the buildings.

A militiaman at the edge of the cordon round the village, below where Gaz hid, where the girl was with her dogs and her goats, looked up. Turned away from those he guarded and tilted his head. He would have been staring directly into the teeth of the wind that whipped across the plateau and swept down the slope. He had heard the clamour from the goats. He was a sentry, at the bottom of any military food-chain, the guy stuck out on the perimeter and who had, as yet, killed no one, had stood there as duty dictated and had been a voyeur. He shouted for his NCO, and pointed up the hill, and the noise of the beasts grew louder. Gaz thought that the militiaman could have been a country boy, perhaps taken into military service from a village far from city civilisation. Could have been a boy with little combat sense but who understood the desert and the life of remote communities. Shouted for his NCO but the wind would have wafted away his call; no one came, so he did his own thing.

The militiaman edged away from his point in the perimeter line. If he was a country boy, he would have known about goats, would have realised that where there were goats there was a herder, a teenage boy or a girl or a young woman – a witness. Would have known that the killings were not yet completed, would have realised that the buildings would be razed and that all the villagers were to be killed. Would have realised, also, that one witness was sufficient to annul the anonymity of what was being done. The militiaman started up the slope. At first he slid back on the mud and was on his hands and knees, then he climbed again and toppled and used the butt of his rifle to steady himself, then slipped and slithered on to his stomach. But he was a plucky boy and tried again – and was seen and his NCO was cupping his hands over his mouth to channel his shouting.

The militiaman stared up and would have seen the dull shadows of the goats on the move and might have heard the throaty growl of the dogs, and he hesitated . . . If he came on up then Gaz would shoot him. If he shot him, then all of Hades would break loose. If he came on and Gaz did not shoot him then the worst of times was launched. The militiaman paused. And now the officer watched.

The load of red king crabs would by now have been transferred to the wholesalers in St Petersburg and Moscow, would shortly be in the hands of the top chefs, and would, that evening, be on the plates of affluent diners in the best restaurants of those cities. There was no justifiable or legitimate reason for the Norwegian fishing boat to remain in that section of the Murmansk harbour.

They argued. The skipper, backed by his engineer, told a story of a doubtful piston in the bowels of the engine that needed more work before they could be confident of not breaking down on the journey back to Kirkenes: dangerous to be sailing alongside that reef-lined coast, having the engine fail and risk drifting on to the rocks. The Murmansk Harbour-Master's representative had bureaucracy to contend with. He would have to justify to his seniors, to the FSB, to border control, all of them, if the boat did not sail by the time its permission expired. A foreign ship was not permitted to sail past the Severomorsk naval quays or the submarine base at Polyarni at any time of its choosing.

The skipper had asked for the rest of that day, another twelve hours. Impossible. The Harbour-Master's man would have the boat towed out by tugs if it could not sail under its own power. What about six hours? The minimum of what was needed for the repair to be effected. Impossible. The office of the

Harbour-Master could supply engineers to verify and repair the offending piston, but it must leave in the slot allocated.

The piston was, of course, in rude health . . . when the engineer took over the conversation, mixing up a patois of Russian and Norwegian and technical English, the skipper gazed over the shoulders of the Harbour-Master's man, and could see the security gate, and the deck-hand who was there to welcome the hurrying 'crewman' who had so obviously overstayed his shore leave. He remembered his passenger across the North Sea from the Orkneys, had liked him . . . which was not relevant. One hour?

"If you can repair your piston in one hour, why did you ask for a half day?"

The skipper smiled. "We go in one hour and hope to get to the open sea, and *hope* it lasts long enough for us to reach Kirkenes. We appreciate your hospitality."

"You have one hour, then you leave."

Hands were shaken, business concluded. He gazed up the hill towards the monument dominating the city, and the apartment blocks, and not even the thin early sunshine could brighten the damn place, and wondered where *he* was, and what had delayed *him*, and the stress ate at the skipper. They had all assumed there would be a party that night after they left Russian territorial waters, and a bottle of Scotch was ready: might have *assumed* too much.

From his window, Lavrenti saw his car.

The windows were misted which meant that the two of them were inside and probably listening to the early morning football talk show, and smoking. They should have been waiting beside the car, finishing its valeting, the motor turning over and a door open for him. Even better if one of them had been outside his apartment door and ready to carry his bag down the stairs. What he saw did little to improve his mood, based on another night's failure to sleep. And there was their increasing disrespect. All difficult to pinpoint if he had cared to raise it with his father, but he had noted it . . . He was about to turn away when he noticed the couple.

He wore his informal uniform, suitable for an office day or one of those tedious occasions when he went to the border and talked with the Norwegian colonel about traffic delays on the E105 route across the frontier or access for the herdsmen who had to be brought from Norway to Russia to take home their reindeer when they cleared the frontier fence. He wore his medal ribbons, and his shoes were polished, although he had cleaned them himself. Breakfast, of a sort, would be served on the flight.

The couple were kissing. She had blonde hair, a strong nose, high cheekbones, and her arms were looped around the man's neck. Lavrenti could not see his face; he was kissing her hard . . . this was something that the two men, Mikki and Boris, should have prevented. Completely wrong that two strangers – he knew, by sight, everyone who lived in the block and used his staircase – behaved so blatantly. That men and women should come to his front entrance and act like teenagers on heat was disgusting . . . Time to move. He could have taken a coin from his pocket and flipped it out of the window and hoped to hear it clatter on to the BMW's roof which might have startled the bastards.

The man with the girl had no face and his clothing was non-descript. Lavrenti had passed out with high marks from the FSB's Academy college, a grand building on Michurinsky Prospekt, across the street from the Olympic Park, and he had done particularly well in a field exercise where every salient point in the appearance of a target had to be noted. It was a paper that he had passed with honours. Lavrenti grimaced, shook his head sharply as if that were the route to a clearer head. Nothing of the man who kissed the blonde girl registered with him.

For the last time, he turned his back on the apartment and hooked his rucksack on to a shoulder. The place meant less than nothing to him, except as a cell block of anxiety, known only to him, admitted to no other. He slammed the door and headed for the stairs, and would give those men grief.

Gaz heard the clatter of footsteps on the inside stairway.

Her arms were still tight around his neck. Gaz had clamped his teeth together to keep her tongue out of his mouth. She did it like it was a game, that they were lovers, not serious, just having fun. Natacha kept her eyes open and he could see the laughter dancing in them. He broke clear. He had told her what she should do in the minutes before and she had broken from the kissing to nod her head in mock seriousness, and would have thought he joked and they would laugh afterwards. Then had gone back to kissing him again and resuming their cover . . . He wrenched away from her . . . down the street was the old woman with her laden plastic bags, coming slowly towards them. The car windows were still misted up. The snoring was steady.

The pistol was out of his belt. Armed, cocked, safety on.

The apartment block door swung open, might have been kicked. The officer filled the doorway; he was scowling and breathing heavily. Gaz read him, not difficult. He was about to bawl out his minders, still fast asleep in the car . . . Gaz relied on Natacha. No time to repeat instructions, no time to gaze into her face, to convey this was 'real business', not fantasy, not pretend.

The men's eyes met. Those of Gary 'Gaz' Baldwin, corporal of the Special Reconnaissance Regiment, invalided out, and those of Lavrenti Alexander Volkov, major in the *Federal'nya sluzhba bezopasnosti* reckoned as a rising star. A few minutes before six in the morning and the apartment block towering over them not yet stirring. Gaz staring, confirming recognition. The target, about to bellow towards the car, saw the girl twisting away from a scruffily dressed man, smaller than himself, lighter and nondescript, who blocked his way and who was snaking an arm around his back then jerking something clear. Gaz saw the scar: needed nothing else, and saw the strip of medal ribbons, and had no time to wonder which was for meritorious conduct in Syria.

Gaz caught him unprepared. He used the weight of the pistol against the officer's neck, below and a little behind his left earlobe, hit hard and true, and the head flipped sideways. What the instructors said in the personal defence lectures, the unarmed combat sessions, was that the blow that jerked the neck and head sideways was the one that stunned. Gaz saw the desperate gulp of shock, eyes big and staring and the head lolling away to the right. The look that said, 'What the fuck? What was that? Who are you? . . .' and the pistol went up hard and under the officer's chin. The barrel and the foresight of the Makarov were tearing into the loose skin below his jaw. The officer might have been stunned, but he was a young man trained in combat, and comprehension would come fast . . . he would know that a pistol was under his jaw and, if fired, a bullet would explode upwards and behind the nasal channels and into the tissues of his brain.

The best chance of breaking clear was in the first seconds, while the wannabe captors were overdosing on adrenaline and stressed half out of their minds. 'Go for it then. Do it then because it will never be as good again.' Could have been that FSB did the same course. The girl was slow. She was dragging a plastic bag from her hip pocket.

Gaz hit him again. A hard slug of a blow. Should not have been necessary. It should not have been the work of an SRR ex-corporal to disable a middle-ranking officer and do it short-handed. The Hereford crowd would have done it with four, minimum; trained guys, brutal and fast and ruthless, and the target out of his mind in shock, and feet not touching the ground. The second blow stunned. Gaz snatched the bag from the girl's hand and shoved it into the officer's mouth. Had to prise the teeth apart but dug it in and heard the coughing and retching. Natacha stared at him, then remembered her instructions, what had seemed a joke, and had the second bag ready. He took it from her and pulled it down over the officer's head and his cap fell from his head. Gaz had the pistol under the officer's chin and his other hand held the officer's left arm, had it wrenched up behind his back, and was trying to run, dragging the target with him. Past the car, down the path, on to the pavement and over it, and into the road. A van came by. What would the driver do? Might just look hard at the far side of the road and see nothing and hear nothing and . . . what real people did who were not queuing to be heroes. The van went by. The officer might have been on the same level of course as offered by Gaz's people. Locked his legs. Swung with his free hand. Tried to buckle his knees.

It was the first crisis. There would be more. Gaz understood that a half measure was useless. 'Go for broke' was what he had been lectured, 'Don't show weakness' was their call. Wondered if the noise of the safety coming off, being slid across with his thumb would be sufficient for the target to realise it would finish badly if he fought back. Gaz ducked under the blow, swung blind, and had to do no more.

Natacha kicked the officer.

The pain would have spread sharp and clean in his shin, and then she kneed him. A gasping and sobbing sound gurgled through the plastic bag in the target's mouth, and his legs went slack. She had hold of his right arm, and Gaz thought the officer was trying to vomit.

Two more cars passed them, going towards the heart of Murmansk, and neither stopped. They dragged him fast and the headlights of the Fiat flashed and he could see that Timofey was out of the car and peering up the road, would have been waiting to hear the sound of double tap, would have wondered why he hadn't. Timofey had the back door of the Fiat open, the engine running, and stared in astonishment, a fag dripping off his lower lip. They passed the old woman with her bags of swedes and turnips, and she had to back away and give them a clear run of the pavement, or they would have flattened her.

They came to the Fiat. A group of kids were watching . . . the officer was pushed forward, his head cannoning into the far side of the back seat. Gaz wrenched his legs into a foetal position and grabbed two more plastic bags from the front seat. Natacha was now in the passenger seat beside Timofey. Gaz tied one of the plastic bags round the officer's ankles, knotted, and knotted again, and the second went round his wrists, at the small of his back, knotted, and knotted again. The tyres screamed, and the Fiat was heading down the road.

"Now what?" A squeal in her voice.

"Now where?" Confusion in Timofey's.

"What did he tell you?"

"Nothing."

"Why did he not shoot?"

"I don't know."

"Why is the bastard not dead?"

"Was not told, Timofey. Used like I am a servant."

"He was going to shoot. Kill, then we take him to the harbour."

"That is what I thought."

"But he did not shoot, why not?"

"Listen . . . he did not tell me. Did not tell me why he wanted the bags."

"Could he have shot him?"

"It was perfect. He was body to body with him. The man had no defence."

"Where does it put us?"

"Don't know. I know nothing. I know nothing more than you do."

"Will we be paid?"

"How can I answer, Timofey?"

"He took him well."

"Took him like a fucking cat after vermin, Timofey. Took him brilliantly. Has not spoken a word to him, not one word."

Timofey twisted, eyes off the road and looked back. "What do we do now? Where do we go?"

A quiet voice behind him. "We go to your apartment, and we organise and you do the last thing I ask of you. Then we are gone, and your part is forgotten, except for the reward paid you. I am going to take him out. End of story."

"Were you frightened to kill him?"

"No."

Timofey drove and Natacha had her hand on his thigh, and the laughter was gone from her and the mischief had fled.

The old woman, moving slowly and gasping under the weight of the swedes and turnips, saw the military cap. She put down the bags and massaged her hands to get the feeling back into the fingers, flexed her joints, cracked them, and wondered what she had seen and how what she had seen might affect her . . . But she always liked – despite a grim and grey appearance – to laugh. And did not deny herself. She picked up the cap and placed it on the bonnet of the German car. Then extracted her apartment keys from her purse. She scraped the sharper side of the main key along the door of the BMW black saloon, then kicked the driver's door as hard as frail feet and her boots would permit. She picked up her bags and was back inside the hallway with a speed that surprised her. She was on the third floor, had hurried up the stairs, and was inside her own pocket handkerchief living-room and at the window in time to see two bleary-eyed men emerge from the car, notice the cap, scratch and fidget, and wave their arms in confusion. She went to make tea . . . an arrogant bastard would have been her description of the officer who had lived two floors higher in the block. But the amusement was short-lived because the taller of the minders saw her and started toward the door.

I am going to take him out. End of story.

The man was straddling him, his neck was ruptured from the blows, he felt he was suffocating inside the plastic bag, and it had taken moments before his mind had begun to clear.

Two young people at the entrance. The girl was a decoy. The man had belted him, struck him hard. Would not have happened if the idiots supposed to watch over him had not been asleep in the car. Done with swiftness and a degree of expertise . . . His initial fight back had been a failure. The pain was still in his privates and his shins were agony where the man's weight pressed on them. He could not shift the plastic bags that gagged and blindfolded him, and bile had dribbled from the sides of his mouth, but he had not vomited. His wrists were tightly bound and his ankles, and he had heard the whisper of talk in the front as the driver threw the little car from one side of the road to the other. They went fast and several times there were choruses of horns as other vehicles were cut up or swerved aside.

Who had taken him? He did not know. At the Academy they taught a reasonable level of English to a favoured stream of recruits. He needed English if he went after foreign diplomat missions, and when he hunted out the western businessmen who came to Moscow and St Petersburg, and thought that Russia was a milch-cow to exploit. *I am going to take him out. End of story.* Not mafia. Not local environmentalists from Murmansk. Not opponents of the President's rule who had, anyway, a negative foothold this far from the principal cities. And not mistaken identity because he wore uniform and a car waited outside for him ... He had had, and scratched in his memory for evidence against the conclusion, no contact with Great Britain, with anyone British: well, other than two businessmen whom he had hustled before going to Syria, and an economist who had written hostile investment reports relating to business life in modern Russia and whose apartment he had ordered to be broken into. But ... neither businessmen nor economists would have involved themselves, or had the resources to, in a violent attack on an officer such as himself. And the whispering in the front of the car, in Russian, was of death, of him being shot dead, and the opportunity had been there and not taken.

Lavrenti could not speak. Could not demand to be freed. Could not demand an explanation: 'Do you fucking know, you peasant shit, who I am?' Could not tell them that his father was a brigadier general and his contact list spread as high as the President. Could do nothing. Was not able to make sense of what he had heard, a flat voice, and calm. *I am going to take him out. End of story.*

Going at speed and quartering the roads and no more talk, and he listened for sirens as evidence of pursuit, and was not rewarded.

Off the E105 highway from Murmansk to the frontier and then the Norwegian town of Kirkenes, and on the east side, the Russian side, of the border checks at Titovka, was a slight track. It might once have led to a natural forest of trees which had long before been felled, and it might once have reached a fortified position for artillery or machine-guns in the defence of the city from the Nazi invaders. It was now used only by Jasha, the recluse. It led to his cabin. He had no power or water, no comforts, nothing of the modern world except for the metal box under his bed where many thousands of roubles were stored. He had wealth, but nothing on which to spend it except for the basic foods that he and his dog needed, and the oil for his lamp, and tobacco for his pipe – essential in summer when the mosquitoes swarmed, and ammunition for his rifle which shot the wild creatures that he sold on those rare visits to the city. His friend was his dog. He loved his dog and its encroaching age upset him. More important now was his belief that he possessed a new neighbour. He had not been out of the hut for twenty-four hours. His neighbour had been inside the hut and had searched its contents but had taken nothing, had destroyed nothing. He could not judge what relationship, other than respect, was possible with the neighbour – with the bear that he had called Zhukov.

All through the night he had heard it. A soft and gentle moaning. A light wind in the leaves of the summer birches. A cry for help. Not a scream or a shriek of agony, not a bellowing roar of anger, but the noise of pain and almost, he thought a call for his sympathy. It was somewhere in front of his cabin but he could not see it from the window. But it was a bear, wild . . . It had moaned for him for many hours now, and the sound of it wounded Jasha. He considered what to do, if anything were possible other than to take the rifle with the heavy bullets from the shelf high on the wall.

Knacker had slipped into the 'waiting time'. Those were the hours that seemed to linger, once his immediate business was concluded. It was now a question of hanging about, tidying up any mess, getting ready for the departure which would be – as usual – at a scamper.

He had been to the airport and Fee had driven. Had watched from a distance. Alice had returned to their safe house, but had been up earlier and had spilled the bad news to their facilitator. Best to get it done early in the morning while the hitters were still half–asleep, half-cut, half-stoned from the previous night; they had been pitched from their pits, barely given time to dress, and were now up and away on the first leg of their flight home, and by the time that resentment kicked in and fury that the job they were recruited for had slid away, they'd be on the next stage of the journey, en-route for Amman: looking for a fast return to the rigours of a refugee camp ... Not for Knacker to ladle out sympathy, but he had allowed himself one mutter of 'Poor bastards, rather them than me'. They were gone, a headache culled.

By now, safe to assume, the trawler would have sailed. By now, also reasonable to imagine, a killing would have been completed. The waiting time was the collection of hours and minutes, seldom days, between something planned with care and the confirmation of its execution. He felt comfortable. He thought that a decent lunch, him hosting the girls and the Norwegian border 'guide', would be appropriate that day if a recommended place existed in Kirkenes ... and his mind drifted. Up in the wild north of his own country, Maude would now be away from the temporary quarters that the diggers occupied and would be lugging her backpack along a platform at Newcastle for her train south. She would be turning her back on a Roman collector of wheat and his adversary who topped up the woad count on his skin perhaps twice a week. Would be back in New Malden that evening and saving tales of mutual derring-do on that frontier, either side of that Wall. Knacker would offer remnants of his own mission to her, tell of a fence, a barrier, a mission and a man far from help and reliant on his own skills for survival. Bugger all had changed over the centuries. She never asked but would have assumed that it had gone to plan, as he'd expect it to, and if she asked him directly 'Win or lose, or score draw?', he would fake annoyance and his eyes would flicker and he'd murmur across the pillow something like, 'What would you expect,' and they'd laugh, briefly. Funny old life and a funny old marriage, and a strong one as long as Maude realised that she took second place to his waiting times on the Russian frontiers. An acceptable one as long as he understood he would never compete with the glories of scratching in the dirt with an old toothbrush ... He'd slip into VBX when he was back, first stop, and would have a sharp ten minutes with one of the Director's team, would brief, then slip away; would hope to see Arthur Jennings and offer up good news, then would go home to New Malden. His dirty washing would make a moderate pile beside the machine – never could work the bloody thing – then back to his Yard and new plans and new thoughts and consideration of how to hurt them, the opposition, in their offices on Lubyanka Square. He had not been there, never would be. By now, the phones would be ringing, and computerised screens flashing news-bites, and senior men demanding answers from juniors, and the air rich with obscenities – and likely they'd not even know the name of James Lionel Wickes – the Knacker man. And laughed out loud, and Fee gazed at him perplexed.

A great team. One to be proud of. They turned away from the harbour and climbed the side street to the rented house. Alice would have heard them, perhaps had nothing better to do than come out to meet them. Had abandoned the preparation of break- fast, and they might just be about to broach a bubbly bottle, and Knacker saw her face. The angel quality gone from it, a hardness replacing the usual innocent prettiness, even the freckles in decline . . . he assumed it heralded the second stage, far worse than the first, of the waiting time.

Alice said, "It's about knowing nothing. There's zilch on their radio bulletins, nothing on Radio Volna and nothing on Big Radio, the principal stations, and the locals here would know if there was a security flap, would have it monitored. If an FSB joker was taken down then it would be top of the show stuff. There's nothing. And the lift out would have sailed. Sorry, Knacker, but it is not looking great – don't know how to dress it up."

If he were punched in the stomach, Knacker would not react, would hide any pain. He walked towards the door, grimaced, went inside.

He had demanded they go back to the apartment because of his need for that rare item, quality time, an opportunity to think. Gaz straddled his prisoner and was satisfied that the lever on the pistol was back on safe, and kept the weapon barrel and foresight hard against the skin on the officer's neck. What he had seen before of Timofey's driving, Gaz would have rated him 'high': not now. The car skidded on bends and when overtaking, and the brakes went on late and the accelerator was stamped on: they careered through the city's empty streets. He had seen a woman with a buggy frozen in fear in the middle of a street, unable to go back or forward and trying to protect her child from the inevitable impact. But Timofey had woven past her. Gaz had reckoned that Natacha believed herself the hard kid, a survivor of the prison system, fortified by her contempt for the regime that had failed to save her father's fellow submariners, but she now cringed and had an arm across her face. Needed time to reflect, to consider . . . The kids did not understand him, and he doubted the officer would have been able to read him.

Gaz had been a trained man. Good at surveillance, at picking the hide needed for a covert eyeball position, decent on a shooting range . . . He would not have contemplated easing back the safety, squeezing the trigger and feeling the shudder through his whole body when the bullet was discharged and he was being spattered by blood and bone and tissue. Not his work. Which was his justification for the remark: *I am going to take him out. End of story.* And be thanked for it? A grim smile flickered at his mouth.

13

Timofey opened the door, waved them through.

The room stank. He could see where he had slept on the floor and where the old man had been, saw the heap of discarded food wrapping, and noted the grime on the windows where thin sunshine tried to penetrate. Nothing had changed in the room but it seemed to Gaz as if he had never been there before. He had had no clear idea in his head of what was possible and what was beyond the realm of what he could achieve. The old man crawled to his feet and had used the sofa arms to heave himself upright. It was for Gaz to lead. He gestured for a chair to be brought forward. Timofey watched Gaz, did not move. Nor Natacha, but she translated the instruction and the old man lifted a chair out from under the table and carried it awkwardly to the centre of the room.

The old man called the officer 'sir'. Showed respect for his rank and his uniform, demonstrated nervousness. Gaz thought the plastic blindfold had slipped enough for the officer to see the chair in front of him, and if he could see the chair then he could see the faces; perhaps good thinking of Timofey's father to address him with deference. In the briefing rooms of the Forward Operating Bases, they often talked of 'collateral'. The prospect of collateral damage should not stand in the way of achieving success in an end-game. Collateral was an acceptable risk in Helmand and in central Syria on the basis that the perpetrators would be long gone, well clear before the damage kicked in . . . worrying about collateral was for the squeamish. The officer would know the faces of those who had taken him if his blindfold had slipped. It seemed to have done . . . the officer knew in what direction he should go as Gaz manoeuvred him towards the chair.

The chair had a tubular metal frame, a hard seat, and a straight back. Was there rope in the apartment? There was not. Was there powerful adhesive tape? There was not. Were there more plastic bags? A handful were brought out from under the sink, some filled with rubbish. Gaz set the officer down in the chair. His head tracked Gaz as he crossed in front of him. Gaz lifted the officer's arms behind his back and eased them behind his spine, and with a bag smelling of rotting vegetables tied the knot, fastened his arms to the chair. He was uncertain as to the reaction of the kids if the officer lashed out with his polished shoes, caught Gaz in the head or the stomach or the groin, disabled him. Might pile in and save the day, or might back off, or might free the officer and push him out of the door and slam it, shut themselves away from the arrival of 'collateral'. Best done himself. Did it from the side and the officer would have known that Gaz's face and belly and privates were beyond kicking reach. He tied both ankles to one chair leg.

Gaz reached at the officer's face, caught at a corner of the bag used as a gag and tugged it clear. There was spitting, coughing, a near choke, and then quiet. Gaz told the kids to get the officer a glass of water. Again, work for the old man. A tap was run, glass swilled out. The father used the hem of his shirt to dry the glass. The water was brought and Gaz saw that the father's hand shook and water slopped from the glass and some spilled on the officer's trousers, and he was addressed again as *sir* and the water was held to his lips. The glass tilted, too much and too fast, more water was spilled and the father grovelled.

Timofey asked, "What now?"

"I look for time, not much."

Natacha's question. "How much time?"

"Until I am ready, that much time."

The officer could have spoken, did not. Gaz assumed that FSB went on the same courses as his own crowd. This was a situation described by the colour sergeants as 'arse pucker time' – so tight a flea wouldn't get in. He would have been taught to say nothing until he had a clear view of his captors' competence, and attempt little until he had a comprehension of their qualities: would hide behind the blindfold and would absorb . . . Would have heard the old man's grovelling acknowledgement of his rank. Would have heard the kids demand to be told the schedule. Gaz wondered if, yet, he had an inkling. He went to the window. He put the pistol under the belt in the back of his trousers.

Gaz saw the huge monument high on the hill and thought of it with the same respect he had for the memorial to the dead of two World Wars in the centre of the village where Bobby and Betty Riley had brought him up. They went there every anniversary Sunday for the eleventh hour of the eleventh day. No enmity towards their veterans, Russia's dead, and would have been ashamed of himself if he had felt hostility. Saw the length of the flight-deck of the old aircraft carrier that had limped down the North Sea and English Channel, past Gibraltar and across the Mediterranean, and he had seen Sukhoi–33 attack aircraft – NATO codename Flanker – roaming in the skies over Syria when they had taken off from the geriatric craft. Saw the church where he'd mingled with the funeral party and been shown politeness and consideration and a priest had smiled at him. Saw the back section of the cut-out conning tower . . . and glimpsed a small cloud of smoke cresting over a tangle of low masts, and knew a boat prepared to get out into the main navigation channel. Saw nothing that was not a distraction. He looked higher, away to the west.

The early sunlight fell on horizons of gradually rising hills, no tower blocks, no pylon lines, no industrial chimneys, only the expanse of tundra. He remembered how it had been when he had crossed a part of it on foot, running with the kids, and more of it when they had circled the roadblock and reached the car. Behind him, the old man gave the officer more water, whining, with a drunk's slur, his apologies. It was the only way that Gaz thought worth considering . . . and how to get a prisoner, young and fit, desperate and trussed, on to that landscape. He scratched in his brain for detail. It was a bleak view confronting him, and with no charity: there had been no charity in any of the theatres he'd worked.

He owed it, and the debt had a millstone's weight. He turned away from his view of the wilderness.

The bear, Zhukov, had come forward and now had its weight on its buttocks and lower back and half of its stomach fur was exposed and one of its front legs was raised above its throat.

Jasha had seen it emerging from its cover. He had not taken the rifle from the wall but knew how long he would need to reach it, and how long it would take to arm it, and his dog lay supine on its sacking bed and growled quietly. Jasha had lived for long enough in the cabin – with no company but that of a dog – to know all the sounds made by animals, large and small, shy and bold. He knew those indicating anger and those that meant an animal was challenged and he should back off, and those when a creature crossed boundaries and regarded him as a companion. He recognised that Zhukov made the same sound, with a chilling and dangerous intensity, as when he had had the wire around its foot and his flesh had been growing over the barbs.

Using his binoculars, the hunter located the source of the bears pain. One leg was a full fifteen centimetres shorter than the one with the long yellow claws and with the roughened dark pads that made the identifying footprint. He studied the stump and his eyes roamed slowly over the skin that had weathered and strengthened. When Zhukov moved, he employed a rolling gait, like that of a bow-legged peasant. There was little grace but his speed was undiminished. In the last days the creature had kept back from him, had stayed hidden, but had tracked him. Jasha had only seen this behaviour once before. When Zhukov had been in intense pain from the wire he had followed and stayed hidden, but had kept company with the hunter. What the binoculars found, Jasha reckoned, was a fencer's staple. He estimated it to be some five centimetres from point to arch, and almost entirely lodged in the stump. It surprised him that the bear could not put the stump in its mouth and use its teeth to extract it. The bear, Zhukov, did not know how to be free of it . . . He had come to Jasha for help.

He thought the bear weighed perhaps 350 kilos. On its hind

legs it would have stood at more than two metres. With either front leg it could break Jasha's neck with a casual blow. With one slash of the claws it could disembowel him. With its teeth, old and as darkened as those of a habitual nicotine smoker, it could bite off his head. It was a wild creature; stories of bonding and friendship were few and far, mostly lies or delusions. His aid was required. He removed his binoculars, and pondered. The dog had not moved, not even a flick of the tail.

Every few minutes, the bear uttered the short and soft cry, pathetically quiet for a creature of that size. Jasha's loneliness, self-appointed, in the wilderness was interrupted by the beast that came to him and trailed him, made demands of him. Two options faced Jasha. Living in the wilderness there were rarely opportunities to fudge an issue of importance. The same as when he had served in the treacherous beauty of Afghanistan. He either killed the enemy or he slipped away unobserved and accepted failure. Both the options were stark. He could go to the far wall of the cabin, could reach up above his dog and could lift down the old Dragunov sniper's rifle. A single cartridge, 7.62x54R, fired at point-blank range – the same bullet could kill at 800 metres – would end the life of the bear, would close a chapter of suffering. He could then go outside, and use his hunter's knife carefully to remove the bear's pelt and hang it out to dry and be cleansed while he dragged away the carcase and dismembered it for easier consumption by the foxes or even have the attention of a pair of lynx. Could sell the skin via his agent in Murmansk, and get a fair price even though a front pad was missing, and be freed of the burden of having the troubled creature tracking him, entering his home and leaving his dog traumatised . . . The second option was both terrifying to Jasha and compelling.

For an hour or more, he would busy himself inside the cabin. The dog would be fed. He would place the tin with his worldly wealth on the table beside his military identity card. He remembered the two kids running in their ridiculous clothes across the rock and bog of the tundra, and remembered the man with them who struggled to keep pace who was military from his bearing, and they came from the frontier and the barricaded border. The memory was a distraction. He would drink tea first, and dry his eyes, and the dog would have to take its chance.

He supposed it to be a matter of trust, and a time when trust and love merged. He eyed his overflowing toolbox, and put his kettle on the ring.

From a high point, Knacker surveyed a vista.

He and the Norwegian, their vehicle left at the bottom of the slope, had trudged up a rough path and the mud from earlier rain clung to his shoes, buffed that morning by Alice.

A familiar moment for Knacker. A chance to look across what seemed an endless expanse of uniformly dull ground, a scrap of the hinterland of the Russian Federation. Never tired of it. Could have learned more by taking out a subscription to a postcard company, but it still thrilled him to have that chance to gaze towards a long horizon. There was little to learn except that the terrain seemed to be difficult and slow-going: on the side of any fugitive would be the lack of roads and trails and the clumps of granite rock and the stunted forests of dwarf birch. There was one blip on the desolation in front of him ... a cluster of high-rise blocks and three industrial chimneys, grey from the smoke they poured out. The place was called Nikel. The reason for the place was the nickel-smelting ovens: seven decades before, it had been a site of ferocious combat as the advancing Germans had fought their way into the complex. Old equipment was still used. The Norwegian said the levels of pollution from sulphur dioxide were way above even Russian standards of safety. The light wind floated the smoke emissions to the south as they had for many years and there the ground had no trace of green.

Knacker said, "You are one of the cleanest and least contaminated countries in Europe and you have to exist alongside this foul mess?"

The Norwegian shrugged. "What else is possible?"

"It is immaterial to them that they poison the air, the ground, the water courses?"

"They require nickel for their armaments programmes and so they must have it, but will not pay the price of modern equipment. They do not care."

"Do they listen to you?"

"We complain, but we are ignored. And they deny ... We believe that town is inside one of the top five most poisoned locations in their country, but they say our data is 'contrived'. They will not admit to a fault, are scared to take blame. You cannot confront them with logic and argument, but you know that."

"That analysis, I do not disagree."

"You have a man there? One man?"

If Fee had been with him, or Alice, they would have expected a slight smile to break on his face, and a little shrug, and a gesture that indicated a conversation straying into such confidences was unwelcome. No smile, no shrug, no gesture. He liked his companion, believed his honesty. "That's about it."

"And you have a target?"

"We do."

"My knowledge of Russians – they are warm, they are generous, they are loyal in friendship, except for one fraternity."

"They are used to being ruled. Serfs and aristocracy. They are docile. A small minority has a grip on authority."

"And that is where your target exists, the contemporary aristocracy?"

"In the heart of it."

"An important man, with status?"

"Not with status but a part of the apparatus. On the lower rungs of the élite. He is a target because of what happened thousands of miles from here, and when he is taken down then I gain advantage, an advantage worth chasing."

"The man you sent . . . I was not able to form an opinion of him."

"Unlikely you would: calm, responsible, quiet. Probably quite dull. No intellect but that is not required of him. Ordinary."

"What do you look for when you search for such a man?"

"A sense of duty, but more than that. Dull and ordinary, yes. You point him in the right direction, tell him what is wanted, give him a shove and off he goes. That sort of man. Not complicated by moralities and ethics. A bit of obligation pushes him forward. Actually, this one rather needs me to regain lost pride, was on a downhill run till I showed up."

"Manipulated?"

"Your word, not mine. Offered an opportunity when he was on the floor, had one of those bloody syndromes. Needed his self-respect burnished."

"This 'ordinary' man had little chance to decline whatever you asked of him. I am sure there is no connection but on the police radio in Murmansk city there are reports of a police officer being assaulted and his personal firearm stolen from him. Any connection? But no report of a killing . . ."

Silence fell on them as if enough confidences, or too many, had been exchanged. Always the same, when the best laid plans were in place, the waiting. All now rested in the hands of an 'ordinary' man.

"I hope you have not forgotten, Gaz," Knacker said to himself, "what he did. I hope you have nailed him. No reports of a body because it's plastic wrapped and hidden and will not be found before you are clear of that place. You should now be sailing homewards, and I'll meet you with a glass, bubbling furiously. Of course you won't have forgotten what he did."

Delta Alpha Sierra, the thirteenth hour

Gaz had resumed his hold on her arm. Occasionally, she whimpered.

She had told him, all that she had ever said to him, that one of those taken from the huddle of women was her sister. The rain seemed to have eased. Digging had started. The charred houses had been looted for tools. Gaz watched the officer.

The activity was at the football pitch. There had been little grass there and it was flat enough and there seemed a good depth of soil. They dug with spades and shovels and pickaxes and forks. Their commander leaned against a truck, and smoked. Made no contribution. The officer was growing impatient, striding along the line of Iranian militiamen, giving his orders and waving his arms in theatrical exasperation because the pit was not being excavated as fast as he wanted. It was obvious to Gaz that the officer would have had no authority over the IRGC men, would have been there as liaison only. The goons with the officer stayed back. Twice the officer turned and seemed to yell at them, perhaps demanded they put down their own weapons and go and find themselves tools and join the digging frenzy, but was ignored. Some of the perimeter men were called down from the higher ground around the village and from its recreation area and were sent to gather the bodies of those who had been shot, had been hanged, bayoneted. Gaz counted four who were brought from inside the smouldering buildings, rigid, scorched from the fire. Some of the men held handkerchiefs over their faces as they scratched at the ground. The NCOs were blistering the men for their poor work rate, and coming behind them was the Russian, and once he aimed a kick in the direction of a trooper who had dropped his spade, and held a rag in two hands over his face.

Gaz supposed it always played out in this way. A frenzy of killing and destruction and then – before the eagles and vultures came to feast – an attempt to hide what had been done. Not that there was, in Syria, any court before which those responsible for the atrocity might be brought . . . no panel of judges who would look down into the dock and face the Iranian commander of the IRGC unit, or his Russian colleague who had killed and now helped organise the burial of the evidence. Nor would any tribunal in western Europe or in the United Nations ever get to determine the guilt of those men. But they would have needed to conceal what they had done, and their anger at being fired on by reckless teenagers many hours before would have slid into the mud, and they would have been cold, and sodden and hungry, wanting to be gone from the place. But the dead – the evidence – could not be left to lie in the slackening rain, the dying wind ruffling their garments. The scavenger birds would come in the morning, but the rats would probably have already crept close and sniffed, coming as near as they dared. The pit grew in length and in depth. Some of the bodies were dragged by their hair, some by their clothing, some by a leg. The dead had no dignity, which would not have mattered to them, but he thought the girl would feel an agony. She would have known every one of them, and her sister was among them.

Somewhere behind him, to the north-east, two vehicles protected with steel plate and heavily armed would have stopped. They would have been miles back from the village and from the pick-up. It would have started as 'You got Gaz?' and 'No, we got Arnie and we got Sam.' 'Did you not see Gaz?' 'Reckoned you had him.' 'Didn't.' 'Nor us, we don't have him.' Then there would be a volley of oaths that would be spirited away on the wind, and short seconds of contemplation and a coming together of the relief party and of Gaz's muckers, Arnie and Sam, and a realisation that they had pulled out and left behind one of their number, alone in that fuck-awful place. Arnie and Sam had had different viewpoints and had covered the road leading up from the south and would have heard shooting and would have seen the glow of fires but would only have known the extent of the atrocity from the texts that Gaz had sent. Would have realised he was grandstanding, could not exit a covert location in daylight, but it was night now, no sight of a star or anything of the moon, and it was safe to assume he'd have bugged out . . . knew they were coming, knew the rendezvous point, but had not reached it. What to do? It would have exercised them, and the messages were going back to the FOB and a spate of questioning that had no answers. Why was Gaz not with them? Who the fuck knew why?

He held the girl. Ant-like activity wriggled below him.

Gaz's error. His mistake. Was not supposed to make a mistake. Mistakes ended with someone killed. One militiaman had been on the slope, sixty or seventy paces below them, and Gaz had lost sight of and interest in him. The last flare of flames in a building must have ignited a gas cylinder, used for heating a bread oven or making hot water . . . it exploded. A sheet of flame flew high towards the cloud base, brighter than the sheets of the earlier lightning. It lit the village and the pit being filled with cadavers, and the men who dug, and the strut of the officer, and illuminated the young militiaman on the slope who was hunched down and would have hoped his own commander and his NCOs had not noted his absence from the work fatigue. The country boy who was unwilling to dig a mass grave, and who was now shown up as a part of the tableau as if it were midday. With the thunderclap of the detonation and the brightness of the light, the goats' final inhibition died. They broke and fled. Scattered to all points, bleating and screaming, and the dogs went after them.

Gaz watched the trooper on the slope. He was alert, half-kneeling. If he had been a country boy then he would have wondered where the animals had come from, who had charge of them – a herd of quality would not have been without a minder, and he listened and he stared around and above him. The cold ran on Gaz's neck, had the chill of winter ice. The officer looked up and would have seen the chaotic flight of the goats and the one militiaman on the slope.

Gaz held hard on the girl.

He started to speak to the kids, quietly, in Russian.

"Perhaps it is mistaken identity. Perhaps you have the wrong individual. I am Lavrenti Volkov. I am FSB. I do not know who you are but can guarantee that our lives have not crossed. This other man, I have no idea who he is. You have no argument with me, and I have none with you."

He controlled his voice. Tried to capture a calmness. Held his breathing steady, did not pant or stammer. Spoke slowly as if the matter was simple, just a misunderstanding.

"You can choose one or two directions. One and you will be involved in the murder of a member of state security. From such involvement there is no escape. If you were fortunate you would be 'shot while escaping' but that would only be after the most rigorous interrogation but there is also the certainty of going to a penal camp high in the Circle, a harsh regime camp. You are young and would probably endure your middle years and if you have no fortune you might enter your old age. You would never leave, and from the moment your trial process ends you would see each other never again. Don't go that way."

Most of the time he spoke, his gaze was towards the kids, simple scumbags. The filth of the gutters. But he also spoke towards the sofa and the old man, where the stench was. The pathetic creature nodded his head fervently at what Lavrenti said, and would join them in the gaol for criminal collaboration. Only rarely did he face the window and the outline of the man's back, his shoulders and his head, and the pistol now held loosely in the man's right fist, and the lever was in place for safety but it was armed. He did not understand why he was there, why he had been chosen, and was confused, but had to exercise control, and had to divide.

"The alternative is good for you. I walk from here. I take this foreign adventurer into custody. You are fifteen-minute heroes. Both of you have shown true loyalty towards the state. You can be named and applauded, you can stay anonymous, but you will be granted the extreme generosity of FSB. I imagine a large sum of money will be pushed into your laps. I promise that such action will be well rewarded. Enough for a new car, enough for a new apartment. I cannot imagine you would take the wrong turn."

Their feet would not touch the cell block floor. Beaten and already bloodied, they would be dragged to the top of the stairwell, pitched down and caught, then pushed into the cells and the doors slammed. Would shout, if they had any energy left, of promises made, and would hear only retreating feet and fading laughter.

"Why a foreign agency has come after me, I do not know. I am employed to protect the Federation from its enemies, but work inside the territory of the state. I have done nothing to hurt you, you have no justification in hurting me. I am a major in FSB, I do not beg. You should free me. Immediately. I offer you the guarantee of the state's gratitude and in return you free me, you help me take this man to an appropriate location, I suggest the one on Lenin Prospekt, and you will receive the congratulations of my superiors. What do you say?"

He thought he had done well. Reckoned the force of his argument would bend the resolution of an idiot. The man at the window never shifted, stared out, took no part in it.

The girl said, "He's going to kill you. Going to shoot you. Don't know why he has not already done it."

"Why? What have I done?" He could see that the boy slouched, shrugged, seemed indifferent, and that the girl had a tight waist and a flat chest and pretty hair and a sweet smile. Faced the foreigner and made no more pretence that the blindfold still obscured his view. In English, as it had been taught him. "And you, what have I done? I am a junior officer in FSB. How are you affected by me? I have done nothing."

The answer, as quiet as the rustle of old leaves in a gentle wind, smacked the breath from his chest. "You should recall your visit to a village . . ."

". . . You should remember, Major, your visit to the village of Deir al-Siyarqi."

He saw the officer flinch. Gaz had turned, only for a moment. He thought that his response to 'I have done nothing' devastated more than the blow to the face with the pistol butt, and more than the kneeing by the girl. Gaz had not understood what he had said, but the tone was a mixture of authority and wheedling reason. Would have been the predictable line of making a deal, getting real, being everybody's friend, and it was all a mistake. What Gaz would have expected. The girl must have answered sharply, behind the cover of her sweet face, because the confidence had drained and the argument had been louder then had spilled into English. First the officer's head went down and his chin hit his chest, then his head came up and his lips narrowed and, somewhere deep behind the slack blindfold, his eyes would have flickered.

Gaz said, "There was a village. I came because of what was done there."

Far below him, out in the harbour channel, Gaz saw the fishing boat. She made slow speed and a launch sailed alongside her. The good guys on board, kind men and decent and the sort he'd have known in the unit, would have talked and fidgeted and rustled up excuses and might have delayed the sailing for an hour or so, but had hit the buffer of bureaucracy, and they were on their way. If they lost the attention of the present escort, further up the inlet and beyond the Severomorsk submarine base, Gaz assumed they would try to use the one back-stop procedure that had been talked of. Discussing it in the below-deck cabin it had seemed fanciful, and thinking of it now it seemed ridiculous. They were good enough guys, all of them, for him to assume they would try to fulfil the procedure. It was a fine-looking craft and the water it traversed was calm and it made a useful bow wave. He thought well of the small crew, imagined they'd be gutted that he was not on board . . . remembered the words of Robbie Burns mouthed when the milking parlour pump went down, or the pin sheared on the field grass topper. *Best laid plans o' mice an' men, Gang aft a-gley.* And the men crewing a small fishing boat would have understood that. Best plans going awry. He might see them again . . . and might not. He held the pistol. He saw that the kids had made no move towards the officer, that he was still trussed securely to the chair. He had not wasted his time at the window, and did not waste it further as the boat went north up the inlet.

"It is about the village, only the village."

"Rubbish, shit talk."

"About the village."

"Not there, never heard that name."

"The village of Deir al-Siyarqi. I think you will remember the day you were there."

"Never heard of such a place. You cannot prove I was there. Show me evidence."

"I saw you there, Major Volkov. I am a witness."

"You lie . . . you could not have seen me because I was never there, have never heard of such a place. I was liaison, I stayed in a barracks. I played no part in operations, and . . ."

"A witness, Major Volkov, to an atrocity."

Like a darkness had come into the room. All eyes were on him. He struggled to break the bags that tied him to the chair, and

failed. Wriggled and contorted, and what Gaz could see of his face
was flushed where blood ran, and he tried to kick out with his feet
but all he achieved was to topple the chair so that he slid onto the
floor. No one helped him. The old man stayed back now as if realising, though not understanding the language, that the major's
claim to power had slipped away, and the kids did not move as he
thrashed against the chair. Gaz understood them both: Timofey
was boot-faced and showed no feeling and would have been
considering what he had involved himself with, and the girl had a
look of malevolence and smiled through it as though this was
entertainment, high grade.

"So, I was there. But I was the liaison. I gave no orders and had
no authority. They were savages, the Iranians. They obeyed none
of the rules of warfare. None of it was my doing. I still have night-
mares because of what I saw that day, I cannot escape them. What
tortures me the most is that I was helpless and in no position to
influence it. They were like mad dogs, the IRGC, but it was the
attack in the night on their camp which provoked their anger. I did
not plan the follow-up operation. I went along in the hope that
some intelligence material could be accessed from the village.
Several times I urged the commander to rein back his militia but
always he refused. I am not a psychologist, but from what little I
know of that discipline, it was clear that a frenzy of hate enveloped
that unit of IRGC. They were beyond control. I had no part in the
killings or the abuse, what was done to the women. I was a
bystander. The weather added to the awfulness of the day, and
into the night – rain, gales, thunder. I have no guilt. Do you not
understand war? It is what happens in war. I have been honest
with you, but I do not believe you were an eyewitness – perhaps
you were there afterwards. Whoever you are, and from whatever
agency, you should free me. I am an innocent man . . . there were
no witnesses."

"I was there. I saw everything you did."

There was a tone of finality in Gaz's voice, as though by trying
to excuse himself of blame the major merely wasted breath. He
looked again from the window and no longer saw the boat, only

the ends of its bow wave and some gulls hovering over its wake. He had needed a plan and the quiet in the apartment had given him the scope to think of it. A workable plan? Not sure, would not be certain for twenty-four hours. It was the only plan he knew. He gestured to Timofey and the kid went forward and took the weight of the chair, and his father helped, and they straightened it. He said that he needed some food and a hot drink, and he peeled off notes from a wad in his pocket and gave them to the girl. He trusted her more than he trusted her lover, but had no right to burden either of them with his trust. She went out, and would have skipped away down the stairs. She could, of course, use her phone and call a police number, or could head off into the city centre and pitch up on the Prospekt and denounce him, and a storm squad would be kitted in bulletproof vests and wear bala-clavas under their helmets and carry assault rifles and gas and flash grenades and would break through the flimsy door to the apartment, and she could then claim the rewards he imagined the major had offered . . . But it would not happen, that at least he was sure of.

It was a quality wake. Most of those that were organised in cele-bration of the life of a Round Table member were good occasions. They mixed anecdotes and what they saw as truisms, and laughter, and powerful doses of criticism were always directed at the new guard, the analysis geeks. Upwards of twenty were in the first-floor room of the Kennington Road pub and on the central table lay the theatrical sword. One founder member was a notable absentee – Knacker – and it was said that his rooms down the road were still locked up and showing no lights; so, not just him away but also his girls. Only a revered death could beat the excitement of the members when one of their own was running a show. Not that secrets were hawked round but small nuggets were talked of with evident joy. At the heart of the occasion was the true veteran, Arthur Jennings, always with a crush of colleagues round him and listening to the observations of the arch enemy of the geek gang.

"Miss him if he's not with us, don't we, old Knacker?"

"First-class man. No formal education but razor sharp. He'll be up on some part of that bloody place's endless border, and they'll know about it, but not until he's ready."

"Serious, a meticulous operator, thorough, with an eye for advantage."

"And a decent nose for ferreting out the sort of asset he can usefully employ."

"I enjoy it when he saunters in here and gives us nothing, except that somehow it always leaks out, delicious canapés of detail."

And the drink flowed and a good friend was remembered, gone on the long journey to the safe house in the skies, and the entry of the Coldstreamer was barely noticed. They believed themselves to be an old élite, whose life span was essential to the safety of the realm. They were confident and cheerful.

The Coldstreamer crouched beside Arthur Jennings' chair. "So sorry, sir, for the disturbance. A summons from the DD-G, sir. You are required to attend, immediate. A car waiting outside."

The officer's rucksack was retrieved. His personal weapon found at the bottom.

Up the stairs, two at a time, Mikki leading. He could have said, or Boris, that the world had no worse outcome up its sleeve than when personal protection lost its 'principal'. Irrelevant whether they despised him. Unimportant if they detested him. On their watch, they had lost the major.

The old cow had locked herself inside her apartment, had barred or bolted the door. They kicked the door and shouted. No response. Then they put their shoulders to it.

Mikki, from Kamchatka in the far east of the Federation was the tougher, stronger, and Boris from Irkutsk in Siberia was the brighter. It was Mikki's efforts that collapsed the door, then Boris had hold of the old woman. Her shopping bags were not yet unpacked. She was on her knees. Nothing subtle in the efforts of Boris. She was a fellow citizen of the Federation. Her late husband had worked loyally for the state. He twisted the lobe of an ear. In between her bleating cries, like a ewe's, he whispered his questions. Each time she did not answer it was Mikki's turn to sweep china from a cupboard and pictures from the walls, and soon the room was trashed.

Done steadily, without impatience, and she was given the impression that the two of them had time to spill, could keep the pain coming without needing to hurry. Could hurt her more than she had ever been hurt, could break pretty much everything she possessed. Weeping and holding her ear, she spat out what she knew. The girl who had carried her bag was the girl who had kissed the man on the step by the front door. The boy who had sat in the car. The car that had taken the officer away. The man who kissed was not of that city, and not Russian. They left her.

Outside, pieces of the puzzle started to interlock, and connections were made.

A car might have followed them the previous evening when they had brought the major back from the Prospekt. The boy who had gone into the bar and had emerged with two vodka bottles had had a foreigner with him. Through the window of the bar they had seen the 'foreigner' go close to the major, then abruptly turn away. The boy who had come to the gate of the headquarters building on Prospekt and had carted away a drunk and been ingratiating and polite. The drunk had been demanding access to an officer to make an accusation of treachery. Work to be done, and fast, at that building.

First, unwelcome business. A telephone call to be made. Mikki behind the wheel and starting the engine and needing to burn rubber, and Boris scrolling through his phone for a stored number. Keys pressed. Face creased in anxiety, dialling tone and ringing out. A clipped military tone answered. Boris gave his name. What did he want? The brigadier and his wife were soon to leave for the airport to celebrate the return of their son from duty in the far north. Why did he call?

Well, for a start – shit – not great news to give. Had lost their son, not mislaid, not like a fucking wristwatch or a pair of spectacles put down, but *lost* like he and Mikki were mugged and had 'lost' their wallets. Called him 'sir' and his voice would have been hard to hear and his jaw trembled. Lost like it was a kidnap. An intake of breath. Where? At the front door of the block where he lived. Where was the car, where were they? Round the corner, just – very briefly – out of sight, which was a lie but necessary. What had they done so far? They had interrogated an eyewitness to the abduction . . . They had a siren going and had a slap-on blue light on the roof . . . What possible reason was there for his being taken? Boris could not answer, but would have to – knew it. Was his son not a middle-ranking officer, principally involved in desk work? He was, Boris was able to reply. Was a fucking nobody, was fucking useless, was a time-server – agreed? No reply from Boris, and the voice ranted on and detailed Lavrenti Volkov's failings, and culminated.

"It could not have been a foreign agency."

A big breath from Boris. It was owed to the man who had saved his life, who'd had the guts, courage, balls, to call down the air strike on to their position as they fought hand to hand and with ammunition low or finished. He blurted.

"It could be about Syria . . ."

"What about Syria? What about that fucking hornets' nest?"

There was a village, there was a day the Iranian militia came to that village. There was that day when the major accompanied an Iranian commander to the village. The village was destroyed on that day. People died. Men, women, children died . . . Boris said it.

"But that was Iranians. My son was liaison. He had no authority, no command."

Mikki was approaching that sector of the Prospekt where the headquarters building was sited. He nodded, encouraged Boris.

"He took part in it, Brigadier. He was at the front of it. Maybe a hundred people died, maybe more. He was active. We thought everyone had been killed so that no witnesses were left to testify. He was – forgive me, Brigadier – like a mad dog there. I know of no other reason for a foreigner to come and seize your son off the street."

He thought he had crushed a man whom he had always respected beyond all others. Had broken the spirit of a man he would have followed anywhere, into the teeth of any battle. He thought the brigadier a man of discipline and of integrity. Who would have been wounded to learn that his boy, disliked and treated with near contempt, but his own blood, had been involved in a matter of such squalid violence. The silence hung on the line.

"We will do all we can, I promise you, to find him and recover him. We do that for you and your wife. We have a start but need a few hours before a general alarm is raised. That way scandal is suppressed. I am confident."

He cut the call. They pulled up at the gate and flashed a card. A camera watched them.

"You said, 'I am confident' – what are you confident of?"

"Confident of fuck-all. I thought he was about to weep. I did not want to hear him weep. What the fuck else should I have said?"

They loosed his ankles, then took him down the inner stairs.

Just before they left the apartment, the boy found his father's phone and chucked it from a window and it would have fallen in the scrub above the conning tower memorial. He had locked the door after him.

The girl led, and the boy held the officer's arm and Gaz was behind them and kept the pistol within an inch of the back of the officer's neck, but touched it with the barrel and foresight often enough to remind him it was there. They went down at scrambling speed. Brushed out of the way was a woman who worked part-time in the Fleet museum, the kids told him, and who would have been on her way to work. Next to be pitched back against a wall was the man who did translation work and was also a tour guide when the cruise liners, rarely, came to Murmansk. In the lower hallway, two young teenagers smoked and scuttled away as if lives were at risk. All of them would have known Timofey and Natacha, and would not rush to a phone. Seen nothing, heard nothing, known nothing, all survivors.

Outside, a little fresh sunshine came with the breeze and fell on Gaz's cheeks. Their prisoner would have assumed this was the start of his last journey. When his feet hit the smoothed dirt beyond the slab in front of the step, he stiffened and tried to drop his weight. But Gaz shoved him from the back and Timofey propelled him from the side. It was only half a dozen paces and the officer was docile. He'd have believed this was the journey that led to a killing site, where there was waste ground and where a body might lie for days, weeks, or months. They had not gagged him again and the blindfold was further down than before. He could have shouted but did not, and he was manhandled along the path, then down to the pavement, then up the hill to where the car was parked.

No further attempt to slow them down, and no yell for help. They used to watch the videos of the killings by the ISIS people in Syria. After, they would go to their bunk rooms and lie in the darkness and wonder how they would be if it were them wearing the jumpsuits, being led out on to the sand, forced to kneel, hair pulled back and their throats exposed, the blade coming closer and laughter circling them. Wondered if they would go to their deaths with bravery – whatever that meant – and defiance. Struggling to make it difficult for the butchers, or just dumbly docile. They had no trouble with the officer. He did not threaten, went with them, and would have believed the man behind him, with the firearm, was the killer who would end his life. Cars went past, and a bus dawdled at a pedestrian crossing, and people on the pavement seemed not to see them.

They wriggled their way into the car. Timofey and Natacha in front, Gaz and the officer in the back. They headed for the bridge and the start of the long route into the tundra, the E105 highway, and he reckoned the Russian prayed silently though his lips moved. Gaz could not say whether he would succeed, or what would be the cost if he failed.

14

"Why have you stopped?"

The Fiat had pulled off the main road and parked outside a hardware store. The trade for the day had started and the front area was filled with piles of plastic buckets, lightweight ladders, and forests of broom handles. They were on the outskirts of Murmansk, well past the aircraft carrier and ahead of them was the misted outline of the bridge.

Timofey said, "I need money."

"For what?"

"Because I need it."

Gaz had his knees up by his ears in the cramped area in the back of the Fiat and his legs were hard against the back of Timofey's seat. Beside him, trussed, was the Russian. There had been no talk between them. Gaz held the pistol, still with the safety on, still armed. They braked close to the display of plastic buckets, and the Russian's weight cannoned into Gaz.

"We don't have time to lose."

"Then give me some money."

"How much?" The sum was named. Gaz had to squirm to get his free hand into his hip pocket and heave clear a wad of notes. Natacha reached back, took the money, flicked off several notes then handed the rest back, and her eyes danced in fun. She was out of the car, walked past the buckets and went inside the hardware store. Gaz fidgeted and his legs hurt and his mind was messed, wondering how he would manage what he intended: and he expected – all the time – to hear sirens and see lights. Other customers at the hardware store walked past the little Fiat. Timofey smoked and the car filled with the nicotine cloud and then the

Russian started to cough, like he was choking, and a window was
wound down. A buggy was pushed past and a small kid pointed at
the back seat and would have seen a man with a plastic bag
wrapped around his head and knotted at the back. It was a bad
place to wait. Timofey dragged on the cigarette then chucked it
from the window, let it gutter on the road. She came out. On her
shoulder was a heavy garden spade. Sunlight caught the metal.

She had a jaunty walk, like it was fun to go into a store and buy
a spade and carry it out, like it helped to move the day on. Natacha
opened her door and squeezed inside and sat with the spade
between her legs.

She reached back and gave Gaz the change.

He said, "Why did we stop?"

"Because we did not have a spade where we live. We have no
garden there, so no need for a spade."

They were chuckling.

Gaz said, innocent and uncomprehending, and distracted by
what he planned and how it would be achieved, "What is the
spade for?"

Timofey was driving fast, and a cloud of fumes belched from
the exhaust. "Charge it on your expenses – except that Natacha
did not bring you a receipt. You want a receipt . . . you want to
know the cost of everything, do you? How much does a bullet
cost, a police bullet? I do not know what is the price of a bullet for
a Makarov. Perhaps we give it back afterwards and tell them that
we are one bullet short and they will not be concerned. What is a
spade for? A spade is to dig a hole. We buy a spade because a hole
must be dug."

"It's what they do in films," Natacha said.

"What do they do in films?"

"Do you not go to the cinema, watch gangster films? They
make the guy dig his hole. They watch him and he digs and they
tell him to get the hole longer and get the hole deeper. He sweats
when he digs but they have no water for him. He knows what is
about to happen but, in the films, he does not sit down, refuse to
dig. We will see if *he* does. See if *he* wants to fight or wants to go

quietly, quickly to his Maker. We free his hands so that he can work but we keep his legs tied. But we did not have a spade and we cannot make a hole without a spade. Do you understand that?" Colour flushed the officer's face and he was about to speak but did not.

Natacha said, "He digs the hole and we put him down in it and then tell him to kneel, and perhaps he will do so, and perhaps we have to hit him with the spade, but he is still tied and cannot run. Then it is for you. That is our part complete. Why we have to take you both out of the city you have not explained. We could have found you a place up by the Alyosha, by the monument, where there are bushes, places to hide, where the whores work in the summer. He could have been put to dig there. I think you were a soldier."

Gaz looked full into her face. His eyes did not waver, nor hers. He had said, *take him out*, it was what was said in the films, the gangster movies. 'Take him out' was the drawled phrase in the American dialogue for a killing ... Of course he was a soldier. Would have been a soldier and would have been highly regarded by his commanders, had been sent on a mission of danger. Would be a trained man, resourceful, without weakness: she almost snorted at the thought, not like the idiots that had been sent by her own government to Britain and other places in Europe and who were identified as assassins. This was a professional soldier and he would feel nothing when it came to the moment of looking into the pit and watching the officer slowly lower himself down and kneel. He would line up the pistol on the back of the officer's neck, or the back of his scalp. Perhaps the officer's lips would be moving, as if he recited a prayer. Might be allowed to finish the prayer and then be shot, might be getting to the last lines of it, and then the trigger pulled. As a professional he would not hesitate, would do it, and cleanly, would *take him out* as they said in the movies. She had never named Timofey. Had been offered inducements of early release, had been threatened with abuse, rape, but had not betrayed him. She did not think that Timofey would have been able to look over the open sight of the pistol, aim, squeeze. Not

Timofey. This was a soldier and it was his training. They had cleared the bridge. No roadblock in place. Fuck knows what they would have done ... scattered, and she and Timofey knowing where to meet eventually, and leaving the other two. Would have been bad if there had been a roadblock, would have been the end of the dream. In the movies, the screen first went to black and the sound was killed and the lights came up. The dream was the money. Because the mission was important enough for the 'sleepers' to be woken, Timofey said the reward would be huge. She did not know where they would go, her and Timofey, to spend the money ... the officer saw her, and would have heard every word she had said.

Part of the pleasure for her was knowing that the officer heard, understood, what awaited him. Like it would be a small piece of revenge, instituted by her, for the men who choked to death, or drowned, in the sections below the conning tower that she could see each time she looked from the apartment, and revenge for the death of her father. She could have done it, but not Timofey. She could not have relied on Timofey to do it, in what the films called 'cold blood'. The soldier could do it ... The officer had heard, had understood, and he breathed harder and his shoulders quivered and his skin had gone pale. It was a fine spade, a strong one, and she had short-changed Gaz on its purchase.

She was laughing, was happy. They climbed on the E105 highway and the ground grew more bleak and trees rarer and an expanse of rock and lakes was exposed. She thought of the killing, closed her mind to the hunt and chase that would follow.

"I cannot believe it. There has to be an explanation that is more rational." From the major who had replaced their man, who occupied his office space on Lenin Prospekt.

Mikki and Boris received no succour from the female captain. "You say he is missing. You say he may have been kidnapped. You are two long-retired men who achieved only the rank of *starshina*. I say that you are juniors and were given some vanity role in protecting Major Lavrenti Volkov. Why did he need protection? Because he was the son of an influential father, or because his mother wanted him put to bed safely each night? Why?"

The replacement echoed the captain's sneered remarks. "Are you telling us that the major has been abducted from in front of you, that you failed in whatever duty you were given, that he has been taken in a criminal enterprise, should now be listed as 'missing'?"

"If that is the allegation you make, then the issue goes to the colonel who commands FSB in the Murmansk *oblast*. He will, I assure you, pass it direct and as a matter of priority to Moscow. There will then be mobilisation of all available forces, the arrival of a responsible person, the closing of the border, and a full analysis of the major's work here."

"And an examination of his past duties. He served in Syria and served in Moscow. All of his history over the last five years would need examination."

"May I offer you guidance? More likely than kidnap is scandal. Open that to public examination and you have no idea where the trail leads – could be a woman of the streets, a prostitute, or could be a boy who sells sex, or could be the result of corruption of fraudulent activity and a bitch fight over the control of the rewards of a roof."

"There are many jealousies in this service. There are those who would rejoice at the discomfort, when displayed in public, of an officer who was universally disliked."

"So, do you wish to tell me that – in your opinions – Major Lavrenti Volkov has been kidnapped, abducted and that a substantial rescue operation should be launched? Yes?"

"And wish also that his previous work here, abroad and in Moscow, should be forensically examined in order to pinpoint motive for this crime?"

They left. Mikki murmured 'Those fucking bastards', and Boris muttered that 'He should be hung up by his balls, she by her tits'. They clattered out and closed the door noisily behind them. And agreed that an audit of the major's recent work, and at the village in Syria, would be a killer blow to the brigadier to whom both owed unquestioning loyalty.

Mikki said, "We do it ourselves."

Boris said, "For his father, not for the little shit himself."

Down into the bowels of the building and along a corridor running parallel to the cell block. A room where the noise of the adjacent heating boilers in winter could deafen a man. In the room, housing the computer's heart and backed up by a considerable archive library, were the recordings from the cameras surrounding the building's perimeter. Neither had the authority to have the clerks run through recorded footage, but it was demanded. There had been a drunk at the gate. Accusations slurred. A demand for an officer. Yelling about denouncing criminals. A young man coming from across the road, and speaking with respect and politeness, carting the man away. And a similar young man at a bar, and . . . the picture was found. A blown-up print of his face was made.

Also in the basement area was the armoury. Two assault rifles, 100 rounds for each, two pistols with belt holsters and fifty rounds of ammunition for each, a pair of smoke grenades and also the flash-and-bang type, two bulletproof vests, a set of field dressings. They possessed identification cards, and were well known in the armoury because of their trips to firing ranges – anything to break the boredom. They should have had additional authorisation, at least the signature of Major Lavrenti Volkov . . . but it was a matter of urgency and they were persuasive, and there was talk of 'someone coming within the hour to provide the necessary confirmation'. They were gone. The weapons went into the BMW's boot.

They went back to the bar where the little shit had insisted on going for a drink. They wore their ID cards hanging on lanyards, and their FSB caps and armbands and had the holsters on their belts, and Boris had loaded the magazines while Mikki had driven. The bar was not yet open, and the owner was deep in paperwork, and they started to kick the door in. Had demanded the recording from the camera behind the bar. Prevarication at first and claim that there was no camera, so Boris had gone behind the counter and had seen the lens wink at him and had cleared half a shelf of bottles onto the floor where they broke, and would have started on the second half, but the manager had darted into his office and had set up the recorder and the link to the screen. They saw the film, froze it on the kid who had come in to buy vodka, then had the image printed . . . and kept going until they had a decent shot of the stranger who had walked in with the kid. Had that printed also . . . and they were gone.

Police headquarters was next on their list of destinations, time running, and no loitering. Police were secondary in Murmansk, or anywhere in the Federation, to FSB. Only showed the picture of the boy: keen eyes that were set deep, fair hair cut short and pushed forward, a strong nose and thin lips and a jaw that seemed to show a lack of compromise, a show of defiance – similar to 1001 boys in the city who were addicted to small-time robbery, pickpocketing, narcotics dealing. Always, in a criminal records archive, there was a keen little beggar who had no value other than being able to match printouts of faces to files. All done fast, and either of them might have given the guy a kiss on each cheek if it had not been for his acne. He was Timofey and there was a family name . . . and a bonus: a secondary file was produced and a photograph and name. Natacha, pretty little thing and familiar in a vague way, and then a larger bonus. There had been a robbery the previous night. A girl had 'deceived' a police officer in his patrol car, a firearm had been stolen, but the girl's hair was not blonde. "Try a fucking wig," Boris had said. Mikki had said, "It's a good word that, 'deceived'. Tell him to keep his bits inside his trousers." Gone again. An address poached from criminal intelligence, that of a small-time drugs dealer and his girl.

They found an old man lying in his own vomit. Would have smacked him around had it been necessary. It was not. Behind them the door hung at an angle from one hinge.

Shown the chair where the shit had been tied. The identity of the foreigner confirmed, and talk of the man coming in through the border and being met . . . and the pleading that he, the old man, be treated with clemency. And he told them how far ahead of them were the fugitives . . . They were going to kill the major, that too was thrown at them in the hope of additional clemency. They did not do arguments, nor debates, did not dispute. Could they handle it? Could handle anything, and Boris had heard the brigadier's shock when Syria and disgrace were spoken of . . . and investigators would be crawling over his history, maggots on old meat.

"Can we do it?"

"Why not?"

"You happy?" Mikki asked.

"As I'll ever be," Boris said and slapped his colleague's shoulder.

They drove, blue light on the roof, and would jump traffic lights and overtake crazily, and took the one road that led towards the Norwegian border.

He recognised that the Fiat was approaching the garrison camp at Titovka, where the roadblock was. He had not answered Natacha, no explanations given.

Broke his silence. "We have a misunderstanding . . ."

A dilemma had faced him, one that he had not before been asked to confront.

He said quietly, "The misunderstanding is because of what I said to you before . . ."

There was a track off the road. Further up, above the tree line, were the higher chimneys of the camp and a watch-tower on stilts. Timofey was leaning back in his seat, yawning, but Natacha was out of the car, gripping her spade. A thought sprinted in Gaz's mind: what about these kids, their future, the danger he propelled them towards, the retribution lining up to sledgehammer them? Considered: Knacker would have said, 'Not your problem, lad, leave the conscience bit outside your knapsack, and I'll take care of it.' Only a fast thought, and other issues chased it away, took precedence. They'd suffer . . . he shrugged, started to explain.

Gaz spoke with no rancour and no emotion. "What I said to you was 'take him out', and that refers to him, to Major Volkov. But we do not need a spade to 'take him out' . . ."

There were no recent tyre marks on the track surface and the sound of vehicles was behind them on the E105 highway and was muffled by the dense birch copse. The major now seemed to breathe faster: in the final stage of this journey the movement of his chest had been slower and regular, and Gaz thought the man had prepared himself for the moment of execution-kneeling, eyes closed and a final intake of breath and the click of the safety being moved. Now he was listening, and so were the kids in front.

" 'Take him out' was what I said and what I meant. But not shoot him dead. Could have done that on the step of his apartment block, or could have gone up the staircase in the night, tapped on his door, got him there, shot him. Did not have to take him this far out of the city and shoot him. 'Take him out' was what I said and what I intend. I will take him out of the jurisdiction of the Russian state. I will take him over the border. Will take him if I have to carry him there and he kicks and screams and wakes the dead."

In their own styles, all of them reacted. Timofey's mouth gaped. Natacha blinked. And the officer gulped.

Gaz spoke, had to. "I was once a soldier, but never a killer. I lay in ditches, in holes, and I watched men and saw them play with their kids and kiss their girls and do their functions, and saw them clean their weapons and had the lenses on them when they had a map and planned where to lay the next anti-personnel bomb. Watched, reported, and moved on and was somewhere else when the heavy men moved into position, lined up the long-range weapon and waited for the schedule to be enacted that I'd told them to look for. Was not a part of it."

He spoke only to the boy and the girl. Gaz did not look at the officer. They were frowning, and each seemed bewildered as if the definition of involvement – what he was prepared to do, was not prepared to do – was incomprehensible.

Gaz said, "I was an eyewitness to a war crime. I was there and I watched. Major Volkov was a party to what was done. He deserves punishment. I am simply a witness, will appear before a legally constituted court of international law. Will give my evidence and hope to see him convicted. I am not a hangman, I do not play with lives. Perhaps that is an honourable principle, worth upholding, and perhaps it is a coward's way to avoid responsibility. Perhaps. But it is what I can live with. I will take him out of the country, will hand him into the custody of a lawful organisation."

Natacha said, "I would have done it, if you were frightened."

Timofey said, "We should have been better rewarded. You have cheated us."

She said, "We took big risks for you – the pistol . . ."

He snapped across her. "He sits with a lawyer, tells them of us. We are taken, locked in a shit camp. Dead, and we are paid big money. Alive and it is us who are condemned."

He did not argue, had neither the breath nor the strength, and thought they both spoke the truth. They were sleepers, had been woken, were unlikely to sleep again. Assets low on the food chain. He himself, in Knacker's world, was merely an instrument of policy. They, to Knacker and his team, were irrelevant once the assignment was complete.

He opened the door and pushed his legs out, the pistol in his hand: reached in and caught the tunic of the major and yanked. The blindfold had slipped further and the man gazed at him and seemed to try to read him and failed and his lips moved but no words came. He stood the major against the car.

Timofey asked him, "If he is allowed to live, what sentence would he get?"

Gaz said, "Life, if convicted."

Natacha said, "Then better dead than for ever . . . and we are sacrificed for your principle that is so valuable."

Gaz said limply, "It's how it is. I am not a killer and not a judge, just a witness."

The officer stared at him, bit his lip, swallowed.

Delta Alpha Sierra, the fourteenth hour

There were few flames left to light the village homes, but the Iranians had fired up their transport, and worked off the headlights.

Gaz watched two of them. Had the glasses with the image intensifier facility alternately on the Russian and the country boy, as Gaz thought of him. Worried more about the boy – could see the outline of his body on the slope where the vehicle lights did not reach – than about the officer. The goats were scattered; the dogs had tried to round them up and bring them back to the girl but they had been spooked by the gas explosion, and had failed. They were back beside her. If he had tried to pull her into the cavity in the sand where he hid, his own Covert Rural Observation Post, there was a better than fair chance she would struggle and the dogs react. Enough eyes were below them that could glance upwards and see indistinct shapes struggling. They were digging a second pit because they wanted to hide everything they had done. If there had been a witness on the hillside they would come searching. He let her stay where she was.

Bodies were dumped in the twin pits. They were thrown in fast, in vague and distorted lines, landed hard and were manhandled to an available slot, and the work went slower because the men were hungry, had not stopped to drink, and the flush from the killings would have dissipated. The Russian had taken a shovel from the hands of a trooper, had started to dig at the far end of the second pit, to deepen and widen and lengthen it. His goons did not help, stood back. Gaz knew this was a country of mass graves. He had heard an UNHCR aid worker comment that 'Pretty much anywhere in this country that you bat a tennis ball, where it comes down there will be a mass grave.' Others said that no grass grew above where bodies decomposed, only weeds. The idea that the pits and replaced earth would hide the evidence of the killing for a day or a month or a year was infantile, but they dug and dumped. The officer seemed to regard it as a matter of pride that he should dig faster, throw up more soil, than any of the militiamen. When he turned or twisted and the headlight beams caught his face, Gaz could see that he was working as if demons overwhelmed him. Behind him, his goons smoked and chatted, and the commander from the IRGC shouted encouragement at his men.

The girl did not move. Her arms were around her knees, her

head sunk low. Sometimes he heard her murmur, mostly she was silent. He rested his hand on her arm. The silence clung between them but they would both have heard clearly the shouts and barked orders from below.

He sent another message. Was hunkered down, could not move. Would come out when safe to do so. The airwaves of that country were alive with encoded signals and scrambled talk, and great dishes swept for traffic. Would not give a commentary and would not invite an intercept.

He watched the country boy. Trouble with him, probably used to minding cattle or sheep or goats, was that he'd have the keen eyesight to go with his work. Would not need image intensifiers, nor the lights from the personnel carriers and the trucks ... Suddenly, a moment of horror. A body must have moaned or twitched and half a magazine was fired into the pit. Might have been wolves where the country boy came from, or big cats, and with his eyesight would come quality hearing. He was on the perimeter line and would have been positioned because both his vision and hearing were trusted. The country boy should have been watching what was done on the football pitch, but a goat had come to him. Gaz did not know about goats, but knew about sheep and reckoned them contrary, easily scared and wanting to be loved, and the boy's head twisted and his eyes would have raked the slope.

Gaz thought the country boy had seen her. He stood, holding his rifle in one hand, cupping the other to his mouth and shouted below him. The officer stopped digging and listened, and the commander threw down his cigarette and listened, and a vehicle manoeuvred and its lights lit part of the slope and caught the goats in their glare.

It took Arthur Jennings no more than a cursory glance to realise the scale of the sea change. Little time taken for the new order to move in lock, stock and barrel. He would be the first one facing it, the barrel ... The pictures so beloved by his friend were still in place but Jennings doubted they'd last until the evening, and the ornaments had not yet been binned, but the framed photographs of the Director-General with the American President and other, lesser, heads of government had been removed.

A quiet voice, with a squeak in it, like an oil change beckoned. "Good of you to come, Mr Jennings. Gather you had to interrupt one of your little sessions. Hope not too inconvenient … My predecessor, sadly, has health problems, is going under the knife in the next twenty-four hours, won't be coming back, if he survives the ordeal – as we all hope he will – but can look forward to his retirement after distinguished service. The world moves on."

No answer required and none given.

"I have no intention of faffing about during any interregnum. I expect sooner rather than later to be named as D-G, have the 'acting' scratched out. Am beginning as I mean to continue. Games of charades in a public house will cease to have any relevance to the actions of the Service. If a few of you, past retirement age or nearly there, wish to entertain yourselves with fabricated tales of the 'good old days', of course you are free to do so. But not with our support, not with our resources, not utilising any individual on the Service staff. Fanciful stories of legendary activities are 'yesterday', and the Service believes in 'tomorrow'. Understood?"

Those activities cavorted in Arthur Jennings' memory. Triumphant successes, victory snatched from clamping jaws, the dismissal of an odious functionary in Moscow or Beijing or Tehran for manifest failure. On occasions the perpetrator of a no-argument win would be brought to a Round Table gathering and a little of what had been achieved would be dispensed, and there would be an ovation: confidence that the ethos of the Service was alive, enjoyed rude health. He stared at the usurper sitting in comfort behind his friend's desk: would probably change the bloody carpet the following day, might even have the decorators in by the end of the week.

"We are a modern outfit. We are, I am proud to say and I've played a part in establishing this, a place of excellence. We employ many of the best intellects that Britain produces. We have graduates with first-class degrees queuing to join us. We are not a building where mumbo-jumbo, sorcery, is tolerated. Let us be clear, Mr Jennings, we are not going to continue as if the Russian Federation is the only enemy on our horizons: simplistic, convenient and flawed. You are hearing me?"

Nothing to say. 'AJ' was always described as having fine eyes. Not a judgement on his vision capabilities, but his ability to bead on an opponent. Even the little inscrutables, the Chinese from the Ministry of State Security, were said to blink or deflect eye contact when it was lasered on them at rare meetings. It was reported to be fearsome. For a moment the DD-G hesitated, might have considered he had lost face, then pressed on and had a page of bullet points in front of him.

"We have endured the circus of Salisbury and relations between the Federation and the UK have been fraught and reached base camp levels. I do not intend to pursue that agenda. We have to talk, find common areas of interest, cooperate against mutual enemies. The Federation shows justifiable irritation in the way that we harbour opponents of the regime, and the extent to which dissidents and spies are awarded asylum here. I want to reach out, while in no way slackening our vigilance, and have sensible conversations. Unless our national security is directly threatened, I will not authorise hostile acts against Russian territory or interests. Most certainly I will not be permitting, on my watch, missions that have little purpose other than to further dubious policy aims abroad, or are designed only to annoy. You are quiet today, Mr Jennings."

And would stay quiet, and would consider . . . too early for sherry but coffee would have been welcome.

"I believe the Service, as it moves forward, will put aside – once and for all – these playground antics. Few of them I believe would survive examination by our risk assessment teams. For heaven's sake, we are dealing with people's lives. We have set ourselves up as Lord God Almighty if we cling to ludicrous clichés such as 'can't make an omelette without cracking eggs'. I won't have it. I will not go home at night and consider that – through my dereliction – some wretch faces execution in the morning in Evin gaol, in some hell-hole prison tucked away from sight in China, and for what? For the grotesque amusement of dinosaurs who were once on our payroll. Will not have it. Am I clear? And my predecessor's links with your Round Table are cancelled with immediate effect. You will appreciate that the clock moves forward so we will be opening discreet channels to agencies we have formerly considered to be hostile. Don't think this a sign of weakness. Absolutely not. It is pragmatism. Any comment?"

Arthur Jennings shook his head. He gripped the arms of his wheelchair and started to turn but it was a slow movement because of the density of the carpet pile. It was good to turn away because the gimlet in the eyes was distorted by a damp mist, like fine drizzle. His back was to the desk.

"Before you go, please Mr Jennings. Are you aware of any operations running at this time? Are there? A direct question, requiring a direct answer."

He thought of Knacker, thought of Knacker and his girls, thought of Knacker and his girls and their quarters down from the pub where the wake would be in good heart and good voice on the first floor. He could have mentioned a couple of people who were high in the foothills adjacent to the Iranian border with Turkey and who had an asset inside. Could have summoned up the face of a woman, ugly as sin and as crafty as a ferret, who had her asset loose in the Democratic Peoples Republic of Korea. Seemed to forget them. Called to his mind Knacker and the girls who stayed close to him and the little office suite, the Yard . . . Within a few hours the usurper would be in contact with those parts of VBX dealing in funding and travel arrangements, and liaison with Norwegian agencies, and there would be a record of Knacker's paper – what could be achieved, and how, and in the briefest timeframe because of the inevitable hazard of information leakage. He never had a running commentary from Knacker, but it was likely one of his girls would have a line into Operations and that brief résumés would be received in London. But the DD-G would have to know what code-name was attached to the mission, might find it hard to expose *Matchless* before the end of the day.

"How would I know, useless old fart like me?"

He steered himself towards the closed door, rammed it with his wheelchair and it opened. As he remembered the schedule, Knacker's man would have been beyond reach by now and the wild men from the refugee camp should have been wriggling through a border fence . . . would have been, should have been. He brushed aside offers of help, passed through the office suite and headed for the elevator.

One of the marine engineers caught her eye.

Faizah was back at work in the Hamburg bar, and it was another busy lunchtime. They had come in, the same group, and had parked themselves at the same table, and on the walls were pictures of old sailing boats, and pieces of antique navigation equipment, and the menu was the same. And their laptop was open on the table.

It would have been easy for her to avoid serving them, leave it to the other girl on duty, but contact had been made and the menu was waved at her. Would have been hard to avoid. All of them peered at her as she reached the table and fished out her notepad and pencil stub. They had fired up the laptop and one of them flicked the keys. A picture erupted in front of her. Remembered him, would not forget him. Then in foul and soaked fatigues and with his skin running with rainwater; in this image, smart and confident and in a pressed uniform, with his cap perched jauntily on his head. The memory was of a man beyond the limits of self-control; the laptop showed someone who believed himself inherently superior to those around him. And they ordered the same as she remembered they had eaten before, and the same beer. She scribbled on her pad and was about to turn away.

One of them said, "We were wondering if it were you."

Another said, "Caused us hassle."

And another, "Found ourselves with security policemen when we got home."

From the last, "An interrogation . . . 'What was the photograph on the laptop of a Russian? What entry on which website? Why were we at that website?' Questions, questions, questions. That Russian and that site. Seemed important."

And another, "Detail on the Russian. As much as possible."

Another, "We are all related in Kirkenes, our home, where the dockyard is. We lose the intelligence police, then I have a call from my wife's cousin's boy, and he works at a website. I am asked, 'What the fuck – excuse me, I apologise – what the something is going on because we have a picture of a Russian officer, months ago, at a frontier meeting, and now the spy people crawl all over us, and it is about the British, there is a connection."

One of them said, "And my uncle's nephew by marriage, he is a fisherman. You know that a fishing boat, a small one, came into Kirkenes two or three days ago and had sailed from the British islands of Shetland, and in Kirkenes the crew had used an agent to buy up all the red king crabs they could get their hands on, and they paid well over the usual price for them. Where did they take the load? They sailed for Murmansk, would go from Kirkenes and east into Russian water, then past Vayda-Guba and on past Zubovka, and so to Murmansk. There was apparently a problem with their own catches of this crab and the boat went to fulfil an order from smart restaurants. Why was it a boat that came all the way across from Britain? It is very confusing . . ."

She took the order, made no comment. She disappointed them. Remembered the tang of the sea in her mouth and nostrils, and the freshness of the wind on her face, and – as sharp as if it had been in the previous hour – each line and movement of his face. Could see him as he had been before, when she had teased with her eyes and never spoken, and how it had been when he had clung to her as the killing had started in the village and then she had broken the silence and said that one of the women was her sister; saw him as he had been in the small Norwegian port, his face thinner and more drawn, and his eyes tired and almost a shake in his hand. She had held it and had sensed his fear. The people with him had said she would encourage him in his mission, but all he had to do was identify. Would he kill the officer? 'Absolutely not.' Would he help to kill the officer? 'I just do my job.' She had snorted contempt at him, had whipped him with her voice and had known stress enveloped him. She had bullied, had dismissed him, and felt belittled and the anger was gone.

She wondered if he were out and back over the border, if a killing had been done; thought if the work were finished then the woman from the Consulate would have told her. She wondered if he were still there, was a free man or trapped. As if she had forgotten the officer, remembered only Gaz. She put the order on the counter, went to clear another table.

It would be, for Jasha, an act of faith.

From his toolbox he took an old pair of pliers. He had drunk a mug of tea which he thought would calm him and stay any shake of his hand. He had fed the dog, but the animal was aware of crisis and had merely toyed with the food in its bowl. His money box was on the table and his military identity card, and the dog's leash: he believed that would be an invitation to anyone who came to the cabin and found it deserted, to pocket the money, take the leash and the dog. It was his fall-back. His narrow single bed was spread with a coverlet, and his dishes and pans were washed and on the board beside the sink, and . . . he could hear the moaning.

The figure from history that Jasha revered most was the Red Army commander, Georgi Zhukov. The creature from the wild that he respected most was the brown bear with one foot already a stump and now a fencer's staple wedged deep in it.

Jasha had heard of men who claimed a relationship with a bear, and they likely lied or had inherited one freed from a circus. He left the rifle, the Dragunov with the telescopic sight attached, on the shelf. He did not think he could play two games and have a fall-back position. He would go to the bear, would help it if his intervention were allowed, but he would not rush back to grab the weapon if the fury of the creature, in its pain, were turned on him. There was an old German song that he had learned before going to Afghanistan; it had been almost a dissident crime to whistle it: *Lili Marlene*. Jasha removed his shirt and vest, folded them and placed them on the table. The song comforted him. He murmured it, tapped his dog's head, felt it shiver, and wiped his eyes with the back of his hand. He went out of his cabin, the pliers in his hand.

The bear did not move. It held its leg upright, keeping the whine deep in its throat. Jasha whistled his song between his teeth. He thought the first few seconds would be critical. He walked slowly, deliberately towards the bear. He saw the bear's head tilt towards him. Everything in the animal's psyche would tell him that Jasha posed a threat by coming close. He should show no fear, should come with a smile and the soothing sounds of the German anthem on his lips, should show the pliers and allow Zhukov to realise that he had no weapon with him. He was within a metre of the bear.

The arch of the staple could be clearly seen. Zhukov could have swiped him and broken Jasha's vertebrae, could have slashed him with his claws. He assumed that if it wanted to knock him down he would see only a blur of movement before he was struck. Jasha had not witnessed the wounds on a man that a bear's claws would inflict but he had seen a moose that had strayed too close to a female with a cub: great railway tracks of blood and the thick hide ripped apart. He watched the bear's eyes and saw a dullness and looked at his teeth, the mouth wide enough to take his head inside, bite it clean off.

Who would care if the bear killed him? Who would remember him after all the years he had lived in the tundra? Jasha was beside the bear. The last steps were at tortoise speed, his eyes always on the bear's, and there was a moment when he almost flinched because the animal showed its teeth. Jasha did not stop. His life was either within seconds of ending, or . . . Enough messing. He reached forward and locked the tips of the pliers on to the arch of the staple. It was big and rusty and caked in mud. One more deep breath. He pulled, and was flung back. Had used strength but the grip had failed. He would try again. The bear watched him and his front leg stayed upright and Jasha saw his teeth again . . . a mad thought, perhaps, but he wondered, had he chickened out and abandoned the job, whether the bear would come after him, whatever the pain . . . He felt himself committed. Raising the level of his voice, singing all the words in German that he knew, he came back close to Zhukov. He fastened the pliers on the staple, squeezed the handles so that his fist was near cracking and put his elbow across the bear's chest to gain better traction, and heaved. Nothing moved. He sang louder, full-throated:

Wenn sich die spaeten Nebel drehn,
Werd' ich bei der Lanterne steh'n

Used every necessary muscle . . . felt the staple move, and saw it emerge, blood with it.

Wie einst Lili Marlene, wir einst Lili Marlene.

The bear watched him, its breath rancid in Jasha's face. He eased his body away. He should not hurry. He was glad that what he had done had not been seen, as if it were a private moment between the two of them and he must not show fear. He walked away, unable to loosen his grip on the pliers. Walked steadily as if nothing special had happened.

He went back through the cabin door and the pliers fell from his hand, and the staple clattered free and he felt his head spinning and his legs crumbling, and he fell to the floor.

The harbour launch had left them. The fishing boat sailed alone.

The skipper studied his charts and used satnav and could only hope that the choice of location was indeed a section of the inlet's coast that was not under the highest levels of surveillance. They were beyond the Northern Fleet headquarters at Severomorsk but were short of the submariners' garrison city of Vidyaevo. It was a simple plan. All the best plans were. He believed that complicated procedures were generally unsatisfactory, prone to failure. It was the last throw. They had waited and had dared to hope that they would see him at the outer gate, flitting in the shadows, and would then be chatting up the security while the stranger came with his bogus papers, and was waved through. There was an emptiness among them and the bottle of scotch was on the table below. It was what they called a back-stop.

They put up black smoke from the stack and seemed to slow and then to veer from the straight as if their steering was affected along with their reported engine trouble. Daylight, but no other way. There was a navigation marker buoy, attached to a heavy weight by a rope long enough to handle the rising tide and a couple of metres below the buoy was a package wrapped in oiled tarpaulin. Inside, deflated and folded tight, was a dinghy. When they were as close to the rocks and the shore line as the skipper dared, and near to an out-of-date iron frame for a navigation light, the weight and the buoy and the package were heaved over the side. Then, as if the engineer had performed a miracle, the dark smoke dispersed and the steering problem seemed resolved, and course for the open sea was resumed.

Gaz said, "So that a mistake is not made you should know what I intend. I will take you to the border, take you over it or under it, and on the far side you will be put into lawful custody. All of your rights will be observed. You will lead and I will be a pace behind you. If you attempt to break clear, then I will shoot you in the leg. As you know, Major, this is wild and hostile territory. You will be crippled, unable to move other than on your stomach, and you can shout but you will not be heard. You will die alone and in great pain. That is what I intend if you play games with me. Now, we start to walk."

He did not make either a heartfelt farewell to Natacha, nor an insincere one. Did not acknowledge that she had conjured out of the night a police service pistol for him, nor that she had kicked the officer when it had mattered. Nor did he give a hug or a hand-shake to Timofey. Might have been because they were kids off the street and nothing in his life mirrored theirs, and might have been because their sense of freedom unsettled him. He bent, his back to them, and flicked open the knots fastening the plastic bag around the officer's ankles, then reached up and tugged down the blind-fold bag . . . It was the first big step, he supposed, the start of the hard yards that, God willing, would take him back to Westray. He gave his prisoner a prod, like he was a dray horse needing encour-agement, and they set off on an animal track, a yard wide. He had his weapon ready, had no illusions about the officer's compliance.

It was what his own instructors would have said to the guys and girls on the Escape and Evasion stuff. The best chance of getting clear was at the start, and that had not worked for the officer, but they also stressed that any time an opportunity came up it should be taken. The alternative was a jumpsuit if ISIS had him, or a Syrian torture dungeon if it were the government. The sun was high, almost hot, and flies clustered on them, and the prisoner could not get them off his face and shook his head violently. It might take four or five hours to reach the fence. Gaz thought it the beginning of the end . . . Was it better to die, quick and clean, or to squat in a cell and see the sky through blistered glass and bars, without the chance of tasting the air beyond a high wall?

They started out over hard ground, and climbed. He heard a siren. He had the pistol close to the officer's neck and twisted his head and saw the blue light through the trees hustling fast up the E105 highway. The prisoner did not slow and the siren passed them.

15

He would try to get close – without the guidance of the kids – to the lake that he had skirted and then the fence where he had come through. They were making good progress, and the prisoner did not fight him.

A handgun had an effective range of ten paces. Gaz would have been rated, on the range with a Glock, above average, but that had been two years ago. To achieve a good shot, a stopper, at ten paces in the chaos of a man breaking away and trying to run, with bushes to deflect a bullet and obscure the target, would have drawn praise from the instructors. A man with his wrists tied at his back was still able to duck and weave.

He had been given no reason to use force against him. Everybody had seen the internet-peddled version of Saddam's hanging, with guys in the shadows bawling abuse at the dictator as he stood upright, steady, on the trap. All the young squaddies had voiced that it was 'out of fucking order', whatever the magnitude of the man's crimes. He did not abuse the officer, nor use violence, just prodded him forward along the animal trails. And the sun was burning through a veil of cloud, and Gaz gave a curt instruction each time he reckoned they should veer right or left.

When he spoke, a necessary few words, he did not use an obscenity, nor call him by his first name, he was Major Volkov. Others would judge the major, but he would go to the end of any road to bring him to a court of law.

Unable to protect himself from the whip of low branches and of bramble stems, the major was beaten across the body and thorns caught at his clothing. Easier for them to move faster if the bag binding his wrists were removed and he could use his hand to shield his skin. There was blood on his cheeks from small cuts. Each time Gaz saw the smears he looked at the line of the scar that ran from near to the ear and almost to the side of the mouth and remembered. He would shoot if the man tried to belt him, struggle with him, or bolted. Would shoot him; but afterwards regard it as failure. Messed-up thoughts careered in his mind and every two or three minutes he needed to blot them out and concentrate on the direction they took and the climb that brought them to the plateau of the tundra. Almost open ground, only sparse low trees.

Gaz knew that complacency was a killer. It was going too well, and anxiety built. There were long silences: he could not read the major. Was he close to springing the trap? Might he pretend to stumble and twist as if falling, then turn and use his head – the weight of the forehead was as destructive as a knot of wood or a rounded stone – to crash into Gaz's face, to break his nose? A sudden movement. Gaz stretched, had the pistol barrel hard against the man's neck and saw the indentation it made, and twisted the foresight so that the skin was caught and blood dribbled. But he said nothing. Remembered the fifteenth hour because that was the one that had collapsed Gaz, changed his life. The fifteenth hour was why he was there, plodding across tundra, bringing home a prisoner.

Delta Alpha Sierra, *the fifteenth hour*

Gaz watched the country boy.

He shouted and gestured, attracting attention. One of the drivers responded. An APC was swung round, had a searchlight mounted. The country boy was caught first, using an arm to cover his eyes. With his other arm he pointed up the hill. The light threw his shadow on the slope, sharp all the way until it rested in the girl's lap, a yard short of Gaz's position in his scraped-out hide. The light edged up the hill – military grade, designed to search out infantry up to 400 metres away. Bizarrely, the Russian officer was the only one left working at the pits, rearranging the new cadavers, the rim higher than his waist. His goons stood behind him. The commander left him there and strode forward, wanting to know why the militiaman was on the slope and yelling for troops.

The searchlight wobbled, steadied, was off course, then found her. A shout of triumph from below. And it found the dogs and they cowered.

The commander might have shouted for the men to come back inside the perimeter line, might have sent his NCOs scrambling up the slope and using their rifle butts to send the militiaman back . . . Or might have thought that this long after it had started, and this late into the evening, it was better to let the business take its course. He would have seen what the militiaman saw: a woman, in wet clothing clinging to her body, wisps of her hair escaped from under the flattened scarf on her head, the long skirt that hid her legs. The country boy was advancing up the slope, the gang of militia coming after him. Some would have wanted to get to her because she was probably the sole witness to have survived . . . some because they had not been on the detail that had taken the village women away from sight and into the gully and the dried-out river-bed. Those who had formed the perimeter line duty had not enjoyed what others had . . . and the light fastened on her.

No chance for Gaz to ask advice . . . no officer to quiz, no senior guy back at the Forward Operating Base, no sergeant who had 'been everywhere, done everything' to challenge for a solution. His legs were locked and his breath came in gasps. He could drop the country boy but another twenty men came behind him and where the light was mounted was also a heavy machine-gun. There would be fleet-footed kids among the militiamen, tired and hungry and cold, but enlivened by this circus ring of excitement. Gaz was stiff, his gut ached with lack of food, and his mouth was dry.

He was about to speak . . . about to make some damn great hero speech. Waste of time, waste of effort, stuff about 'going down fighting'. Did not speak, did not have to.

She was on her feet, brushing off his hand, a slow and considered movement. The light was full on her and the dogs hid behind her skirt.

In front of her, like a pack that had spotted prey, there was first a pause, and then the country boy was flicking at the belt of his trousers, and Gaz saw a grin playing on his face, and he would be the first to reach her.

She hitched her skirt and began to sprint down the hill and would have known it better than her hand, and chose a narrow track, made by her goats over the years. Her dogs galloped with her.

Had never had a conversation with her, only eye contact and long days of it since he had first come to the village. He had worked the duty roster with the people who did the tasking, made certain that he always went to the village to replace the batteries in the camera and to collect film. He saw her run and he saw the pack following her.

An English master at school had been besotted with Dickens: *It is a far, far better thing that I do, than I have ever done; it is a far, far better rest that I go to, than I have ...* Had loved those words when the teacher had declaimed them: now understood them.

The searchlight stayed on her as she ran. He did not know her name, knew only that once a happiness had bounced in her eyes, and she was a peasant girl from a remote village who had bonded with a foreign soldier and had seen it as her duty to protect him. He blanched at the depth of her loyalty, and saw her fall. Maybe her skirt caught at her ankles and tripped her, maybe a stone on the track was enough to pitch her forward. She was down and he saw the dogs had gone to her. Saw that the country boy had his trousers already flapping at his knees and saw others snatching at buttons and belts, and lost sight of her because of the crush around her, and heard a dog yelp. He was a soldier, presumed strong, and he blubbered like a child. He saw the country boy come back through the crush, lifting his trousers and feeling for his belt, and others pushing closer and making an untidy queue ... He wept until no tears were left.

From the trench, the officer watched, his goons behind him. A pistol out, perhaps another movement in the pit, and another shot fired ... and he went back to his digging, and the last bodies were dumped, and he shovelled earth, and was alone. And darkness fell as the searchlight by the hatch of the personnel carrier was switched off.

"Who are you?"

"Does it matter?"

"What status do you have?"

"My own status, Major Volkov, that of a witness."

"What name?"

"I don't have to give you a name."

"I wish to address you. What do I call you?"

"When I was a witness I was a corporal. You can call me that – Corporal."

"But you have an officer with you, of course you do?"

"I do not answer any questions on the mission, Major."

"You were there?"

"I told you that I was a witness."

"Is that a witness to a satellite transmission? Or was there a drone up even in that weather? Perhaps you dream of what you *think* you saw."

"A hillside south-west of the village. I had a hide in the lip of the hill. Was there from the time you reached the village. I saw the killings, the destruction of homes, I saw . . ."

"You were a reconnaissance soldier? A British army reconnaissance soldier? You were by the goats?"

"By the goats, and the girl."

"We thought them formidable troops, the British reconnaissance unit. Why were we opponents? We had the same job, killing the terrorists. Why?"

"Above my grade, Major, those decisions."

"Were you romancing the girl?"

"I was not."

"Just a village girl, all she was."

"As you say, just a village girl."

"Only a girl. What happened, it is what soldiers do."

"You have no need to tell me. Tell a judge. If it is your defence against a war crime that she was 'just a village girl' then you must say so. And there were many 'just village mothers' and 'just village old men' and 'just village children'. Say that to the judge."

"By now they will be looking for us. A big force will be out. A cordon . . ."

"I do not hear the helicopters, Major."

"And I do not, Corporal."

Through days, nights, weeks and months it had been welling in him. No one to tell. Only the loneliness of his own company to hear his whispers so that walls and doorways would not betray him. Here, he had only his gaoler to share his thoughts. His head rocked at the thought of this man, a pace behind him and holding a pistol, mannered and courteous and without anger, but with determination. He thought of the Iranians unlucky enough to be captured, taken alive, and thought of the long passageways in the Lubyanka and the men and women who ruled there, and how prisoners, some of them he had sent there, were treated: dehumanised, broken.

"Can I say something, a truth, Corporal?"

"You don't bargain with me. Nothing is on the table for negotiation."

"I have shame, Corporal. I live with it and it is more persistent than the malarial microbe. For that I can take medicine, which may work. For shame I cannot find the antidote. It is guilt . . . I make the excuse that it is just war, that war breeds crimes. Back there I said 'just a village girl'. I live with it, Corporal, the guilt and the shame."

"We keep going, Major. If you try to trick me then I will shoot you. Do not try to deceive me."

"No one else. I have told no one else."

He did not know if he was believed. Nor did he know whether it had been good to speak with this junior, whether the burden was lifted.

Timofey was in front, Natacha a pace behind.

They never disagreed on tactics. The officer could be taken into custody, or he might break free and run; either way he would be at the head of the queue to denounce them. The reckoning was that more money would be on offer if the officer was dead.

Timofey had said, "He stays alive and the FSB will be at our home. How do you run here, where do you go? Nowhere to run to . . . Imagine we have the money and we cross the border, and the money is useless, has no value. We have to do it."

Natacha had said, "No future, no hope, not if he denounces us. I will do it."

"We both do it."

Like a bonding, like the blending of blood, both stopped the pursuit and crouched down, using their fingers to gouge through the lichen of the trail, to scrape and dig for stones, to prise them from the dirt. They were heavy stones, hardened from the eruptions of millennia before. Not as good a weapon as the pistol would have been, but the best available. It was not difficult to follow the trail because foot prints and broken twigs and crushed weeds were markers. She would have said that he had the stronger will for survival. He would have said that she had the better instinct for avoiding danger. Natacha thought that he would want to strike the first blow on the officer's head. Timofey would have said that she would demand to hit first.

At times they could skip from stone to stone, miss the patches of bog where water lay till far into the summer: at other moments they sank in the pits and he had to lie on his face and reach into the dark mud and drag out her shoe. Would not have said so and would not have shown it, but the girl was more important to him than flight over the border, the escape to a life beyond Russia . . . he would lose her if they went. He would appear gauche, awkward, and she would dance for a new music player, and they would be lost and helpless and always running, and she would drift from him. Both were city kids and knew Murmansk and could trade in any of its districts and had friends of a sort there who hung out with them and drank sparingly with them, and dealt dope and 'phets on neighbourhood pitches. They would not go. To stay they had to destroy the chance of the major naming them, identifying where they lived.

He saw them first, and she had them in view a moment later. They sank down on their knees. The pair were less than 100 metres ahead and going slowly. The Russian had stumbled, and it was clear to Timofey and Natacha that the younger man had heaved him up. Not a kick and a punch but a helping hand. They crept forward, and he had his stone behind his back and she had shoved hers down her anorak. He was twenty-two years old and she was twenty . . . and he thought that if he were not leading her she would slip away from him and be gone towards brighter lights. She thought him reliable and dependable but also beginning to be predictable. Both would have said that, for reasons known only to them, they needed this moment of violence and authority. They started to run.

They were on a stretch of drier ground and they could go fast and the gap closed.

Natacha was jostling to get past Timofey, to be the first to strike. The shock was wide on the stranger's face and his prisoner was cowering. She held her stone high and was clear of Timofey, realised that momentum was important in any attack: could be out in the middle of tundra, unseen, or could be in a dark corner by the Kirov statue, or among the trees behind the *Kursk*'s conning tower. She seemed to have a fury about her and her arm was up, the stone bigger than her fist.

Gaz reacted in the way he had been taught.

Retaliate and do not back off. No other options, no place he could run to. His prisoner was on the ground: could not escape. The pistol was in his 'wrong' hand and it would have cost time to swivel and aim. He used his spare arm as a shield and deflected her blow. She recoiled. Timofey came after her. Gaz caught his wrist and pushed the boy back, and Timofey's feet were entangled and he fell backwards. She came again at him. Gaz was from a culture where fighting women was degrading, would not have expected to use his full defence techniques: the heel of his hand across the throat, fingers extended and reaching for the eyes, a hard knee jerk up and into the lower belly, grabbing an ear lobe and twisting it . . . belting her across the face with the pistol as a last resort – or, the big call, aiming at her. She pounded at him and wriggled like an eel. He wasn't her target so she fought, scratched, tried to reach the officer. He would take blows and bruises and blood, but would not permit her to harm his prisoner. He fought with one hand. The other held the pistol.

Timofey was back on his feet and lurching towards them and she had registered the pistol, and went for it. Hard against his body, writhing, difficult to hold unless he grabbed a fist of blonde hair and yanked it back, but she could survive pain. Had absorbed it all her life, had the pallor of Arctic nights, tower block life and prison cells. He had been forced to his knees and covered the prisoner, who was helpless, his hands tied behind his back. He supposed, vaguely, as the blows rained on him, hers with feeling and his with less enthusiasm, that he would give his life to protect the Russian major, and it would only take for him to lose hold of the Makarov pistol, or one blow of the stone in his hand or hers . . . if he were concussed, knocked unconscious, then the prisoner was dead.

He remembered the arguments. More money as a reward for them if Major Lavrenti Volkov was dead because that was the aim of the mission that had sent him to scout out the location for a murder. More chance of them sliding back into the anonymity of dope peddling if the life of the man who could identify them was terminated. Gaz could not fault the arguments, but rejected them. One blow, and he had failed in his responsibility, might as well have stayed on the island, kept up his little chain of jobs, kept space in his home for the black dog.

He hit her. She squealed, fell back. Without hurting her he would never get off the tundra, reach the border, cross to the safety of Norwegian territory, all tantalisingly close. He lashed with his boot at Timofey's leg, and doubled him. Gaz did not know what happened in the next two, three seconds. Perhaps when her fingers had been groping for the pistol, one had found the lever for the safety and had shifted it. Perhaps, when he hit her or kicked the boy, his grip had altered and a finger had gone inside the guard. He was reeling, pushed himself up and the prisoner was still, barely breathing and face down. She had hatred in her eyes and part of her face was flushed from his blow. She glanced behind her and caught the eye of her boy, and it would have humiliated him that she led, not him, that she challenged him, and Gaz knew that the next time they came for him it would be . . . .

They did not do wounding shots on the range when SRR practised combat shooting, nor in the field. The card they sometimes carried spoke of justifying lethal force in the belief that their lives or those of others under their protection were now at risk. They did not do wounding shots because then an adversary might pull a grenade pin, detonate an Improvised Explosive Device, or have the strength to use a knife. The training was for killing shots, those that ended life. She would have taken the first two bullets, mid-chest or centre of the forehead – either where her thin anorak was torn open and her blouse had lost buttons in the struggle, or above the blaze of her eyes. He stumbled as he readied himself, and the prisoner was trying to turn and the officer's feet caught in Gaz's.

Only one shot fired. The crash of the firing in his ears and a moment of lost hearing, and the smell of the discharged bullet, and the flash of the ejected round.

Timofey dropped his stone, stepped back, raised his hands. Natacha froze. Not a surrender, but she ducked her head and knelt. The prisoner had jack-knifed into the foetal posture. His hearing sang with the sound of the discharge, but the quiet and the emptiness had come back to the tundra. Gaz pulled the officer to his feet.

Gaz said, "I understand, Natacha and Timofey, that you feel you would be paid more if this man were dead because that was the purpose of the mission. I understand that my prisoner has seen your faces and can identify you and I do not know how to protect you from that risk. I understand the gravity of the risks you have taken but Major Volkov is in my custody. I have to guarantee his welfare. I cannot feed him because I have no food, and I cannot give him water because I have none. But I can defend him, and will. I will go to my grave to defend him so that he can be delivered to a court and go in front of a judge. That is the way it is and your hopes of payment, and your anxieties about identification, are secondary. That is where we are."

Gaz walked tall, the prisoner a pace in front, and gritted his teeth; sweat ran in his eyes, and he felt the pain where she had hit him with the stone, and where her teeth had bitten.

He heard them following. He did not look back at them and had the pistol tight in his fist with another round ready to fire but with the safety lever raised. A sort of peace fell, and the intrusion of a shot being fired seemed long past, as if forgotten.

He lifted down the Dragunov, checked the magazine, armed the rifle.

Jasha had been asleep. Exhausted, he had lain across the front step of his cabin, his head on the bottom of the door jamb. He did not know how long it had been before he had lost the trembling in his hands, had put out of his mind the size of the teeth and the strength of the claws. And it was not just Jasha who had collapsed under the weight of the stress, but the bear also. Zhukov had lain on his back, his stump still raised, had not yet stuffed it into its mouth to suck the wound clean. Both man and beast shattered.

He put on his vest and shirt and slung the rifle on his shoulder. It would have been the same for both of them. First sleep, then slowly waking, then disbelief that it had happened, then the sound of a single shot. Near to the door was the debris of the experience. Spatters of blood, the rusted staple, and the pliers. He stepped over them. The dog did not follow him. Both Jasha and Zhukov had a rooted suspicion of intruders on their territory. Uppermost in his mind was the memory of seeing the two city kids skipping among rocks and bogs with a military man struggling to keep up with them.

The sun on his face, Jasha looked for Zhukov. He might have seen the bear's haunches between low trees. But they were still heavy with leaf and it could have been the back of the bear's head.

He set off. He could go fast across this terrain, and the bear would likely follow him. He went towards the place where he believed he had heard a pistol discharged.

Alice reached Fee.

"How is he?"

They stood together on the coast line, could see past the repair yard and the quays for the cruise boats and up the inlet, almost to the open Barents Sea.

Alice answered, "Just quiet, as when stuff stacks against him. Focused."

"And said?"

"Don't think he really said anything."

"End of an era."

"End of fucking everything as we know it . . . It was pretty specific what came to us. That Operations Group Executive didn't mince it. Back home, and soonest. Seems there's been a *coup d'état*, and that the D-G's gone off to meet a surgeon's knife and the DD-G has his hands on power. All the pantomime stuff, the Round Table, it's gone to the trash can. And *Matchless* is for the fairies, the Service won't go up that road any more. Dominic told me all that, more than he should have, along with the 'homeward bound' bit."

"Wants to get his hand in your knickers."

"That is disgusting," Alice pouted. "Probably true . . ."

They made a point, Fee and Alice, of discretion. Their relationship was not an open secret. Had it been, they'd have likely received overtures to join up with splinter groups bent on advancing the cause of their sexuality: and fuck-all business of anyone. But they were not observed in Kirkenes, and Alice had slipped her hand into the crook of Fee's arm, had a hold of that muscular elbow. A couple of relaxed lovers . . . not a pair of girls who had heard that the purpose of their professional lives was disintegrating, that their boss was surplus to requirements.

". . . Dominic says that the best Knacker can hope for is a berth in Finance and Resources. No more fieldwork. No chance of him being where he is now, on a border and staring into the haze and the mist, and waiting."

The message had come through. Alice had taken it. She had gone to find Knacker up on the border, watching the fence, escorted by their Norwegian guide. Had passed it on . . . Had been greeted with an impassive face, something of a shrug: no obscenities, no collapse of the shoulders, barely a twitch at the sides of his mouth . . . It was payback time for Knacker, the D-G's protective parasol under which he had thrived, now gone.

"We're casualties, poppet, go down the plug with him."

"I will fucking miss it, really will."

Fee had the fags out and Alice lit them. They would stay put and wait for the arrival of the small fishing boat, and the Harbour-Master's Office had told Fee it was out of the main shipping channels and at the north end of the inlet, and they'd see it within an hour. No indication of whether their man was aboard. That was their vigil. Alice threw away her cigarette and it buried itself in fresh seaweed dumped from the last high tide.

Alice said, "We're doing a vigil and so is he. He'll stay up there until we know where our man is, and whether it's been win or lose. He'll work until they cut his legs off at the knees . . . Tell you something – all of those guys and girls that he recruited, then put in harm's way, exploited and used, never let them cop out while they were still functioning, they never complained. Bizarre. Why not? They'd cause to . . . If not dead, they could have queued right across Vauxhall Bridge, and marched on VBX, then slagged him off. Didn't. Never bitched about him, seemed almost grateful to him. Funny old world."

They gazed out at the sea, focused on the headland around which the trawler would come, and, held each other tight.

Mikki said, "That is a pistol shot."

Boris said, "It would be nine mills, a Makarov."

"One was stolen, a Makarov."

"Stolen from a cop, taken off an idle fucker."

"And being pleasured?"

"Good chance it's the one from the cop. Where was the shot?"

"Towards the border, where else?"

Quietly spoken and with a minimum of fuss they put a call through to the barracks at Titovka, and their presence in the ranks of FSB was repeated to a duty officer, and the advice that intelligence indicated an attempt would be made later that day to breach the fence dividing their Federation from the NATO country of Norway. Not specific, but emphasised that FSB did not expect their warnings to be discounted. A map had been dragged out and spread wide. Boris said where he thought the shot had been fired. Mikki stood at his full height and sniffed the air. They would both identify where the sound had come from, could factor in wind strength and direction, estimate how far from the road the pistol had been fired. They parked off the road.

Mikki said, "We're having two platoons up on that sector of the fence. The line we're going would give us a two-kilometre probability zone, where they'd be looking to cross. Two platoons and vehicles on the patrol track."

They went forward at a good pace, and had the fire-power drawn from the armoury.

Mikki said, "As long as this is understood, we do not walk through this shit-hole territory in the interests of that bastard. Not for him . . . Could have been that shot sent him on, and not a wet eye from anyone I know."

"His mother might weep but not for long. And nothing from his father. We are here on this fuck-awful piece of ground to do things for the reputation of the brigadier. We had the contract to watch for him."

"Had the contract and were pissed."

"Pissed and asleep, and the contract paid us well."

"Were asleep when he was lifted."

"Which is?"

"Which is not something to be shouted from the rooftops."

Two peals of laughter, but both grim and shorn of humour. They moved fast and their legs pounded the rough ground like they had decades before when they had trained to go to

Afghanistan. Tiredness would kick in later . . . Nothing to do with rescuing the young FSB major and nothing to do with the possible, or probable, incursion of a team from a hostile state. Only to do with the loyalty felt for the brigadier.

Gaz had realised the change. The kids were behind them, at a distance, but keeping pace. No one spoke. Gaz did not talk to his prisoner about the weight of responsibility, nor about what he had seen from his position on that day more than two years before, made no accusations. The major had denounced himself, declared his guilt and shame, but said no more of it. Did not complain about the lack of food or water, did not try to free his arms, or speak of the kids' attack. Gaz reckoned that soon they would break away and might shout a farewell and might not, but would head back, would want to be in their dealing zones when the peculiar half-light of the Arctic summer came to their city.

Soon they would be, if his navigation was proven, at the lake, and they might rest there, and he would be wary and have the pistol ready, and consider how they would do the last leg to the fence perhaps an hour and a half away. His concentration roved. Knew it and could not stop it.

Part of his mind dribbled in the direction of what would follow his crossing – after he had climbed high, and to hell with the barbed wire on the top, and no concern for the alarms that would be shrieking in some control centre. Where would Knacker be? How would it be received, bringing back a prisoner? The man in front of him kept his own counsel, did not query where they went, how they would go across the frontier. Would have wanted a corpse and the ability to filter word to a broken community that vengeance of a sort had been inflicted on those responsible. Not able to get at the Iranians, their commander and militiamen beyond reach, but a Russian officer was a bigger prize. Except they would not have that: instead they must make do with a man – ordinary and seeming harmless, respecting the instructions of the court guards, standing in front of robed lawyers. Would have wanted a body, and were not going to have one. Thought also, accessing a different section of his mind, of the danger of the lack of concentration and his inability to create a full sense of danger. Knew of men who had been in Afghanistan and who had done long-range patrols or had been in the business of defusing the IEDs, and who had been either careless or too tired to register what was around them, and had died – like the devils stalked them and watched for weakness. And switching back in his mind, the people on the other side – Knacker and his girls – would have to make do with what they were given.

A big bird circled high over them, and sometimes he heard the kids talking, and did not know why they followed. He listened for sirens and for a helicopter, heard neither. Sometimes Gaz was aware of wheezing noises and thought it was the kids, and sometimes a twig snapped, and he thought that was the kids' feet. And he tried to up the speed but was too tired and the ground too rough, and they managed only a plodding progress on the old animal trails.

16

Close enough now to the lake to see the reflections bouncing off it, and silver ripples.

It was the biggest, best, marker point since he had started to walk the prisoner across the empty landscape. Felt almost proud – not about the mission, not about its success, but about the simplicity of navigation ... didn't think many would have been able to locate it. Getting close to the lake deflected what was more serious – the border. But, still surprising, there were no helicopters and no drones, and no baying dogs. The kids followed them and he did not know why, were just a distant tail ... At the water, fish were leaping, leaving increasing circles. He stopped and motioned that the prisoner sit on a rock, and was refused. The prisoner pointed to his flies. Gaz had the role of gaoler which he took seriously. Half the men he had known in the military, maybe even Arnie and Sam who were the last he had worked with, and maybe even 'Bomber' Harris who piloted the Chinook when they had been taken to the village, would have told him to go 'piss his pants'. Not Gaz. He fiddled with the officer's flies, and worked the necessary gap in his pants, and might have grinned sheepishly. It came in a flood and some went down into the lake. He thought it was an obligation, and the prisoner finished, and shook his backside and let the last drop go, and Gaz put him back inside and zipped his flies, then motioned to the rock.

His prisoner sat. "Thank you."

Gaz grunted. It had seemed the right thing to do, and he had done it, and nodded to acknowledge the gratitude, and reckoned it was genuine.

"And I do not know your name."

" 'Corporal', just that."

"And I am 'Major'. Why did they give this work, this mission, to a man so junior, to a corporal?"

"Because I was there and because I could identify you."

"Why did they not send trained men with you, men from the special services?"

"I cannot discuss operational planning."

"You are very formal, Corporal."

"I think that is as it should be, Major."

As an afterthought, Gaz pushed the Makarov down the back of his belt. He went to the edge of the lake and stood on pebbles, crouched and leaned forward and cupped his hands. He filled them with water. Then went back to the rock and his prisoner lapped at the water, wet his mouth but slopped most of it. Did it again, and repeated it until the prisoner indicated he had taken in enough.

"Tell me something, Corporal."

"I will not discuss the planning of the mission, its end-game."

"This question, did your family push you into the military?"

"It was my own decision."

"You did not join because that was the wish of your father and mother?"

"It was nothing to do with my guardians. I do not know the name of my father and I have not seen my birth mother since I was very young."

A sigh, a shrug, a roll of the eyes as if to say, 'God and were you not fucking lucky . . .' and then, "Are you still corporal, in the military? Will you be promoted if the mission is successful? Well rewarded? I ask to learn your motivation, Corporal."

"I am no longer in the military. I am a civilian. I had the rank of corporal, but not any longer. I garden for people and repair their homes. It is what I can manage."

"Because?"

"Because of illness."

"In the Russian military we call it the Afghan Syndrome – that illness?"

"Because of what I saw, was a witness to. I was violent, hit someone I was close to, a woman. I also can be ashamed of my actions, and feel guilt. And that is enough, and neither you nor me is a therapist. Enough."

"Thank you, Corporal."

"For nothing, Major, and we are going to rest another half-hour, then push forward, and we will go through or under or over the border fence."

The smile that greeted Gaz was sardonic, almost mocked him. He had not yet read the man nor knew what reaction to expect from him as they came close to the wire, and having the pistol in his belt was reassurance of a sort. The kids stayed back.

The Norwegian brought two collapsible stools from his vehicle, and a thermos and other gear.

"What's necessary, if it's for the long haul."

"Appreciated."

Knacker had been sitting on the grass, under birch trees and within sight of the wire fence, but hidden from view. One patrol had gone by, a four-wheel drive vehicle with only a pair in the front, and he had stayed still and it had not slowed. He sat on the stool, had the same view, but the Norwegian was not satisfied with their cover. From a rucksack, he took two tunics and a jar of camouflage cream. Helped Knacker off with his coat, emptied the pockets, folded it, packed it away. Gave a hand for him to shrug into the military tunic with the camouflage shapes of general NATO markings, and did the same for himself. Opened the jar and dug with a couple of fingers. Knacker offered his face, was daubed. The Norwegian's fingers moved briskly across Knacker's features. He recognised an old smell and the taste of the cream when his upper lip was done and his tongue flickered to it involuntarily. A grin, ironic, from the Norwegian.

"Familiar? Back to the good old days? Not recently?"

"Used to, in the Irish times."

They had been happy old days, not just good. Pretty much anyone who had made a name, positive or negative, awesome or disgraced, had served in the Province, cut their teeth there. The experiences were used as a raw kindergarten, before they'd all dispersed, gone on to confront supposed Russian opponents or those from ISIS, home and abroad. And pretty much anyone would have recalled those days as among the best that life had so far offered. Most of his time in Northern Ireland had been running assets, meeting in darkened pub car parks, or in remote lay-bys; on a few occasions he had worn uniform, done CamCream on face and hands, a Browning 9mm on a webbing belt, and had gone out to do some ditch time, or get buried in a hedgerow with a clear view of a farmhouse. Remembered all the stuff about cows' curiosity, and sheep gathering in a half-moon and staring at the camera lenses and the binoculars, and the damn dogs that roamed ahead of the farmer when he came each morning to walk his parcels of land and would have a pocketful of enmity to carry with him. There was no danger here, not to him, Knacker was not threatened. Gaz was. He understood, after reflection, that the Norwegian – no name required and no ranking – would be an officer in the PST organisation, or might have been from E14, but he had no need for detail. Sufficient to realise that the man would have known as much about the life of the fence as would a train-spotter at the end of the platform at Didcot, knew every scheduled engine on the down line, and the up. Knacker did not mind help, was not stubbornly resistant ... and who cared, who gave a tuppenny toss, because the era of Knacker's Yard was wrapped in cling foil, gone in the can. Did not have to be told, but had the minutiae of danger for Gaz explained to him, a soft voice and insufficient to frighten the songbirds that flipped close to them.

"What we are hearing makes a picture."

Gazing at the wire and noting the camera and the cables that would flash alarms if yanked, Knacker followed the progress of a pair of chaffinches, brightly coloured, pretty and confident, who perched on the barbs coiled at the top. And listened.

"It is confusing. We have nothing from the police networks, but have material from the confidential networks of FSB. An officer is listed as missing. He is a major, Lavrenti Volkov. The circumstances are vague. There are also reports of a foreign asset having crossed the frontier, and met by a nonentity couple, drug dealers. More reports indicate that a force of a hundred border guards will be deployed on the border within the next hour ... May I ask if it has been an aim of your organisation to bring a prisoner into Norway and ..."

"No bloody way."

"The prisoner being taken to the border is an assumption based on what we know."

"About as far from reality as is possible to stretch."

"A prisoner brought with coercion to the border, and across it, would signal a grave and embarrassing situation. Repercussions would follow."

"Our guy, he has no mandate."

"Your man's brief, as I understand, is to report on locations and schedules, not more."

"Or do the business there."

"I have been, perhaps unwisely, selective with the information I have passed back to my superiors. If a prisoner were brought across the fence there would be a greater fallout than if such a prisoner and your agent were to be intercepted on the far side of the fence. It would be bad, would destabilise the narrow agreements that are in place. Nothing then could be covert, hidden. Is there a situation where your agent might believe it within his remit to bring over a prisoner?"

"Absolutely bloody not."

"Effectively to kidnap a major of FSB would provoke a very considerable issue."

"Not authorised. Would be in flagrant violation of any instructions given him."

"Why then would he act in such a way?"

"Don't know. I'll take his fucking balls off, watch me as I do it."

"So, we wait and we see."

They did not have long to wait. A small convoy of military trucks laboured up the track parallel to the wire. An officer dismounted from a jeep. Uniforms jumped down from the tailgates. And a dog handler came with them, and a machine-gun with a forward bi-pod. Orders were given and a field of fire back towards a forest track was identified. The convoy moved on and cigarettes were lit, and weapons were armed. Knacker's hand, as if he needed comfort, went to his trouser pocket.

The coin was easy to find. Lightweight metal and frayed at the edges and with the indents on its surfaces almost eroded in spite of the girls' hard work at cleaning it. His fingers turned it over . . . He reflected. He was the intelligence officer, painted and was crouched over his stool, and he wondered how many times that man, the keepsake in his imagination, had taken up a position within sight of the Wall, had been there damn near two millennia before and had watched for the return of his asset . . . And on the other side, hidden behind the Wall, behind the fence and the tree line, was the sector's garrison commander. He saw himself in both roles, held the coin between two fingers, and one would win in the next several hours and one would lose – and neither would ever have believed they could trust an agent, an asset, to do as he was bloody told. He let the coin fall and it was subsumed amongst his small change. One to win and one to lose, predictable for both Knacker and his adversary.

The sea was millpond smooth.

The wind had gone, a little sunlight pitched through the cloud. Fee and Alice disentangled their arms, stood apart, as if they were at work.

"The betting?" Alice asked.

"Turning out to be that sort of day. I'm taking a no-show."

Not often in their lives, tramping in the wake of Knacker and running affairs from the Yard, that they knew failure. Fee had no trust that their man would be on board. The instructions had been for the minimum of phone contact firstly from their man, and then from their boat. Taking it into Murmansk with the hold full of red king crabs, gourmet stuff, had been a master stroke, and having it there as an evacuation vehicle, along with decent documentation, were matters for pride.

A few gulls flew in its wake. Not many, because it was coming back without a catch. No gutted carcases were heaved overboard and the birds had nothing to clamour for. Fee had the better eyes of the two and had a hand at her forehead to shield the glare off the water, and it was hardly necessary but she shook her head. Had he been on board he would have stood at the bow. Would not have waved or jumped about because they were only a few hundred yards from the well-stocked Russian Consulate, and would have been too street-wise to blow the cover prematurely, but would have been there. Nothing to say, just a feeling of growing emptiness. They saw three crew on deck and could make out the silhouette of the skipper in the wheel-house. It came to the quay-side, docked carefully. One of the boys jumped ashore and lashed a rope to a ring, and then the engine was cut. He didn't look at them, avoided their gaze. Another rope was lashed and the boat lay still.

The skipper took it on himself . . . the engineer slid away and went to the harbour office to do the formalities . . . came towards Fee and Alice. Cigarettes were lit.

The skipper spoke, with something near to a doctor's bedside tone, sombre, "We waited. We stayed at the quay as long as we dared. To have stayed longer invited even greater suspicion than we had already attracted. You bluff, and you attempt to make a best friend of a harbour official, but it wears thin. Impatience replaces cooperation. We had to sail. We were ready to hustle him on board as soon as he passed the security checks, and would have sailed within minutes. He did not come. We were sorry to have left without him. We cannot explain it. There was no extra security at the fishing docks. What has happened? A last thing. When we were far up the inlet, at an agreed place, we launched a buoy close to the shore and a small inflatable is packaged beneath it. We had talked of it with him. Very frankly, it is little more than a craft suitable for a beach in summer. I am sorry."

He broke away, went back on board. Fee and Alice walked towards the town.

Alice said, "I hate this goddamn place."

Fee said, "It fucking stinks."

"Just a little nothing town, barely on a map."

"And under the perpetual shadow of that bloody monster across the border. We're screwed up, at the end of the road."

"Best then is to get pissed, make a proper job of it."

Both kept walking and neither wept and both wished they could.

"We do things differently, Dominic, today and in the future. The sooner that lesson is learned the more comfortable we shall all be."

Dominic, considered a rising star, had been called to the office now occupied by the acting D-G to report on his communications with the far extremity of northern Norway, where it was adjacent to the frontier with the Russian Federation. He had been able to relay the message that Knacker – called him by that name which raised a serious frown and a shaken head – expected to be out within twenty-four hours, and would be bringing his team with him. 'All of the team?' Which was more than Dominic could answer.

"The Service is held back by the presence of a group of decrepit veteran warriors, playing games as if they were still at their preparatory schools. Playing God with people's welfare, even their lives – which I understand to be this Knacker's speciality. Has some poor wretch over there, has he? Something quite repellent about men and women who sit in safety while they consign others to risk, often to death. I won't have it."

Dominic sailed close to impertinence. He asked if the old adage of 'rough men' who might 'visit violence', at night, on the folks likely to harm us was now inappropriate.

"That is an attitude, no doubt hawked round by the 'old guard'. But on my watch it will not be tolerated. Might have been acceptable a century ago, not today. State-sponsored assassination no longer has houseroom, and those who object can go and find themselves alternative employment. Root and branch these 'rough men' will be removed from the Service payroll. I won't have it. It's a new age that I will preside over . . . and this Knacker, he has a man on the far side of the Russian frontier, no doubt with a hue and cry up his backside ... It will be a new dawn and it starts tomorrow. So, get him home, and his team, before more pain is inflicted. I read a résumé on the justification of this mission. It is preposterous, some woolly idea about a centre of intelligence in some ravaged village in Syria. Should be bottom of any list of priorities, and a Russian citizen to be murdered in cold blood. Might have been acceptable in the past, no longer. They're going out to grass, all of them. I'll not permit hankering after the Dark Ages. They are redundant. Understood?"

"Very clearly," Dominic answered. "I'll get back on to them. Tell them to find a decent verdant pasture. Have them on the first plane out, those that have a chance."

"Let's go do it," Natacha said.

She was bored, uncomfortable, and tired, and the mosquitoes had taken a liking to her. She reached back and took Timofey's arm and heaved him up.

They went together, in step, but neither carried a stone. Her idea, not his. Timofey would have turned away from the two men and headed off back the way they had come. He thought, ruefully, that too often he listened to her and did as she said. Had reason to: she had been the one arrested and he had been the one to break free, and she had been the one who had kept her mouth shut during interrogation and he had been at liberty. He sensed a sort of madness about her and wondered what show she would enact. There was always a show with Natacha which made her fun to be alongside, worthwhile when they worked. Was a pain in his gut when she plagued him with the *Kursk* business – not prepared to move on and 'get a life' as he urged. He knew each detail of the *Kursk*'s sinking and how long the survivors of the initial explosion had been alive at the stern end, and the telling made him shiver each time she parroted it, and what the navy had done and what fucking Putin hadn't done. Knew it – and loved her in a rough, unsentimental way.

So, they went to 'go do it', and she was in front and skipped gracefully off rocks and on to hard grass tufts and stayed out of the bog, and Timofey laboured behind her. He did not know how she would do it, but supported her aim. She wanted money . . . He thought it a bad day for them, which had got worse because they had failed to retrieve the pistol, shoot the fucking officer, then get back home. Their only consolation was that they *might* stay free. Money would help. Money, in his opinion, usually helped.

Her show, and he would stay back. He was confident for her. If she could take a cop's gun off him then he thought her a certainty. She reached them. The officer watched her, hands still tied behind his back, and something beyond contempt on his face, and Gaz never took his eye off her and removed the pistol from his belt. She was covered by the officer's eyes and by the pistol.

The silence could have been what Timofey hated most about this bare, desolate space. It seemed to close in on him, then begin to throttle him. So he started to clap, rhythmically, as if they were not by a lake in daylight in the tundra but under the strobe lights of a strip club. It was the part she played. Her dance, and Timofey kept up his clapping but sank on to the ground. They would need money if they were to disappear, shrink off the stage and move on, perhaps reach as far as Archangel and start again there. She was a few feet in front of the Englishman and the officer, and her thin little anorak came off first. A girl by the railway station had been desperate for a spliff last summer and had paid for it with this anorak and Natacha was rarely without it. She threw it down by the officer's feet. Her dance was sinewy, what they might have done in an oriental dive, not that either of them would have known.

After the anorak came the blouse. After the blouse came a flimsy vest. More pirouettes and more fast-foot shuffles, and then the speed of his clapping grew and her hands were at her waist and her belt was hanging loose.

She kicked off her trainers, then her jeans and came to her underwear. She did not look at the two men, did not know whether they watched her, were entranced, or were embarrassed, irritated. She went into the water, until it covered her ankles, and her dance splashed them. Flesh as white as if it had come from under a stone, went further and the water cascaded off her thighs, and her hair dripped and she went in deeper. Took one step more than she had intended and the bottom of the lake must have sloped sharply . . . and she was pitched forward. The clapping stopped, and she shrieked, went under. None of the men came forward to drag her out.

She surfaced, spluttering. The bones in her body seemed to jut out, sharp enough to break the skin at her elbows, her shoulders and her pelvis. Her hair was lank and tangled.

She chose Gaz. "You liked that?"

Hands on hips in front of him. "You thought I danced well?"

Made no effort to dry herself, had struck a pose, no modesty, and the smile cracked her cheeks. Her cabaret act was complete and attention was riveted on her, as she required.

"Did I do well enough?"

She stretched out her hand and the water dripped from her, and it would never have warmed during the brief Arctic summer, but she did not shiver.

"You will pay me?"

She played her role, thought she did it well. He took a wad of money from his hip pocket, tossed it at her and she caught it, grimaced, then threw it towards Timofey.

"And him?"

The prisoner had his back to her.

"Because he will name us, denounce us. His money."

He turned. And blanched. Saw her, all of her, raked a gaze over her body, every angle of her. The officer whispered into Gaz's ear. Gaz's hand was in a pocket of his tunic and lifted out a smart crocodile-skin, wallet. Peeled out the bank notes, all high denomination. She came close and they were handed to her, and the wallet returned to his pocket. She took the money, as a whore would have done, and grinned.

"And he will denounce us?"

Gaz shook his head. For a moment, confusion knitted her forehead, and suddenly she was small and no longer pretty and her boldness was gone. She covered herself with one arm and scampered clumsily among the rocks for her clothing, and turned away from them while she dragged on her clothes, and it was hard to fasten clasps and buttons because her hands shook.

It was over, like a curtain had been drawn across a stage.

In a few minutes they would move. They had heard no sirens, no helicopters, no barking dogs or the shouts of a cordon closing.

Gaz hardly dared to consider that in a handful of hours he would be touching down on Westray, his island refuge. Never a smooth landing, always a series of lessening bumps and usually a skid, most often to the starboard side as the wind came off the west coast and ran clear across the makeshift strip. A hut there, with a closed but unlocked door, and a chance to call up the hotel and ask who was doing taxi duty that day . . . Wondered if they would ask, from the far end of the line, whether he had been far, anywhere nice, and had he had better weather than was hitting the island. Just a bit of business that had to be attended to. Would feel the wind on his face coming off the Atlantic, and would hear the gulls' screams. He gazed out over the lake and saw reflections and felt the cold of the ground and the rock he sat on and the sunshine was brittle. Allowed himself the chance to dream because the last stage was almost on him, and on his prisoner.

The officer was silent. The kids were near him but not joining him, and the money would have been bulging the boy's pocket. Gaz was surprised that the officer had murmured in his ear a promise that the kids would not be denounced by him, but it had been said. Only a few minutes. The memory was a sharp pain, not welcome.

He had been told that in his condition, which they took seriously, the Orkneys were ideal. An escape from stress, withdrawal from anxiety, an opportunity to regain his health and to prosper, a chance to make strong reliable friendships and to 'make a difference' – this was emphasised. Would he go back? He did not know, and the peace at the lakeside disturbed him.

*   *   *

Delta Alpha Sierra, the sixteenth hour

It ended quickly.

Shots were fired into the pits before they were filled with piled earth. No point in the shooting except that it might have reminded the militiamen that they had confronted dangerous enemies. The vehicles were manoeuvring and the headlights spinning through all directions, and sometimes they burned out the vision through his image intensifier lenses, and sometimes he saw men running. He saw the officer work in a frenzy at the second pit, the last bodies going in, and the last soil and dirt covering them, and then the officer was gesticulating to the personnel carrier drivers, and the Iranian commander stood with his hands on his hips and allowed the Russian to give instructions. The APCs were driven up and down over the pits and where they sank too deep in the loose earth, more soil shovelled up to level off the ground . . . and then chaos. One body had been forgotten, and the pits were already closed over. Gaz thought that it was from the first group to be executed, left beside a goalpost. Petrol was tipped on it and a match thrown. There was shouting from the NCOs, and the final men came running towards their vehicles.

Gaz had seen the pits and the burials and the work the officer undertook himself. Had watched because the alternative was to have turned his head away from the football pitch and the destroyed buildings of the village, and to concentrate on the gang, sprinting with the excitement of a pack in pursuit. He knew where she was, where the chase had ended. Knew also that she had broken clear of him and had run so that she would divert attention away from him. He saw the last one break from the place where they had caught her. Yearned for the opportunity to use his rifle, take aim and lock, get the range and density of any cross wind, line him up and squeeze . . . and the militiaman stopped, turned, and aimed down at the ground, into the rocks. Gaz thought he identified a piece of her clothing, and saw her bare leg. Aimed, fired, had a jam. Cleared the breach, aimed and fired, and again silence. And in frustration the boy hammered his weapon against a rock . . . but was not going to strip it down in the dark and clear it. He might have reached for a knife at his belt. If he was a country boy he would have thought little of taking a knife to the throat of a goat or a sheep. There were yelling for him. He went, and fast. If he were a country boy he'd have the sure-footedness of a youngster able to go at speed in near darkness. A crescendo of noise as the engines gained power. He saw a light come on at the back of a carrier and hands reached down to grab him, peals of laughter, and then the heavy noise as the armour-plated door clanged shut.

They left. He watched the headlights turn off the dirt track to her village and straightened on the metalled surface of the highway, fumes belched and they were gone. The lights faded and then disappeared. Night was allowed to settle, and it was quiet. And then a soft sound of whimpering. He knew where he would find her.

Gaz reverted to type. He did not crawl out of his cover, take off in leaps and bounds, charging down the slope and away to his left. He did what was drilled into him as the correct procedure when working behind an enemy's lines. Folded the scrim net, stuffed it in the Bergen, packed what he had collected in tinfoil and the bottle. He could have gone down to the wall beside the highway and set about changing the batteries on the camera, testing them and seeing if the problem were with the internal electronics or was merely power outage. But he did not . . . Could have been that the cameras had failed because of the fierce rain getting inside the casing, and he worried that he turned his back on the problem – but he did. He went toward the sound of the dogs.

The smells around him were of burning – the buildings and their contents. But most powerful was that of the scorched flesh of the body that had been noticed only when the grave pits were already filled in. The dogs were his guide. He came to them and the soft growling snarl dissolved when they scented Gaz. They were reluctant to move but came on their stomachs. When he crouched down, and had the Bergen and his rifle and needed one hand to steady himself, he realised that his fingers had moved from the fur of their necks and on to taut skin. Seemed natural to

Gaz, the first thing he did, was to find the hem of her skirt and lower it until it reached her sandals. He put his fingers on that place below her neck and on her shoulder where a pulse was felt. He knew she lived. He held her, and the dogs leaned against him. She started to push herself up, came half-way, hacked a cough, then let his arm take her weight and stood. What to say? Nothing to say. He owed his life to her, and did not at that time have the words to express what he thought of her.

The rain had stopped. Small mercy. She leaned heavily on him and he thought she would walk awkwardly and in pain because of what had been done to her. He assumed that she bled there and he would not have known how to ask her. Did not ask her anything and did not speak, and his tears had dried. She had none, and her breathing was steady. He had his phone out, hit the keys, not the text. Darkness cloaked him but he had the stars now, and a moon, and also his compass. She did not trip or stumble. He heard sounds around him that at first he could not identify, but the dogs showed him. Goats had materialised; not as many as at the start of the day. Some would have stampeded and were lost, some would have been shot for sport, but the dogs were alerted and brought the stragglers together.

It was cold: they pushed on. She no longer leaned on him, did not seem to need his help. Gaz could not think of a bigger debt than the one he owed her.

He had watched them for more than a quarter of an hour.

As an old soldier, one who had learned his trade well, Jasha had a rooted belief that problems were seldom solved by the man who hung back. And it was proven.

Time was lost, would not be regained. It interested him that the small group seemed to be resting beside the lake. He had watched. Old excitements had stirred. He had seen the girl do a striptease on the lake shore, had almost chuckled. There had been a whore-house in a wooden shed by the gate in a perimeter fence around an airfield south of Kabul, and the women had come from Bulgaria or Romania, all a long time ago, and he had thought this girl to be skinny and bony and likely to give a ride to remember. But that was of passing interest ... More important, he recognised her. Recognised her and remembered her boy, and the man he assumed to be a trained soldier who had come across the open spaces with them the day before. Knew them, and saw that they had another man with them. Jasha's binoculars identified the bound wrists and the military tunic of the type favoured by the FSB units. Jasha had gone towards the sound of a single shot. Perhaps he had heard it only because a momentary bluster of wind had carried the noise. Perhaps they had assumed the shot's retort would have vanished in the wilderness, gone unnoticed.

Jasha had heard it, and others had heard it. He watched them. Two men, both well armed, wearing civilian clothing. Not hunters who had strayed off the permitted areas and were after trophies. They were dressed for the city but had military-issue footwear. They were in pursuit, moved well, had a knowledge of dead ground and would not have been seen by those at the lake. Clear to Jasha that these were former fighting men, skilled in fieldcraft and presumably in marksmanship. Their route would take them to an intercept point that was halfway to the fence from the lake side.

And he had seen more that disturbed him. Before he had spotted the two men who would block, or trail, the fugitives, he had been on a heather-covered knoll, had lain on his stomach, had enjoyed an all-round view. The road from the east, the E105, climbed and was in clear sight. A military convoy was on the move but branching off to the west where there was nothing except the feeder roads used by the border militia to patrol the fence.

And ... and the bear was still with him. Old Zhukov, the warrior and survivor – the one who had saved his skin and lasted through the Stalin purges – and the one who was an old scarred beast with his combat scratches from fights over territory or feminine favours, and his three good feet, he tracked Jasha. Why? He did not know.

He hurried. He could cross rough ground at speed. It was a hunter's skill. He did not know why the bear did not just disappear into the dwarf birch and find a tree to sit under and sniff happily for berries, worms, a small deer it might outrun . . . but it followed him. Remained hidden but was close. He did not know the mind of the bear, but understood his own. His military career had been brought to an end because Jasha could not abide the posturing of the officer class. His obstinacy had ruled him. They had sought to belittle him, withdraw what was owed to him as a combat veteran because he had spoken a truth. He sided with victims, talked his mind on the treatment of wounded, frightened, conscripts in that distant war. Then, alone in his cabin in the endless winter months, reliant on the food he had stored in the summer and his supplies of heating oil, the hatred of them had germinated.

Had not met them, had never spoken with them, but was too gnarled in his temperament not to follow and watch. And the bear would easily keep pace with him and he had that reassurance. Also had the Dragunov rifle on his back.

"It will be me who shoots," Mikki whispered.

"You are likely to miss, I am the better shot," Boris answered him.

Both were supreme infantry-trained marksmen. In the late stages of the Afghan campaign, their unit had become increasingly involved in front line combat. The new conscript recruits had proved ever less reliable. With their officer, following where he led and with true faith, they had been deployed into increasingly hazardous patrols and strikes. The time when that officer had called down the air force on to his own position, because the hairy-faced bastards were within metres of them and the ammunition stock had dwindled to fuck-all of nothing, had been the culmination of their exposure to combat. And, that evening, after an apology of a hot shower and a visit to the casualty section of the military hospital to see comrades, the two had retired to a corner of the sergeants' mess, had drunk beer, had talked of hits. Mikki had claimed eight hits but Boris had said that he knew his count was nine.

"The compromise is that we both shoot."

"But only one will have the hit – me."

They laughed together. What was not discussed was the degree to which the target must be clear before the bullet was fired. They had both fired in Chechnya, and their officer had been on short-term secondment, and it was an ambush set up by an informant. A good informant because otherwise his wife and elder daughter were likely to have a 'bad time' in the barracks where they were held. It would have been a tricky shot to drop the prime target guy, and he had been alongside the informant. Both had fired . . . the target lived another hour before heading off to the martyrs' paradise and the waiting virgins, but the informant went down stone dead, half his head missing, Never agreed which of them had had the better aim.

"That target, he's for killing, done outright."

"Wouldn't want him in court, blathering his story."

"Not welcome, him regurgitating Syria."

"Put him down, close his eyes, forget . . . and we take our man, shit-face Lavrenti, home to his adoring mama. Assuming we haven't dropped him."

Neither was a spring chicken, and neither spent time in the FSB basement gymnasium, and neither of them took care over their diet: it was a sense of duty to the brigadier that pushed them on. They were to the east of the lake where the innocent group had stopped, and a girl had stripped and paraded herself. It confused them. The chance had been given them to get ahead and stay hidden while they moved and still they sat at the lake.

"What range you looking at?"

"About a hundred . . . Good enough?"

"Heh, they're moving. Sat on their arses, gave us time. Left it too long."

Time, as a sergeant used to say, to 'put the show on the road'. Gaz stood. He gazed around, did the full turn, watched and listened. A Sicilian moment: saw nothing, heard nothing . . . knew nothing. A pair of crows circled. Gaz always watched birds: these were moving steadily and showed no panic.

He had the pistol lodged in the back of his trousers. He took hold of the officer's tunic and helped him upright. He had not spoken since the girl had done her act, been pensive, his head bowed. The statement, that the kids would not be denounced from a courtroom on the far side, or in confidential talk with a lawyer, had surprised Gaz. He had wondered whether to believe it, but had not challenged it.

Gaz said quietly, "We go now. The last leg . . . Be quite certain, Major, that if you attempt to break free I will shoot you. It is your choice. You live and go across the wire, you decide to end your life here in a self-inflicted suicide. Be very certain, Major, that I will kill you rather than have you go free. I was there, I saw it, I am determined that you will face a court, a process of justice. There are people who believe that revenge is acceptable. Not me. That brings us down to the same level as those responsible for a crime. Had I only wanted revenge then I could have shot you at the start. My opinion, Major, that would have belittled me but for you would have been the easier option. You should sit each day in a cell and look at a barred window, peering out 'upon that little tent of blue we prisoners called the sky,' and should think each day of where you were, what you did. If you are a man then you walk with me, if you are not a man then you break and I shoot."

He tapped the major's shoulder. Gaz did not fancy himself as a speaker. He had said a few tongue-tied words from the dock, had addressed the magistrate's bench and made a piss-poor job of it, and his hands had shaken and the bench would have noted that he was no longer a fighting man.

No argument. The major moved. Ahead was a plateau of ground, carpeted in low birch, in full leaf, and dotted with green patches marking bogs, and there were reflections off little lakes, and dotted over the landscape were rock formations. They had a path of sorts to follow. It would be the same route as he had taken when he had come across. He glanced at his watch: anywhere else but here the light would be failing and the comfort of evening and darkness would be around him – not this far into the Circle. It would have been good to have had darkness, but he was not that blessed. His immediate target was higher ground, in a tree line, and the tree – taller than the rest – that had taken the lightning strike. First was the open ground. He had heard no helicopters nor the dawdling engine of a drone, and no sirens.

He turned, and gave a cursory wave to the kids. They were woken sleepers and he owed them nothing and they were paid, more handsomely than intended, and had made their own bed. Without them he would have blundered . . . but they were not friends which was the creed of the instructors. They were Locally Recruited Assistance, and he had no responsibility for them.

17

The officer spun and Gaz had the pistol out from his belt. Cocked it.

The kids ran towards him. He waved them back, was ignored.

Had he been on his own he would have moved faster and with more attention to his security. But he escorted a prisoner who had his wrists pinioned at the back. The major could not walk easily and often stumbled, and there were times that he might have pitched forward and gone down if Gaz had not grabbed him and held him upright. He had twice found his own footprints, and knew that he took the best route as he headed for the dead tree. It surprised him that the prisoner did not complain about his treatment, did not try to flop down and refuse to go another step. It seemed to Gaz that the major had weighed up his situation, had decided that the fence was as good an option as any. Would Gaz have shot him? Possible he would have aimed and pulled the trigger if he had been kicked, a blow in the groin, or if the major had used his forehead on Gaz's nose – and then had run. Might have fired then. If the prisoner had collapsed, could have claimed he'd turned his ankle, would he have put the barrel tip against the back of his skull, and squeezed? How he had won the prisoner's cooperation was beyond fathoming. The man had his head down and concentrated on the ground ahead, on the next step and where he could keep his balance. They were less than an hour from the border fence and making good progress, and still there were no sirens, no tracker dogs, no helicopters. The kids were a diversion and an irritation, a further drain on

Gaz's focus. He was tired beyond exhaustion, hungry and thirsty.

He had not heard them, should have done.

"You stay back. Go back. Not your place and not your time."

Nothing from Timofey, but the girl laughed in his face. He had spun, had the weapon raised and realised the lunacy of standing in the centre of a wilderness and aiming a loaded Makarov pistol.

"You have no business at the fence. I don't take you with me. You did what was asked of you, and that finishes your involvement."

Maybe Gaz should have threatened them with a show of ruthless and uncompromising temperament . . . Some of the Hereford people would have frightened the knickers off her and made him flinch, but they were the men who would not have questioned the Knacker instruction. *Gaz, I trusted you, and a host of people have that faith in you. Find a way, always a resourceful soldier, weren't you?* Enough of them would have done. He had not, and had a prisoner and would receive little gratitude from the big cats when he handed him over.

"The last time I tell you – stay back. Get under cover. Don't follow."

Did not know what else to say. He could not shoot them, had used both of them and she still had the same damn grin playing at her mouth, taunting and teasing. The boy did not break stride.

"At the border, I don't know what I'll find. Patrols, maybe. Shoot to kill. Go back."

Gaz almost believed what he said. Guns, danger, troops, directed at all of them. Would have bottled it before, now showed it.

She did not answer but Timofey did. "Be good to see, the border, see into Norway. Never been there, never done that."

"It is not a theme park. Stay back and do not interfere."

"Will be a show. Something to remember you."

He did not know how he'd lose them. Madness, as if he led an asylum party, and . . .

"May I speak, Corporal?"

"To say what?"

He was Lavrenti Volkov, he held combat decorations awarded for service in Syria, he was a man identified for fast-track promotion, he had performed tasks inside the *Federal'nya sluzhba bezopasnosti* that had advanced his own career, and had delivered influential men to tongue-tied impotence. He was the son of a prestige-laden senior officer – and had been broken by the civility of a soldier, a mere corporal, who was a witness. Arrogance was stripped off him. Might as well have walked as naked as the girl had been but without fun on his face, only abject apology. He looked ahead, kept up a good stride, spoke firmly.

"I deny nothing. I was there. I killed – old people, women, children – killed them or helped to kill them, did not prevent the killing of them. There was a frenzy in the air. It consumed me, and when my face was scratched and blood drawn I lost control of my actions. That is not an excuse, but a fact. I veered to the edge of 'evil', became a creature beyond the norms of behaviour. Before that day I took delight in humiliating men through the uniform I wore and the power given me. Took pleasure from inflicting fear, and could grade it so that a man in front of my desk might be only discomfited, but might also piss his pants. That, Corporal, is power, and it is enjoyable. It is like a drug. At the village it was different to the Lubyanka . . . I called it 'evil'. I have been punished, not as I ought to have been, but still punished. I have not had a girl since I came back from Syria, only a whore and rarely. I do not sleep at night whether it is the Arctic winter or the Arctic summer, and pills are useless. I am destroyed, Corporal. Because of what I did, I should face justice for what happened in the village, and face retribution. I understand the punishment that should be presented to me. I sincerely regret what I did . . . that is what I believed important to tell you."

"I am not a priest. I cannot absolve you."

"Am not asking."

"Nor offer any level of mercy."

"Not requested."

"I do not debate what you did. They wanted you killed, my people. They wanted your murder, chopped down in a street in Murmansk, broadcast in those small enclaves of Syria where the government does not have support. Dead, you were a good image to demonstrate the limits of your country's power. Your corpse would be a fine symbol, an encouragement to keep fighting. Because of what you have said, I do not think the better of you, or the worse of you. I was a witness and am scarred. We keep walking, and I will shoot if you try to break away, shoot to kill."

Hard going and difficult ground, and the kids were behind them and he heard the boy's voice and the girl's laughter. They were on open ground and it was hard for him with his arms pinioned. He thought he left behind him an old world: hatred and contempt would fall on him. He slipped, fell, and was tugged up without ceremony. He had not meant to gain sympathy, but had earned none. He regained his balance, was shoved forward. He did not know why they were not tracked, and why the helicopters were not up, nor the drones, did not know why he was not hunted . . . They approached a dead tree, wide branches that were grotesque and ill-shaped, where crows perched, gazing down on them – and the girl laughed again, like it was a school jaunt.

Delta Alpha Sierra, the seventeenth hour

They walked in darkness. Gaz had draped her arm over his shoulder and she clung to his Bergen. The village was far behind them. The cloud had broken. Stars shone, and a miserable moon threw slight light. It was a skill Gaz had, to navigate across open and featureless ground.

Around them were the goats from her herd and her dogs. Gaz had offered her the biscuits from the bottom of his Bergen but she had refused. The dogs had wolfed them down. There were enough small indents in the ground for rainwater to have gathered and the animals – both the goats and the dogs – could drink. He did not talk because he had no idea what would have been appropriate to say. She had been gang raped and the price she'd paid was his life.

They were briefed on Russian military tactics, and command structures in Syria's theatre, and were told about living conditions for their troops, had a fair impression of life for their air force personnel and the special forces units. None of their own intelligence people had turned up at the Forward Operating Base with thumbnail sketches of existence inside a camp of IRGC militia, how it would be to board and lodge with the Iranians . . . and after any fire-fight the chance was that the Russians would hightail it to a place of their own and do their report.

. . . and he'd be telling his story to their intelligence people and main force unit officers. 'We got ourselves involved in a confused small-arms contact. There was an attack on our garrison camp from terrorists; they were beaten off. This morning the local IRGC organised a counter-strike at company level. I did not feel it necessary to involve myself in the operation and they seemed competent in what they intended. The night attack came from a terrorist-controlled village, Deir al-Siyarqi, just off the main highway crossing our sector. They met resistance there, a full-scale fire-fight developed. Passions ran high and there may have been civilian casualties when the village was finally taken. I cannot rule out the possibility of reprisals against non-combatants, but I would stress the Iranians believed the community to be a nest of anti-government dissent. I and my escort stayed back because there was no reason for us to be directly involved. It took longer to complete than expected because, in very poor weather conditions, there was continuing sniper fire. When the enemy combatants had been neutralised, the fatalities among the villagers were given a decent burial by the Iranians. I saw little of what happened in the village when it was taken. There may have been excesses but I did not witness them. In my opinion, the Iranian allies acted correctly. Were there captives who our interrogators should get a run with? Unfortunately that is not possible. There were no captives. Were there terrorists who escaped from the village before it fell, subsequent witnesses? I think not. My conclusion – the highway is safer for travel by our forces now that this village has been rendered harmless.' An easy story to tell. The colleagues, professional soldiers, who had extracted it might have noticed cheeks drained of colour, a stammer, or obviously rehearsed sentences, might have seen a tremor in the officer's hands. He would not have been challenged, contradicted. An old adage of military life: only the losers get hauled in for crimes in the field. He could imagine that but did not know what he should say to her.

She stopped. The goats' cries had reached a crescendo.

He saw her sense of duty. She squatted. The animals pressed close to her, could no longer be ignored. She reached out, took the teats on the udders of the goats, and did the milking movement she would have been familiar with. Worked a line as milk was jetted out and splashed on to the dirt below. Went on, looked after them, took time for it. He did not interrupt her, stayed close to her until she was finished, had a hand ready in case she toppled. He tried once to put an arm around her shoulder as she relieved the goats, give her comfort, but she flinched and then shook it away. At the end she turned, looked up, and a gleam of the moon's light settled on her face.

She said, "I had to survive because there must be a witness who lives."

They moved off again in the dark and the goats were quieter and the dogs shepherded them. He sent the text, gave an estimate of his arrival.

Gaz's mind contorted with images of the Russian officer, of his face, his actions, of his guilt. He did not know what to say but made his pledge silently, and saw the officer and did not dare to lose sight of him. Who would listen? Likely no one, and likely no one would care. He draped her arm across his shoulder and her hand gripped the Bergen and they walked. Who would ever give him a chance to be that witness? No one would.

"You have the better angle on him," Boris said.

"I think I might have," Mikki said.

They were both aiming. Boris was on one knee and had a low granite slab to rest his elbows on. Mikki was on the ground and had found heather and low scrub and was comfortable. At the range they had chosen, some 175 metres – as veterans of combat – both would say, in estimating range and the deflection that wind might make to the passage in the air of a bullet, even with assault rifles, it was a simple shot.

Mikki said, "At the next stride he takes."

Boris said, "Best for you, better than me – go, drop him."

They had open sights on their rifles. Those issued to the FSB, through the armoury on Prospekt, did not have telescopic attachments as the front line infantry would have had. They fired on the rare enough occasions that the weapons were issued, over open sights. Mikki had the V and the needle together and calculated the distance and the lever at the positioning for the range; in the distance beyond the sights was the blurred shape of the man's body. The target was to the left of the officer and a half pace behind. Easy for them both, at that distance, to note that the officer had his wrists tied with a supermarket plastic bag, then he rocked and was unstable. They both knew that reward and praise would follow the successful rescue of the major, that rewards and praise would come, and they would be paid off and generously. Mikki had the necessary elevation. Would have fired, could have, but the officer slipped sideways, only a quarter of a metre, but the target was immediately reduced. The kids – scum brats, criminals, should have been beaten to pulp – trailed by at least fifty metres, outside the loop of his vision. Did not matter, would be dealt with in the aftermath. He had slowed his breathing, readied himself.

"Fuck, but the next time."

"Do it, do him the next time – heh, if you fucking miss . . ."

"No chance."

"Don't miss."

"Did I ever?" Mikki murmured.

"When we did Jalalabad, you missed at . . ."

"Shut the fuck up." But Mikki had to smile. The target on that day, thirty-three years ago, had been a big hairy bastard with his turban flying behind him having been loosened in a charge over the stones in a dried river-bed. Their detachment had been rushed in to save the lives of a two-man crew from a downed helicopter gunship. Since that day, the target had always been the 'big hairy bastard' and Mikki had been on 'single shot' mode and not 'automatic', had missed and would have been dead but for the big hairy bastard's own weapon choosing that moment to malfunction. Boris had put him down . . . A hell of a fucking good story and part of the lore that bound the two of them. Beside him was the granite rock, its surface coated in a froth of pale lichen and on it were Boris's elbows, but Mikki had the better angle, and it improved for the few seconds of delay. Their man was ahead, the bodies separated, and the aim was clear except for the blurred waving of tall grass.

He squeezed. And saw . . . Did not know what he saw. A movement among the dwarf birches ahead of the major and the man held in the gap of the V, a definite movement . . . Squeezed further. Smelt the fumes from the breech, and saw the flash at the barrel tip below the needle, felt the impact of the butt against his shoulder, lost hearing, and saw the target drop, and could have cheered. Had not known the elation of a hit for close on fifteen fucking years, riding the armoured jeeps on the roads near Chechnya's border with Dagestan.

Like he had been hit with a sledgehammer.

Had been in mid-stride, close to his prisoner, one arm reaching forward to steady him and the other an angle to improve his own balance, and stones under their boots as they crossed a shallow pool and concentrating on his next footstep, and hearing the kids chatter behind and without the energy to shut them down.

The officer froze.

Gaz was draped over stone and stubbed bush growth and some of its flowers were in his mouth. He was aware the water in which his chin rested, was opaque, first pink and then reddening. Something they'd talked about – guys in the regiment. What was it like to be shot? How did it feel? Only Chalkie knew because he had taken a bullet in the upper thigh in some arsehole corner of southern Iraq, and the skills on the casevac airlift had been sufficient to save him from fatal blood loss, and he was fine now: never joined the talk, would say he hoped they'd never find out. After the blow of the sledgehammer had been the fall and no time to break it. Gone down with the impact of the proverbial potato sack. A numbness and a coldness spreading, and not knowing for two or three moments whether he was actually alive ... If he'd survived the bullet, was he going to stay alive? Did not know where 'Bomber' Harris was, and his big Chinook, where Sam and Arnie were and any of the rest of the gang who did fast first aiding to get him through the Golden Hour when wounded men needed serious medical intervention.

The pool by his face was deep red, colour of the Galway Bay rose that Bobby and Betty Riley grew in the front garden of the farmhouse, and it had thrived from the undiluted horse shit piled over it, and been dug up to go to Criccieth with them ... And he was already rambling in his thoughts, and more of the red was on the foliage and he reckoned he was bleeding badly.

He looked up. Could move his head but his upper body seemed crushed. The pain had not started ... Gaz knew ... that first would be the numbness, and the pain would come later. He was beginning to think about detritus, how much of his jacket had been drilled into the wound, and how big a piece of his T-shirt was in there, plastered against the sides of the bullet's passage. Did not know yet what had been hit, if an organ had been damaged. Had not tried to move his legs, might have paralysis, what they all dreaded, whether a part of his spine had taken the impact of the bullet and fractured ... Talk was that a trooper was better off shoving the barrel of his weapon into his mouth and fiddling for the trigger if his future was a wheelchair. He thought the wound was in his upper chest, right side, and below the armpit ... and could not know whether the bullet had broken up, splintered, bits buried in many directions, and if there was an exit wound and whether it had stayed whole.

The officer was beside him, flat down on his stomach. Gaz looked up and past him, and saw them.

Like his life had travelled fast. A fistful of seconds since the hit. Had the training that located where a shot had been fired from.

Saw them clearly, one man knelt, and he could see the head and shoulders of a second. They both had an aim, and he reckoned both were about to fire . . . and recognised one face but was too tired, too screwed, to think from where.

Both about to fire, about to pitch Gaz off his perch. Both barrels had him marked out, were lined on him. Pretty much point-blank, fairground shooting for a cuddly toy, pretty much Gaz's last moments. He bit his lip, felt the pain, bit hard. And heard the shot.

The bullet struck the granite rock underneath the barrel of his assault rifle, then ricocheted. It cleared Boris' head, but did a glancing contact with the rock and then sang like a plucked harp-string as it careered away. Mikki did not know, nor Boris, where it had come from. Under fire, the overriding priority was to learn the source of the shot, the position of the gunman, then to take better cover.

"Was that lucky? Or was that aimed?"

A croaked answer. "How can I fucking know? It went under the barrel, had less than a hand span to get through. I don't know."

Neither moved. Neither would stand up and look around to try to get a line on a rifleman's position. To find out whether the shot were luck or skill was to make him fire again.

"You scared, Boris?"

"Not feeling great – that good enough?"

"We going to lie here, have a sleep?"

"Never did, never will."

"He's starting to wriggle."

"Then he's mine, and cover me good."

Mikki had seen his target go down and had reckoned the shot good enough to kill but could not deny that the target moved, a hand had gone up and then sank. But they were confused: it seemed as if the officer was sitting up and looking around and then was assessing the state of his captor. Should have been on the move. Pushing up and running, staggering, but putting in distance. He thought the officer was about to get close to his target. An eye behind the V and the needle and a view of the target's head, not a difficult shot for him, except that he was shivering and the weapon floated in his hands and his breathing was crap, and his finger slid from the outer lip of the guard and found the trigger itself. Would not hurry, would do it in his own time, would bank on the incoming round, from whoever and wherever as a lucky shot, not aimed, and . . . it whipped in his ears.

He was deafened. The lichen was blown free, thrown up and then floated down. Fragments of the granite stone had splintered, and had spattered on his face.

This second shot was over his barrel. Boris thought the contact with the rock had been no more than fifty centimetres from his eyes. The bullet wailed after the initial impact and was gone. Not luck. Not a rifleman but a marksman. Not an infantryman but a sniper.

Boris took his hands off the assault rifle and lifted his head clear of the sights. Dogs would roll on their backs, put a tail over their bits, raise all four legs and look away: dogs did good submission. He would not have done that in Afghanistan, nor in Chechnya. This was the territory of the Russian Federation. In the places where he had fought in the military units of FSB, he would happily have gone to his grave rather than permit himself to be captured: in Afghanistan the men would have done it with blunt knives. In Chechnya it would have been the women, the Black Widows and the Allah's Angels, using blunter knives to mutilate them.

"Mikki, you are my friend, and you trust me."

"I am your friend and trust you."

"We get the fuck out."

"Get the fuck out, get clear. Let him show himself."

"The message I get, leave the firepower. No threat offered."

"Leave the guns, back off. You pray, Boris?"

"Not often enough."

Both pairs of arms were raised. A good display of surrender. Mikki would have said that the accuracy of the shooting meant that a sniper's rifle was trained on them – the Dragunov carried a powerful telescopic sight. Probably the sight could identify the hairs on his face, those sticking out from his nostrils. He would not play games with the guy. Both of them were standing. One rifle was on the granite stone, the other was leaning on the rock, close to where the second bullet had impacted. Mikki picked up their rucksack. Hands still high they started to walk away. Did not look behind but Mikki was able to slip a glance out to the side, to where they had left the weapons.

"Don't question me, just do as I say." He kept his voice low. "We are in a bad place."

"What are you saying?"

"Saying that we run – don't argue. Just fucking run."

"Why?"

"Seen a bear," Mikki hissed. "Full grown, half again, and coming behind us."

"What? A bear? What . . . ?"

And Boris turned and broke ranks. The biggest fucking bear he had ever seen. Bigger than anything in a circus, or stuffed and displayed in a bar. It came to the rock of granite they had used and sniffed at the weapons and would have noted the chemicals from the discharge, and then it came after them. The bear did not run, but loped, covering ground fast. They ran, then stopped, both heaving breath into their lungs. The bear stopped, about 100 metres back from them. Mikki thought that firing a pistol, the one at the bottom of the rucksack, would only have stopped the beast if the barrel were put hard up against its ear, or down its throat. He saw that it was club-footed and reckoned a swing of that old leathered stump would break his neck, and that a slash of the claws on the good foot would slice him like he was ready for barbecuing.

The bear had small eyes for the size of its head. Bright and cruel. They ran again. Then collapsed. They were at the tree line. One tree stood higher than the rest, petrified. Mikki thought it was worse than before because he could no longer see the bear. The trees were dense, heavy in summer leaf, and scrub grew underneath the branches. They could not see it but heard it.

"Do you understand anything?"

"I understand fuck-all. What do I want? I want away . . . I never been so scared, not anywhere. He let us go, the sniper. Might have said we are useless, not worth two rounds more. Useless . . ."

Far behind them, gone from sight, were their target and their officer, forgotten. It surprised them that the animal seemed happy now to make a cumbersome noise as it went unseen, near to them. They threw grenades, pepper spray and flash-and-bangs. The beast seemed close to them but was hidden in the trees.

"If you want me to help you."

The shock and cold had settled on Gaz and the pool by his face had reddened further. The officer shoved his hands, bound at the wrist, towards Gaz.

"Why would you?"

The officer sounded irritated. "If you want to talk about it, you sitting in a chair and me on a therapist's bed, we can discuss my childhood, my home life, my attitude to military work, and the security industry. Could spin it out for a month of appointments. Then come up with 'why?' And wait till you are dead, then . . ."

He heard his own voice bubbling from his throat. "Why should you help me?"

Gaz assumed both would have known the necessaries of the trade, what all military were taught – the same for *them* as for *us*. Made sense in Gaz's mind, but weakness was setting in. They would both know about a bullet wound taken in the chest. First up was 'debridement' which was the business of how much filth penetrated the wound; then 'fragmentation' and if the bullet had held together; and then the dimension of the 'cavitation' the bullet had made in his chest. He'd have had five litres of blood in his veins and a portion of it was in a rainwater pool and if more than two litres were lost then he was food for the crows. There was 'calm', how he must be and how the man who asked for his wrists to be freed must react if he were to be saved. His mind struggled. Why would his prisoner save him? He knew he needed 'pressure' on the wound and needed to be 'sat upright'. Had seen all the procedures done. And he was supposed to hate the man who offered help, and was supposed to have stepped from a side street or waited by a doorway, and faced the man and shown the Makarov. Seen his self-control disintegrating and hopefully had waited long enough for fear to set in, long enough for him to beg, then have shot him dead. Clutching, as they said, at a straw.

Gaz groped with his fingers. He was losing the numbness and the pain had started and the weakness grew, but he found the knot and started to ferret at it. It had tightened over the hours, but he worked at it and time must have slid and his efforts became more feeble . . . The officer did not complain at the pace, and the thinning sunlight bathed them and the voice betrayed raw excitement.

"What do I do?" the girl asked.

"Undo it."

"For what reason?" the boy asked.

"Because I asked."

Gaz thought that if the officer had snarled at her, they would both have refused. He did not, just held his arms out behind his back. Two kids who dealt Class C drugs round the city and had been 'sleepers'; an officer in the country's premier law and order and counter-espionage outfit; himself, a reconnaissance expert, psychologically damaged and an illegal – and somewhere further back, unseen, was a marksman who could put a bullet at 200 metres, on to something the size of a saucer. All together, fused . . . a good enough answer, and the kids did it. Hardly liked it but would have noted his colour gone and his forehead screwed in pain. He had abandoned the kids, put them out of his mind, had not considered his obligation to them, what he owed to Timofey and Natacha . . . was humbled. The officer's wrists came free. He worked his wrists hard, pummelling and massaging them.

"I'll take the pistol."

Had read him wrong.

"If you can move just a little then I can reach it."

He heard the kids protest, but in their own language. He thought of the magic bits that every fighting man knew of, the words that mattered: debridement, fragmentation, cavitation, blood, shock. Did not want to die, not here, so Gaz rolled a little. A hand took the weapon from his belt. A military man, and his first act was to check the safety and the status of the next round. Said nothing, pocketed it. Gaz realised he had come far, was not going farther, and that authority had switched. Not thanked, no gesture either of trust or of hostility. The officer, to Gaz, was from a world of which the Englishman, of corporal's rank and mired in sickness, had no place. He wondered if talk about shame and guilt had been mere subterfuge, done to distract him, but that was irrelevant now.

Gaz asked, "Who shot me?"

"Scumbags, people from the gutter."

"It was a clean shot."

"You were a witness. You saw them if you were there."

"The two men with you?"

"Behind me, and absolved from blame because they did nothing. They did not kill and did not help to kill and did not hide what we left. Supposed to guard me and keep me safe, were likely pissed and asleep in the car when they should have met me. There was a second marksman, I know nothing of him, and he fired twice and terrorised my people, and they ran, and they were hunted and have thrown grenades, and I know no more. Good fortune. You are correct and are decent, and I wish you well. But I have no optimism. Do not forget me, Corporal, and do not forget what I said to you."

The pistol bulged in the major's pocket.

He had a good stride and the kids made way for him but in Gaz's opinion he barely saw them, as he took the same animal track that Gaz had used when getting from the tree to the lake. Had gone only half a dozen paces when Timofey raised a finger to the major's back, and Natacha gurgled in her mouth, then spat noisily. The major gave no sign he heard.

Gaz asked the kids to lift him, to raise his head and shoulders, clear his face from the blood red of the little pool. He would ask them next to find some material that was clean – clothing, fresh on, if they had any – to make a casualty type dressing and use it as a plug for the outer wound. When he was upright they could iden-tify if there was an exit wound, or the bullet was still inside . . . Then he would tell them the back-stop concept: perhaps they would help, perhaps they would not.

The officer moved as if he were a man determined on a mission and ready to organise and carry out the obvious when he reached communications. Gaz had many confusions and was tired to the point of deep sleep, but he knew that if he let his head loll and his eyes shut, then he would be gone, would not wake again. As confusing as all the rest was the question of a man firing on his attackers, frightening them off, but not showing himself. Too many confusions. The kids lifted him and their clothing was smeared with his blood. He could see up the hill, towards the spread-eagled branches of the dead tree, but no longer saw the man who had been his prisoner. Had lost everything except his life – had failed. Said so.

Natacha answered him, "You cannot have failed yourself as long as you live. To die is failure. What do we do with you?"

He had lost sight of Zhukov, had lost sight of the men he had fired towards, had lost sight of the man who had been a prisoner. He was on his own territory, and pondered.

Jasha did not enjoy surprises brought to the wilderness. Two shots fired from the Dragunov and his position still secure, Jasha could have backed away into thick undergrowth then moved off in a wide half-moon and left the scene behind him. Could have gone back to his cabin. There, might have heated a tinned meal for himself and given biscuits to his dog, and could have sat in his chair in front of his door and lit a pipe to keep away the mosquitoes. Could have wondered if Zhukov would return to him, or whether their relationship had run its course. Could have, except . . . the man had a bullet wound, and was being treated by two city kids who would have known nothing. The success of Jasha's life since he had moved to this corner of the Kola peninsula was based on his caution and his shyness. He did not seek out strangers but hid from them. Did not involve himself in the affairs of others, was rigorous in the defence of his privacy. He went with a sniper's skill, did a slow crawl and would eventually reach a rock that stood out as a marker. He came to the crushed foliage around it. He could see where his bullets had struck, where he had made grooves in the lichen, and he picked up the one spent cartridge case, then took the two abandoned rifles. He could not have explained why he had intervened, broken the core belief. They were crap weapons and carried the serial numbers given them by an armoury, and the metal insignia of FSB was hammered into the butt of each.

He thought the man was grievously hurt, and thought the kids out of their depth in matters of reaction to a gunshot wound ... and he had heard the explosions past the landmark tree and knew that his confidant, Zhukov, had tracked them as they ran, and they'd have had good cause for fear. He sat back from the rock and had a clear view down, and his camouflage gear would blend well. He watched, waited, and his decision was not yet made.

"It's like a movie."

"No music and no fade out."

"But real, and blood," she said.

"I never seen a man who's shot," he said.

"There was a girl got stuck in the gaol, but nobody stayed around," Natacha said.

"I seen a man knifed, down by the railway station, was mugged, wouldn't give his phone, and nobody helped him," Timofey said.

"Don't get involved."

"Get clear."

"Anyway," she said, "other people, the paramedics would have known what to do."

"Except there's only us," he said.

"And we're ignorant."

She knew he listened to them. His eyes moved, lethargic but aware, and rolled, took in whichever of them spoke, and his breath came badly. Natacha knew nothing of medical care. Had never done a course in first aid or trauma response. Instinct demanded she back off, and Timofey would want to put ground between the Englishman and themselves. Would have been an old instinct, deep set. When she had been taken by the police, she would not have expected him to fight to free her, get clubbed with batons, and go to the cells with her. No one who sold on other pitches in the city, or the Chechens who came from St Petersburg with fresh supplies, would have stayed. There would be no help here and no chance of escape. If medical treatment arrived it would be because the bastards who had shot him had alerted a recovery team. They had been fired at and had run, and Timofey did not know what had happened, nor she. They put themselves at greater risk with each minute passing. His eyes watched them, waiting. He would have known what decision they had to take. She thought that he, Gaz, would not chew on blame and spit that in their faces if they left him. Whether it was a bad wound, or only looked bad, she could not have said. Each time she looked up at Timofey he seemed to step back from the business, like it would be her call, her shout. She tested Timofey.

"Do we start walking?"

"Start walking, and take him. Fuck knows how."

"Not dump him?"

Done with a rueful grin, a trademark of her man, Timofey. "Can't see you . . . Turn our backs, give him a goodbye kiss, start walking, then begin to run . . . Keep going, don't slow. Leave him, ditch him. Up for it?"

And she tested some more. "What's he done for us? All take, no give. We owe him nothing, owe his people nothing . . . We'd have to be lunatics to stay with him, help him."

Timofey shrugged, a little gesture than seemed to say talk was cheap and wasted time. She reached across the head that she held and kissed her guy lightly on the forehead, like it was a sober moment – and a decision taken. Was for 'better or worse', seemed to her to be for 'worse', and defied common sense.

They lifted him. A big bird was circling, screaming at them. It was hard to hear his voice. Would have hurt him as they raised him up and she took part of his weight and Timofey had more. He spoke in Timofey's ear, slow but coherent. One of his legs was lifted and one trailed.

Timofey said to her. "The guys who shot him went up the hill towards the border. No future there. Blocked off. Have to go down, where we started . . . he says there's a back-stop. I think that means an alternative, an idea if all else is fucked."

Natacha laughed. "Would you call that 'well fucked, truly fucked'?"

Both guys smiled with her, but it hurt Gaz more. They went slowly and headed for the lake, and he was heavy.

Knacker stood back, waited to be told.

The Norwegian had his phone in front of him and text spewed on to it. Of course, Knacker knew bad times, as the wheat collector or the garrison commander would have, and the man with whom he identified more closely, blue woad plastered on him. Had done the vigils, had waited for his man to show. Could always justify the frustration at losing an agent: having to recruit again, change codes and procedures because, for certain, the asset would have a hard time in an interrogation cell. Would have to begin again – and he always cursed that his agent, his asset, had failed to survive that 'last' mission. Too careless and too desperate, and a net closing . . . Could have done with a cup of strong tea, and a biscuit to dunk in it. Instead let his hand fiddle in his pocket until he had identified the *denarius* coin: flicked it, turned it, scratched it to feel the markings, had started to regard it in the same way that some of the Mid-East veterans used the local worry beads. He thought it went badly, how badly he would soon be told. He did not interrupt but the sights in front of him – seen through layers of the branches of close-planted pine, and through the wire fence – offered little encouragement. The initial military force, described to him as border detachments of FSB, had been reinforced. More men, more trucks, more sense of impending drama: the job of preventing illegal crossings of their bloody fence would have been in the high areas of the boredom threshold and the guys in front of him looked to be motivated. Not quite baying for blood, the border boys, but close to it, and ammunition would have been issued and the chance of action was high, and . . . The Norwegian tugged at his sleeve, spoke softly.

"I believe we approach, friend, an end-game. Our monitoring

of their airwaves provides interest. There are reports of both shooting and grenade explosions, about six klicks from here. They believe that an officer of FSB, named as Lavrenti Volkov rank of major, has been kidnapped and is being brought to the border by an illegal alien. Who fired the shots is unclear. Why grenades have been used is also confused. Much is speculation, but what is without argument is that no fugitive will make it across the frontier in this sector. I am sorry, friend, but that is a clear conclusion."

Knacker, murmured, "Why could he not just do as he was told, why?"

He started to rap his own phone, call Fee or Alice, whoever would pick up first: anger coursed in him. A mountain of work and all wasted, because a man did not perform as instructed.

"You want to stay?"

Knacker answered, "Yes, to the end. I pride myself on an ability to treat those two impostors, Triumph and Disaster, just the same. Rough with the smooth, that sort of thing. Be here at the death, yes."

He needed to rest and they did. Not for long but, for a few gulped breaths, they would lean him against a rock, and flop down. They were past the lake. No sirens and no helicopter engines, only the drone of the mosquitoes and the chirrup of songbirds.

Not often, but sometimes, a twig was broken in the tree line to their left, or dried leaves were scuffed. His hearing was better than his sight. Gaz's eyes misted over. He ought to have been brutal with the kids. Said that he was prepared to take his chance, be alone, ride whatever diminishing luck came his way. 'I'm grateful for what you've done. Might not have said it and might have taken too much for granted, but it is appreciated. We are where we are, cannot escape that. I have no right to have you jeopardise your future freedom. Put me down, leave me, and get the hell out. Keep running, never look back. Deny everything if they throw shit at you. I'm trying to tell it simply, you don't have to stay with me. Just go home . . . Do that, please. Please do it.'

Might have parroted all that, given it them as a demand. But he stayed silent other than to have the breath heave in his throat and whistle out through his teeth. He did not cry out when the pain surged. He thought he asked too much of them, but they had bought into the concept of the back-stop. Should not have, but had, and Gaz thought himself damned for not refusing them. They went on. It was a summer night and there would be no darkness to hide them. But they were tough, committed, and they did not lay him down.

The numbness had gone and the pain came on hard, and each step was worse than the last. But they had cleared the lake and were among trees, thought they were watched and cringed from a sort of fear, and insects buzzed his wound, and . . . He tried to imagine who would care if he came through.

18

Not gone far, not fast, and Gaz had started to struggle. The kids held on to him. He attempted to break free.

"Let me go. I don't need you."

Had they let him go, he'd have fallen flat on his back or his stomach, and the bleeding – internal or through the entry wound – would have come on worse, and the pain.

"Don't need you, don't want you."

Difficult ground to cross and they were among low trees; he would have had to accept that the kids understood the need to be clear of the open ground where the heather and short bracken grew, and the bushes with the berries gave no cover. If they had not supported him then he'd have tripped on a rock, gone down slithering into a bog . . . Gaz was alive, and angry. Would not have had that anger if he'd been in Helmand or central Syria because a Chinook would have scooped him up, and alongside the protection of the machine-gunners aiming down through hatches would have been the team of trauma geeks: the needle going into his arm, and chasing him. Could not hand over responsibility for his safety, his survival, to the kids.

"Let me go. Christ's sake, free me."

They were high up on the tundra plain. Before going into the dark of the close-growing pines he had been able to say where he'd be heading – not to the west and towards the frontier, but to the east. Would not have had that chance now as the cloud was thickening and the wind pressing against his body. When they had started back he had been able if he squinted, and bit at his lip for concentration, to see the ribbon of water that ran out to the north and into the Barents Sea. Had definitely seen it. Had promised himself that the inlet was the sole route out that remained to him ... had been told it, had been given the promise of the fishing boat's crew.

"Go back to flogging skunk, whatever. You owe me nothing. Get the hell out."

Neither of them had a spare muscle in their body. They were both thin and pale and breathing hard, but their hands gripped him. They shielded his face from the stinging whip of branches flicking back on to his face. The sight of the inlet that led out to the open sea was lost and he did not know if they headed in the direction he had demanded or whether they merely blundered into the depths of the woodland – or whether they went in a circle which would have been the worst of catastrophes ... There had been a Scots boy in the regiment, known as 'Bare Arse' because he wore a kilt off duty and shunned underpants, and he had been lost on a plateau on the north part of the Helmand sector when fog had come down, and had suffered flat batteries on his communications, and had walked twice in big circles and had lost thirty hours, and a big hunt was on for him and then the fog had lifted and he'd been sitting on his haunches, his head on his knees, and weeping, because he had screwed up big time, two huge circles and each time back where he had started, and he was a skilled navigator. Truth was, Gaz would not have known if they had walked in circles unless they had splashed in the pool where his blood had coloured the water.

"Just leave me, walk away."

If anything, they held tighter to him. He wanted to walk, put the wound behind him, control for himself what destiny was left him. Pretend that he had not been shot. Reality was a wound in the upper chest that would not have been life-threatening if the Chinook had come in fast and the expert care was on board. He had his right arm around the boy's shoulders and most of his weight rested there, and the girl had snuggled herself closer to him and had an arm around his back and clutched the waist of his trousers to keep a firm grip, but struggled to sustain the burden. What he was, a damned burden.

"Am asking you, ordering you – I am pleading with you. Leave me."

He flailed with his arm. He might have caught Natacha's chin with the heel of his hand and he saw her head rock but she rode it. He kicked at Timofey's shins, to better effect. Two results of his efforts to free himself: when he hit her he widened the entry wound, and aggravated the dirtied tunnel of the bullet's passage, and felt pain along the depth of the wound, seemed to split his chest in two on either side of its passage, and the agonies crumpled him . . . And because he kicked and Timofey hopped one-legged and lost balance, they almost fell and the boy had to reach down and steady himself before straightening. He thought he saw a shape that moved alongside them, tracked them. Thought he had seen it before. Delusions, a degree of madness. Gaz wanted to be free of them, dependent on himself, and they did not permit it. Trees were close around them. The wind came on harder and riffled the branches over his head . . . and without them he was dead.

"You help me and I've the right to know. Why?"

Timofey's answer: "We have to."

He was a city boy. Some of the kids of his age were a part of the *Nashi* youth group. A favoured arm of the regime, they had summer camps in the forests, and hung banners of flattering portraits of the leader, called him Vova, and girls wore knickers celebrating the 'close relationship' with the President, the hero. A brutal version of the Komsomol of Soviet times. Inside the ranks of the non-believers they were the *Putin-jugend*. Timofey avoided them because he, or Natacha, would have had a beating off them if they had trapped him on the street . . . would have stolen his stuff, would have smoked it, would have beaten him for amusement. The *Nashi* boys and girls might have had an idea about how to move across this barren, frightening place, and hold the direction he was asked for. But they would have been in the wilderness if recruited in Murmansk . . . the ones who strutted on the parades for Defender of the Fatherland celebrations. He did not know whether they went forward or sideways – could have gone backwards – but reckoned the injured man had the strength to guide them in the right direction, had to. Each time that the direction was set, Timofey took charge. Why? Not easy to answer without baring something that was private to him, shared only with Natacha – and only then within limits. Started slowly, and was thoughtful, but would grow in confidence.

"Because of what you brought us, friend. I call you 'friend'. You are a soldier, I am a dealer in narcotics. You would have a uniform to parade in. I have a uniform if I go to gaol. She wore a uniform in the prison. We are so different, but you gave us something. What we did not have. First, the start. Who I am. The result of a bastard's birth? Have your blood in me, some of your people's blood. A sailor's blood. Would have been ordinary, not an officer. Met a girl in the shadows, in winter. And a child born. And the child would be a grandparent, mine. That is how I feel I am joined to you. I tell you something you bring to me and why I have a love of you, friend. I am not a serial killer, I have not stolen millions, have stayed at a humble level and sell drugs. Good weeks and bad weeks, and I have Natacha. What I despise is the corruption. Who am I, a criminal, to speak of wrongdoing? I am entitled. I see it. We are stopped in the car. The car is searched. The cannabis weed is found. We can be handcuffed, arrested, sent to court, sentenced and imprisoned. You would not want to spend days in a gaol here, friend. Or, I can feel under my seat, where I keep trading cash, and I can pay them, and come back again the next evening and pay some more, and again. You give me a chance to kick their testicles. I think you made them angry, and I think they will be angrier if they do not have you imprisoned, where it would go badly for you. The way it is, I give one kick to one testicle, and you give the second kick to the second testicle. I see them, then, at FSB on the Prospekt, doubled in pain. That is why I help you. Please, friend, do not hurt me again, it slows me. When we reach the Kola inlet you have not told me what we look for, what will happen. Because, friend, you do not fully trust us?"

No reply given him. Nor did he know if his words were heard. He thought they were watched from the deeper undergrowth, and sometimes he looked behind him, and sometimes he thought a shadow passed between the trees. But the wind had freshened and the noise from the trees clattered in his ears. When there was wind, there would be rain chasing behind it.

"You have given us something, friend. That is enough. We rejoice in it, the freedom, the opportunity to kick. And you are heavy, friend, fuck, you are heavy. And I tell a truth. You should have killed him and now he is free, and he will be back with the snakes he lives with and they come for us, and all we can do is kick. You should have killed him."

Lavrenti hopped from rock to rock, and sometimes jumped to clear the bog pools. He could have been out in the carefully preserved woodlands – accessible only to residents of the gated *dachas* near the President's own palace – where he had walked as a teenager, before his father had decided that he should go to the Academy of FSB, and start the fast track. A great weight, one that had bowed him, was lifted. His mother was not in his thoughts, nor his father. No longer any consideration of what curtains he should have in his new Moscow apartment, and what girls he should take to dinner, nor which businessmen entrepreneurs he should offer a protective 'roof' and what rewards would accrue and how his promotion prospects could be enhanced.

The rain was hard in his face, came from ahead of him where the border was. It flattened his hair and ran down his face and added to the weight of his military tunic.

Lavrenti Volkov's decision was made. Not usually generous in handing out gratitude, but in his mind, Lavrenti was prepared to give thanks to the man he now knew as the corporal. He held the pistol in his right hand and his finger rested on the trigger guard and the rain washed it and highlighted where the paint had been scraped from its body. He had not fired his own pistol while in Syria, also a Makarov, except on that day. If the corporal had been a witness to the long hours spent at the village then he would have seen him shoot. Of course, the two sergeants were also witnesses but their loyalty was to his father and no mention had ever been

made of his behaviour and actions at Deir al-Siyarqi. Their attitude towards him had changed, formality turning to scarcely
disguised contempt. They had eked out their time with him, would
shortly – with his father's blessing – retire to their dream of the
restaurant with chalets on the Moscow-St Petersburg road. The
day had never been spoken of, nor had he challenged them if they
were late, slovenly dressed, or the car smelled of their sweat or fast
food . . . neither possessed the corporal's dignity.

It was as if a way had been shown him: what the corporal had
done.

Through the rain sheeting on to him and below the cloud that
bucked on the tips of the trees, he had seen the two men who had
been at his side on that day. They should have driven him to the
airport, grunted a farewell, and he would have boarded his flight
south and they would have spat an insult. He would never meet them
again. He could not remember when he had last met a man, uniformed
or civilian, who had been with him, close, for only a matter of hours,
who had been able to cleanse him. A good man, only a corporal but
with behaviour that could not be faulted. The arrival of the witness
had brought conclusion to a nightmare. He was at peace.

He barely noticed the rain, and the wind. His sergeants would
beat him to the fence and he assumed by now that the militia
would be deployed. Everything was clear in his mind. There had
been confusion back on the path, with the kids trailing them. A
single shot from an AK47 assault rifle and the corporal had
pitched over. Not dead but hideously wounded. Then, two more
shots. A Dragunov sniper rifle, he'd judged. Had seen no
marksman. Had realised the shots were aimed to intimidate his
sergeants, had been successful. He'd no idea who else might have
been out in that wilderness.

Delta Alpha Sierra, the Eighteenth Hour.

The dogs, ahead of them, realised first.

Soft growls, would have been showing their teeth then scurrying, low on their bellies, to bring stragglers to the main group. In

the heart of the goats were Gaz and the girl. The goats picked up on the danger and started to blast. Neither Gaz nor the girl were alert enough to recognise the dull shadows ahead of them, too exhausted, too mentally stripped. A searchlight came on, caught and blinded them. The growling went up a pitch and the bleating become a chorus. And the light went off; they had been illuminated for some five seconds, again were in darkness and clouds must have covered the moon and the stars.

Gaz shouted his name.

Was answered, "Is that a fucking zoo you're bringing?"

Gaz did not know whether she understood Dusty the Scouser's crack, but she seemed to stiffen beside him. She had done well to walk that far, bloody well, had not complained, had just slapped one foot in front of another, and her body had been violated and her mind would be turmoil: she was bereaved, in shock. He had his arm around her waist. The light came on again. Now, she looked straight into the beam and did not blink, showed no weakness and the herd was buffeting her legs and the dogs ran rings round them.

"Brought the missus with you, Gaz?"

"Shut the fuck up, just shut . . ." Never finished. It was like he had already been removed from the comfort zone of the regiment, had lost the protection its cordon gave. Black humour was their way of handling bad times, the worst exposure to experiences. One they liked was, 'This trooper on his deathbed, shot to Hell, was asked by a priest to renounce Satan before he passed on, and he replied that this was no time to be making new enemies.' That was a favourite, was all right between them but not in the presence of an outsider. Not acceptable after what she had endured, what she had seen. There must have been a whip in his voice. The lights were killed. He was with the Golf Charlie team. The goats milled close to the wheels of the vehicles, started to search for anything to eat and found filled sandbags, started to chew.

He was asked, "You all right, Gaz?

"I'm good."

"Who's the lady?"

"Just someone I met at a bus-stop."

"Don't fuck about, who is she?"

"She has a herd of fine goats, I don't know her name."

"Get your goodbyes done, and we'll be off. Not a place I care to hang about, but you'd know that. Took your time, but all's well that ends . . ."

"She's coming with me."

"What about that bus she was waiting for."

"Needs medical treatment."

"So does half this fucking country."

"And she saved my life."

"I'll take her with you, but we'll not manage the goats and the dogs."

A formality. Had to be done. One of the boys, a fellow corporal, came forward from the darkness and patted her down. Arms, spine, thighs and shins, and nodded that she was clean: just doing his job. She was indifferent, probably hardly noticed. Gaz told the girl that the goats and the dogs would stay where they were. Told her that it was not up for argument, she would be seen by the medic team. Reluctant, seemed to pull away from him, but he only freed her when she crouched down and spoke into her dogs' ears, then stood and her eyes blazed as she looked around her and would have taken in the sight of armed men, masked faces, protective vests, heavy machine-guns, and might then have been half-choked at the spill of exhaust as the engines were revved. A hand came down and hoisted her up, and that was Dusty, the Scouser, and he called her 'love' and seemed soft, caring. Gaz had tears and wiped them on his sleeve. She was at his feet, down on the floor, squashed in, and the weapons were manned. They bumped away. Just used side-lights and it was the knack of the drivers that they could follow a seldom used track, and they went fast and her shoulder thumped against his knee. He choked back tears, made a noise of it, but never heard her weep . . . He thought that all she had in her life, only bloody thing left her, was her goats and her dogs, and now she had lost them.

The memories came in waves, surged in his mind, and always

the image of the officer. She had said, *I had to survive because there must be a witness who lives.* Had made a promise, had shared it with him, passed on responsibility for it.

"And you," he asked her. "Why?"

"Better we move than we talk. Talk is empty."

"I have to know. Why?"

Her steps were shorter, and Timofey heaved. Exhaustion weighed them. The man, named as 'friend' by Timofey, seemed heavier to her and her arms ached and her shoulders were bowed, and the forest of low trees they moved through was darker than before. Rain pattered down and the upper branches shook in the wind. She did not know how much longer she would be able to support him. His problem was to know why? Why did she help him? Did it fucking matter: more important was whether he would reach the coastline of the inlet, somewhere between Polyarni and Vidyaevo. Her answer . . . staccato . . . breath harder to suck down.

"Because you are against them. Because your navy would have rescued some of the *Kursk* boys, if it had been allowed. Because you stand for something they would not comprehend. Because you have a principle, friend, would not kill him – as you should have. Because you are destroyed by the principle, but do not regret it. I tell you, as a fool, I think every day of *Kursk*, the crew, the death. Every day, and the guilt of it killed my father . . . And because it has been good, has been fun, is excitement. Beyond anything I knew. Getting clear of the cops by the railway station when selling is big but you brought the biggest, the best."

"Would you come out, after . . . after whatever happens to me, would you come out? Go to that banking island, Guernsey, go to the counter, empty the account, take it in notes . . . keep walking, be at the airport. Take a plane – somewhere, anywhere – would you?"

"End a dream? That is boring, friend, is bourgeois. That is what 'they' would do. They are from the Prospekt and they would go to this island and try to keep moving the money, make an industry of it. We stay, and then we can hold the dream. We try to help you, and may succeed, and may not, but we try. But we will not follow you. You want me to sing? Do I strip again to make you laugh? Your principle, friend, it has fucked us all."

She felt tears well in her eyes. Did not care.

They came to a clearing, only a few metres across. She paused, as did Timofey. Their 'friend' seemed to sniff the air and there would have been only the scent of the wind and the taste of the rain, and her hair no longer blew because it had been plastered on her scalp. It would have been a good afternoon, the right sort of weather and the police and militia anxious to stay in their patrol cars, and trade would have been brisk when the great snaking train came in from Moscow or from St Petersburg. There was no horizon to guide him, just a cloud that sat low on the treetops ahead of them. She thought he smiled, and his voice was faint and hard for her to hear, but it was a remark about a helicopter and no visibility, and the clouds' low base, and she thought that a small victory. A hole in his chest, and blood leaking, and damage inside . . . Quite often, down by the cutaway section of the *Kursk*'s tower, she would let tears run. Would stand, feel no embarrassment, just cry – would be the same if they lost him. She thought him weaker . . .

"Come on, our 'friend', don't fucking fail us, keep your eyes open."

. . . and slapped his face. A light blow but not a caress.

His voice was a whisper and she strained to hear.

"You owe them nothing. You should have gone home, never been here. Listen to me while I can still talk. They are never grateful. Should you ever get to London there will be no trip to the Palace, and no posh men in pinstriped suits to grip your hands, and no medals dished out, and the 'thanks of a grateful nation' on offer. I know, I've seen. We had wonderful people in Afghanistan, in Syria, put their lives, and their families' lives in our hands. Fought alongside us . . . Then we were bored, or could not afford to fight any longer. We went home, and the Yanks did, and these good people were abandoned. Do we give them asylum in UK, a safe refuge from the Taliban, from the Damascus regime? We do not. Charities make a bigger effort to bring a mongrel puppy in because it used to have the run of a soldiers' garrison camp, and a guy is lonely without it. But the heroes who fought alongside that guy, they don't get the treatment. Nor will you."

"Talking just tires you."

"You ought to have left me."

"You, friend, should have shot him."

"I've told you who they are, what they are."

His head dropped, chin on to his chest, and he would have seemed heavier to her and to the boy, and the rain came down and the cloud was lower. He wanted to sleep, to lie down on the pine needles, and . . . She slapped him again. They went forward, but slower.

Knacker and the Norwegian sat close to each other, had a decent view, and he'd dozed, and in front of him the troops beyond the wire showed no sign of immediate action.

His phone vibrated. Alertness returning, and ignoring the rain that dripped on his head, his shoulders, found its way under his shirt collar, puddled in his lap. He saw the source of the call . . . had dozed and had dreamed. Had been up on the Wall, and Maude had been somewhere within shouting distance. Plastic sheeting had jumped and arched over her, and mud swilled over her waterproof clothing, and she had been at the cleaning job with her toothbrush. God, it must have been foul for them there, stuck by that rampart, watching that frontier, waiting for the bastards to come out of the mist, screaming and shrieking and wanting blood . . . And on a similar day, the chap in the woad, their intelligence officer who plotted moves against the wheat collector and garrison commander, would have been huddled – pretty much as Knacker was now – in bushes or under trees, waiting for an agent to come through the gate ahead of him, and leave Roman territory and keep walking with his mules. All the time that individual would have been, near as dammit, messing his pants for fear that a Roman voice would peal out into the rain. Might have an accent of empire from Spain or from North

Africa, or from the Tigris River where the bargemen were originally recruited, might have called the wretch back. Probably
restless and gasping, because twice the Norwegian had elbowed
him, but dreaming and understanding the future. Him up on the
Wall, squatting on a shooting stick and watching the horizon,
and Maude with her archaeology friends. Knacker had a skill
that was much envied by those of the same trade: he saw little
point in Canute levels of obstinacy.

"Yes, DD-G, how may I help?"

Actually, Knacker was told, it was 'acting D-G' who called him,
not 'DD-G'. Had he received communications?

"I have, yes."

Was he at the airport? Was he flouting instructions? Did he
regard himself as emanating from an independent fiefdom?

"Just wrapping things up, tying loose ends, not wanting to leave
any untidiness."

Had matters been made plain to him? A new broom and a new
mood, and a new acknowledgement of ethics and morality, and a
new rubbish bin for outdated attitudes towards the Russian
'enemy'. Did he not realise that times changed, attitudes moved
on, techniques grew more sophisticated in the light of electronic
advances? Putting these unprotected wretches in harm's way for
the sake of some hypothetical advantage to be gained in central
Syria. All ridiculous. Quite apart from justifiable annoyance felt
by the Russian agencies. It was over, and the stable was to be
cleaned. Did he understand?

"All understood."

He would have expected a fight. Probably, in front of him and
at the desk where he sat – hopefully on borrowed time – would
have been a crib sheet of clever lines to throw back at Knacker if
he'd argued. Would have slapped him down and would have had
around him a room full of Young Turks, or Albanians, or Egyptians,
wherever they came from these days. Would have seen himself as
a prizefighter with an opponent on the ropes and a stadium baying
for blood. Knacker gave him a trifle of ducking and weaving, and
then silence. To the point of impertinence, he frustrated, gave no

cause for the crib sheet to be used. Would he not, at least, stand his corner?

"Just those loose ends, then be on the plane."

And his man? How was the 'wretch', his man, doing? Going to make it out without repercussions off the Richter? Or in a holding cell, waiting to be shot dead on the wire? What was happening?

He terminated the call, then switched off the power. The Norwegian would have heard it all, gave a sardonic grin. The top of the thermos was unscrewed. Fish soup was offered. A foul night, and cold, and hope dying and any form of intervention beyond his capabilities . . . taking the rough with the smooth . . . win some, lose some . . . worth the risk, wasn't it? Through the wire he could see that the border troops huddled in their oilskin capes or crowded close to their trucks for shelter. The sort of evening, and sort of weather, where optimism was difficult to purchase.

"So, this is the end for you . . . will you miss it?"

Knacker held the coin, felt each indentation. He said, "I am going to be a wheat collector and plan the decapitation of my opponent, or I am going to be wrapped in a wolf pelt, my face painted blue and plotting how to slit the collector's throat . . . Sorry but no large lady has yet sung. Not the end, not yet. What we call the dark hour, but then there's dawn . . . A hell of a good soup."

"Is that them?"

"Could be, I'm not sure."

The wind pounded them and the rain was relentless and the light faded and clouds hugged the hills either side of the entry to the harbour at Kirkenes.

Fee said, "Just can't tell."

Alice said, "Would they have just fucked off without a word? I mean, after all we've done for them, and what we've paid them up front."

"Rats getting out early, sinking ship and all that," Fee said.

"You've got the glasses," Alice said.

Which meant that Fee had to get her hands out of her pockets and then root in her ample handbag, and it was sods' law that the pocket binoculars were at the bottom. Swore softly because the rain was now coming into the bag. She had the glasses, wiped the lenses on her pullover.

"It's them. Pretty much have the registration bit. Not a hundred per cent, but near enough. Bastards . . ."

"The same old trouble. You bring in outsiders and they say the right thing, then haggle over the washers, then reckon they're your best friends, then fuck off out without a word of what's been done for them. Predictable."

They were on the coast road. Deep in the mist was a fishing boat, a dark grey outline and chucking back a small wake from its engines. Grey sea, a grey mist and grey hills.

"And us? What about us?" Alice asked. "Are we joining the rats?"

"Could sign up. Rats have a trait of survival. Would be sensible," Fee answered.

"Knacker wouldn't. He'll not compromise."

Fee said, "Truth is, best will in the world, this has been a right shambles. This is 'piss-up in a brewery' stuff. I'm not listing them, but it had no right to work for us."

Alice said, "Looks like he's going to be dead or banged up in a cell. That's worse than a shambles."

"Too rushed."

"Never had a chance. Sensible to be a rat."

"Knacker'll be out on his neck. We'll get a billet somewhere. Keep our heads down, and mouths shut."

They held hands, had lost sight of the fishing boat.

Fee said, "And our boy, he wasn't wonderful, was he? Pretty ordinary."

Alice said, "If he'd had the balls he'd have plugged that fucker, Volkov. That's what it was all about. Sending a message to allies and friends in Syria, little people on the ground. There would have been a right old jump-up of pleasure in every Jordan refugee camp when word spread that a Russian, an officer, a war criminal, had gone off to the big gulag in the sky. But he bottled it."

Fee grimaced. "Know what's worst, poppet? Having wet ankles. I hate wet ankles."

"That flight out?"

"Two hours till check-in. We go, whether or not Knacker's back from safari."

Alice bit at a lip, distorted a pretty face. "Be a rat, get along the hawser, be safe and have a life . . . Come on."

They scurried away, headed for the safe house and a change of clothes, and a whisky. Not their fault that it had fouled.

The seas would be difficult once the fishing boat was clear of the hills on either side of the inlet. They made the harbour at Kirkenes a haven in the poorest weather. Out beyond the twin headlands and the island of Kjelmoya, uninhabited and ribbed with granite strips, was the Barents Sea. Few would treat the open water lightly, certainly not the men who had experience of the northern gales, winter and summer. On the fishing boat, among the four of them, there had not been a rancorous debate as to whether to leave Kirkenes as the weather closed and the visibility shortened. All of them were from families that had sailed from the Shetland islands on the bus routes to the Norwegian coast, and had only gone in winter because then the perpetual darkness gave protection from air attack, but those months were the most savage in terms of mountainous swell and the force of the gales. They were fuelled up and the engineer had pronounced himself satisfied that the engine would – if God blessed them – survive what the elements threw at them. Everything on deck that could be loosened by the pitch of the boat was strapped down. They would not use the radio, would give no indication of their route to the Harbour-Master's Office, but before casting off had spoken about heading for the Norwegian ports of Alesund and Bergen far to the south. The radio would not be used again and the predicted bad weather would reduce their footprint both in terms of satellite imagery and shore-based radar.

Why? . . . None would have been clear in giving an answer. All were men of few words. Each of them, if challenged would have grimaced, would have gazed from a porthole or out of the reinforced wheel-house windows, would have looked anywhere other than into the eyes of the questioner. Then an answer of sorts . . . 'Because it's what sea people do, who sea people are.' It would be a big moment when they were clear of the inlet, the hills lost in the mist and the cloud behind them, and the decks glistening with water from the rain and the spray off the crests. The skipper would swing the wheel and they would go to starboard and catch the gusts and be shaken and rocked. The boat would lurch and swing and waves would hammer it. It would be a gesture.

"Don't fucking shoot. Lower the fucking rifle."

Mikki would have said, under any circumstances, having a rifle aimed at him, and an eye squinting over sights was an unhappy place to be. He could barely breathe and his mind had lost coherent thought. They had run but neither had helped the other. Supposed to be the best of friends, men who would stand together in whatever front line confronted them . . . had been 'each for himself' in headlong flight. He had fallen, tripped on roots and stones and fallen and Boris had raced past him, had not stopped to heave him up. And Boris had slumped and had been holding his guts, but Mikki had left him and gone on ahead. Where was the bear? Mikki had no idea. A full ten minutes before he had shouted back at Boris. Had he seen the bear? Seen the bear in the last kilometre? A guttural response from his long-time friend, future business partner; had not seen it. Had he heard the bear? More gasps and more coughing to get air down into the lungs. Had not heard it . . . Might not have seen it and might not have heard it, but Mikki would not advocate standing still, cocking his head, straining his ears and gazing into the rain . . . looking for the bear, listening for it. So, he had kept running, and Boris had chased after him.

They were near the wire, in the last line of stubby fir trees. He would be from the border guard. He held a shiny new rifle, and aimed it. Mikki stood, statue-still. Boris cannoned into him, jolted him, then saw the guard and the rifle.

Boris had an arm out, leaned on Mikki. Croaked at the militia kid. "Point that fucking thing somewhere else, boy."

The 'boy', a conscript far from home, soaked and cold, and likely no food or drink provided, and told some shit story about an officer taken prisoner, kidnapped, dragged towards the border, might have thought a NATO armoured division was running escort, and might have his safety lever up and might have it down. Mikki said, trying to find authority, that he was putting a hand in his pocket and would take out his identification card. And did so, and held it up so that the boy could see it. The kid looked scared, not half as scared as he'd have been if he had first dropped his rifle and then had that fucking bear coming after him . . . only one foot at the front end of it, just a stump, but the other foot had claws that could have sliced him to spaghetti lengths. And now he might be shot by a kid.

Mikki said, "Aim it somewhere else, kid, or I'll eat your dick off – see if I don't."

They were taken to an officer. Mikki's mind went at flywheel speed. What to say, what to tell? Both spoke.

"I am the driver . . ."

"I am the bag carrier . . ."

"For FSB officer, Major Lavrenti Volkov. He was kidnapped this morning."

"We are both FSB personnel. Immediately we reported to the Prospekt. We had information . . ."

"From an informant, that the foreign agent would attempt to cross the frontier . . ."

"Do that at this location. Take the major with him. Why you are deployed . . ."

To the complicated part. The officer barked into a handset, relayed what he was told.

"We had weapons."

"Had drawn FSB weapons."

"Were following, had a sight of them."

"Fired a single shot, put down the foreign agent, dead or wounded."

"But . . ."

"We were fired on ourselves . . ."

"Almost killed – had to drop our weapons, then . . ."

"A bear chased us . . ."

"A brown bear . . . Major Volkov is behind us. We could not stop to wait for him."

"Because of the bear."

The officer left them, went to his truck and his communications.

Mikki said to Boris, "That was fucking awful."

Boris said to Mikki, "Fucking awful and worse."

"They won't credit us until he comes."

Kneeling, hidden, Lavrenti watched the squirming performance of the two who had been tasked by his father to protect him, and had failed. It no longer mattered to him. Could tell from the shifting feet and fidgeting hands and slumped shoulders that the buck was being passed. He saw an officer take charge. Men were despatched, and it was necessary for Lavrenti to lie flatter, stay still, as they pounded away noisily on the path close to where he hid. They would find where the British corporal had been shot and, in spite of the deluge of the rain, there would still be blood, though thinner. That would initiate the chase . . . and nothing he could do would alter it. On other matters his mind was clear, sharp. Almost ready, and still at peace with himself. He would have liked one more chance to speak with the corporal, regretted that he was denied the opportunity. Would have liked the chance to speak with the kids who had likely wrecked their lives by following in the wake of the corporal's escape; for excitement and to imitate something out of the movies. He had only paused once when he had gone up the last hill before the tree line, had followed the pair of them, the idiots on his father's payroll, and had looked back and seen the two kids, the girl and her boy, struggling to lift him and then beginning to go back the way they had come. Alive, but almost certainly dying. The corporal had affected the kids as he had affected Lavrenti. Only a few more minutes, on his knees or on his stomach, and sheltered from the rain, and then he would move.

Almost certainly dying, which hurt him, and all chance of a decent ending long gone. He felt a strange calm, one he'd not known before.

Jasha stepped out and blocked the path.

He did not have to. Very little of his life since he came – phsyically injured and mentally scarred – from the military and lost himself in the wastelands of the Kola, was not decreed by himself. Not told when to wake, what to shoot, how to feed himself, what to earn for survival. He was that rare individual in the society of the Arctic north, 'his own man'. They were just kids . . . city kids and had the wrong clothing and the wrong footwear and seemed to blunder erratically in the hour, or more, that he had watched them. They were cowed under the weight of the man they tried to help. More confusion for Jasha: they did not go towards the fence but headed inland instead and would very soon have crossed the main highway, and where they aimed for was a headland on the inlet that was between the two submarine bases, Vidyaevo and Polyarni. He thought, quite soon, they would drop the man and let him sink into the undergrowth. They might collapse alongside him and rest, or they might manage a shy sort of farewell and make excuses, head off . . . There was an old saying: 'the enemy of my friend is my enemy'. He supposed it had as great a relevance to a Russian as to an American, an Afghan or a Chechen. He could make a 'friend' of the wounded man. Could make an 'enemy' of an FSB officer being taken to the border.

Jasha had tracked them since they had first hoisted him up, set off with their burden. Surprised they had gone so far with him, taken that weight for so long. He had stopped once only, and allowed them to get ahead, and had heard that noise close to him – broken dried twigs and rustled leaves and the clatter of branches sliding back after being pushed aside. He had been firm. Been too many days and too great a familiarity. Had said in a clear voice, against the wind and the rain. 'Get this message, Zhukov, I do not want you. I helped you when you needed help. What anyone does, gives help. Now, bugger off back to your own territory. Stop following me. And stay away from my home. Stay away from my dog. Stay away, Zhukov, from me.' Would have sounded decisive.

He was in front of them and they stared at him. He would have made a frightening figure: in camouflage clothing, his rifle with the barrel topped by the bulk of the telescopic sight, a balaclava unravelling at the slits, two more rifles slung on a shoulder. He missed the beast already, did not have the peculiar feeling of company and assumed Zhukov had taken him at his word.

The kids were close to collapse. It was not Jasha's argument and he owed nothing to an unknown casualty, and nothing to the kids . . . But had owed nothing to a bear with a limb poisoned by wire and then with a fence staple stuck in its pad. He told them to lower him, and gently. The kids gazed back at him, had the same defiance in their faces: took orders from no one, were from the city streets and high-rise shadows. If he did not involve himself then he could have retreated to his cabin and barricaded the door, and let the storm beat against the grimed windows and be with his dog. He took his lead from the kids, both thin and pale, sodden and shivering.

Jasha said, "Put him down, please. Trust me. Accept help. Whatever you try to do, I am your only hope of achieving it."

They laid him down, wary movements, and there was no shelter. The rain careened over them. He crouched over the man and passed the Dragunov to the girl. She took it. That was trust, passing her his rifle. He spoke only Russian, but had a smattering of key words in Pashtu from the Afghan days. The girl said he was English, that she spoke a little of it, and her boy spoke some from school. Where did they try to take him?

To the coast, and the boy took from his pocket a scrap of paper on which were a line of pencilled numbers, and the wet caught it . . . any sniper could navigate from co-ordinates, and he understood them, and had an idea where the lines would cross, vertical and horizontal. And what was there? The boy said there was a marker and the girl said it was green. The girl had her anorak off, a pathetic little garment that would be right for a shopping mall and she held it, stretched fully, and it deflected some of the rain from the man. They told him his name.

He started to peel back the clothing from around the entry wound.

The wound at the front of his chest was examined, then he was gently rolled over and his back was exposed after his jacket and T-shirt were delicately cut and pushed aside. A single-bladed hunting knife was used and he thought it wickedly sharpened. They had no bottled water and used what came on the wind: his T-shirt was used as a swab, and the pain came bad but he did not cry out. Supposed there was no alternative to what was being done. On the Chinook he would long ago have had the needle, morphine draining into his blood stream. Might have started to hallucinate and wondered where 'Bomber' might be – at Benson or at Odiham or still piloting the big bird out of the Forward Operating Base. Thought of Aggie, perhaps did not do her justice, and she was talking about her pottery, and the temperature for the glaze, 'I don't care,' he was telling her. Might also have been on the edge of a dream and not sure if he believed what he saw. The girl, little Natacha, crouched and laid the anorak across his back, then wriggled out of her vest. No fuss, and her skin white and wet, and she was ripping the vest into pieces, then passing them to the man who was dressed as a hunter – the sort of backwoodsman who hid in wildernesses. But might have been a dream . . . until the pain woke him.

He saw an old face, lined and leathered and with pepper stubble on his cheeks and chin. The knife was used to ease back the entry wound to see how clean was the flesh at the start of the cavity the bullet had made. The same was done at his back. The knife was handled with delicacy.

She told him, "If we are to get there, in this weather when the helicopter is unlikely to fly, then we go now . . . The question, what can you manage?"

Gaz pushed himself up. Slipped back to his knees, then pushed again. He stood, they steadied him. The wind flapped at his sliced clothing, and he wiped rainwater off his face, and the cold chilled him.

"What is his name – what is my friend's name?"

The answer was given him. "He is Jasha."

He would have been an old soldier, a veteran. Would have been a marksman, a combat sniper. Would also have owned a cussed and obstinate streak of independence. Would have been confronted with a platoon of arse-lickers and page-turners and all of them trying to whip him into the conventional; had turned his back on them, been self-sufficient, would have gone to the aid of any suffering human being or creature, and had nurtured a love for freedom in whatever form, whatever it meant. Lucky to have been found by this man, lucky he was with the kids.

"Can we get it on the road, move the show along?"

He put his arms around the girl and felt her warmth and allowed her to be close enough for the wound to spasm and hugged her, and she was giggling; then the boy and held him tight, then broke from both of them and lifted the arm sufficiently to create more bad pain and let his hand fall on the man's shoulder, Jasha's . . . and let his mouth touch the rough growth on the cheek.

"Thank you – all of you."

Words exchanged, more translation. "Not your business to know I have today lost a friend, my best friend. Told my friend to fuck off. Have been successful, have not seen my friend in the last hour. He is Zhukov. He is a brown bear . . . so, I need a new friend."

They were all laughing. Unreal and impossible. Laughter helped erode the reality. The wind came in a gust, shook him. But he took a first step . . . and a second, then his knees buckled and he was caught. The kids tried to support him, but were brushed aside. No ceremony. He was lifted, was slung over a shoulder, was gripped behind the knees and had two rifle barrels hard against his throat and head. They were on the move and the man went quickly and easily. Gaz remembered a sergeant who had told it to them like it was before a mission that promised a shed full of difficulties: 'Of course the plan is daft, idiotic, but it's our plan, the only plan in town.'

Into the teeth of the gales and of the rain, the man carried him and the kids bounced along behind and chattered, had no idea of the dangers they faced – or did and ignored them. Lucky to have found them all, blessed, and giving him one chance – a small one, but a chance.

19

No one had ever accused Gaz of stupidity. Might have been called 'dull', could have been accused of 'lacking imagination', but had never faced a charge of 'idiocy'. He had wriggled; stupid. Had come down off the hunter's shoulder, demanded it; idiotic. Was into the realms of 'not wanting to be a burden' and insisted he should not be merely dead weight. It was permitted. Clumsily, Gaz walked, allowed himself to be supported but not carried. It was from pride, but was idiotic.

The physical effort he made, throwing one leg in front of another, increased the risk of haemorrhage, doubled the probability of more internal bleeding, would cause the deep cavities to rupture further. Whether the two men and the girl had the resolve to slap his face, twist his arm, hoist him up again, let him struggle to no purpose, was doubtful. He was dependent on no one – not on Timofey, not on Natacha, not on the hunter. He thought of them, in his scrambling mind, as having less relevance to him than the gulls following the fishing boat on its journey across the North Sea. They went faster and the trail was narrow and the branches were low on the trees, and they buffeted through them. He thought the hunter was best equipped for the branches, and the girl managed them better than Timofey.

They heard the low baying of tracking dogs, held on long leashes and tugging the handlers' arms. They'd be leading a section of militiamen. A long way off, but the sounds carried on the wind. They had a good start, but the dogs had no 'passenger' to slow them. Perhaps because she had heard the dogs, and perhaps she sought escape from growing fear, Natacha tugged at his arm.

"Go there, take the money. Maybe you with us, Gaz, run and hide. Go where we cannot be found. That is a good dream?"

"It is a bad dream."

"Into the bank. You vouch our identity. We get the money – and are gone."

"Maybe not simple."

"The money is there?"

"Perhaps."

"Why is there doubt?"

"I don't know, can't say. They might require more proof of identity, and Timofey's father. And 'come back tomorrow', and perhaps a problem with a visa. They are not generous people. How do I know? I don't know. I no longer trust them."

"You have faith with us?"

"Yes, you and Timofey. Yes, and this man. I trust all of you. Those who sent me, they are plausible people, good at persuasion. Always talk of the national interest being served. They promise gratitude and reward, but they walk away. We cannot go faster than dogs."

"You want what?"

"I want not to be the reason that the dogs get to you."

Jasha led. The way he took them might have been good cover for a wild cat or for a fox. They crouched. It was a long time since Gaz had been able to see the grey waters of the inlet, and the low cloud settled on the hills on the far side. Among the trees and protected by the canopies the rain was less fierce. He imagined how it would be for the handlers, perhaps a mile behind them, and held back by the dogs tangling interminably among the trees. There would be little discipline in such dogs, big and hungry and aggressive; not the ones that sniffed for explosives and IEDs where he had served before. If the dogs came close he would not be able to increase his speed, nor would they go faster if they had to carry him. If the hunter used his rifle against them, it would be almost impossible to get anything other than a close-range shot among the trees. Would only be able to halt the dogs when they were within a few yards from him. And it was, truth to tell, the first time that he had considered the possibility – probability, certainty? – that it was here the business would be concluded . . . Remembered a training exercise when he had been in the recruit camp in Herefordshire, with the rookies, and they had done an exercise and had to lie up in a wood for two days and nights and then dogs had been put in to find them. Others had been located, not Gaz. Good fortune, not judgement. Pepper sprays might neutralise their noses . . . but the handlers, with rifles, would be close behind. Beginning to nag at Gaz: in an Arctic woodland of dwarf birch it would end and with him would be the newfound friends.

"Will you, please, leave me? Get the hell out. Please, as I ask."

What the English boy said to him, earnest and heartfelt, had been translated by the girl, and the look on her face was droll, and her boy seemed offended that the demand was made. Jasha laughed. Doubted there was humour on his face. Seldom saw reason to laugh. And now?

The idea of him allowing a friend, an opponent of his 'enemy', to be dropped on the sodden leaves, was not worth a moment's thought. Turn his back on him, allow him to linger with a bullet wound incapacitating him? Nor would he have considered leaving the kids to run on their own. He would have backed himself to find a river course, or a natural drain where the rainwater plunged and use it to lose the dogs. Not a problem for him. If he had abandoned them he would go back to his cabin and shoot his dog, and then sit in his chair and kick off a boot, and place his big toe inside the trigger guard of the Dragunov and put the barrel end in his mouth. Could not have lived with himself had he abandoned them.

Jasha said to the girl, "Tell him what he asks for is not possible. Tomorrow we have a smaller chance. The window now is good. Foul weather, but in twenty-four or thirty-six hours it moves away and then it is clear. The whole area of the Kola will be covered by helicopters, and troops swarming. No chance of using the fence because the patrolling will be too heavy. The way you have chosen offers that window, but it is small. Do not rely on luck. A fickle lady. Does not come to the undeserving. You earn luck."

It was translated. He pointed to the two rifles hooked on his back.

"You want one?"

Translation, then a nod.

"You can use one?"

"You were a soldier? You were in Afghanistan?"

Gaz spoke, and the girl listened, then told him. Had been a soldier, had been in Afghanistan and in Syria, a reconnaissance specialist, the same breed as a sniper, worked beyond the lines of safety. Spoke the words of a poem. And the girl translated, struggled but took trouble. *When you are wounded and left on Afghan's plains, And the women come out to cut up what remains, Then roll on your rifle and blow out your brains, And go to your God like a soldier.* Jasha liked it and recognised it as a truth.

His answer was to hum softly, the lilted tune of the anthem, of his *Lili Marlene*. He could hear the sounds of the dogs, and they went on down the hill, and could not go faster. He thought the man knew the tune of the song and his lips moved with it but no sound came other than the steadily more frantic cough and bubbling spit in his throat.

Natacha said, "Timofey reckons that the major will have told them everything about you. And you will be a great prize to them. Everything, right to the colour of your socks."

He answered her, "I don't think so. I don't think he will tell them anything."

Which was ridiculous; she did not understand him, nor did Timofey.

Often the leashes snagged as the two dogs tugged in different directions, searched with their noses, snorted, chased after fragments of scent in the wet ground under the trees. The handlers were pulled over, were bruised, cursed. Not a difficult decision. Had they sufficient control over their animals if they were let free? They thought so. The bond between dog and handler would likely be sufficient for the dogs to stay within a reasonable distance of the pursuing group. From the actions of the dogs it seemed clear to their handlers that the quarry was close, would soon be confronted.

They were let loose. Big beasts, good on the fence. Intimidating when tracking the illegals who attempted a crossing from the Murmansk side into Norway. Poorly fed which encouraged their aggression. The handlers followed and the guns came close behind.

It was the last leg of his journey. It had started at the check-in desks for service personnel at the military airbase at Latakia, a pretty enough place, kissed with Mediterranean sun, and unmarked by the war. Lavrenti Volkov had been troubled then, but had not believed how severe would be the scarring. Many on that same flight would harbour bad memories of the war, but he believed none would have incubated such despair, that extent of guilt.

He had never been a drill freak. Had been able to hold his place in the second rank of a parade in uniform for a VIP. Not one who would have been visible or barking orders or carrying a pennant on a lance. Adequate . . . He walked well now that it was – almost – the culmination of the journey. Straight back. Measured stride. Negotiating hazards that might have tripped him, going through water, stepping over protruding rocks, keeping his arms against his side. In his right hand was the corporal's pistol: while he had sat he had cleared the breech, checked the magazine, loaded and armed the Makarov. He had passed at least three-quarters of an hour before a small group from the border force, drawn along by two dogs and handlers, well-equipped troops. He had broken stride only to accept their greeting and he had gone on and had allowed a sergeant's urgent question – where was he, the fugitive? – to die in the noise of the wind. He had the rain on his back. It fell as hard as it had in the village.

He went through the last line of trees, emerged and crossed the military road that ran the length of the fence, and next was the ploughed strip. Lavrenti could have given, two days before, a formal lecture on the importance of the barrier on Russia's border. Could have spoken of the need to prevent those who threatened the security of the Motherland from entering the territory he was tasked to protect, could have waxed enthusiastic on his country's ability to withstand threats, repel invaders. Beyond the wire was a dense line of fir trees. He had lost his cap but the medal ribbons were bright on his chest, and mud spattered his military trousers, but he would have cut a fine figure. There were shouts ahead of him. Their officer ran forward . . . He saw the pair of them, the old sergeants who had dropped their weapons and who had bolted. They seemed to stiffen at the sight of him. He gave no indication of his mood. The young border troopers who had known that an FSB officer was kidnapped, then in vague circumstances had been freed, gazed at him with open admiration. Still the powerful stride, leaving his footprints in the ploughed strip, he came to the track inside the fence where vehicles were parked. The officer left a radio dangling on a coiled wire at his jeep and hurried towards him. An arm was outstretched, a hand offered to Lavrenti while receiving congratulations on his safe delivery from evil, from danger, from the clutches of the enemy. He noted all of that.

The pistol was used to reinforce his gesture. The officer was to stay back, was not to impede him. Another flick of the barrel and troops edged away, stood at the side and watched, confused, and the officer flushed at the slight. No word spoken, but the Makarov in his hand gave a clear message. He was over the track and stood a few paces back from the wire.

Still holding the pistol, Lavrenti's hands came together, made the image of a man in prayer. But his eyes had a deadened look.

He flicked the barrel of the pistol towards those who watched him. No one knew what to say, how to react. He gazed ahead through dulled eyes. Beyond the wire, clouded by mist and the weight of rain, was thick pine woodland. He assumed this was where his captor, the good corporal, was taking him and here the wire would be breached again, and he wondered what trick, what clever subterfuge, had been used to bring the man in at this place. And remembered that he lived because his life had been protected by the corporal. Many men watched him and held firearms, and if he had run towards the fence and tried to scramble over it he would have been tackled at the legs, or shot, or merely overpowered and treated with the same fickle concern shown to any gibbering wreck suffering 'combat fatigue', whatever psychiatric title was now in vogue.

Had more to remember . . . The cordon going into position and a few slipping away, and many encircled, some with fear on their faces, more with hatred, all with defiance.

The hooded informer, and boys named – and one taken to the football area, and the rope, lifted and kicking.

The crossbar breaking, and bayonets used.

His face slashed by a woman, and her and others taken to the gully where the stream ran fiercely from the severity of the rain. Could feel the shallow depression on his skin . . . wore a gallantry medal's ribbon, and many assumed it was a combat scrape, shrapnel.

Old women and young women abused by the militia boys, then shot. And children shot. And homes burned

A body in the trench, life not yet extinguished, and aiming, and the unblinking eyes watching him. Do not beg, not plead, but hate . . . All remembered, making shackles on him.

He was watched and they did not know how to respond.

The scream was carried on the wind, muffled but clear, a cry of acute pain and an awful fear.

A noise such as neither of the handlers had ever heard from their dogs. The sergeant and his militia boys were rooted behind them.

A noise to wake the dead, and one handler knew it was his dog's cry.

Both blundered forward and the low branches scraped their faces.

One was sick, vomited the entirety of his last meal. The other howled in anguish.

The lead dog, there was always a pecking order with the big border patrol animals, and would have been a couple of lengths in front and closing on the source of the scent; it was on its side, its stomach ripped open, its intestines displayed loosely. Life was slipping but still it screamed. The skin and coat of its belly seemed to have been cut with the sharpened tips of a rake, many lines and all savagely deep. The other dog, usually cocky, confident, fearless, lay on its back, posture of total submission. The first handler took his pistol from his holster, choked on his sobbing, shot his dog.

He said, "A bear. They bounced a bear."

From his colleague, "Not another metre. We go back. Not another step forward."

"I think my man got to him." Knacker murmured to the Norwegian, as the little grin played at his lips. "He's not going anywhere. It's as far as the road goes for Major Lavrenti Volkov. Funny old world."

Not even up on the damn Wall, when Maude was scratching at mud with a toothbrush or the trowel he'd bought her at a Christmas fair five years back, had Knacker felt so cold, so wet, and so elated. Always best when the unexpected dropped in his lap. The Russian stood still and moved not a muscle. His face was impassive, his hands raised in a gesture of supplication, except when an officer had approached and a pistol waved at him. Entreaties for him to lower the weapon or give it up were ignored.

And quieter, "Don't you chicken out on me, my boy. Don't do a tease."

The officer had a radio at his ear, was relaying messages that came over the link to his principal NCO, and was calling on additional manpower and tried to explain, obvious to Knacker, the bizarre behaviour of their supposed kidnap victim. The militiamen watched bemused . . .

The Norwegian, dry, in a few words, told him what he heard.

Knacker responded. "He wants redemption, and won't get it, and is a murdering little shit, will get no absolution and knows it. Will have to do it for himself. He was good, my man, didn't know he'd have this sense of theatre. I think, never afraid to admit a fault, that I short changed him. I suppose he's out there, alone – better out of his misery. Yes, sooner the better if not already."

He was told about a bear, about a dog, about the abandonment of a pursuit. Was told that helicopters would fly in the morning. An additional two companies of regular mechanised infantry from the garrison camp at Titovka would go into the field for the search mission. The wind would stay strong but the rain would be gone.

"In the military they've a bit of a yardstick about getting their people back, injured or corpses. Started in the US effort in Vietnam. A man down, send in a platoon to recover him. Not enough so make it a company, still can't get to him so it becomes a battalion and then a regiment and full-blown close support air strikes, and an air cavalry intervention, for one man who is alive or is dead. Not our way, friend, not in my trade. A funny old world and a tough old world. Stand on their own, or lie on their own. They know it, are all volunteers, all signed up understanding the way things are. Rum for him that it didn't work out. Not that we'll be repeating."

A stand off had developed in front of Knacker. The major, drenched, coated in slime and mud but with his medal ribbons still prominent, remained motionless and the detachment's officer was uncertain what action to take. Knock the damn pistol out of his hand, wait for a psychiatrist to show up, keep talking gentle crap in the hope that the lunatic would start blubbering and chuck the weapon down. Knacker glanced at his watch. Had a bit of time left, not much. Would want to catch the flight out of Kirkenes that evening, then the red-eye from Tromso back to the UK.

Knacker said, "We've a new broom back at the shop. Not in favour of this sort of caper. Going to rein us in, and put the old ones, me and my ilk, out to grass. Don't see the value of this type of mission. I tell you, should the shit do the decent thing and go to his Maker, there will be riotous pleasure in a couple of refugee camps, firing in the air, singing and dancing and a carnival night, because of what happened, and we will have won lifelong allies in that neck of Syria. Sorry, but it is now regarded as old fashioned, better left to satellites. The bullies and the dictators, and the killers, are – anyway – going to be our new friends . . . Come on, I'm here till the end but get a bloody move on, can't you."

But the pistol barrel did not waver, remained pointed to the leaden sky, held by hands in prayer.

Delta Alpha Sierra, the nineteenth hour

"He's called Knacker, agent runner. Don't mind him. Seems fierce but he's all right. From the Sixers. Just tell him what you saw."

His officer escorted him to a closed door. Two women were waiting outside: one was fluffy and small and blonde and with pretty freckles, and the other was taller, heavier, had a serious tattoo on one upper arm and bulged in a T-shirt and floppy shorts.

"This him?"

His officer answered them. "Well, it's not fucking Father Christmas – and he's had a tough time so treat him well."

The door was opened. The women followed but not his officer. Behind a formica-topped table was a small man, stocky and powerful and greeting his visitor with a decent smile. The sort that would put Gaz, a little, at ease. An apology. Food and water were waiting in the Mess for him, and a medic on standby to run over his condition, but this guy, Knacker, would really appreciate his take on the last twenty-for hours. Seemed it had been this Sixer's shout, way back, that had caused them to target the village, get the camera in place, and line up a friendly location in an area of hostility. He'd said he was fine, could wait for food and drink, and had talked.

Started with the camera and the schedule for the batteries and the life they had, and the need to clear out the recorded images. A set of batteries might have been faulty and the need for replacements had come sooner than anticipated. All routine stuff and all rendered with a dry monotone voice. And the move into position up a slope and under a lip below the plateau, and a girl with goats, and boys coming back on pick-ups, and then the convoy advancing up the highway. He told of some specifics, of the first boy to be hanged and of the corralling of the women and children and old men. Described how the crossbar had collapsed under the weight of four suspended youths. The woman who had slashed the officer's face – a fair-haired Russian officer. Had struggled but had gone on to describe the long day, and the longer evening, the burning and the shooting, and then the Iranian militiamen lining up for their turn, their belts loosened and their flies undone. Spoke of the girl who hid close to him and who never spoke except to say that her sister was among the dead. Had remembered pretty much everything, and it had seemed to hurt more, now, in the recall, than when it had been played out live in front of him. Tears came.

"It's all right, Gaz, take your time. Nearly through, but it is important we have a record, an honest and truthful appraisal which is what we are getting. We have ways of making people answer for their actions, not always obvious and sometimes far from sight, but that's what we do. Have done in the past, will do again. Those sort of bastards, particularly the Russian officer, imagine themselves above any creed of the legality that we believe in. I promise you, Gaz, if anything can be done then it will be done. I don't chuck them around lightly, promises. And at the end . . . ?"

He spoke of the darkness and of the pits, and of the shooting of those already in the pits who showed faint signs of survival. Then talked, with a choke in his throat, of the girl, and the stampede of her herd, and of militiamen running towards his hiding place where she, too, had taken shelter. He would have been identified, would have been captured and paraded, but she had run, had drawn them off. He said, would have sounded infantile to this man, that when he had been a youngster on a farm that a hind would bolt from cover to take dogs away from the place where a fawn, too young and too weak to run, had shelter. Told what had happened to the girl when she was caught. Told how she had escaped being shot dead, was a witness. Told this man, Knacker, he owed his life to her.

Knacker said, "What can be done will be done. As we said about the genocide people in Bosnia, 'They can run but they

cannot hide'. We go after them. It's not something we forget.
Thank you."

Had seemed decent, had reckoned him to be a caring and
honest man. He went out. Went to look for the girl. Was told she
had been taken to the medic. Went to the medic. Seemed not a big
deal. 'What the local kid? Yes, saw her. Gave her a 'morning-after'
dose.' Had they provided her a bunk in the women's quarters?
'Didn't have to. She's gone, pushed off. Said something about
some goats and her dogs. Just as well, would have been difficult,
impossible, to square with regulations, her sleeping here.'

Had gone outside the collection of Portakabins and converted
freight containers. Had gone to the entry point where the sentry
was positioned behind a wall of sandbags. Was told she had come
through, was alone, was walking, that no transport was deemed
available. Had borrowed the sentry's night-vision glasses, had
scanned the track leading away from the Forward Operations
Base. Had not seen her, had not thanked her, had failed her. He
owed his life to her . . .

Timofey freed him, then Natacha did. He sagged. They left him
to be held up by the hunter.

They ran, as best they could, down to the shore. There was a
half-light of grey, the rocks and the sea and the far side of the inlet
and the cloud ceiling, but a little brighter as if the worst of the
night was over and a new day tilted forward. A desolate headland
stretched away in front of them. Not a place that either would ever
have been to before. No school party, no youth section, would
have come here. Not fenced in but no road reaching the place:
inside a restricted zone, halfway between the two Northern Fleet
bases for submarines. When they were close to the water, they
looked back, needed the final directions of the hunter.

Because he was soaked and because the wind off the open water
snatched at his clothing, Timofey thought it a bad place, one
without life, without hope. He saw the concrete flooring of abandoned buildings, and the roofs long collapsed. The place would
have been built for the Great Patriotic War effort, what they had

drilled into them at school. The weed came up out of the water and seemed to squirm on the rocks, made them treacherous. Far down the inlet, back towards his home city, Murmansk, was a flash of white set deep in the uniform grey. He squinted hard, and blinked to get the rain from his eyes, and saw the shape of a naval vessel and the white was the bow spray that it threw aside. He turned, gestured to the hunter that he had seen the warship and received a curt duck of the head, indicating the man had seen it maybe minutes earlier. The man knew much . . . matters that had never concerned Timofey, nor Natacha; knew when the tide was at its highest, when it would turn and run back towards the open sea, when the wind would shift, when the rain would end, and sunlight lie on the wilderness behind them. They needed the tide and the wind, and needed to be gone before the storm ebbed. His thought was savage: better to have been at the railway station and meeting the long distance trains, better to be dealing there and dodging between shadows and using cover, better to have been at the apartment and changing clothes and going into the city to dump a plastic bag filled to overflowing with the bloodstained clothes they wore now. The sea water broke on the rocks by his feet and he thought the tide almost at its highest point.

He asked her, "What colour is it?"

"It is green. He said it was green."

"I can't see it."

"Nor me."

He shrugged, admitted his failure to locate it. The hunter might have sworn and if he did his voice was lost in the wind. One hand holding the man, their friend, and one pointing to the right of where he and Natacha stood – or crouched as the wind gusted stronger. Looked at the waves and their crests, looked at the swirling weed carried up to the surface, looked at the shades of grey that were constant in the water, looked at the wave that the naval vessel made as it came up the inlet, looked again where the hunter pointed, and saw it.

It was green, the colour of springtime's grass, what there would be in a pasture. It bobbed and half the time, when a wave came on to it, was doused and then disappeared, then would spring up again. It strained to break free from a rope but was tethered. He could not have dreamed of doing it. Timofey understood that the hunter had absorbed the coordinates on the slip of paper, had programmed them, had made his own map and puzzled on the mathematics. Then had brought them through the denseness of the scrub and woodland, and they had emerged close to the shore and within 100 metres of where they were directed. He could not have done it, nor Natacha. He showed her the buoy. It seemed so small and the sea so big ... She shivered. He held her close. Thought, was not angered and not surprised and not broken, that his Natacha – his soulmate – would probably have gone with the Englishman across the frontier if he had been able. Would have followed him, gone for the brighter lights, louder music, or might not. Thought it, accepted it, held her tight and tried to squeeze warmth into her. The hunter, Jasha, called them. Together, they scrambled back over the rocks.

"He's a fucking lunatic."

"Never good, what I say, that combination – a lunatic and a loaded firearm, not good."

They stood behind the officer who gabbled into his radio about a crazed major who had a pistol and seemed not to want rescuing but indicated he would shoot anyone who closed on him, but had not spoken.

"You want more?"

"No."

"Are you looking for a decoration?"

"Meritorious service, one hanging from a lanyard, don't think so."

Mikki and Boris had been given coffee and had fed on bread and sausage, and the officer had no time to quiz them. The pistol had been waved decisively in the officer's face and he had backed off. The attitude of prayer was resumed.

"Front row of the veterans' parade on Armed Forces Day?"

"Not for me."

"Going to turn in those kids, the druggie kids, him who deals and her who waves those little boobs in the air? Going to?"

"The price of a decoration? Don't think so. No thanks for it. Agreed? We turn our back on the fucking hero of the fierce combat for that village, Deir al-Siyarqi, on him."

They slipped away. Would get a ride down from the fence and back to where their vehicle was parked. Would be on a plane and headed south, gone by the time the inquest came to dig into detail. Unnoticed they eased back from the fence, left their major. Loyalty? Neither would have reckoned to know its meaning.

"Me first. And you. Me second, and you," Mikki said. "The way this country works – and me third, and you."

He was helped. Gaz tried to find the strength to walk unaided but the rocks glistened from the rain and were coated in weed . . . Had seemed to come to a decision which was the spur. No drugs in him but a variant of delirium. About a future. Seemed important and worth living for. Must have been a fantasy because he stood on rocks and was nudged forward, firm movements and not brooking weakness, nor delay: and ahead of him was the channel where the waves surged and a future was an illusion. A dream and likely beyond reach but still a comfort: who he would be with. Would hold to the dream as he weakened, slipped.

The man spoke to the girl, clipped words and not for argument.

She told him, "You have to fight. At the darkest hour, you fight. Put an image in your mind, and fight for it, or put a person there. You will never dream if you do not fight."

The officer called to him, "For God's sake, however unpleasant your experience you should not threaten with a firearm, should behave like a man of honour. Show some fucking balls, man. Stop simpering like a college girl. You are behaving in a disgraceful manner, not fit to wear a proud uniform, you . . ."

He did not look at the officer. Lavrenti estimated where the man stood. He lowered his right hand and swung his arm and his aim was into the dirt. He slipped his finger inside the guard.

Squeezed in a disciplined way, and fired. One shot, and the voice had strangled in the officer's throat . . . He heard the metal scrapes as other weapons were armed, cocked. He resumed his posture. Hands together . . . He had noticed, from the corner of his eye that the two men given him by his father, Mikki and Boris, had left. Justified. Now he surprised those who watched him . . . thought of his father and thought of his mother and there was no affection, no respect . . . and he started to take slow and deliberate steps towards the fence.

He did not consider the village. He did not think of the corporal who had brought him to this point.

Lavrenti was now two paces from the wire. It stretched taut in front of him, showed grime and wear, was ochre – coloured from rust, and in places plastic strips had been ripped by the winds and had scudded on to the barbs. Saw the smooth tumbler wires that were alarmed and would flash lights, activate cameras, howl a chorus of sirens if he disturbed them. Would they shoot him if he careered the final steps and jumped and was prepared to lacerate his bare hands and try to heave himself up? Or would they just drag him back, drop him in the mud, talk about when a strait jacket could be brought up?

He looked ahead. He peered into the trees. He saw the shadow shape of the man's shoulders, set low as if he sat on something short, perhaps a stool and perhaps a log, and thought he caught also a momentary sight of a second man but in fatigues and better camouflaged . . . It was where Lavrenti would have expected to find the corporal's officer, his control. The man would be close to the frontier, waiting for his agent . . . Would not know that he waited in vain because of a single rifle shot: a bad wound and no medical treatment was a sentence of death, might already have been exacted. The corporal would have been there for identification, a reconnaissance trooper, and the assassin would have been due to travel in his wake, a week later or two weeks, could have been a month. Refused to do the killing himself, accepted the role of gaoler to escort Lavrenti to the border, across it, into a courtroom. Had achieved much, had cleared Lavrenti's mind. He thought himself grateful, the weight was shed. The lie and the guilt were no longer lived.

To the wire, Lavrenti said, "He was a fine man, the finest . . . dead. I owe him much. I am in debt to him."

He smiled. Of those who watched him, only a man crouching beyond the wire and hidden by low branches would have understood, and those in a half-circle behind him would have thought he rambled . . . For guilt there was a punishment. For a crime there was no atonement.

He lifted the pistol, the corporal's pistol. He put the barrel between his lips, bit on it. He pushed the barrel deeper, felt the metal grind on his teeth. His finger was on the trigger, and the foresight of the Makarov gouged the roof of his mouth. The corporal had been his teacher. His finger tightened, squeezed.

Knacker murmured, "Well, fuck that for a curtain line."

The Norwegian was impassive.

The noise of the single shot faded. The blood spout and the bits had long scattered. The body did some spasms but was lifeless now and the top of the head was fractured. The officer, first to move, bent, crouched, then knelt, shrugged to confirm the obvious, prised the pistol away, without fuss, made it safe. Walked off.

A stretcher was brought from one of their trucks and the remains of Lavrenti Volkov, major of *Federalnya 'sluzhba bezopasnosti*, was heaved on to it, no ceremony and little respect. And somehow fitting . . . Knacker thought it the way that a condemned, pronounced dead, would have been treated in the pit below the trapdoor. He thought those in the camps adjoining Syria and with especial attention to those who had come from that village, that region, might enjoy a telling of the circumstances of the retribution. Might egg it a little, might give more satisfaction that way, might upgrade the role and responsibility of a young British trooper – out of retirement from the front line but determined to avenge the savage atrocity meted out to loyal and innocent friends – that sort of stuff – and gave his life in the act. Might be the end of the road, but always a requirement to leave matters neatly in place.

The body was hoisted into the back of a truck. Some mud and leaves, sodden and clammy, were kicked over the blood stains. There would be sufficient carrion feeders out here to clear up. They were moving on, no longer required.

His phone vibrated. Alice. If he wanted that flight it was time to quit his location, come direct to the Kirkenes airport. He was asked if there was word of their man, and he answered quietly that the belief was that he had been shot, dead probably. Likely hidden somewhere in the squat forest of the tundra and might lie there for weeks, months, years. Too wet for the dogs, and too windy for the choppers to fly, but the forecast was due to improve for the rest of the week. Best if their man were not found and if Gaz, done better than expected for all his queasiness, were left to lie in peace, the rain and winds would scatter the scent of his failed flight.

The lorries drove away. Knacker emerged from the trees and his Norwegian friend folded up the stool he'd provided.

He went up to the wire, stood inches from it. Knacker rummaged in his pocket and found the coin. Maude might have understood but if she did not then it hardly mattered to him. It would be a good place for it to rest. He took it out of the pocket. A silver *denarius* from the reign of the Emperor Hadrian, the image of Pietas, 'duty', still visible. He imagined himself as one of the *Frumentarii*, a wheat collector, alone and gathering lethal intelligence. Was, briefly, also an officer trained to conduct counter-espionage on the Wall, and keep it safe, secure . . . Or could have been the dirty little beggar in pelts and covered in woad who did the job on the other side. Not important which role he, Knacker, performed 1800 years later. He held the coin, brushed it hard against his camouflage to retrieve some shine on its surface, and threw it.

No sunlight to glint on it. It rose in an arc, dived, and fell.

The coin, pressed in that precious metal, landed near to where the blood had been thickest, but the rain was already dispersing it. It made a feeble splash, and sank. He had been here, the wheat collector or the intelligence officer or the spy master, had left his mark. An honourable profession and he had no shame for any of his achievements and no regrets for the price others – always others because that was the nature of his work – might have paid. The airport would be called, told he was on his way, the flight would be held. This section of fence was silent, like nothing had happened there, and a few birds chirped without enthusiasm.

Knacker said to the Norwegian, "Always remember what delivers intelligence is agents. They are motivated by money and ideology and compromise and ego, any of those or all of them, so MICE puts agents in the field, on the ground, and they deliver. Deliver a hell of a sight more than bloody machines. Been a good day and a good evening. Ended well for us. One or two things not quite in place, but mostly satisfactory – and left tidily."

She was in the water. The estimate, before Natacha went in, was that the naval vessel would power past the green-painted buoy that rode in the waves and would head on for the mouth of the inlet. She had stripped down, wore her jeans and not much else, and had shaken off her trainers and socks. Any other time, Gaz could have done it, but not with an entry wound, not with an exit wound. She was in the water and at the buoy, and the vessel should have been hammering up the inlet, but it had slackened power, and was crawling. She swam well enough, clumsy but effective, and could flip up her legs and do a shallow dive and had already dragged hard enough on the rope to show them the package fastened to it, then had wrestled with it, would have had cold fingers and been shivering through her body, and had freed it, and had showed them, and . . . the vessel had slowed and twenty of the crew, could have been more, were on deck. She was pointed at.

Timofey swore softly. The hunter, Jasha, was stone-faced. Gaz, and most of them in the regiment, would have said they believed in the true faith, in Murphy's Law. 'If it could go wrong, it would, bet your shirt on it.' A biblical level of certainty about it. An officer was being called. It had to be Natacha who went into the water because Jasha said he could not swim, and neither could Timofey. Shouting and running on deck, and decisions to be made: time passing, and him weaker, and the best of the tide was now, and the best of the wind. She rose out of the water. Sat, astride the buoy.

Gave the guys on the warship a view of herself. Waved to them. Would have heard the cheering and the wolf whistles.

Let them bounce, did an eyeful for them, blew kisses back. And seemed, and Gaz did not know how she managed it, to waggle her hips ... She was a great girl, a unique kid, and he counted the blessings that she was the girlfriend of Timofey, a wakened sleeper. Had never met anyone in any way similar.

A belch of dark smoke breeched the funnel vent. Like an oil problem in the engine had been dealt with. The whole length of the deck was filled with sailor boys, all rewarded with the full sight of her white skin and her breasts and sodden blonde hair clinging to her shoulders. The vessel gathered power. The sailors might have been on their way out into the Barents for a week-long sea trial, or might have been at the start of the journey down to the Mediterranean and warmth. Gaz doubted, wherever they went, they would find another girl with the supreme talent of Natacha, drug pusher from Murmansk, and his friend.

She had the package, and swam back to the rock where they sheltered.

Timofey helped her ashore, shivering and sliding and coughing water, and they had no towel to dry her, but that job was done with the fleece that Jasha wore. He used his knife on the package wrapping to reveal the folded shape of the folded rubber, and air hissed and the shape filled, became a dinghy. Might have been six feet across, and the sides might have been a foot high, and the wind caught it, and Timofey grabbed it.

Farewell time, but not protracted. The kids took the dinghy down to the water; it seemed feather light and rose and fell and slapped the rocks and the weed. Jasha had hold of Gaz. Just a few words from him and they might have heard him and might not, and the business in hand was getting him into the craft. They had no water to give him, and no food. He was in the middle of telling them that they were good people, and the pain had lifted in his chest, and he could barely hear his own voice. The tide pulled away, the tide did the job and the wind caught at the dinghy's side and propelled it. It was the back-stop.

The girl had not covered herself and shook from the cold. Timofey might have choked on tears. The old hunter gazed down at him 'Did what I could, could not have done other.' Gaz saw Timofey point once, back down the inlet and towards the city and then they were scrambling to get clear of the open rock and regain the cover of the undergrowth. He did not need to use his hands as paddles because the elements took him out into the flow and away from the shelter of the headland.

Gaz felt a desperate sense of tiredness. Wanted to sleep and reckoned if he did, could, that the pain would go and the sleep would be deeper.

The tide took the dinghy, and the swell was around him and spray splashed on to him. If it had not been for the water coming over the smooth rubber sides he would have slept. One hand was draped over the side and in the sea, and was intended to act as a rudder, futile because the craft now had a mind of its own. The tide and the wind dictated that it went effortlessly towards the central water of the inlet, and here the current was more headstrong and the wind funnelled up between the two hillsides flanking it. Almost starting to dream. Of warmth. The rain seemed to have slackened but not the gusts, and he made good speed . . . and he was thrown from one side of the dinghy to the other. Water cascaded over him, was in his wound and in his face and down his throat and stung his eyes. The dinghy shook and he gripped the fine rope looped around the inside of the tiny craft. He was close to capsizing and the rain came in torrents, and his movements must have further opened the wound and damaged the interior cavity. If he went under he would not regain the surface, knew it. A great dark shape was passing him, a ship surging on down the inlet and towards the sea. Later he would see the lights of the bridge, then would be flung about again as the screws churned the water.

He felt that the fight had left him.

Would drift and would wait for sleep to claim him.

Did not know his name, nor where he was, nor why. And the tide raced faster and the wind flicked the waves and the swell was fiercer.

20

He had no sense of time. He wore a watch but it was on the arm that trailed in the water; his hand was frozen numb and he could no longer move it. Not that the time mattered, other than that it was a fraction lighter on the far horizon. The cloud blanket was still capping the hill line on the east side of the inlet, but he reckoned it softer. Could have slept . . . The rain had stopped, but not the wind.

Gusts caught at the inflated sides. The dinghy was pushed forward and spun as it went. Gaz's head lolled and sometimes he was facing out to sea and saw the cloud and the horizon merging, and sometimes he was facing the west's hills that bordered the inlet, or the east's, and there were moments when he faced where he had come from and could see distant pricks of light. There were navigation beacons on rocks close to the shore, and buoys flashed intermittently, but he did not know their pattern or their importance.

A cargo ship had passed him and he had smelled the wet coal loaded in the hold, but it had not seen him, had gone past at speed and he had again been shaken by the waves it created. He might have slid overboard but had, again, a sufficient grip on the rope, and that further tired him. The combination of tide and wind moved him but he had no destination, only the fading hope that he might clear the inlet, be carried towards the west, might leave Russian territorial waters, might be picked up if he were seen, if he lived. Spray climbed the sides and washed across him.

With his free hand he made a little cup of his palm and scooped out minuscule quantities of the water that now settled at the bottom of the dinghy. His buttocks were in water, and his boots, and the part of his back from which the bullet had exited. There was no cup, tin mug, bowl or plastic water bottle which would have helped his feeble efforts to bale. And the water, deep enough to lap against his body, further chilled him. Gaz supposed there would be a time when exhaustion married a loss of hope and then the best answer was sleep. A long sleep and a dream of warmth and of the sun, and of a girl and love.

A light caught him.

Bright and firm, locking on him. Then was gone. The dinghy rode a wave, sank into the following pit, shipped more water, then surged up again and the light caught him a second time. Eyes wide open now. He waited for a shout, yelled commands in a language that he did not understand, but the light lost him. He was aware of rocks and they obscured the light. He drifted on. The dinghy collided with the shore. A rock was towering above him and he was against it and there were weed and barnacles, and the waves beat against it. The craft smacked into the rock, rode it, then dropped and wallowed in a swell, and came again. Gaz fought to trigger the little coherence left to him. Realised . . . the light would have guided fishermen working close to the shore, simple. Men who used little boats would have relied on the light, and he realised he was now wedged.

Big moment. The failure of the back-stop. The light caught him, dropped him. He was between two rocks and the waves beat against him. How would it end? A good chance that he would be pitched off the dinghy and dumped into the water and the first wave would hurl him against the rock face. Would be a quick finish . . . Tried to look for the girl's face. He used a leg. Managed to find the strength because he had the image of her, and the wind tore her hair, a small sad laugh, and . . . he stamped and pushed and the dinghy was freed, went in a tight circle, then bounced him against the far edge of the rock and he lingered there for tantalising seconds, then the dinghy moved and the current held it and the wind caught the sides. He moved on, and looked back, and saw a big shadow on the shore. It moved with a rolling, uneven gait as if it were disabled. The light on the rock swerved again and held it for a moment, then disappeared and found Gaz and left him and shone out across the open water. When the beam completed its circle and again lit that part of the shore above the rock, close to low twisted trees, the bear was gone. Gaz rubbed at his eyes. A delusion? An hallucination? Something that he had seen or imagined, or dreamed of? Where it had moved, and where the light had made bright diamonds of its eyes, was deserted.

Two more ships passed him. One was a fishing boat and the other was a freighter, and they were far out in the inlet channel and he was tossed some more by the waves they threw at him. More spray came in and his efforts to ladle out the water failed to match what splashed in. He thought the cold was worse. He had a question in his mind. Wanted it asked and needed it answered.

'What I did, had it any value?'

Not a big voice, he hardly heard it. Waited for the reply but in his ears were only the swirl of the waves and the singing of the wind, and carried to him across the white caps were the diminishing sounds of the engines of the trawler and the freighter.

'What I did, will it make a difference?'

He listened. The grey cloud still blanketed him and a mist had formed. Harder to see ahead and the current was still strong and the wind was prodding him towards the open sea. Listened for Knacker and his smooth talk, and for Alice and Fee who would be encouraging and talk about assessments still being made but the picture, on the whole, being good. Listened for the words from Timofey and Natacha that would lift him, and those of the hunter who had carried him to the back-stop opportunity. Listened for what the officer would tell him, and wondered where he was, what he did, whether the reading of him had been true or was merely wishful thinking. Heard nothing.

'Was it failure, was it for nothing?'

Too tired now to care.

"If anyone were to ask me, was *Matchless* a failure, all for nothing, I would say to their face that they are ignorant. Of course it made a difference, and one of value. Might just be that you and those now posturing on the fifth floor have not the wit to realise it."

Knacker faced him, the new broom's message-boy.

"I understand your irritation. Way above my pay grade. The instruction is from Internal Security." The young man, Dominic, had a gentle voice and a shuffling step and a wobbling lower lip, and had shaved poorly that morning, but did not back off.

"I have personal items inside that I wish to collect."

"Am very sorry, but my instructions are clear. *We* have first call on the rooms and after completion of our work then you may enter, also your assistants, for a supervised period not exceeding ten minutes. Then the area is to be locked, sealed, and finally returned to the landlords. I am very sorry, but it is over, on D-G Acting's say-so."

A church clock chimed the half hour. Thirty minutes past seven o'clock, steady rain falling on the pavement and traffic queuing to get north over the bridges for the run into central London. Unlikely to be play that morning at either the Oval cricket ground or at Lords, and even more unlikely that Knacker would get past Dominic, rated as an able and boring recruit who would go far because of his lack of eccentricity. And behind Dominic were a pair of men in the usual rubbish uniform of the security detail: jeans, leather coats, shades – and it was raining and half dark.

"How long will this charade take?"

"Three or four hours. My apologies but matters are out of my hands. Could be longer. Your assistants are upstairs, Alice Holmes and Tracey Dawkins, and have proved most cooperative, so it may be nearer three. Should be out by late morning. We started at five, both of them here then. I really would suggest that you go and find some breakfast and a cup of tea."

That hurt ... but Knacker had lived a life of inciting men and women to turn against their own, did not champion loyalties. They had landed forty-five minutes after midnight at Gatwick. He had gone back to his suburban home, been there barely two hours, showered and changed and dumped soiled clothes and the sodden suit in which he had travelled, had catnapped beside Maude before his alarm had gone. Had caught the train to Waterloo, then

walked along the embankment to Kennington Lane, and had seen
the knot of men and women on the pavement outside the Yard.
They'd been on a fag break, and piled inside the door were plastic
bags bulging with files and electronics, even the bloody raincoat
that he kept there . . . Hurt more than he would show that his girls
had jumped ship. Problem was for Knacker that he preached
betrayal, gloried in it. He supposed that he could go and find a
sandwich bar where there would be hot coffee and a builder's
breakfast, and when he returned the door would be double-locked,
and there would be a note with a number and an address further
along the road where his personal items were temporarily held.
Clients at the taxi company counter, next door, watched them
with interest, and a wry grin was on the face of the principal at the
gentlemen's tailor on the other side where they performed mira-
cles letting out trousers for older men and . . . He smiled. Could in
fact have knifed the little bastard, Dominic, then could have
packed him off to a *souk* in Aleppo or Mosul and wiped the smug-
ness off his face. But just smiled.

"I wish you a good career – and a good day."

He walked away from Dominic and the heavies with him, then
rang Arthur Jennings. God, the poor wretch sounded low.

Knacker was asked how it had gone, 'your show'. Had he been
able to tie all the loose ends, as he usually did?

"Went well. Good result. The creature we targeted is up with
the angels. Lost our man but we think it's clean and deniable. Will
be well received in the camps and where people from the region
of that benighted village are gathered. Will get us solid support . . .
except that we may not have a footprint in those parts if this
vandal, illiterate and unimaginative, has his way on the fifth floor."

He was told the rug had been pulled, that Arthur Jennings had
wanted to call a meeting of the Round Table the next day at lunchtime. They could not do it, the pub management said, had a
booking for a *Pilates* class. Have to be another day.

He rang off. If there was 'another day' he doubted he would
attend. He would not enjoy the obsequies for his work, his style.
He walked away. A dinosaur, a representative of a species that

teetered on the verge of extinction . . and wondered if, in that great building at the end of the road, Ceausescu Towers, he would ever be missed, indeed if his name would ever be spoken again. It had been a good show, no regrets, what a wheat collector might have said, and saw that spinning coin flying high, stalling, then dropping, splashing into a mud pool. Had left his mark there.

He walked tall, no slouch of failure. A good show, and on Knacker's watch. And all finished neatly, tidily, his hallmark.

He was nearer to sleep. But as the cloud lifted so the wind freshened and blew cold from the east. The dinghy was tossed, and each time Gaz was thrown against the side, and each time he snatched at the rope, then the pain came, was more fierce. He doubted there would be much longer, and wondered if when the moment came he would continue to fight . . . but had the face, clung to the image.

The two most recent disappointments, crushing for his morale, were when the circling of the dinghy had meant he looked out towards an unbroken expanse of sea, and he had squinted to focus better. Half the time he had been below the level of the wave caps that tossed him, but when the dinghy came up to mount the swell, he had seen a fishing boat, a big trawler. It would have been heading far out into the Barents, not after the inshore crab stocks but chasing bigger and more challenging fish. The time no longer existed when he could have stood and peeled off some clothing, waved it with ever-increasing urgency. His craft – had it been noticed – would have been taken for a plastic container, or a length of driftwood. The boat had not slowed and not diverted from its course. The second moment of hope, despair, then resignation, had been a tramper making a lonely progress on the horizon. Let alone stand up and wave, shout, Gaz could no longer shift his hips and his legs, and half of his chest sodden and being lapped with water, and he thought the level in the dinghy grew higher. How long? Not long.

Another face gouged into his consciousness.

Kindly features. Natural that Gaz should speak to a new friend. Elegant whiskers sprouted by his friend's mouth, and its eyes were dark, but the head was well out of the waves and rode with them. His friend would have been curious had no ability nor wish to harm.

Gaz said softly to the seal, tilting his head with difficulty but making eye contact, "Won't be around long. Apologies for coming on to your territory. Where I come from, used to live, we had plenty like you. They gather off Noup Head and Inga Ness and also they get to be at Castle O'Burrian. It's where I'm supposed to be going but the chances of it working out are going down the plug. I think there must be a time when I'll get past caring."

It was gone. Did not rise up, somersault and dive, just seemed to sink back without disturbance. A wave pitched the dinghy, and then it dropped and he struggled to hold his grip on the rope, and when the craft steadied there was no sign of the seal. Difficult to imagine that it had been a part of the dream, but he was edging closer to sleep.

He said, "I did what I could, did what I thought was right. Won't be thanked for it. I was sick before I came to your place, your territory. Not now. I think well of myself. Good to have known you, friend."

His head sagged.

The seal was back with him. Not as close as before, but moving slowly enough to keep pace with him. It was huge, heavy, but had a grace in the water and he wondered about its enemies: orca whales and polar bears. Off Westray, out at Noup Head, he had seen the killer whales – and Aggie was usually with him and they would sit on sheep-cropped grass. He did not know what day it was, what date, and so could not say if it were one of the mornings that she would come across from her island to restock her pottery in the craft shelf of the hotel. He did not think he had anything further that he should say to the seal, and let his head rest on the side of the dinghy and the water splashed around him, and he drifted and did not know where he was – nor knew if, any longer, it mattered. He supposed he had honoured his promise, had done his best.

Delta Alpha Sierra, the twentieth hour

He lay on the bunk bed allocated him.

Arnie and Sam did the honours. Not much to employ them. They packed his gear, his personal kit. Had already taken his issued firearms and the grenade canisters back to the armoury. Used the same Bergen that had been with him through all those days. Next to nothing that went in the bag had any sentimental or emotional importance to him. Some of the guys, and most of the girls, brought pictures and mementoes to the Forward Operating Base, wanted to be reminded of wives and girlfriends, of small children, of dogs at home. Gaz had not. Just essentials. His bag was by the door. Their suggestion, he should get off his arse, put a bad day behind him, come on over to the bar. There were dispensation times when the cupboard under the counter was unlocked, and beers could be served, and the normal intake of fruit juice and Cola and Sprite were ignored. Their officer would have accepted that his experience had been bad, damaging, needed lubricating. Refused . . . It was not pressed. The guys and girls in the regiment were individuals, did not require herding. He was entitled to decline. The door closed on them.

He had told his story coherently. Had good recall. Had talked little of the girl, had been calm and composed and professional, but then had broken, shed tears. He had noted how they had waited for his composure to return, had not hustled him. Had done the bit about the girl, and her sacrifice and him undiscovered. He lay on the bunk bed, and wondered whether he had emphasised sufficiently her role in his preservation: they had seemed interested but it was not milked. An attitude that seemed to be: 'War is shit, tell me something new, what I didn't know, it's bad shit, and never pretty and never glorious'. He wondered what *they*, across the table from him – the girls and the debrief officer who they referred to as Knacker – knew of warfare: not games of intelligence officers parking cameras in concrete walls, but shooting war and the consequences of war. Doubted they knew much ... Gaz didn't play chess. Did not know of the game in which little people, 'pawns', got to be knocked off the board.

They came back for him. Arnie helped to tidy him, and Sam hoisted up his bag. The Chinook was ready. It would be the regular run into Kurdish territory and the airport there, would do rotation of personnel and load up with supplies for this Forward Operating Base and a couple of other locations. Would be routine for them, but nothing was routine in Gaz's world. He was reluctant to leave the bunk. Both of them, Arnie and Sam, would have realised that their colleague was damaged. Going to be shipped out and soonest. Would be fast-tracked. The helicopter to Idlib, another supply flight, and into RAF Akrotiri on Cyprus, and the big bird out later in the day to Brize Norton, home. An early assessment that the damage might be terminal to his career ... Some would have shaken out of the experience, others would not.

He stood in the centre of the room. Looked around him, saw blank walls of plywood. There would be another guy there by the time the next dusk came down over the desert.

Gaz said, "I don't ever forget what happened. Owe it to them there, and owe it to her who saved my life. Don't forget it, and I promise that I will do what is possible to repay those responsible with a degree of harsh justice. I pledge that."

Arnie said, "Yes, of course, Gaz, well spoken."

Sam said, "Quite right, Gaz. Nice thought. Fuck knows how you will, but nice."

It would have been all around the FOB that a girl had endured a gang-shag in order that Gaz stayed hidden in his covert observation position. That Gaz must have been soft on her, her on him, that she herded goats in the village that had been taken down. Would give them something to talk about.

They went out. Arnie and Sam stayed close to him. Out past the briefing room where the intelligence man and his girls were with their officer and glanced up momentarily at the beat of the boots on the corridor floor. Past the Mess that he would not be returning to, and a chorus of 'Good luck', and he was already gone from the ranks, no longer a part of them. Out into the night air and across the apron and towards the arc lights close to where the Chinook was parked, engines rumbling.

He said it like it was a commitment that needed reinforcing. "I promise . . . what is possible . . . a degree of harsh justice. It is owed to you."

And his voice was drowned by the thrash of the rotors.

Timofey said, "It was good to have known him."

Natacha said, "Was the best time of my life, most fun and most excitement."

"I don't have hope for him."

"He will be alone and frightened."

Jasha said, "His trade would mark him as a solitary man. Not a frightened man. If he is not overboard he will sleep; if he sleeps he will not wake . . . Good to know you."

They hugged awkwardly. In truth, something of them unsettled Jasha. He thought they possessed a freedom that he did not have. Were as liberated as Zhukov, and would have hung around him while there was a value in his friendship, then would have drifted away, returned to a world from which he was excluded. It was a long time since Jasha had held another man in his arms, many years, and even longer since he had clung to a young woman and felt her dampened contours, bumps and angles against him. He had guided them back, first, to where his vehicle was parked up, well out of sight of his cabin, then had driven them to the point where the little Fiat had been left. They said they would go back to the apartment where his father was. Would be cautious, careful, suspicious, would spend time watching the entrance and looking for cars that mounted surveillance. Would be wary of any indication that an FSB investigation searchlight was beamed on them. Would spend most of the day loitering and watching. If it were clear, then they would be inside, check on his father, might feed him, then would draw down stocks for sale from the cache behind the wardrobe, and would be off to the railway station in time to meet the slow train up from the capital. Would they ever be used again as 'assets'? Jasha doubted it. He had done his farewells with the boy first, then the girl. She kissed him, wet lips, and shivering, and then they were into the little car, and they bumped away and swung on to the slip-road to the highway for the run down to the coast and the bridge over the inlet, and then to Murmansk. He thought it unlikely they would talk of him after they had gone two kilometres, and that he would soon be forgotten, an unpredicted interlude.

A last wave from her, then the bend in the track.

Jasha could have taken them to his cabin. Had not. Might have fed them and lit a fire, and given her a blanket to drape over herself while her clothing dried on a bar in front of the flames. But they had no place in his space, and the only common factor was the stranger inserted briefly into their lives. He would have enjoyed more time with the agent, learning something of where he had been and his philosophy and where he stored the anger that was common to those of the lone wolf breed. Could have spent two days, or three, but then each would have exhausted the other . . . Jasha imagined that the man was long dead and would now be swirling among the mixed currents of the Barents. Might float for a bit after being toppled from the craft, then would sink. Might snag on deep rocks, or be dropped in weed beds, or be beached on isolated rocks and become food for the gulls. Had not told the kids.

He reached his cabin. He looked around when he was out of the pick-up. Stood still and listened to the sounds of his dog scraping the inside of the door, but listened also for Zhukov. Heard only the dog and the wind in the trees. He did not expect that he would see the bear again . . . unless the idiot creature suffered more injury, required help. If it stayed fit then their companionship was unnecessary. He would miss it, missed any friend who moved on. He fed his dog, lit the fire, then stripped out of his wet clothing.

But he was troubled. Remembered how long he had watched the dinghy as it spun and twisted, rose and fell, and seen it into the rain mist of the inlet, and looked long and hard for it after it had disappeared. He supposed he was touched by the man ... which was weakness for Jasha. But they were all flawed men and made friendships only from necessity, and ditched them when they could, which was their pedigree – missed a friend, regretted the passing, and moved on.

He was in and out of sleep.

Gaz did not know, nor care, how long he had been in the dinghy. Time no longer had meaning. What had changed were weather conditions and with them the sea's motion.

The cloud blanket was gone and through his near closed eyes he watched as the sun teetered on the edge of the horizon, did not dip further in this Arctic Circle summer, but would hover and then rise for the start of a fresh day. The wind had dropped and the wave movements were now gentle, soothing, and he lay in the dinghy with the water heavy around his body and rolling.

He had tried to fight sleep. Reckoned he had made a good fist of it for as long as his strength held out, but that had slipped. When he finally slept he would not wake again. Regrets? He would have said, had his thoughts been cogent, that he was a small man in a big system, a tiny cog in a large motor, that he had performed a use and delivered as comprehensively as he had found possible. Could not have demanded more ... No more pain in his upper body and it might have been the cold water in the bottom of the dinghy that lapped against him that had achieved the numbness. It would be good to sleep.

Gulls were with him.

Not the seal. Doubted now whether he had *actually* had a seal riding escort, and was now near certain that he had not *actually* seen a full-grown brown bear on the rocks as he had moved towards the northern mouth of the inlet before drifting into the Barents Sea. The gulls shrieked and screamed over him, might have suggested that he hurried up with the business of getting himself asleep so that they could begin the feast. One, the boldest but not the biggest, had landed on the side of the dingy, had pirouetted there and perched more comfortably, and Gaz had managed to tilt his head sharply and it had realised that he still lived and that patience was demanded. It would go first for his eyes, then the slack skin of his cheeks, then try to burrow its beak inside his mouth having prised open his jaw. He would have liked to have the seal alongside, if there had *actually* been one. It could have ridden shotgun. Always on the wagons that the regiment boys drove were some who were never behind the wheel but were crouched over the barrel, and its sights, of the big machine-gun, fifty calibre. They were capable of keeping bad things back, and the seal would have been the nearest thing to match them.

No seal and no bear, and the gulls biding their time and circling him. Only the one face to hold on to. He had seen men die, eking out the last moments of breath and heartbeat, and some held crucifixes and some gripped worry beads and some shouted prayers. He only had the face . . . but the shape of it, lips and nose and the dance of the eyes and the hair that the wind carried over it was fading in his mind.

No ships to look for and only the ripple of water and the gulls' cries. And ever more difficult to keep his eyes open.

It was an ability much prized. Both Mikki and Boris had the skill. Each cupped a lit cigarette in the palm of their left hand.

The funeral service would be a brief affair, but both would have time to smoke a filter tip during the priest's prayers and there would be a short address from the brigadier on the loss of his son, tragically taken.

They stood behind the principal mourners. Other than the family there was a decent attendance of older cronies, men from the former KGB days, and their wives, many of whom showed off loud jewellery. Not anything that either man would have commented on to Lavrenti's mother and father, but it was striking that very few colleagues from Lubyanka had chosen to come to this cool, shaded, flyblown place of ostentatious headstones. The burial was in the Kuntsevo cemetery, out at the end of Kutuvovsky Prospekt, and both had arrived early. There was good history in the ground there and they looked for the 'famous' graves of Kim

Philby, a hero and a defector to the Russian cause and a Briton with an Order of the Red Banner, and those of the Krogers, husband and wife, both quality agents, and there were those of Russian military men who had given their lives for the Communist state. The brigadier would have had to pull strings, use influence, to lay his hands on a precious plot here.

The mother looked broken. The father had aged but stayed upright, straight-backed, kept his head still and looked imperiously into the middle distance. Not suicide, of course not. Not a self-inflicted wound. Not a war criminal for whom a mysterious sense of conscience had driven him to seek his own punishment. Not an officer of FSB who had allowed himself to be captured by a lone foreign operative who was aided by a pair of low-life narcotics dealers . . . It was the funeral of Lavrenti Volkov who had distinguished himself in combat in Syria, who was marked for promotion, who had been out on the north-west border of Russia and engaged in vigilant patrolling of an area notorious for its use by criminals and spies, and who had suffered a fatal wound from the malfunction of his service pistol. A tragedy. A young, honourable man cut down when not yet in his pride.

Had Boris spoken he might have said, 'I need a smoke, a good drag, after all the shit I've had to listen to.'

And Mikki might have said, 'Typical, took the coward's way out. I tell you something: if anyone from that village is left alive, and is stuck in some fucking camp over a border, then it will be time to pop the corks, whatever they do, celebrate big time.'

'And the guy who came for him.'

'No chance, not at that range, not with the way he went down. Be there somewhere and loss of blood, or sepsis, will have screwed him. The kids will have dumped him.'

'Heh, that bear might have fucking had him.'

'Big bastard, the biggest. I've never run that fast.'

'Scared the shit out of me.'

Had the exchange taken place there would have been a peal of laughter from Boris and a growled chortle from Mikki – inappropriate at that time, that place. An honour guard arrived, did a goose-stepping approach, formed two short ranks, and were cued in by the priest, and a volley of shots was fired over the open pit where the coffin now rested, then marched away . . . Trowels were used to scatter the first dry soil. The coffin had not been open for any part of the service: it would have been considered unnecessary to show the extent of the head wounds resulting from the 'accidental discharge'.

They stuck around at the end. The main party would go on for a meal. Both men had wriggled into tight suits, shirt buttons barely fastened, and ties clumsily knotted. They waited until the gravediggers had started to shovel earth noisily on to the box.

Both finished their cigarettes, down to the filters, then tossed the ends – still alive – into the grave, and left.

"I need to know . . . the guy who came and took him, what do we say?"

"Just a crazy guy – who got himself shot, for fuck-all. Proper crazy guy."

There would be rumour and gossip. Stories would travel 'word of mouth' and on internet chatroom pages. They had a single factor in common . . . they were second-hand stories. None was verified, but had a tenacity, and some were driven by what people feared and some by what they wanted to hear.

'What I was told, good source, just on the Russian side of the frontier with Norway, quite close to the main highway going down to Murmansk, there is a cairn of stones. Newly built. Quite big stones and might well have needed machinery to carry them into place. It's not where there would be a marker for a summit, and not on a site commemorating a World War Two battle, and there is no plaque indicating why it has been built. The suggestion is that under the stones, proof against scavenging wildlife, is a grave. Another guy I spoke to had suggested to me that he'd been told a military detachment had been there when the cairn was erected, might have been an honour party and might have been cheap available labour. But it ticks plenty of boxes. You can't see it from the fence, nor from the highway, but I'm told it's there.'

Other people said, 'There was a grave dug by border guards in the woods that are four, five klicks back from the border fence. There was security in place, and the guys who did the digging were warned, pain of something worse than death, that they would face supreme punishment if they talked of that night's work. I heard – it was a Baltic states fisheries minister who told me – that in fact the grave was not dug sufficiently deep and was excavated by wildlife. Could have been foxes or bears, and if the flesh was still comparatively edible then a lynx would have had a feed. I mean, up in those parts, nobody turns down free grub. Nothing in the local media, but there are whispers of an agent crossing from NATO territory, not substantiated, but it was said.'

A few said, 'I talked to a man, a deck-hand on a trawler, and he had been told that another boat, sailing out of Murmansk and up into the Barents – quite near, in fact, to where the *Scharnhorst* lies, a war grave and a thousand drowned there, Germans . . . but that's not the point – anyway, another boat retrieved a small dinghy, the sort that could be used in harbour to get from the shore to an anchored pleasure boat. Far out and drifting, not capsized, but no evidence of a holiday-maker or a survivor in distress. It had no safety kit, was just drifting, and in rough seas. Visibility was good but there was a fierce swell. No one had been reported missing or overboard, so perhaps it was there by chance and had been carried that far by tides and currents. Not a nice thing to hear about, makes one think of a desperate end . . . but then it might have just broken free from a mooring, never had anyone clinging to it. Only one thing certain, it was not a Russian dinghy, most likely southern Norway or Sweden. FSB were told of it but showed no interest.'

More said, 'I heard, I was in a bar and fishing crews were talking, of a corpse being washed on to the rocks out on the headland, east side, of the inlet. Had been in the water a long time. Too damaged to be identified. That's the crabs, do the damage, or the big cod, no eyes and no hands and most of the flesh on the face taken. No one reported missing so he stays in the icebox at the hospital, the one on ulitsa Pavlova, and no one has yet been forward to claim him. Like no one cares . . . it's what I heard.'

One man said, and was hesitant, seemed fearful of being over-heard, but told what he had learned, third-hand, could not confirm, but shrugged. . . . 'A man was picked up at sea or on the shore and brought into harbour, not Kirkenes but further west and nearer the Cape, and the local doctor and the nurse were never called but a military helicopter was at the quayside. He was flown direct to Bodo, to the Nordland hospital, and there's a wing there for air force use and for NATO people. Went into a secure room and even the hospital authorities were not told his name, armed secu-rity for him. What I did hear was that his condition was grim, infected combat wounds and the talk was that he'd need big luck to win through. Did he die, did he live – if he existed? Don't know, no one ever said.'

Someone said, 'There were people in the bar of the hotel on the island of Westray, in the Orkneys, one of the smaller islands. They said that they had heard, not directly, but from friends, that lawyers had been up from Aberdeen on the mainland. There was a croft up towards the Noltland Castle and it was owned by an incomer, nice enough chap but kept to himself. Except that he went away, all of a sudden was gone and his grass-cutting contracts were left unworked. Just vanished and a plane had come to take him south in a storm when no one in their right mind would have moved out of their living-room. The lawyers had travelled up to arrange the sale of his home . . . and more to it. He had a woman friend on the smaller island, Papa Westray, and they were almost an item, not quite. She packed in a fair little business, craft pottery for the tourists, gone without explanation. She was Aggie and he was Gaz, and both gone and no explanation given. Like they were running and like they were hiding. It's what was said.'

Another man said, 'People up here, Orkney people, they can guard your privacy. A stranger comes by boat or by air and walks to the first house he finds and asks for directions to a particular man or woman's home. He'll not be told. They protect their own. The one they're looking for could be in the next house, could be in the kitchen drinking coffee, could be out at the back fixing the sewage pump, but the stranger will not be told. It was explained to me, and I was told that a man came back, was unwell, damaged, came back from away over the water, and a nurse called three times a week to change his dressings, and he's out somewhere close to Inga Ness and down from Fifty Hill, but no one will say. Who knows? It's like he's guarded ... Myself, I never saw him, could just be for the fairies.'

He stood in the doorway.

Bright autumn sunshine lit that side of Rostocker Strasse. His body threw a dark shadow into the bar area. He leaned heavily on the surgical stick, let it take his weight. The last few steps from the *Hauptbahnhof* had been a struggle. Probably should have queued for a taxi at the rail terminus, but there had been too many indignities in his recent life and convalescence. To have paid a cab driver would have seemed feeble. He collected his breath, then was nudged. Not rudely, but unpleasant. It was the lunch hour and men and women had disgorged from the office blocks along the main drag and needed to eat, and wanted to get past him. He stepped awkwardly aside, was not thanked. He would not be hurried. The wind was on his back and at two tables clients turned and scowled and one flicked his fingers as if to get him inside or out, and the door shut and the draught excluded. He was impassive. There was little that any of them inside, eating or waiting for service, could have done that would have fazed him.

He saw the pictures of the big masted ships on the walls and most had full sails, all faded with age and needing cleaning. Saw the memorabilia stacked on shelves, navigation equipment from centuries before, and wood plaques that commemorated ships of the nineteenth century. Crowded with beer bottles, the tables were heavy, of weathered wood, scratched but well scrubbed. The chairs looked hard, uncomfortable. A manager hurried between tables and tried to placate the most impatient customers, and he was pointed out. A complaint: could the street door please be closed?

He was elbowed aside. Latecomers, going to be lucky if a free table were found for them.

The door stayed open. The manager advanced on him.

He would have been determining how considerable his annoyance should be at the cold air, at the open door, at the noise and fumes of Rostocker Strasse entering his premises. But the remark was swallowed. He would have seen what Gaz was confronted with each morning on getting into the bathroom, wherever he had slept, and staring at the mirror, barely recognising himself. The manager would have known he faced a man who had stood his corner, had looked death in the eye, had turned his back on it, had survived, had come a long road. Would have faced a pale complexion, and seen eyes that were deep set and dull and lips that were thin, almost bloodless and chapped, and hair that had lost lustre. There was a presence about the man, as if he had been in a bad place but had turned away from an inevitability and had crawled out. Other customers waited for admission behind Gaz but he waved them back imperiously. Did he understand? Might have done, might have made the link. How could he help and how could he oblige?

Gaz told him, hesitantly and in a soft voice. Spoke her name. Not easy for him to say it. He thought of what the manager might have known . . . of the customers who had pored over a laptop and had read a local blog from far up in the Circle: that she had been tracked by an intelligence officer, had been ferried up to the small frontier town, had been there for a few hours before being sent back to her job. The manager said, poor and accented English, that she was in the kitchen. Should he get her? Gaz shook his head.

Was as frightened of seeing her as he had been nervous of speaking her name. The door was closed behind him. He stood close to the line of hooks on which bags and coats were hung. In front of him was the entrance to the kitchens, those swing doors that waitresses kicked open. The manager had left him . . . Being here, in the Rostocker Strasse bar, marked a late stage in his planned, hoped for, journey. The place was at full capacity. She might look through him. Might acknowledge him but seem disinterested. Might scowl, glower . . .

He had finally been turfed out of hospital. Had been there several weeks, seen out the summer there. His pick-up from the Barents was usually described by the nursing personnel as a miracle: a fishing boat that had been idling in that area, no reason given, had spotted him, needle in a haystack, and him unconscious. The second miracle was that he had survived a poisoned wound. One of the girls had come to take him back to the UK. She'd said on the journey, rather casually, that whatever overstretched umbilical cord had linked them was now being scissored. They, the department she now worked for, did not expect to see or hear from him again. He would not have asked her, would have thought it demeaning. Had said, instead, that he would have enjoyed a beer, a chat, a reminisce, with Knacker, who had not visited him while his wound was being cleansed and his health rebuilt. She had said that he had left the Service, no longer required, spent his time up at Hadrian's Wall, where his wife was a digger, a site close to Hexham: should not have told him, probably could have bitten off her own tongue.

He had flown back, was allowed a month's free stay in a one-bedroom apartment in Hereford, close to his old barracks, and she had waved him off. Gaz had taken a train north, then a taxi, had been left at the Roman town of Corbridge, had walked among flattened ruins, then had come to an archaeological site. A score of men and women were scraping and digging and brushing. He had called out, a loud voice, though still with a croak, 'I am looking for Knacker, can anyone help me?' One woman had looked up. Pleasant enough face, a resigned smile, had wiped her muddied hands on filthy clothes but had not bothered to shake earth out of her hair. 'You one of his old chaps? They booted him out, surplus to needs. Got you into trouble, did he? Not here, up by Turret 36B. You have transport?' He hadn't. She would have seen that he was on two sticks, thin as a rake, pale as parchment. Nice woman, and he wondered how she survived alongside Knacker. Transport was arranged. He had been driven close to the location, then dropped.

Not a farmhouse in sight, open rolling countryside. He had walked to the Wall. Seen a hunched figure, gazing out into the middle distance from close to the small square base of the turret . . . and nothing much to say. "How are you . . . Good to see you . . . On the mend I hope?" He asked about the girl, was told where to find her. Without her, on the ground and above Deir al-Siyarqi and when the goats had stampeded, he would not have lived, and without her picture in his mind his life would have failed in the dinghy. Knacker had said, "Was always proud of you and of the operation. *Matchless* was good, one of our best results. I like that image of my 'rough men'. Don't suppose you know what I'm talking about."

Gaz, in his hospital bed, no visitors other than tight-lipped staff, and short times of day for talk with the guards, had made the big decision: no more the island and Aggie – no more the dream of the feisty girl whose anarchy made him laugh. And he had dumped his fear that being with the goat herd girl would be the equivalent of living inside a shrine of gratitude. "You went visiting, visiting violence, know what I mean. Sleeping safely because rough men stand ready to visit violence on our enemies, wonderful stuff. Me, I'm out of it. Not wanted. Just have memories, fuck-all else. But we bashed them, Gaz, hit them hard and where it hurts. One of my best shows, and . . ." But Gaz was edging away, retreating, and left Knacker hunched and quivering with excitement as he gazed out on a wilderness where a mist was thickening. Thought the man who had played God was now little more than a husk, and sad . . . He'd hitched a lift into Newcastle, then bought an air ticket for the morning,

He had spoken her name. She might come bouncing out from the kitchen and be wearing a ring on her finger. Might come out and manage a smile. Could recall seeing her outside the hotel. She was supposed to 'encourage' him, was a manipulated puppet of Knacker and the team. He had denied he would kill the officer, only 'help' to end his life, and she flared anger at what she'd have believed to be backsliding. He had told her that he merely did his job. She might look straight through him, might see him and spit on the floor.

She came through the doors.

An older face than he remembered. A uniform of a navy skirt and a white blouse and flat shoes for comfort. No make-up, no jewellery. She carried a tray with four plates, and beer bottles, and came towards him. A cheer rang out. Four big men, crowded over a laptop, and from the Scandinavian north Gaz reckoned, seafaring men, and a smile flickered on her face, but was transitory and was replaced with sadness. They were clapping her. She saw Gaz.

His surgical stick took his weight. He tried to straighten, find some pride, and smoothed his hair, and wished he had shaved better, and wished he had stopped at the *Hauptbahnhof* when coming in from the airport and gone to one of the kiosks where flowers were sold. She put the tray down. The shock was stark on her face. He went towards her, skirted clumsily between tables, banged chair legs with his stick. They were together, arms around each other, and tears wet their faces.

She said, "They told me you were lost, had gone on the sea, missing, was thought drowned. I was never told that . . ."

A big man came delicately past them, took the tray, chuckled, carried it to his table.

Gaz said, "We are going to find somewhere that you can have goats and dogs, where we can live and where we can be free of them. Going where rough men cannot find us, cannot find anyone. Going . . ."

When she had retrieved her coat and her bag, they went out on to the street and a blustery wind blew leaves and rubbish at their legs. He doubted he would tell her about a bear and a seal, and a friend who was a recluse and more friends who peddled quality skunk, and about an officer in the security apparatus of the Russian Federation who was dead, or about Knacker who was let go and was alone and thought himself worthless, tell her anything about the madness of days gone. They walked together, her hand in the crook of his arm.

The End.